CASTAWAY CHARLIE

THE DRAGON MAGE 10

SCOTT BARON

"We must accept finite disappointment, but never lose infinite hope."

– Martin Luther King, Jr.

CHAPTER ONE

It was pure chaos out in the cold void, far, far from Earth. Unexpected magical blasts buffeted Charlie from all sides, slamming him to and fro in the harness that strapped him firmly to Ara's back.

The mighty Zomoki, despite her impressive strength, was faring no better than he was as the relentless assault bombarding her violently tossed her about.

Bawb and Hunze were only mildly better off, and that was merely because they were "safely" riding inside Kip's magic-tech hybrid ship, while his Chithiid pilot, Dukaan, did all he could to try to keep them from being torn to pieces in the chaotic whirlwind of howling power. And they were not alone.

Gustavo, the other AI ship who had joined them on this mission, was accompanied by Griggalt, a large dragon of substantial power. Both found themselves likewise caught in the middle of a relentless bombardment.

It was not what they'd expected when they began this mission.

They had set to their task with urgency, flying off into space in a rush. All of them exited their respective warps and jumps interlinked, traveling to this location together as intended. But that was where things went horribly wrong.

The coordinates they were following had spat them out right on top of a massive phenomenon the likes of which they'd hoped to never encounter again. And as bad as the initial shock had been, it was only getting worse.

"We're being sucked into a wormhole!" Charlie yelled, his voice carrying over the comms unit inside his helmet. "This is the shittiest deja vu I've ever had!"

He had almost foregone wearing the helmet entirely, as he, Ara, and Bawb, all shared the same silent, magical link between them. But if he wanted to speak with Kip and Dukaan, or the others flying with them, he would need regular old technology to do the trick. As it turned out, that inconvenience had very likely just saved his life.

"*Ara, can we jump?*" Charlie asked as he reached out with his mind, clinging to his friend for dear life.

"*I think so. Hold on tight.*"

"Everyone, we're jumping out of here. Go, go, go!" Charlie bellowed over his comms just as he saw Griggalt get sucked into the wormhole. A moment later, Gustavo was pulled in as well.

"Bob!" Charlie shouted, but it was too late. His friends had crossed over to wherever this thing led. He had to make a decision. "We need to get backup before we do anything," Charlie reluctantly said. "Kip, warp home and—"

The comms line blasted static as the AI ship tumbled end over end through the wormhole, vanishing from sight in a flash.

"Jump, Ara!" he shouted with both his mind and his lips.

Charlie felt the power within Ara surge. She was about to jump when a tendril of colored power slapped her hard, driving her into the event horizon of the wormhole. A sinking feeling washed over Charlie and Ara both as they realized they were going through, whether they liked it or not.

A painful flash hit them as they rocketed through the

wormhole. Only, it felt different than a wormhole. Charlie had been through one of those before, and this was different. Different, but familiar, in a way. It wasn't quite the same, he was sure of that, but it was definitely not a natural phenomenon. This wasn't a wormhole. It was a portal. One created by magic. He could feel its presence all around him.

And then the sensation was abruptly gone.

He and Ara were spat out the other side, the bright orb of the world below them looming dangerously large. Wherever they were, they had just been deposited right above the exosphere of a fairly large planet. And while that would have been disconcerting enough, it was something else that was far more worrisome.

"*Ara?*" Charlie silently called out. "*Ara, can you hear me? Bob?* Anyone?"

He was still on her back but couldn't sense his friend at all. That changed a moment later when they began a tumultuous entry through the planet's outer atmosphere. And that wasn't the strangest part.

Ara, normally protected by her powerful magic, was turning orange-hot from the friction as she streaked burning into the skies. With great effort she positioned herself as best she could to protect Charlie, but even so, he felt the heat threaten to burn him alive. Then, without warning, the harness broke loose from the stress, and he found himself tumbling through the sky.

"Ara!" he called out, utterly disoriented.

She had protected him from the heat of reentry all the way into the atmosphere, but now he was falling, and fast. Worse yet, despite his frantic casting, his magic wasn't working at all.

Oh, shit. Charlie realized he was going to plummet to his death unless he thought of something and fast.

"Charlie, we are coming," Bawb's voice crackled over his comms. "Look down."

He pivoted in the buffeting wind and saw Kip had positioned

3

himself below him, his hatch open and lined up as best he was able. Outside the door, Bawb had latched himself onto the hull and was waiting, arms outstretched to catch his falling friend.

"I'm coming in too fast!"

"Flare your arms and scrub off speed," Bawb instructed.

"I know what to do, but the atmosphere is too thin up here to give enough resistance," Charlie replied.

"On it," Kip said. "Dookie, we've gotta drop faster to match his pace."

"Tracking him already," Dukaan replied. "We are within acceptable parameters, but only just. This will have to suffice."

"You hear that?" Bawb asked.

"Yeah. Not too happy about it, but we'll make do. Here I come, ready or not!" Charlie called out as he flew right at the open door, far too fast for his liking.

At the last second Bawb shifted and lashed out with his foot, kicking Charlie as he passed into the ship, sending him into the interior airlock wall as he entered before slamming into the far door. Bawb immediately swung inside behind him and sealed the airlock.

"We are in," he called out, helping Charlie to his feet.

Charlie yanked his helmet off, the adrenaline in his veins making his hands shake. "Dude! You *kicked* me!"

Bawb flashed the tiniest of smiles. "Yes. Into the wall."

"Dick move, man."

"It helped scrub off some of your speed before you hit the far door. I fear you may have suffered greater injuries had I done otherwise."

Charlie hated to admit it, but he knew he was right. "Well, thanks for kicking me then, I guess."

"Anytime."

"*Only* time. Let's not do that again, okay?"

Hunze's frantic voice burst over the internal comms. "Charlie! There is a problem. Ara is falling!"

Charlie and Bawb both felt their blood go cold as they raced for command.

"What happened?" Charlie asked as he tried desperately to find his friend on the monitors. "Where is she?"

"There! The smoke trail," Dukaan pointed out. "She appears to be unconscious."

Charlie looked at the image in horror. Ara was limp, falling toward the planet below. And she was burned. Badly, from what he could tell. Something that should have been impossible.

"We have to save her!" he blurted, his mind racing a million miles an hour.

"She is a powerful Zomoki," Dukaan said. "What can we do to help? We have no magic. The ship's konus has failed. Can't you assist her?"

Charlie dug deep and reached for his power, but no matter how hard he tried, he couldn't sense it. None of it. Not one tiny bit. His magic was gone. He was just a man.

He looked at Bawb and Hunze and saw the same looks of confusion on their faces. Whatever had happened, their magic was gone too.

"Okay, we need to get close," Charlie said, snapping into his old spaceship engineer mindset. There was a problem to fix, and he was going to fix it the old-fashioned way. Namely, without magic.

"What do you want us to do?" Kip asked as he and Dukaan worked in tandem to draw close to the tumbling Zomoki.

"We get beneath her and adjust our rate of descent slowly to compensate for her mass."

"But we cannot possibly carry her," Dukaan said.

"We don't have to carry her. We just have to slow her down as much as we can," Charlie said, his eyes darting from his smoldering friend to the monitors showing the surface below.

It was a fairly verdant world, with some volcanic hot spots, crater lakes, and lush forests as well as oceans in the far distance. But right below them was what they needed.

"We slow her down and guide her there. That lake."

"She will drown," Dukaan said. "She is unconscious."

"So we aim for the shoreline. Enough water to help cushion the impact but not so deep she drowns. And the water will stop the burning."

Bawb looked at Charlie with deep concern clear in his eyes. "Why is the Wise One burning? It should be impossible."

"I know, man. I know. We can try to figure that out once we make it down in one piece," Charlie replied. "Where's Gus? With two ships we can do a better job of it."

"No sign of him," Kip said. "I've tried on all frequencies."

"Okay, we deal with that later. And Griggalt?"

"Nothing as well."

"Then we do this ourselves," Charlie said, watching as the ground grew closer and closer. "And we'd better hurry."

Kip didn't wait a moment longer, gunning his engines and dipping underneath the unconscious Zomoki, shifting his thrust until her massive weight rested atop his airframe. "Got her," he said. "Going laterally toward the water is actually taking some of the strain off. I think we may actually pull this off."

Charlie winced. He didn't want anyone giving Murphy an open invitation to make an appearance, but it was too late to worry about that. The ground was approaching, and fast. One way or another, they'd be touching down any second. He just hoped they would survive.

CHAPTER TWO

Twenty-four hours prior, a different sort of deadly situation was unfolding out in the depths of space far from Earth. But Charlie, Ara, and their friends were not present. At least, not all of them. Only the quirky AI and his pilot were there, and they had no idea what they were dealing with.

"What in the world *is* that?" Kip asked, sounding more than a little flustered, which was quite unusual for a powerful AI mind.

"I do not know," Dukaan replied. "*You* are the AI. *You* are supposed to know everything."

"Well, apparently I don't, because I'm at a loss here," the ship replied as they banked hard to avoid what was looking very much like a writhing Aurora Borealis in space. A spectacular light show that was wreaking havoc on their comrades.

Judging by how the other ships in their little group were affected by it so far, they had no desire to get a closer look. The churning mass of color was pulling the weaker of the ships to pieces and beating the others something fierce. Even the larger command ship was not immune.

"Evasive maneuvers," Captain Donlin called out to the

remaining craft from his battle cruiser. "I want everyone's shields on maximum."

It went without saying that it was an order they were all happy to follow. Kip had already cranked his up the moment the strange phenomenon had popped into existence all around them. Of course, he was one of only two AIs on this particular mission.

The other ships required their flesh-and-blood crews to engage their defensive protocols. Or, in the captain's case, defensive, and *offensive*. And he had more than enough armament for that purpose.

Captain Donlin's flagship shifted course on its axis with a powerful blast of its maneuvering thrusters then fired off a salvo of pulse fire directly into the anomaly. The weapons' blast diffused harmlessly as soon as it reached the strange light.

"This is bad," Kip said. "I sense some sort of magic here."

His airframe had a powerful konus welded into it, the magic allowing him to do far more than a conventional craft could. It also gave him a whole other range of sensation, a little of which was apparently coming into play. Whatever they were dealing with, it was not a naturally occurring phenomenon.

Dukaan had a sinking feeling as he watched yet another of their ships succumb to the power. All four of the Chithiid pilot's hands flew across the instruments as he tried to get a better fix on the chaos unfolding around them. He used every trick he knew, but to no avail. Whatever was attacking them, it was beyond his means.

"Are you recording this?" he asked the ship.

"Of course I am. I record everything. You know that," Kip said, quickly adjusting his shield phasing to deflect the incoming light energy that continued to pummel their small fleet of exploratory craft. "I don't think we're equipped to deal with this, Dookie. We're going to lose."

It wasn't something he wanted to admit, but Dukaan had

come to the same conclusion. They were exploring, far out in deep space and nowhere near their own solar system. And for that reason, Earth and its robust armada were unreachable. They were too far for any call for help to reach them before this conflict was over. Worse, there was something jamming their communications.

"Someone cast a blocking spell," Kip said, probing the magical barrier keeping any and all signals from escaping. "This is bad."

"Captain Donlin," Dukaan transmitted. "Kip says there is a spell blocking our long-range communications."

"You think I hadn't noticed?" the captain growled back as his ship launched a pair of mini-nukes into the far end of the deadly light show. "Hold tight, detonation in five. Four. Three. Two."

Nothing happened when he reached one. Not for several seconds. Then two flashes of light ignited behind the aurora. The nukes had gone off, but later than they were supposed to and in a decidedly underwhelming manner.

"What do we have that's bigger than that?" Dukaan wondered.

"We don't," Kip replied. "Those were the biggest."

"What could possibly do that?"

"I don't know. But whatever it—"

The AI was cut off as his shields were abruptly battered by a flurry of incoming magic, the force of which sent him tumbling off his level axis end over end. Even if battle in zero-Gs was lacking up and down, spinning the ship like that was enough to overwhelm the craft's artificial gravity generation system, all while driving its organic pilot deep into his cushioned seat.

The violence of it threatened to strain Dukaan into unconsciousness, but he did as he'd been trained, clenching his legs, butt, abdomen, and arms as tight as he could to force as much blood as possible to stay in his core and, ideally, his brain.

Even so, he felt the lightheadedness from so many Gs threatening to drop him.

"Hang on," Kip said, then punched the engines hard, using the main drive systems rather than the maneuvering thrusters to force the uncontrolled spin to slow. It was enough. Dukaan felt his senses sharpen and keyed in a recovery sequence, leveling out the ship as his vision cleared back to normal.

What he saw was horrifying.

"Captain, there's incoming," he transmitted, but he could see that his warning was already too late.

A dark shape lurched through the swirling light, powering right toward their friends. The command ship was heavily armed, but also vulnerable at that angle, and a broadside of what looked like conventional firepower slammed into their shields just as another flurry of magical attacks sought to drop their defenses.

Two more of their ships felt the flowing tendrils of the light storm latch onto their hulls and pull. Like a giant octopus searching for its next meal, the strange power slowly pried their hulls open.

"We have to get to them," Dukaan said.

"We can't. If we go closer we'll get dragged in too," Kip said. "And they've just lost pressure," he added as little puffs of air could be seen escaping then freezing in the void as their last intact compartments gave up the ghost.

"Captain, we've lost two more. What do you want us to do?" Dukaan called out to the damaged ship. "We have all weapons primed but need a target. What are your orders?"

A pause hung in the air before Captain Donlin spoke. "You're at the edge of this," the captain replied, a pained rasp in his voice. Apparently, the command ship had been more severely damaged than they'd originally thought. "I want you to make for open space and get the hell out of here," he continued.

"But, sir!"

"That's an order! Get to Earth. Tell Cal and the others what happened. They need to know what we're up against. You're our only hope."

Dukaan knew he was right. Some incredibly powerful magic was in play here, and while their most powerful casters would normally be a simple call away, Charlie was on sabbatical as Leila grew close to her due date. And while Rika could step up in a pinch, she was also unavailable, having flown off with Jo on a task for Zed and the AI high command.

Plain and simple, someone had to get to Earth to warn them. Or at least close enough for a transmission to reach them unhindered.

"We can help," Kip transmitted. "We have weapons and can—"

"I said that's an order," the captain repeated. "There's no time for—"

His ship exploded in a flash of ruptured warp core energy and unexpected nuclear detonation of the remaining warheads aboard the craft. The others were sure to follow his demise. Without the battle cruiser's firepower, it was a foregone conclusion.

Dukaan quickly adjusted their trajectory and plotted a short warp. It wasn't in the direction they needed to go, but there was one tiny gap in the power blocking them in. It was their only hope, and it would be threading a needle to say the least, but there was no other option.

"Kip, we have to go," he said, taking one last look at the wreckage of their friends' ships scattered behind them. "Warp us out of here. Now!"

Reluctantly, Kip did as he was told, engaging the warp without a countdown. The magic was speeding right toward them, and there simply wasn't time. The tendrils of power lashed out at them, but only the crackling remnants of their hastily executed warp remained.

They had managed to escape, but only barely, and once they exited their unplanned warp, they would set a course for Earth. Command had to know what was going on out here. And once they did, whoever had done this would face the full might of the united fleets of Earth and its allies.

CHAPTER THREE

The sun floated high in the azure sky, a golden orb shining down not only its warmth onto the sandy beaches of Malibu below, but also its nourishing magical power.

When he was just an ordinary man, Charlie had never considered that there might be anything more to his solar system's burning star, but after bonding with his Zomoki friend in her distant galaxy, his physiology had changed, and significantly at that. He was sensitive to things he'd never known existed.

Now, what had once been no more than a pleasant source of heat was also slowly charging him with more and more power every time he stepped out into its rays. And he was not alone in this reaction. Hunze's golden locks absorbed the power like a sponge. And Ara? The ancient Zomoki's magic was greatly bolstered by it as well.

But there was no need to wield their ever-growing strength. Not anymore. Not since they had defeated their nemesis once and for all.

Malalia Maktan, also known as Visla Dominus in her galaxy-conquering days, had her ass handed to her in a most spectacular fashion less than a year prior. Despite all of her planning and nefarious trickery they'd defeated her soundly, and with her considerable powers gone in the process, she was no longer a threat.

As punishment, she'd been quietly secreted away to a distant planet with almost no magic from its sun and only the slightest of traces in the native wildlife, and that variety would be poison to her should she try to take it for herself. The world was a prison without walls, but nevertheless no means of escape.

She was provided a shelter in which to live out her days, and there was certainly enough native flora and fauna there to keep her alive, but that was about it. At long last, with her safely out of the picture on a planet only a very select handful knew the location of, Charlie and his friends could finally enjoy a well-deserved rest. And they had certainly earned it.

Rather than a vacation, however, Charlie and Leila had decided to stay home in their Malibu estate and nest as her belly grew larger and larger, and not from an excess of their friend Finnegan's penchant for culinary surprises, though those were as frequent as they were delicious.

Months and months passed, and as the expecting mother and father were from not only two different races, but two different galaxies, no one really knew how long the pregnancy would last.

It was all so very new, not just to them but to everyone. So, with no firm timeline to rely on, they decided to just take it day by day and enjoy the ride. And part of that process was a lot of relaxing on the shores of Malibu's pristine beaches. It was, for all intents and purposes, idyllic.

"Can I get you anything? A snack, maybe?" Charlie asked as he gently rubbed Leila's taut belly.

"No, I'm fine for now, thank you," she replied, enjoying the sensation of the peptide-rich lotion soaking into her skin.

"All right. But if you want anything, just ask, okay?"

"You know I will," she said, flashing him a smile as warm as the sun above.

Charlie felt so happy he wondered if the joy might actually burst through his rib cage like an over-enthused xenomorph. He chuckled to himself at the thought, then wondered if the rather miraculous lotion might heal even that sort of carnage. Likely not, he mused, but it was pretty impressive stuff.

The lotion was a potent concoction containing several compounds that not only nourished her epidermis, but also healed the stretching tissue, keeping it supple and elastic no matter how large her bump grew. The formulation had been something of a clever breakthrough. Several of the ingredients were not typically combined in this manner, and certainly not in a form that remained stable at room temperature.

It was a chemistry conundrum, no doubt, but an enthused novice in the healing arts had become enthralled with the project and spent his every waking moment working on the formulation until he got it just right.

That in itself was not surprising. The aspiring healer's identity, however, was.

Grundsch was a Ra'az Hok, and a particularly large one even by their standards. A race of brutal killers who conquered and obliterated entire civilizations without batting an eye. At least, until his kind were wiped from existence. All but Grundsch. He had escaped that fate by being sucked through a wormhole into another galaxy. One where his forced servitude had eventually not only broken him of his former ways, but had even helped him grow as a person.

And despite many people's misgivings about him when he had first been brought back to Earth not so long ago, he had stepped up and proven himself in the battle against Visla Dominus, putting himself in harm's way repeatedly as he fought to defend his new home.

Those who had once thought his entire species to be

monsters of true evil had a change of heart where he was concerned and had actually forgiven him for his people's misdeeds. Grundsch was given a second chance. A new life, free of war and death, if he so chose.

And he did just that.

Once the final battle had been won, he gladly put down his arms, parked his attack ship and powered it down, and settled into a new existence. One where he would not raise his hands in anger again. Not if he could help it.

He'd taken quite an interest in botany as he got to know this planet from a resident's perspective, relishing the beauty of nature and ebb and flow of the world's wildlife. The former soldier was evolving, and without a queen directing his every move, he could do as he wished. And what he wished, to his surprise as much as anyone else's, was to learn how to heal.

His transformation had taken even the most ardent of Ra'az Hok haters by surprise, and in less than a year he had endeared himself to the very people his kind had nearly driven to extinction.

Even Daisy was fond of him, and given how she had pretty much fought his kind to the death in the Great War, that was really saying something. In fact, she had even said on more than one occasion that it was too bad there were no female Ra'az to set him up with, as he'd become quite a catch.

But Grundsch seemed quite content with his bachelor's life, spending his time either studying in the lab Cal and the other AIs had set up for him, or roaming the hills with Bahnjoh, his massive Graizenhund friend. Baloo would often join them in the early days, the enormous canine relishing his playtime with his pals. But as Leila's pregnancy advanced he began to stay close to home more and more, protective of his mama as he sensed something important was on its way.

Baloo's ears perked up and his nose twitched as he lay quietly beside Leila, but he didn't get up. Someone was coming, but this was a friend. And from the smell of her approach, they all knew who it was well before she arrived.

"Ripley, nice of you to visit," Leila called out to the girl as she trekked out of the trees, a large box in her hands.

"Hi, guys!" she chirped.

"What've you got there?" Charlie asked.

"My dad wanted me to drop this off for you," she said. "He was on something of a roll and made waaaaay too much."

Charlie chuckled. They knew her father's love of cooking all too well by now. "You sure he wasn't just trying to fatten us up?" he asked, patting his love's belly.

"Hey! *I* have an excuse!" Leila said with a laugh. "You, on the other hand—"

"I don't know what you're talking about. I am the very model of fitness."

"Uh-huh. Well, Mr. Model of Fitness, if you want to be helpful, how about give Ripley a hand and get that out of the sun and into the refrigerator. It looks like we'll be having something of a feast later after all."

Charlie rose to his feet and leaned down to give her a kiss. The kiss itself was wonderful, as they always were, but the disconcerting thrum of the Magus stone hanging around her neck was still a sensation he had to get used to.

"Okay, back in a jiff," he said, leading the way.

Leila lay back and basked in the sun's rays, the stone resting on her collar bone quietly absorbing the sun's power. It was a strange thing, the Magus stone, and one that no one could normally sense by design. But now that Leila was pregnant something had triggered within the magical pendant, tied to her family line as it was.

She felt it, and Charlie could feel it, but only the very powerful outside of her immediate family would ever sense even a hint of the sheer magnitude of magic the stone held. A magic that was now protecting her and her unborn child twenty-four-seven. Benign enough in daily life, but heaven help anyone who dared lay a finger on her. Or, more accurately, *attempted* to lay one on her.

With the added security, however, came a cost. Namely, protecting her and the baby was *all* it would do. Leila couldn't tap into the stone's power for anything else no matter how she tried. Ara posited it would return to normal once the baby was born, but with one of the arcane Magus stones, no one could really know for sure.

Charlie found Leila resting comfortably when he returned a few minutes later.

"Okay, it's all squared away," he said, sitting down beside her. "Now, where were we? Ah, yes." He picked up the lotion and began rubbing more onto her belly. "It looks like Ripley and Arlo are going to take the girls on a little trip," he said. "She seemed pretty jazzed about it."

"A trip? Where?"

"Taangaar. I guess Kara and Vee are planning on coming back across the portal in a few weeks for a visit, and Ripley and Arlo promised them an adventure."

"I don't really see how visiting the Chithiid homeworld is an adventure," Leila said. "Especially after all they've been through."

"Well, it's them trying to get back to normal, I think. An adventure in the old tradition of road trips."

"There isn't a road to Taangaar, Charlie. They need to fly, and it's—"

"Yes, yes, I know there's no road," he said, leaning in for a quick kiss. "Just a figure of speech. Anyway, it's kind of a teenage rite of passage. And I think it'll do them some good to have an adventure of the good old-fashioned, boring variety that isn't trying to kill them."

"On that we agree," she said. "We've all had more than enough of that for a lifetime."

"You can say that again."

"We've all had more than enough of that for—"

"*Charlie, are you there*?" Cal's voice blurted out over his comms unit.

"Cal? What's up? You sound upset."

He did, and for the most powerful AI on the planet, that was almost always a bad sign.

"*There's been an incident*," Cal replied. "*I need you at my downtown command center as soon as you're able. And bring Bawb as well. Ara too, if you can reach her.*"

"I'm on it," Charlie said. "Be there as soon as we can." He put the cap on the lotion bottle and rose to his feet. "Babe, I've gotta go."

"I'll come with."

"No, you rest up. I'll fill you in when I get home."

Leila was about to protest but decided that rushing to get dressed and to downtown might not be the most comfortable thing for a very pregnant woman to do. Everything took a bit longer these days, and she had finally grown accustomed to it.

"Okay, but you get back in time for dinner."

"Of course."

"And tell Bawb and Hunze they're welcome to join us. I'm sure Finn sent us enough to feed an army."

"You got it, babe," Charlie said, then headed off to summon his friend. *Feed an army*, he thought. *I really hope we won't need one.*

CHAPTER FOUR

Ara was the last of her kind. A mighty Zomoki of the highest intellect and great power. One of the few that had been known as the Wise Ones. The lesser variety of Zomoki still existed in relative abundance, flying between worlds if they possessed enough power, attacking travelers and being general nuisances, as one would expect of ravenous space dragons.

They were close relatives, yes, but those primal beasts lacked higher thought, or even the ability to speak. And what little magic they did possess was dwarfed by Ara's enormous reservoir. A fount of magic now fueled even more by Earth's powerful sun.

But despite having power and the ability to travel through all of space, Ara was still lacking something. Something she hadn't even known she had been missing.

Camaraderie of her own kind.

While Ara and Charlie were bonded by blood, and Bawb as well due to recent events, it was still not the same as flying free with others like her. But after giving up hope centuries ago, quite unexpectedly, something had happened. Something marvelous.

Orgalius was his name. A deep cobalt-blue dragon with

bright platinum eyes. The largest and most powerful of this galaxy's own indigenous variant of the species. Not the same as Zomoki, exactly, but rather a distant cousin.

He and his many siblings and friends thrived in this new galaxy, and Ara had managed to stumble upon them. Well, not exactly stumble. To be fair, she had gone searching after hearing tales of creatures similar to her own kind told by local tribespeople on other worlds in this galaxy. And in that effort, she had been successful.

Ara had brought Orgalius and the others to Earth, introducing them to her friends, as well as the magical power of the system's sun. While they did not absorb the sun's rays to the degree Ara did, Orgalius and the others nevertheless felt a great surge in their power in this solar system. On top of that, it seemed they had just made even more new friends. An entire planet worth, in fact, not including the allied worlds in two galaxies.

Now that the war was over, Ara had taken it upon herself to play tour guide to groups of dragons, guiding them across the portal tethered just above the sun's molten plasma into her own galaxy. It was something she found she enjoyed far more than she'd anticipated. The fresh eyes taking in the galaxy she simply took for granted made her appreciate her own home in a way she hadn't in centuries.

"*Ara, are you there?*" Charlie silently called out.

Their bond allowed them to connect across great distances, even more so when she was soaking in the sun's rays. But if she was on the other side of the portal he would have to wait for her return. While perhaps the powerful Bakana rods could forge a connection across that gap, their natural bond, strong as it was, simply could not. Fortunately, today he was in luck.

"*I am here,*" she replied. "*I returned late last night with Nixxus and Gazz. They greatly enjoyed the visit and are contemplating spending more time across the portal in the near future.*"

"*That's great, but we've got a problem,*" Charlie replied. "*Cal wants to see us immediately.*" Connected as they were, he could feel the surge in power as Ara's magic flared with concern, ready and alert.

"*I am on my way. I will pick you up in two minutes.*"

Charlie felt her grow closer almost at once. The Zomoki could move incredibly fast when she wanted to, and this was one such occasion.

One thing Ara did not take for granted was the intellectual prowess of Cal and the other AIs overseeing the alliance. If they said there was a problem, then there was a problem. And if she and Charlie were being called in, in a hurry, it was almost certainly a bad one.

Charlie was standing in the open space near his home atop the bluffs in Malibu where Ara liked to make her landings. While the beach was spacious, the buffeting of sand from the wind her wings kicked up was something she tended to avoid for her friends' sake. A shadow flashed overhead as she dropped from the sky. Charlie didn't flinch.

The deep-red dragon flared her wings and landed softly beside him. Charlie quickly scrambled up onto her back, settling into place in the new harness Cal had crafted for her.

"Hey," he said. "That was quick."

"I was just out on the Channel Islands. Hold tight," she replied, then surged into the air with a powerful flap of her wings.

The flight to downtown was a short one, and Ara set down atop the reinforced structure that was Cal's home base of operations. While in the old days some buildings had helipads to accommodate choppers, this structure had been modified to hold the considerable mass of the enormous dragon. The perimeter of the rooftop had also been outfitted with a series of hardened display screens and audio hookups so Ara could fully participate in the meetings taking place in the command center below.

"*Thank you for coming,*" Cal said, not even waiting for Charlie to descend into the building. "*We thought it would be best to have your eyes on this as soon as possible.*"

"Eyes on what, exactly?"

"*One of our expeditionary groups has had an encounter.*"

"Well, we've been looking for new cultures to join the alliance, so one could argue that's a good thing. I mean, yeah, there might be some violence, but that's to be expected with first contact sometimes."

"*Zed, would you please relay the data?*"

"Of course," the command AI replied. He had massive amounts of information at his digital fingertips as the military head of the entire combined fleet. "Admiral Harkaway sends her apologies she's not on the call. She will join us shortly, but she's rallying the troops at the moment, so to speak."

A familiar ship flashed onto the display screens. It was Kip and Dukaan. Around them were other larger and heavily armed craft. A typical survey team consisting of smaller, faster recon vessels and bigger, badder muscle to support it.

"What are we looking at?" Charlie asked as the images shifted between the craft.

His query was answered moments later when an enormous flash lit up the display. The largest of the heavy cruisers was engulfed in an aurora of writhing, multicolored flame, its shields failing rapidly despite shifting phase to handle the attack. It shouldn't have been possible. They were sporting the latest, most robust equipment in the fleet, courtesy of Joshua himself. The greatest tactical AI ever to live had done all he could to provide them protection. But it was not enough.

Not against this.

This wasn't normal enemy firepower. This was something far different. Something that made his blood run cold. The signs were unmistakable, especially in the void of space. This attack was magical in origin.

Charlie gasped as he watched the battle unfold, though it really couldn't be called a battle. More of a one-sided rout would be more like it. Kip spun away from the incoming spells, the larger ships taking wave after wave of the assault. It was only their bulk blocking him from the onslaught that spared the much smaller craft. Had Kip faced them directly, he would have been destroyed.

The command ship fired off nukes into the heart of the attack, but they had no effect. It was Captain Donlin's vessel, Charlie could now make out. And the captain was throwing everything they had into the fight. Even so, the heavy cruiser and command ship never stood a chance. Despite all of their advanced technology and powerful weapons systems, they were both losing their shielding and suffering massive structural damage under the swirling barrage, exploding in magical fireballs.

Then, when it seemed the magic might actually be letting up, the aurora parted, and what looked very much like conventional weapons' fire blasted through, combining their force with the magical attack. The large ships shattered under the barrage.

Charlie felt the blood drain from his face. "How did you get this footage?"

"Kip was tied into the other ships' live streams the entire time. He saved everything to his data stores right until he warped away."

"Kip and Dukaan survived?" he asked.

"Yes. They are in my hangar bay debriefing as we speak," Zed replied. "I was out near Venus, but I am currently flying farther out to monitor the periphery of the system for threats."

Charlie and Ara shared a look. Both were thinking the same thing even without their magical bond.

"That was immensely powerful magic," Ara said.

"That's an understatement," Charlie said. "Cal, what's going on? No one has that kind of power here. Almost no one. Did Malalia escape?"

"*We are monitoring her at all times. She is still in exile on her planet. Uncharted, hidden, and quite devoid of power.*"

Ara slowly nodded her head as she processed this information. "Then this is something new. Something new and *very* dangerous."

Charlie felt anger rise where shock had previously resided. "Where did this take place?"

"A short warp away in solar system B-127. It was supposedly a system devoid of technology. Obviously, we were mistaken."

"Okay, that's what we need to know. We're going to fly out there and kick these guys' asses."

"Not as easy as it sounds," Zed said. "The bastards have already jumped away. It would seem the assailants, whoever they are, moved out to the emptiness between systems."

"But there's nothing out there."

"I fear they may be setting up for a larger attack. Perhaps even on Earth. I've sent fast recon ships to track the enemy craft as best they can, but they have to stay clear. They're no match for this kind of firepower."

Charlie climbed back onto Ara's back. "Like I said. *We* will take care of this."

"*But the strength of these adversaries is enormous,*" Cal noted.

"Yeah, but we've got a helluva lot of power ourselves," Charlie said. "And no other power users are on this side of the portal, so that settles it." He banged out a message on his console and hit send. "Hopefully Rika's close enough that she gets the message. We could use her in on this too."

"*We could send for help from across the portal,*" Cal suggested. "*More power users would only help in this instance.*"

"No time," Charlie said. "We have to do this, and we have to do it now."

"But the additional power—"

"Oh, we have power. I just need to get home and pick up a few things that might come in handy, then we'll be off. Send the coordinates to Ara's harness navs system and we'll be on it."

Ara leapt into the air, making a beeline for Malibu. So much for relaxing in the sun it seemed. They were going into battle.

CHAPTER FIVE

Bawb and Hunze were standing in the small clearing near Charlie and Leila's home when Ara landed. Both were already decked out in their going-to-kick-some-ass gear. Leila was standing with them, a look of concern on her face, and for good reason.

"If it isn't the Geist," Charlie said, using his friend's assassin name, given his current attire.

"Charlie," he replied.

"You two going somewhere?" Charlie asked, dismounting and giving Leila a kiss.

Bawb cocked his head slightly. Hunze did the same in unison. It was almost unsettling how bonded the two were, and that had only increased in the months they'd spent not fighting for their lives across two galaxies.

Hunze stepped forward, confident and tall, not even a shadow of her formerly timid self remaining. "We are going with you, of course."

"But how did you—"

"We just know," she replied, flashing a grin at Bawb.

There it was again. That spooky ability the Ghalian had.

Their way of somehow seeming to always know what was going on. In this case, however, it was likely Bawb had picked up on something from Ara. His bond wasn't as strong as Charlie's, but if there was trouble in the air, he would have sensed it. And to the Geist, trouble meant taking action. There was no other conceivable option.

Charlie shook his head and chuckled. "So, I guess we'll be riding together. You good with that, Ara?"

"It won't be an issue," she replied.

Bawb, however, shook his head. "We will require a ship for this excursion."

"A ship? What's that about?"

Bawb rested his hand on Hunze's shoulder as she placed her own on her stomach. "We were waiting to say anything—" she began.

"This is wonderful news!" Leila blurted, wrapping her arms around her friend. "Congratulations!"

"It is a little early for that," Hunze said. "Ootaki gestation is lengthy and uncertain for the first several months."

"Which is why we said nothing. This is a *very* recent development," Bawb added.

Charlie took it all in stride. This was going to be awesome. Their kids would grow up together, just like Daisy's and Sarah's had.

"Okay, I understand the ship now," he said.

"Yes. A more secure mode of transit, just in case," Bawb said.

"Of course." Charlie opened his comms to Cal and Zed. "Hey, you two. Do you think you can rustle us up a ship for Bob and Hunze?"

"*Of course,*" Cal replied.

"I have one ship prepped and teamed up for an attack at the edge of the system, but I'll be done with Kip and Dukaan in a few minutes," Zed said. "I'll send them to you. They're armed, fast, and Kip's got a pretty strong konus mounted to his frame.

Plus, he's already got plenty of experience linking with Ara when she jumps."

"*And he has encountered and survived this enemy once already,*" Cal added.

"Yeah, but are you sure they're up for this after what just happened?" Charlie asked.

Zed chuckled. "I can assure you, they are itching to get back out there. They want payback, and when they hear it'll be you dealing it out, I'm sure they'll be quite happy to fly back into the thick of it."

"We should also have additional magic native to this galaxy with us for this effort," Ara mused. "Orgalius is not close at the moment, but Griggalt is quite powerful in his own right, and I know he would be glad to lend his assistance. He is currently basking up the coast at a secluded beach he and his friends have taken a liking to. Plenty of sea lions and other food in the area make it a relaxing retreat. I have cast a request for him to join us."

Charlie nodded his approval. "Thanks, Ara. Good call."

Griggalt was not quite as large as Orgalius, but he was still a rather sizable dragon, and one possessing rather substantial magic. His contribution to the effort would most definitely be appreciated. And with a Zomoki, a dragon, and two attack ships working in unison, the odds of success against this magical adversary were very much in the team's favor.

"Who's the other ship?" Leila asked.

"His name is Gustavo," Zed said. "You actually met him briefly just after the portal was reclaimed. He can be somewhat overenthusiastic at times, but you couldn't find anyone better to have your back when the shit hits the fan."

"The ship who used to be a man?" Charlie asked.

"One and the same."

"*He was heavily modified during the Great War,*" Cal noted. "*When he suffered catastrophic injury when his ship crashed, his mind was already linked with the ship's systems. It is a highly unusual occurrence, but his consciousness was able to be retrieved and mounted to an unimprinted AI drive.*"

Charlie let out a low whistle. He hadn't really interacted with Gus, but he'd definitely heard of him. "And his crew?"

"A crew of ten. You know Tamara and Shelley, of course. They run tactical ops for Captain Sorkin."

"Sorkin is a good man," Bawb noted with an approving nod.

"*He is. The rest of his crew you don't know, but they are all skilled in their roles. Zed would not have sent them otherwise.*"

"I'm confident we'll be in good company," Charlie said just as a small magical jump nearby swirled the clouds and tickled his senses.

Unlike warp technology, using a jump within the atmosphere was no big deal for Zomoki and their cousins. Most didn't waste the magic when they could just as easily fly in not much longer a time frame, but Ara's request had sounded urgent, so Griggalt had felt the expenditure was worthwhile.

He dropped down surprisingly quietly for so large a creature. He was red, like Ara, but a far lighter shade and with a different morphology, which was to be expected as he was a cousin from another galaxy.

"I am here, ready for whatever you need of me," he said matter-of-factly.

Once Orgalius and Ara had sized one another up and forged their alliance, the familial support between the cousin races was unwavering and complete. Though they had only just discovered each other's existence, the bond was rock-solid.

Ara bowed her head slightly. "Thank you for coming so quickly, Cousin. We are facing a threat. One that possesses great magical power."

"The woman who so vexed you less than a year ago?"

"No, she is still in exile. This is something new. And something deadly. Our friends have already lost two of their vessels to the intruder's hostilities. With no warning and no mercy."

Griggalt nodded. "Then whoever these newcomers are, they must be dealt with. Harshly, and at once. The plan?"

Charlie stepped forward. "We fly out with two heavily armed, fast ships. We'll have conventional weaponry as well as casters on board. You and Ara get to do what you do best. Namely, unleash hell."

"I approve of this plan so far."

"I'm glad you do. And then, once we find these bastards, we kick their asses so hard they'll never even think about trying anything against us again."

"I like the way you think," Griggalt said with a toothy grin.

"Then we're set. All we need is for Kip and Dukaan to pick us up and we're good to go. Now, if you'll excuse me, I've got some goodies to pack for the trip. In this instance, I think I'm leaning toward an overwhelming show of power. Bob? Hunze? You guys need to gear up?"

"We shall gather a few additional items, since we have the time. Then we will meet you back here for our departure."

Charlie turned, put his arm around Leila's shoulders, and headed toward his home. "All righty then. Let's all get to it. Kip'll arrive soon, and then the ass whooping begins. See you all back here."

Ara and Griggalt found themselves alone on the field a minute later, sitting in the awkward gap between planning and action.

"So," Griggalt said, "I hear you have taken Nixxus and Gazz across the portal."

"Yes, I showed them around my galaxy. They greatly enjoyed it, especially the transit."

"Well, this system's sun does emit particularly potent energy. I would imagine that crossing in such proximity to it would be quite refreshing."

"Indeed, it is," she replied. "Perhaps after this threat is dealt with you will accompany me for a visit."

Griggalt smiled wide. "I would enjoy that very much, Cousin. Thank you for the kind offer."

"It will be my pleasure. But first things first. Victory, then recreation."

"Do not fear," he said with a cocky grin. "With the magnitude of your and Charlie's combined powers I do not think anyone would stand a chance."

CHAPTER SIX

Kip was already decked out with an impressive array of weapons to go along with the powerful konus welded into his framework, but seeing how he had just cheated death in a most spectacular manner, Zed had seen fit to have his techs do a hasty retrofit with some of the newest armament and shielding devices at his disposal while he and Dukaan were being debriefed.

Kip was an odd AI with one very unusual personality, but damn if he hadn't proven himself on more than one occasion. As such, he'd made some very connected friends.

In addition to the improvements made to the bond between the konus and his inner core, Kip had also received a special gift, one designed by Freya herself. A special invention of hers that was only shared with the most trusted of AIs.

A tiny swarm of nanites.

The microscopic machines spread across his hull in the thinnest of sheets, creating a solid covering from tip to tail. Eventually, they would draw from elements in the environment and reproduce, expanding his personal swarm, but for the time being they were just enough to enhance the auto-repair properties of his hull. But more than that, they also dialed into his sensors and shielding array, adapting to the environment to project images across his entirety and make the ship appear as though it wasn't there.

Kip was not a *true* stealth ship by any means. Even with his countermeasures, he could still be detected on a variety of sensor arrays. But to the naked eye he could vanish, the adaptive camouflage redirecting light around his exterior. It was an upgrade he really could have used *before* he and his friends had been attacked so unexpectedly.

But better late than never, he supposed. And once he was done with Zed, he would be as prepared as he could possibly be to carry his friends into harm's way.

Again.

Down on Earth a conflict of a far different variety was underway, and it was a heated one of type that no amount of armor could protect you from. Even Baloo, formerly curled up on the floor as Leila dropped him scraps, had retreated from the room. Mom and Dad were having an argument, and he was not about to wind up in the middle of that.

"I can't believe you expect me to stay here!" Leila yelled as she crammed more food into the cooling bag on the kitchen counter. "Unbelievable."

Charlie, to his credit, kept his tone level and his motions slow and unalarming. With the Magus stone around her neck, Leila could be a hazard, even to him, without realizing it. The stone defended her from anything it perceived as a threat, and that included the father of her child if she got worked up enough. Charlie had no desire to bear the brunt of that particular magical defense.

"You're pregnant," he said calmly. "And I don't mean just a little bit. You're ready to pop, and that means you are not in any condition to fly into combat."

"We are about to start a family, Charlie. We should be together. Period."

"And under any other circumstance I would agree. But like this..."

"Like *what*? Are you saying I'm helpless just because I'm pregnant? I'll have you know—"

"Babe, please, that's not what I'm saying at all," he said, moving closer.

"Oh, really? Because from where I'm standing, it—"

A small pulse of magic burst from her magus stone, knocking Charlie back a few feet. Leila paled slightly. She had been upset, but she had *not* intended for that to happen. As for Charlie, he was unharmed by it, but his point was made.

"I'm so sorry," Leila said, her anger extinguished in an instant, or at the very least reduced to a low smolder.

"It's okay," Charlie replied. "Actually, I'm kinda glad that thing's working the way it is. It means I won't have to worry about you while we're gone. No way anything's getting near you, though I do want to leave a couple of the strong konuses from the vault with you, just in case."

"You expect problems?"

"No. But by now we know better than to take anything for granted."

Charlie walked over to her and slowly wrapped her in his arms. The belly made for a slightly awkward embrace, but he wouldn't change it for the world. The Magus stone changed its vibration for a moment, bringing Charlie into the fold, creating a little bubble of perfection for the two, soon to be three.

Leila let go first and stepped back, wiping her eyes as she turned her focus to packing even more food for the voyage.

"Hon, I don't think I'll need that much food," he said. "Kip has a galley, and I'm only eating for one, you know."

"You will be well-fed if I have anything to say about it. And I do," she replied with a grin. Charlie knew far better than to object. "You're about to be a father, and that is going to require you at full strength."

"Well, if you put it that way," he said. "I'll be right back. I'm going to get you a few things from the vault."

"And for you."

"Yes, dear, I'll grab a few to bring with me as well. But without anyone to fight these last months, my power has been building up almost exponentially," he said, effortlessly creating a small fireball in one hand, tossing it to the other, then transforming it to a ball of ice.

"Nice trick, showoff," she said with a laugh. But behind the joking, she truly was glad he and Ara had grown so strong. He wasn't impervious, and neither was she, but they were starting to feel that way.

Charlie headed out to their vault and returned a few minutes later with a small backpack of gear for himself and a pair of very powerful konuses and a few enchanted blades for Leila. Normally, he would have simply left her to wield her Magus stone, but in protecting her baby it had a mind of its own, and that mind was fixated solely on protecting mother and child. So, a konus it would have to be.

He dropped the heavy bands on the counter along with a small metal cylinder.

"You're bringing the Balamar waters?"

"Like you said, I'm about to be a father. Better safe than sorry."

She grinned broad and kissed his cheek. Charlie redirected and went for the lips, holding her close a long moment. Then he hefted the overflowing bag of food and treats over his shoulder and headed for the door.

"Lord, woman, what did you pack in here?"

"Everything a growing boy needs. And a few surprises."

"I can't wait," he said as he picked up the helmet he'd be

wearing with his light space suit so he could communicate with the others in space.

They stepped outside and walked to the clearing where Ara and Griggalt were waiting for them. Bawb and Hunze were ready to fly, their Vespus blades strapped to their backs and their most powerful magical weapons tucked neatly in small bags. It was all they needed. He was a Ghalian, after all, and she might as well have been, and heaven help any who stood in their way.

Bawb also had the reinforced case for his wand strapped firmly to his thigh. It had been absorbing the sun's power for as long as Charlie and Ara had, as well as Hunze's golden locks. They, and their weapons, were all brimming with magical force just waiting to be unleashed.

"Okay, the gang's all here, but where the hell is Kip? He and Dukaan should have been here by now."

The AI ship popped into the visible spectrum parked right in front of him.

"We're here," he said, popping his hatch.

Dukaan stepped out to greet their friends. "Pardon Kip. He is rather enjoying his new upgrades."

"I can see why," Charlie said. "Or more accurately, I couldn't see."

"Zed wished for us to relay a message to you. He was able to reach Rika and Jo with a piggy-backed long-range transmission. They are quite a long way away, but they will be joining us on this mission. We will refine our trajectory and dial them in as we pursue the enemy."

Charlie smiled wide. They were up against a powerful enemy. A *really* powerful one. But they possessed a hell of a lot of magic of their own. And adding Rika to the mix only put them on even better footing. It might take some effort, but he was more than confident they would emerge victorious. And once they'd put these aggressors in their place, maybe then they'd get some answers.

He gave Leila a final kiss, scratched Baloo behind the ears, stowed his gear aboard Kip to spare Ara any additional mass on her harness as they flew into combat, then mounted up, looking at the amazing collection of friends he had at his side.

"Okay, you wonderful bunch," he said with a full heart. "Let's go save the world. Again."

CHAPTER SEVEN

"So, where exactly are we going, Sid?" Gustavo asked, settled in beside Kip on the far side of the moon at their rendezvous point at Dark Side base.

Dark Side's AI overseer checked his records. "No one is exactly sure," Sid replied. "We've been compiling flight data and tracking the trajectory of the fleeing craft, but it is still a moving target. Joshua, do you have any updates?"

"Not as of yet," the mind formerly running all tactical operations for NORAD replied. "But once the crew has completed the adjustments to your drive system konus, you should be able to lock into Ara's jump path without any problems."

"Okay, then. I guess we'll be hanging out a bit longer before we open that can of whoop-ass," Gus said.

"Not too much longer," Sid noted. "My techs are almost done. Charlie, Captain Sorkin, your teams should load up in about ten minutes."

"Copy that," Charlie replied, sipping a cup of hot coffee from the comfort of the base's mess hall. "Looking forward to it. Captain Sorkin, is your group good to go?"

"Ready and waiting," the captain replied. "Wilson's finished the final flight check with Gus. I have to say, we're all looking forward to a little payback for our people."

"Yeah, a great quantity of ass-kickery is about to be unleashed," Tamara added, crushing the cup in her ceramisteel hand for emphasis.

"Did you have to do that?" Shelley asked. "I mean, yeah, it makes the point and is, admittedly, pretty cool. But now Sid's gonna be one cup short."

Tamara laughed and jabbed her with a friendly elbow. "I think he'll manage."

It was an unplanned adjustment to Gustavo's onboard konus that had required the stopover, but spirits were high among the crews about to fly into battle. Sid had an extremely efficient crew running his repair and upgrade department. Also, having the most brilliant AI couple in existence living in their formerly secret fabrication lab just outside the base's perimeter didn't hurt.

While Freya was out on a run to the other galaxy with Daisy at the moment, Joshua was home tinkering with some new ideas in the lab, having left his larger ship body in orbit and opting for his smaller, incredibly armored, and more maneuverable housing to descend into their shared abode.

It was there that he and Freya had spent a great deal of the past year studying how magic worked. After all, magic is just science they haven't figured out yet. Or so people say. But the more they delved into the strange power, the more they realized it was not quite so simple as that.

"Hey, do you want to take the left or right flank when we warp?" Kip asked the other ship.

"Doesn't matter to me. Whichever way we go, we'll be warping right on top of them if all goes according to plan. They won't know what hit 'em."

"I hear that. I was thinking of opening with a spray of railgun sabots trailing an initial pulse barrage. You know, something to soften their shielding spells and get them to shift their defensive strategy from the onset. Then Ara and the gang will do a one-two punch with their magic when they're off guard and knock down their casters. Sound good to you?"

"Works for me," Gus said. "You're the one who's dealt with the magic side of things the most. Me? I've used the konus to tie into jumps before, but it's still pretty novel to me."

"Yeah, it took a little getting used to. But then, you've got experience with that."

"Ain't that the truth," the formerly human AI ship replied. "Ooh, that tickles!"

"Sorry," the tech welding inside of his airframe called out. "Almost done. You'll be able to launch in less than ten."

"Thanks," Gus said. "Looking forward to getting underway."

Ten minutes later, as promised, both crews had taken up their positions on their ships and were streaking through space, magically tied to Ara and Griggalt's jump magic. Their first stop was the coordinates of the initial attack, but when they exited their warp-jump, there was nothing there. Not even a trace of wreckage. There would be no unexpected survivors discovered here.

"This is unexpected," Dukaan said. "When we were under attack, the other ships were breaking apart. There should be at least some debris."

"Yeah, this is weird," Kip agreed. "Where did it all go?"

Ara and Griggalt sniffed the magic residue all around them. It was strong and everywhere. And it had an unusual flavor to it.

"There was extremely powerful magic used here," Ara noted. "Familiar, but not. Most intriguing. And their jumps appear to be muted, as if they were attempting to hide their true direction. No wonder Zed's trackers were having trouble."

"Can you follow it?" Charlie asked.

"Of course. But it does seem it will take a little longer to track this adversary than expected."

"I'll let Rika know," Charlie said, firing up the comms unit on Ara's harness. "Hey, Rika, are you close?"

Even with the relay units deposited all across the solar systems they had visited and the space in between there was still a long delay. Finally, her reply crackled over his comms.

"Almost to the coordinates. Just need to let the warp drive cool a minute. Solar winds in the last system pushed us a little off course. We're running hard to meet up with you."

Charlie keyed his comms. "Don't worry about being precise. Just follow the fighting when you arrive. It looks like they're playing hard to get, slippery bastards. They're jumping, and trying to mask them, so it'll take a little more work to track them down than we thought. I'll send you updates as we move." He shifted his attention to his Zomoki friend. "*You ready*?"

"*I have their scent,*" Ara replied.

"Okay, guys, we're on the hunt. Weapons hot, spells ready. We should be dropping in on these bastards relatively soon."

With that the team began following Ara and Griggalt as they jumped, their keen senses following the hidden path. Charlie updated Rika at every waypoint as soon as they had the next destination plotted. They repeated this several times, warping then popping into a new system, or space between, ready for a fight. But each time there was nothing. No one there.

"It is stronger," Griggalt said, sniffing the space around them. "I think we have them."

"I agree," Ara said. "They appear to be close."

Charlie had already sent his message and was calling up his most potent spells from the deep well of magic within him. This was it. Time to back up all of that big talk with actions.

"Almost there," Rika's reply reached him a few moments later.

"Okay," he said. "We're good to go. If there are no objections, let's do this."

There weren't any and a moment later, they jumped.

A mix of magic and warp energy flashed in the vast darkness of the void between systems. The last coordinates Ara and Griggalt had tracked the mysterious enemy to. The mighty beasts and accompanying ships arrived in a blaze of glory, deadly power bristling and conventional weapons primed and searching for a target. But there was nothing there.

Or so it seemed.

"I don't see any—" Gus began to say when he abruptly snapped out of existence with a faint crackle of magic.

Charlie and Ara looked around. Griggalt was nowhere to be seen, nor were there any enemy craft. The magic was strong here, but there was no one to fight. But that didn't mean they were safe. Not by a long shot.

"*Ara? What was*—" Charlie began to ask when the two of them were abruptly yanked through what he now realized was a hidden portal, floating invisibly in the inky black of space.

Kip, likewise, spun about like a tiny boat in rough seas and vanished just as Rika arrived, exiting her warp a little off course, the solar winds having altered her trajectory just a fraction. It was that fluke of luck that landed her just outside the portal's reach.

She sensed incredibly powerful magic, but not in a good way. This was danger, and it caused a violently repulsed reaction.

"What is it?" Jo asked as Rika yanked on the controls and banked their ship hard, pulling away from the portal.

Rika played back the images her cameras had captured at the instant of their arrival. There it was, clear as day. Ara and Kip vanishing without a trace.

"Rika? What's going on?" her cybernetic friend asked. "What the hell just happened?"

Rika swallowed hard as she scanned for other threats then executed an emergency warp away to a safe location.

"I don't know, Jo," she said. "But it's something very bad."

CHAPTER EIGHT

While the entry into the hidden portal had been only moderately violent, albeit startling, the exit proved to be quite the opposite. In fact, one could call it catastrophic.

Ara and Charlie were tumbling out of control as they were spat out the other side, the violent spin only compounded by the fact that they were being assaulted by something hot and painful.

Magical blasts buffeted Charlie from all sides, slamming him to and fro in the specialized harness that strapped him firmly to Ara's back. The mighty Zomoki was faring no better than he was as the relentless assault was bombarding her just as strongly.

Kip seemed to be faring no better, the poor little ship spinning out of control as he re-entered normal space. Only this space wasn't normal. This was somewhere unexpected. Unexpected and dangerous. The bright glow of the world's surface far below made it quite clear. They had been ejected right into the outermost edge of a planet's exosphere. And they were taking a beating.

"*Ara?*" Charlie silently called out. "*Ara, can you hear me? Bob? Anyone?*"

He was on her back still but couldn't sense his friend at all. That changed a moment later when they began a tumultuous re-entry through the planet's outer atmosphere. Ara was turning orange-hot from the friction as she burned into the skies. She positioned herself as best she could to protect Charlie, but even so, he felt the heat threaten to burn him alive. Then, without warning, the harness cracked, and Charlie found himself hanging on for dear life.

"Ara!" he called out, utterly disoriented.

She seemed to be conscious and was attempting to right herself as she plummeted toward the gravitational field of the world, but she did not reply. Stranger, she also seemed to have had frost forming on her thick scales from her space flight. Frost that was now turning to vapor as her scales heated up as they bumped along the edge of the atmosphere. That should not have been possible.

"*Ara?*"

Bawb's voice blared into his helmet. "Charlie, I cannot establish contact with the Wise One. She appears to be in distress."

"Our link is severed," he said, only now realizing that he felt absolutely nothing of the omnipresent connection that had bound the two of them for so long. He would have said more, but he suddenly felt the violent increase in G-force as he was flung from his broken harness, sent tumbling toward the atmosphere.

"Charlie!" Dukaan called after him as he and Kip struggled to gain control of their chaotic descent. "Kip, we have to get to him."

Bawb was already in motion within the little ship, quickly suiting up and locking himself within the relative safety of one of the space suits stowed aboard. Normally, his magic would have been enough, especially with Hunze beside him, but he could not feel his power. Nor hers. And without it, the emptiness of space was a most inhospitable place.

It was only because they would need to communicate over radios that Charlie had even suited up for this flight, and it was that seemingly inconsequential thing that had just saved his life. Without his and Ara's power protecting him, the human would not have lasted a minute.

"Charlie, we are coming," Bawb's voice crackled over his comms.

"Any time now would be great."

"Look down."

He pivoted in the buffeting wind and saw Kip had positioned himself below him, his airlock hatch now open and lined up as best he was able. Outside the door, Bawb had latched onto the hull and was waiting, arms outstretched to catch his falling friend.

"I'm coming in too fast!"

"Flare your arms and scrub off speed," Bawb instructed.

"I know what to do, but the atmosphere is too thin up here to give enough resistance," Charlie replied.

"On it," Kip said. "Dookie, we've gotta drop faster to match his pace."

"Tracking him already," Dukaan said. "We are within acceptable parameters. This will have to suffice."

"You hear that?" Bawb asked.

"Yeah. Not too happy about it, but we'll make do. Here I come, ready or not!" Charlie called out as he flew right at the open door, far too fast for his liking.

He flew into the open airlock, receiving a kick from Bawb as he did, sending him into the bulkhead where the impact helped scrub off some of his speed. It sucked, but he had made it aboard in one piece.

After a quick check that all of his parts were still attached, and a little griping for good measure, Charlie and Bawb hurried to command.

"We have to help her."

"How? She's a full-grown Zomoki."

"We get beneath her and adjust our rate of descent slowly to compensate for her mass. That lake."

"She will drown," Dukaan said. "She is unconscious."

"So we aim for the shoreline. Enough water to help cushion the impact but not so deep she drowns. And the water will stop the burning."

Bawb looked at Charlie with concern in his eyes. "Why is the Wise One burning? It should be impossible."

"I know, man. I know. We can try to figure that out once we make it down in one piece," Charlie replied.

"Where's Gustavo?" Hunze asked. "With two ships we can do a better job of guiding her."

"No sign of him," Kip replied. "I've tried on all frequencies. Wait a minute. I think I may be reading survival pod signatures."

"Are you sure?" Hunze asked. "How many?"

"I can't be sure. My readings are all over the place. Something slammed my systems hard. I can barely sense anything. They're coming back online, but it's a slow process."

"We'll deal with that later," Charlie said. "What about Griggalt? He could carry her at least a short distance."

"Nothing. Not a trace, but again, my scans are all out of whack."

Charlie weighed the options in a flash. "Then we have to do this ourselves," he said, watching as the ground grew closer and closer. "And we'd better hurry."

Kip didn't wait a moment longer, dipping underneath the unconscious Zomoki and shifting his thrust until her massive weight rested atop his airframe. "Got her," he said. "Going laterally toward the water is actually taking some of the strain off. I think we may actually pull this off."

Charlie winced. He didn't want anyone giving Murphy an open invitation to make an appearance, but it was too late to worry about that. The ground was coming up on them, and fast, and one way or another, they'd be touching down any second. He just hoped they would survive.

CHAPTER NINE

The unconscious Zomoki's scales were orange-hot in the whipping air, leaving a trail of smoke as the poor little ship tried his damnedest to guide her mass toward the water's edge. It would be a hard landing for her even with his help, but at least now there was some hope that she would survive it.

"Kip, we're coming in too fast," Charlie said.

"I know."

"You need to slow us down."

"I said I know. This isn't exactly easy, okay?" the AI said as they zoomed closer and closer to the muddy shore below. "Everybody strap in."

This particular body of water growing larger by the second appeared to be freshwater, part of a great lake system from what they could tell, but until they were able to get a sample to test there would be no telling for sure. But it was looking like they'd be down sooner than later, so that would not remain a problem much longer.

"Can you tell if the atmosphere is safe?" Charlie asked. "I see trees growing here."

"Not sure," Kip said. "But signs point to it being stable at the very least. Hold on!"

The ship bucked and dropped abruptly, then banked hard before leveling off. A moment later it settled down on the shoreline.

Hunze scanned the area outside the window, a questioning look on her face. "What just happened?"

"I rolled her off as we came in to land. It was a little tough compensating for the sudden lack of mass."

"That's what that was?" she asked.

"Yes. And, thank you very much, I managed to get her right in the shallows, as requested."

"Nice job, Kip," Charlie said, already rushing to the airlock door. "Make sure the air is safe when you can. I'm already suited up so I'm heading out. Ara needs me. You got it?"

He didn't wait for a reply, quickly sealing the airlock behind him and exiting the ship. A moment later Bawb cycled the airlock doors and joined him.

When Bawb reached Charlie, he was calling out to Ara but she just lay there, motionless and partly submerged in the shallows, steam rising from the water around her. She was breathing, but she did not respond. He reached out and rested his gloved hand on her flank. He yanked it back immediately.

"Bob, she's burning up. We need to cool her down," he said, quickly scooping up handfuls of water and splashing them on her as best he could.

Steam flashed where the water landed, but it was like using an eyedropper to fill a bucket. Bawb rushed to his side and joined in the effort, making a tiny improvement, but it was still nowhere near enough. Two more figures clad in light suits with helmets hurried from Kip's airlock a minute later and began helping as well. It was a valiant effort, but wholly inadequate.

"Thank you," Charlie said. "But this is *not* going to cut it. Stand back."

The others moved several paces away as he reached out his hands, drawing deep from his inner reserves of power, summoning a massive wave to wash across his burning friend.

Nothing happened.

Again he tried, straining to connect with his magic, but once more nothing came of it. Not even the slightest ripple in the water. Charlie's brow furrowed deeply.

"What the hell?" he wondered, pulling a pair of powerful konuses from the pouch on his hip and sliding them onto each wrist.

With all of his might he called upon the power they contained, willing it to bend to his demands and do his bidding. But instead of summoning a cooling wave to wash across Ara's flanks, the konuses merely sat dormant, as useless as ordinary bracelets.

"My magic, it's gone," he gasped, his mind racing. "It must be because Ara is hurt. Our bond is somehow causing it to fail. Even the konuses."

"Allow us," Bawb said as he and Hunze stepped in to pick up the slack. But even the naturally powerful Ootaki and her bonded mate could not cast so much as the most minor of spells. Try as they might, they too, it seemed, were entirely without power.

Dukaan, the only completely magic-less person among them had seen enough. "No more of this futility. Ara is in need. Kip, we require your assistance."

"What can I do?" he asked.

"Ara is in peril. You must help extinguish the burning."

Kip didn't say another word, but rather fired up his drive systems and lurched into the air. Only he didn't fly high, but, rather, stayed low. So low, in fact, that he was skimming the surface of the water. He flew back fifty meters then rushed forward, abruptly dipping down into the water itself a little bit before lifting up just as he reached Ara's inert mass.

The water rose and sloshed over her, releasing a massive, hissing cloud of steam. Again, he backed up and performed his unusual fireman's drill once more, quenching the last of the smoldering scales once and for all before settling back down onto the shore.

"Nicely done, Kip," Charlie said. "Thank you. That last bit diving into the water was inspired."

"Thanks. But it wasn't exactly intentional," the ship said, his power spiking and dropping erratically. "I lost some drive control for a minute there. Wasn't sure if I'd be going for a swim or not."

"Are you okay?"

"No, I'm definitely not. But I can at least tell you that the air here is safe to breathe. I would have a more specific analysis, but after that surge, my scans are now entirely down. Something totally overstressed aspects of my systems, and I'm rather blind now."

"Is this permanent? Can they be repaired?" Bawb asked.

"Repaired? Almost certainly, but I need to reroute power so my drive systems can cool off while I troubleshoot and run a full systems diagnostic. When we popped out of whatever the hell kind of portal that was and were thrown into the atmosphere, I felt something slam into my power systems. The warp core stepped up and picked up the slack and kept me aloft, but it was touch and go for a minute there. It knocked just about everything out."

Charlie felt a sinking feeling deep in his gut. Magic and technology alike were failing them, and they had no idea why.

"Oh, and my konus?" Kip added. "Yeah, that's totally dead. Not an iota of power from it that I can tell. And I'm saying that as an AI. Tracking power fluctuations and that sort of thing is kind of my forte."

Charlie turned and began pacing the shoreline, walking back and forth as he ran the situation through his mind over and over. Things were wrong. Very wrong. And though it was full daylight, this planet's sun was casting the strangest light. The wavelength felt off. Bent, almost. Charlie couldn't exactly put his finger on it, but wherever they'd wound up, it was not normal.

"What the hell just happened, guys?" he wondered. "We were totally prepared. Overprepared, even. Anyone have any ideas?"

"Nary a one," Dukaan said, shaking his head in disbelief. "This is utterly unprecedented."

"I am in agreement with Dukaan," Bawb chimed in. "And while I am well-accustomed with the taking of power, we do not appear to have been drained, as such. But, nevertheless, our power appears to be negated and untouchable. Yet I did not sense it being actively taken."

"But *how*?" Charlie asked.

"*That*, my friend, is a mystery," Bawb replied, scanning the treeline for any signs of danger. "And one we need to solve, sooner than later, if at all possible."

CHAPTER TEN

"Captain Sorkin, do you copy? I repeat, Sorkin, are you there? Tamara? Wilson? Anyone? Transmit if you are receiving this."

Charlie waited a long moment then tried again. "Gustavo? Anyone on this frequency, do you read me? Rika, Jo, are you picking this up? We've been pulled through a portal and forced down on some planet. Habitable, but not without issues. Come on, somebody respond."

Again, silence, and the worst kind. There wasn't even static. Just the complete absence of sound.

"I don't think they're out there," Kip said. "They would have at least squelched the comms line or something."

"Or they are incapacitated and unable to reply," Bawb noted.

Charlie groaned. "Always a frigging ray of sunshine, aren't you?"

"I am merely stating the facts as I see them. Sugarcoating them, as you say, does not benefit anyone."

Hunze stepped close to him and rested her hand on his shoulder, the two of them feeding off of one another, drawing strength even if there was no exchange of magic at the moment.

"He does not mean to distress you, Charlie," she said. "Bawb is merely being pragmatic."

"I know, I know. It's just our situation is not so great, and I could use a win right about now."

"I understand. But he is correct that false hope is of little use to us in this situation."

Charlie knew she was right. He also knew what he had seen as they were streaking down toward the surface. He'd hoped he was wrong, but deep down, he knew he wasn't.

"Kip, do you have any access to your external video files during the descent?" he asked.

"Most are still inaccessible, Charlie. Sorry."

"It's okay. I just thought I may have seen something on the way down."

"What?" the ship asked

"Some of Gustavo's escape pods."

Bawb and Hunze both perked up at the mention.

"But that would mean the ship was critically damaged," Kip said. "For anyone to punch out during a rough re-entry like that? There'd have to be a catastrophic failure."

Bawb stroked his chin as he pondered the possibility. "But even if they did, we have no means to track them at the moment. Without any functional technology to search with, and lacking the power to cast even the most basic of spells, if they did come down, we simply do not know where they may have landed."

Charlie merely gazed off into the distance over his friend's shoulder.

"Charlie, did you hear what I said?"

"Yeah, yeah, I heard you. But I don't think we need magic or even a tracking device to find them. I know where they landed."

Bawb cocked his head slightly. "How? I do not sense anything."

"And I'm not getting any signal," Kip added.

A little grin creased Charlie's lips. He pointed over Bawb's shoulder. The others all turned to look where he was focused. There, perhaps five or so miles away, a long wisp of dark smoke was rising into the air.

"With Kip experiencing flight issues, that will be a fair trek," Bawb mused.

"Yeah, but that means he can keep an eye on Ara while we're gone," Charlie replied. "Someone has to look after her. She's totally vulnerable like this."

"I will stay at her side as well," Hunze said, drawing her Vespus blade.

The sword's blue length shone in the sunlight, as one would expect of the expertly crafted sword, but its signature magical glow was notably absent. It was just a sword, it seemed, not a magical implement of death. But in skilled hands, that would be quite enough for most situations, and Hunze's most certainly fit that criteria.

Bawb eyed the blade with discomfort. He did not need to draw his own sword to know its blade was likewise lacking power. It was impossible enough that both of them possessed one of the few remaining Vespus blades in existence, but to have them simultaneously lose all of their formidable power was unheard of.

"Are you certain?" Bawb asked, his concern for his love clear despite his calm expression.

"Yes. Ara needs us now, and more bodies on the ground will not make your approach to your destination any stealthier. I can do more good here, protecting our friend."

Bawb nodded his approval.

"I will remain with her as well," Dukaan said. "Not for her protection, of course. I believe, should danger present itself it would more likely be Hunze defending me than the other way around. But I will do all I can to repair Kip's systems and get him in proper working order as quickly as I am able."

Charlie turned to the Chithiid pilot. "You expect trouble?"

"Don't you?"

"Well, yeah. I kinda always do at this point. But a guy can hope, right?"

Dukaan gave him an amused look and handed him a pair of adhesive bone-conduction comms patches.

"Spec-ops comms?"

"Zed supplied us with them as we geared up for this mission. Just in case, he said. It would seem he was prescient in his foresight."

Charlie stuck the patch behind his right ear. "Testing, testing."

"I hear you," Kip said silently in his head, the tiny receiver vibrating the bone at the back of his skull, transmitting sound silently rather than out loud.

It was a device he'd played with once back when Sergeant Franklin was showing him some of the toys he and his human comrades used on their missions.

For Charlie, however, it was not a common part of his kit. He could communicate far more efficiently and over greater distances with his magic, after all. But now, powerless as he was, it was a godsend.

"Great. Let us know if there are any developments back here. We'll be as quick as we can," Charlie replied. He turned to fetch his friend, but the deadliest man in the galaxy was momentarily occupied, and not even Charlie would interrupt this intimate moment.

Bawb and Hunze were saying their farewells, their foreheads pressed together, his hand on her stomach and hers resting on the back of his neck. She twinged slightly, then regained her composure, but the look of concern on the assassin's face was immediate.

"I am fine," she said with a warm smile. "It is merely my body's way of reminding us that there is a new life growing."

"All the more reason for you to be careful in my absence."

"And for you to come back to me safely," she replied. "Something of which I have little doubt, love. Now, go. Do not worry about me. Our friend needs my assistance, and our allies need yours. There will be plenty of time for us later."

"A lifetime, one might say."

"Indeed, one might," she replied, leaning in for a gentle kiss. "Go. Charlie looks antsy."

"Charlie *always* looks that way," he replied with a low chuckle. "We shall return shortly. Charlie, come, let us depart."

The two men took off at a quick jog, a pulse pistol strapped to each of their hips in addition to their other weapons. Of course, with the trail of smoke rising in the sky, any hostiles that might be around would quite possibly follow it back to its source. That would be enough to attract unwanted attention without weapons fire. Avoiding notice was the priority.

If they had to dispatch anyone, it would be silently if at all possible. The pair moved with speed and precision, their footing sure on the uneven terrain. Soon they melted into the tree line and were gone from sight.

Dukaan stepped inside his damaged ship and set to work. Hunze, on the other hand, leaned close to examine her burned and slumbering friend. The damaged scales had been badly charred, and the flesh beneath them was inflamed and raw. Despite all of that, Ara appeared to be in a deep, restorative sleep.

Hunze had seen this before, when the Zomoki was soaking in the rays of the sun back on Earth. But there was no magic to be had here, and Ara was sleeping, but her body was not healing.

She paced back and forth beside the enormous creature, her feet sloshing in the mud as she tried to think of a way, *any* way she might help. Hunze pulled her boot from the sucking mud and hopped a few steps toward firmer ground, then stopped, remembering her lessons from Leila.

She bent low and scooped up a handful of the mud, brought it to her face, and sniffed. From what her herbalist friend had taught her in their time together, this was clean, helpful clay-type mud. Ideally, she would have asked Kip to verify her observation as to the mineral content of the mud, but he was short on resources at the moment, and she was confident enough in her assessment to proceed.

Scooping with both hands, she pulled free a sizable quantity of mud with a wet smack then leaned in close and spread it along a tiny fraction of the burned Zomoki's flank. The mud seeped into the cracked scales, and the radiant heat that had remained even after being quenched with water began to tangibly dissipate.

Hunze smiled to herself. Leila would be pleased. A very valuable lesson, indeed, and far, far from the land it had been taught upon. Some things, it seemed, transcended planetary boundaries. She bent down and scooped up more mud and began the Herculean undertaking of covering an entire Zomoki head to tail.

CHAPTER ELEVEN

"Look at this stuff," Charlie said in a hushed voice as he and Bawb weaved through the lush growth of the alien forest. "It's like the frikkin' Amazon down here."

The trees had been somewhat densely packed for a few miles, but when they shifted course slightly and moved inland, away from the moisture of the lake's edge, nature, it seemed, had seen fit to space out the trees a bit more to best utilize the precious resources.

Close to the water, however, everything grew like a weed. Charlie almost wished Leila was there with him to see it. Her skill with plant and animal life would be a huge help, not to mention she would undoubtedly find the new species fascinating. From what he could tell, the water was rich in whatever nutrients the plant life required. Whether that translated into something people could drink was yet to be determined.

"Have you noted the tracks?" Bawb asked, his eyes constantly scanning the terrain as they moved.

"Animals. Mid-sized, likely herbivores," Charlie replied.

Bawb smiled. "Excellent. Your tracking skills are improving."

"Good teacher," he noted.

"The teacher is only as good as the pupil."

"Well, this pupil sees some interesting separations between the trees up ahead. I assume you see what I see?"

"Yes. Either larger animals have passed that way or—"

"Or we're not alone down here."

Bawb squinted as he followed the wisps of smoke growing closer with every step. "We know we are almost certainly not alone. But to create a notable trail? That would imply local inhabitants frequenting the path."

"Or space cows."

"Yes, Charlie. Or space cows."

"Man, a burger sounds good right about now."

"No killing local fauna. For all we know, the highest form of sentient life on this world may look like one of your space cows."

"I know, man. I'm not a barbarian," Charlie griped. "I'm just saying. A burger? Sounds pretty damn good."

"No, Charlie," Bawb chided.

"Dude, chill. I'll use the replicator when we get back to Kip. I can't remember the last time I had *actual* meat from an animal. But do you really think it could be space cows?"

"Whatever it is, judging by the smoke, our course will bring us near to that area. We will find out soon enough."

While her partner trekked into the unknown, Hunze was hard at work applying mud to as much of Ara's body as she could reach. She was careful climbing up on her friend's back, as the damage to her scales was more severe where she had twisted upon entry to the atmosphere, using the thicker scales to deflect the burn while protecting Charlie's far more fragile body in the process.

It spoke to the strength of their bond and friendship that went far beyond the mere blood ties. Their invisible, magical connection may have been severed, but Ara was still looking out for him even in the most dire of circumstances. And it had almost certainly provided Kip and Bawb the window they needed to save his life.

Hunze had stripped off a layer of clothing for the effort, though she kept a decent assortment of weapons on her person, as was the Ghalian way. But cleaning additional mud from her bulkier gear would be an annoyance, and one she would rather avoid if possible, especially as it was a rather warm day.

It felt strange, standing in full sunlight but receiving not a single iota of magic from the sun's rays. She had grown so accustomed to the constant flow of power in her time on Earth that the absence was somewhat disconcerting. Like a sensation you hadn't realized you were experiencing until it was gone. Of course, as magic was neutered in this place, it wouldn't have made a difference one way or the other, but it was an unusual feeling all the same.

She dug her arms elbow deep and flung as much mud up onto Ara's flanks as she could, repeating the process a few dozen times before carefully climbing the slumbering Zomoki's side to spread the healing balm across her body. It was incredibly time consuming, but Hunze was nothing if not perseverant, and someone she cared about was in need. There was simply no other logical course of action. She saw the problem that needed to be addressed and set to work.

Dukaan stepped out of Kip's hatch and sized up the Ootaki's work.

"She is covering her in mud," he mused.

"Yep. Been at it a while too," Kip noted. "I don't really have the resources to do a proper scan, but I was able to determine that the soil directly beneath me appears to have an interesting mineral composition. If that holds true everywhere in the area, my guess is the mud likely has some healing properties."

"But it is mud."

"So? Come on, Dookie, haven't you ever used mud on your skin?"

"Why would I do that?"

"It's something people do. Good for the skin."

"You do not possess skin."

"Gee, ya think?" the ship snarked. "Just because I'm not in a meat body doesn't mean I haven't paid attention to what all y'all do with yourselves."

"Did you just say, *all y'all*?"

"It's a thing. Shut up," Kip said with a chuckle. "Anyway, I'd do a more thorough analysis, but I'm still experiencing a serious power drain. Check the bottom of my hull, would ya? This doesn't feel right."

"You just want me to crawl around in this 'healing dirt' of yours, don't you?" Dukaan grumbled as he ducked down low to better examine the lowest part of his AI friend's hull.

He got down on his hands and knees and made his way toward the landing gear, as it was the most elevated part of Kip's lowermost area. Strangely enough, there actually *was* something unusual down there. Something that was clearly not naturally occurring.

"I see something," he said.

"What is it?"

"I am moving closer for a better look, but from what I can see, it appears to be a large disc of some kind stuck to your hull."

Dukaan's griping reluctance had been replaced with both curiosity as well as concern. Something had latched onto Kip's underbelly, and he had no idea what it was. And if his suspicion was correct, this could very well be what was hampering his scanners. He moved closer, reaching out to touch the foreign object.

"It appears to be metal of some sort. Perhaps as thick as my palm."

"So, it's kinda thick, then?"

"I suppose you could say that."

"You do have manly hands, Dookie."

"Oh, shut up, Kip. This is serious."

"So am I. Can you pull it off?"

"I am not sure. Stand by."

Dukaan slid his fingers along the edge of the disc. It wasn't that large, all things considered. Perhaps the size of a small serving platter, though made of far more robust stuff. He pulled, gently at first. It did not budge. Again he pulled, this time with more force. A shock made him snatch his hands back.

"Ouch!"

"What happened?"

"It shocked me."

"Rude!"

"I have a few other choice words to describe it, but yes," Dukaan said, rubbing his fingers.

"Hey, come back inside," Kip said.

"Not yet. I see more of these things down here."

"More?"

"Yes, at least five of them stuck to your hull."

"Not cool. A bunch of nasty space remoras hitching a ride. I bet that's what's messing up my systems."

"Perhaps. Now you see why I must stay here and come up with a solution. I know there must be something, I just have to think."

"Stop thinking and come inside."

"Did you not hear anything I just said?"

"Yeah, I did. But I've got something that'll help. Sid's techs hooked me up with a new set of non-conductive tools before we headed out."

"Well, why didn't you say so?"

"I just did."

Dukaan bit his tongue and began crawling out from beneath the ship. He could be maddening at times, but Kip was a good partner despite his quirks. Arguing would not serve their purposes, so he let it go. That, and Kip could draw out a circular ramble ad nauseam if he continued to engage with him.

Three minutes later Dukaan was on his hands and knees again, this time sporting not only a tool that *should* protect him from any unwanted shocks, but also protective eyewear and gloves. This was alien tech, after all, and there was no telling exactly what it might do when he tried to remove it.

As it turned out, the answer was not much. A few sparks crackled across the device, but once it had lost contact with the ship's hull it seemed to become entirely inert. He passed a handheld scanning device over the now-silent unit. Its origin was utterly alien, a technological variant the likes of which he had never seen before. But there would be plenty of time to study them later.

With the first of the troublesome devices removed, Dukaan now knew what he was dealing with. And more importantly, so did Kip.

"I can feel my sensors regaining some capability," the ship said. "Get the others, Dookie."

"That was my plan," he sighed.

In short order the remaining discs were removed. It turned out there had been seven of them in total once he made a more thorough search of the craft. It appeared they had been attracted to the metal, clinging to it as he flew into them.

"So, it was like some kind of debris field?"

"Not debris. A deliberate hobbling technology."

"I know, it was a figure of speech. But you get the idea. Someone left these things floating out there, waiting to zap anyone who came close. That might explain why we haven't been able to talk to Gustavo. He was probably hit by the same things. Hopefully when Charlie and Bawb find him they'll be able to get him back online."

"I will relay our findings to them," Dukaan said.

"I can do it."

"No, you need to focus on restoring your systems," the Chithiid replied. "For if someone has laid this sort of complex trap, I fear we may find ourselves dealing with them sooner than later."

CHAPTER TWELVE

Charlie and Bawb were making exceptionally good time now that they were on more solid terrain. A narrow strip of marshy swampland where an inland water source flowed into the large lake had provided a brief delay, and minus the convenient use of magic, the duo had been forced to resort to more conventional means of traversing the obstacle.

Fortunately, the water was shallow, and finding, then relocating, a fallen log to provide a little footbridge had proven easy enough. However, when they moved to place it, they discovered something surprising just upstream. Surprising, but not entirely unexpected.

"Is that a little footbridge?" Charlie asked, stating the obvious.

"Yes, most definitely a bridge," Bawb replied.

Of course, it had been a rhetorical question. Charlie was an engineer, after all, and identifying a bridge, even on this alien world, was well within his expertise.

"So, there are people here," he said. "And if they're building bridges, they're obviously not just stopping over. This place is inhabited."

"It would appear that way, yes," Bawb agreed. "We must be at least somewhat close to wherever they call home. And look, over there," he said, pointing to the diverging paths. "Clearly used by bipedal individuals, wearing footwear, no less. I am sorry, Charlie, but it seems your space cow theory is not going to play out after all."

"I'll survive. So, you think we should hit the trees the rest of the way? I'm not liking how exposed we'll be on those trails."

"I was thinking the same thing," Bawb replied. "We will go off-trail and move silently from here on. The smoke is not far."

Charlie zipped his lips and nodded, stepping off into the trees close behind his friend. They had still not seen any actual people, whatever that meant on this world, but it was now abundantly clear that *someone* was here. Until they knew if they were friend or foe, the two of them would stay out of sight.

Charlie and Bawb had been trekking for well over an hour when they finally reached the source of the smoke. One look at the place and they knew one thing for certain. This was not a landing field. It was a crash site.

Parts of Gustavo's formerly magnificent ship lay scattered about the area, trees and shrubbery crushed by the impacts. Now that they were at the actual location it became apparent that the craft had broken apart before reaching the surface, its pieces slamming into the soil across what looked like a square mile or so. Smaller fires were still sending up smoke in thin tendrils away from the main crash site, but the largest portions appeared to have descended together.

It was that massive impact that had kicked up a sizable amount of dirt, much of which snuffed out the flames. It was blind luck, but it had left a great deal of the wreckage intact as a result.

"Look," Charlie said, pointing out the empty indentations in the ruined hull. "Escape pods launched."

"Or were torn free and landed somewhere else," Bawb posited.

"No, they launched. Look, the chemical separation rockets burn hotter than a normal fire. That's what those char patterns are, see? They burned the hull when they ejected."

"So, it would seem at least some of the crew may have survived. We should look for them," Bawb said, scanning the area.

"I want to, and we'll look for survivors at this location. But as far as trekking off into the wilderness, there's some salvage here that we could really use, and they could have landed miles away in any direction. The instinct is a good one, but without knowing even rough coordinates we'd just be wandering around aimlessly. No, we need Kip for this. Once his electronics are functional we should be able to lock in on their location within a few feet."

Bawb's shoulders relaxed a fraction. "Yes, that would be more efficient," he said.

Charlie walked to the most intact section of the ship and began rooting around inside. It was a long portion of corridor and parts of the adjoining compartments, all of them now broken and in ruins. But some of the storage racks had survived the crash, and at least a few of their contents had to be salvageable.

But there was something else.

"Hey, Bob. Check this out," Charlie quietly called out, his eyes scanning the tree line.

The Ghalian strode to his location, his fingertips tickling the ends of his matched daggers, ready for action. "What is it?"

"Nothing. At least, not yet. But look at this. There should be another bin attached here."

"The vessel did crash, Charlie."

"Yeah, I know, but see this?" He pointed to a shiny bit where the char had been scraped free. "Whoever took this did it after the ship crashed and the fire was out. That means this thing's been scavenged already. Someone got here before us."

"The surviving crew?" Bawb wondered.

"I don't know. I really don't think so. This doesn't look like the work of anyone who knows the ship. It looks more random. Like they were just hoping to find something of value but didn't know exactly what they were looking for."

"So, as you said, then. Salvage."

"Precisely. But there are still plenty of things we could find useful. We should get them back to the ship."

"Or the ship should come to us," Bawb replied. "Kip, how are your repairs coming?" he transmitted.

The ship's voice came through loud and clear inside both of their heads, vibrating their skulls as it did. It was such an unusual sensation, Charlie almost sneezed for a moment.

"Quite well, actually," the AI replied. "Dookie found some weird disc thingies stuck to my hull all along my belly. Definitely weren't there when we left Dark Side, so I must've picked them up on the way down. They were wreaking merry havoc with my scanners and drive systems, but now that they're off a lot of that is coming back online."

"A passive attack of some sort?" Charlie asked.

"Yeah, seems that way. Like a bunch of remora sucking resources. If I had to guess, I'd say they latched on right after we popped out of the portal."

Charlie and Bawb shared a look. This was getting very interesting, and not in a good way.

"Okay, you keep your eyes peeled. There are definitely people on this planet, and with our luck they won't be the kind that want you to marry their daughter."

"This could be awkward, depending on morphology," Bawb noted.

"I'm flexible," Kip said with a cheerful laugh. "But I do see your point. Dookie should have the drive systems cleared within the hour."

"Good. We may need you to fly out to our location to pick up some salvage." Charlie immediately regretted his choice of words.

"*Salvage*?" Kip asked. "How badly damaged is Gustavo? It's his landing gear, isn't it? I told him to have it reinforced, but he said there wasn't any time. Well, let me tell you, there's *never* time until you're suddenly forced to make a belly landing. Why, I bet—"

"He's dead, Kip," Charlie said. "I'm sorry, but Gus is gone."

A long silence hung in the air before the AI spoke again. "What do you mean, *gone*?"

"I mean he broke up long before he even hit the ground. And from what we've seen, he hit *hard*. There's no way he survived this."

"You're sure it was Gustavo's ship, not some other one?"

"It wasn't the *Fujin*, if that's what you're getting at. There's been no sign whatsoever of Rika and Jo. And besides, the wreckage is quite distinctive."

Kip processed this information both passively, as a machine would, but emotionally, as was his AI nature. Gus was a friend. Not a good one, but a friend all the same. And now he was gone. Kip was now the only AI on the planet.

"What about the crew?" he finally asked.

"From what we can tell, some of them may have managed to eject in escape pods, but we have no idea where they might be. That's where you come in. We need you to run a scan for the pods when you come to pick us up."

"Pick you up? I thought I was guarding Ara."

"And you are. But a short hop should only take a few minutes, and we need to get this salvage aboard. The faster we do that, the better our overall situation will be."

"So, there's a lot?" Kip asked.

"A fair amount," Charlie replied.

"And we may have something else," Bawb added.

Charlie looked at his friend with a puzzled expression.

Kip had already made up his mind. Of course he would fly to get them. Hunze was anything but helpless, after all. Even without her power. She'd be fine.

"Okay, I'll do it," the ship finally said. "I'll let you know as soon as my drive systems are checked out and online."

"That's all I can ask," Charlie said. "And, Kip, I'm sorry about your friend."

"Me too," he replied. "Me, too."

The line went silent.

"Come on, help me gather everything useful they didn't already take," Charlie said.

"Of course," the assassin replied. "But once that has been done, we will need to procure food for our friend."

"We have food, Bob."

"Yes, but the Wise One is injured and weak, and when she wakes, she will require sustenance. Far more than we have aboard the ship."

Gears began to turn in Charlie's mind. "What exactly did you have in mind?"

Bawb's fangs shone as he smiled. "We shall hunt."

CHAPTER THIRTEEN

The *Fujin*'s warp core was hot from constant use, the ship's systems pushed hard in the aftermath of whatever it was that had happened to Charlie and his team. Rika had been flying fast and furious for hours, warping to every system within range as well as stopping over in the void between periodically.

It was more than the ship's systems were designed to endure in such a short time frame, but she had been pouring her power into the *Fujin*'s airframe the entire time, her magic-channeling tattoos glowing faintly as she drew from whatever sun they might be near.

Even so, the ship needed a break, and her copilot was not shy in saying so.

"Goddammit, Rika, you've got to ease off," Jo said when they popped out of yet another warp.

"I ease off when we know what the hell happened to them," she replied.

"And we *will* find out. But if you push the ship much harder we're going to wind up needing rescue as well. Remember, you don't do anyone any good if you go and make yourself into a casualty as well."

It was something Rika had yelled at Charlie on more than one occasion, and hearing those words redirected her way drove the point home. Reluctantly, she unclenched the knot in her belly that had been pulling every ounce of nearby energy she could, and as she did, she realized she hadn't even been aware just how hard she was working.

A little shiver ran through her body.

"Here," Jo said, handing her a tall mug of enriched chicken soup from the ship's replicator. "You need to replenish all of those calories and protein you've been burning through."

Rika didn't argue, greedily guzzling the contents of the mug and handing it back with a satisfied burp.

"More, please," she sighed, slumping in her seat as the warmth spread through her belly.

"You got it," Jo said, heading off to the ship's small galley to get her friend a refill.

Jo had made a point of keeping an eye on her human companion in times of physical as well as psychological stress. Rika was a stubborn woman with exceptional drive, and while that was a good trait when the chips were down, it also meant she sometimes neglected herself in the process. Being a cyborg who never slept and always paid attention, Jo was not only her friend, but also the perfect babysitter for her.

When Rika would let her, that is. Being the wielder of a particularly potent magic in not one galaxy but two, her human pilot sometimes let her bravado get the best of her. Fortunately, this was not one such moment.

A second mug of soup later Rika was in a much better mood as her blood sugar returned to normal levels.

"Thanks, Jo. I didn't realize how much I needed that."

"You know me. *Jo, Bringer of Soup*, they call me."

Rika grinned wide then turned her attention back to the displays in front of them. They were floating at the far edge of a nine-planet solar system, reviewing the footage they had captured when they narrowly avoided the same fate as their friends. What they saw was just as disconcerting now as before.

"I didn't feel it connect with the other galaxy," Rika said. "None of that power."

Jo enhanced the visuals to show a rough outline of the invisible portal that had sucked in the others. They'd only just barely arrived in time to witness the disappearing traces of Kip and Ara, but it had been enough. That, and the uncomfortable lack of magic in the portal made Rika's tattoos itch something terrible.

"So, they're still somewhere here," Jo said. "But we're not receiving any distress signals. No messages at all."

"I know. But if they were damaged on the way through, they could be stranded and needing our help. I can't gauge how much power that thing is putting out, but to pull in a creature as strong as Ara, I have to assume there's enough magic powering it to send them at least a few systems away if not more."

Jo nodded her head as she traced her finger along the route they'd followed trying to find their friends. They had flown an expanding sphere from the point of disappearance. With only one ship to perform the search, and with space spreading out in all directions, it was the best shot they had.

Rika had wished she could fire up her mech and launch in it to divide their efforts, but she'd left it on Earth. Besides, it was too big for the *Fujin* to carry anyway, unless she strapped it to the ship's belly.

"There was something off about it," Rika said. "I keep coming back to the way it felt. Like it was grating my own power the wrong way."

"The Kalamani have said there are many types of power, and some should never mix. After all, look what yours did to Malalia's people. Maybe we finally stumbled upon the Yin to your Yang."

"Maybe. Whatever it was, I don't like it. And I can tell you, there's not a doubt in my mind that Charlie and Ara felt it too."

"So why did they get pulled in?" Jo asked.

"My guess is they landed too close to avoid it, and by the time they realized they were in trouble it was too late. You and me? We were both late to the party and a little off course. It was just blind luck that we got there far enough away from the portal to escape."

Jo nodded in thought. Or in the appearance of thought. As an AI superbrain, she had already processed the finer points of those parameters in microseconds. "So, you think it was a trap," she finally said.

Rika ran her fingers through her hair as she replayed it all through her head again. "Yeah, I think it was a trap."

"We have to warn Zed and the others."

"I know. And we will. But time is a funny thing, and we have to do all we can while the trail is still warm. By the time we warp all the way back to Earth we'll have lost what little edge we have. And we're way, *way* too far out to send a long-range transmission. Hell, we're so far out into the uncharted regions that it'd take decades for a signal to even reach one of our repeater satellites from here."

Jo knew what Rika was thinking. They'd flown together far too long for her not to. But she still had to ask, just to make her say it out loud.

"So, what do you want to do, Captain?"

Rika tapped six more systems on the screen, highlighting each of them with a flashing dot. "We search a few more systems before heading back is what we do. I know it's a needle in a haystack made of more needles, but this is Charlie we're talking about. If he's in trouble, you know it's bad."

"True," Jo agreed. "Run of the mill is definitely not in his vocabulary."

"Not in the slightest," Rika agreed. "And another thing, I

have absolutely no desire to be the one who has to tell Leila her man was sucked into an enemy portal and sent god knows where in the galaxy when she's just about ready to pop. One should never deliver that kind of news to a pregnant woman if at all possible."

"Especially if she happens to be the owner of a Magus stone," Jo added.

"Oh, most definitely not," Rika agreed. "I can only imagine what might happen. No, scratch that, I don't want to imagine it." She slid back into her pilot's seat and strapped in as she powered up all systems. "Warp core is cooled and good to go, and the primary drive systems are humming like a happy puppy. We're as ready as we're going to be, so let's get to it. Charlie and the gang are out there somewhere, and I'd bet the farm they could use our help."

CHAPTER FOURTEEN

"No space cows, huh?" Charlie muttered as he and Bawb followed the unmistakable trail of some sort of large quadrupedal beast endemic to this world.

"Shh," Bawb chided, pointing to a fresh pile of scat.

"Just saying."

They were getting closer, clearly, though what exactly they were tracking they weren't quite sure of. There was actually a decent assortment of animals in the trees from what they could tell, many of them utterly unafraid of the two men stalking through the brush. Unfortunately, it would have taken many dozens of them to make a dent in Ara's inevitable hunger. They needed something bigger.

The Zomoki's appetite was normally quite impressive, even when she wasn't attempting to recuperate from an injury or particularly strenuous exertion. But given her current condition, even the largest of animals would likely only begin to take the edge off of her hunger.

They had seen her feast after battle plenty of times and knew the extent of her potential intake. But this time it was different. She had been burned, and it would take more than a snack and nap to restore her.

The hope was that once she had at least a little nourishment she would be able to fly and hunt for larger prey, and more of it. But incapacitated as she was, for now it was up to her friends to provide for her.

A shriek pierced the air, but by now they were aware of its origin and ignored it. There were flocks of bird-like creatures in the skies above, their loud calls breaking the quiet of the woods below. Charlie and Bawb had been moving together for nearly twenty minutes, following a meandering trail of broken brush left by the animal's hefty stride. Judging by the depth of the indentations it left in the fecund soil, this creature, whatever it was, would suit their needs just fine.

They had been far more fortunate in their unplanned landing than they had initially realized. This world was clearly square in the Goldilocks Zone. Not too hot, not too cold, possessing a breathable atmosphere and potable water enough to support a thriving ecosystem. Under other circumstances, Charlie could easily see bringing Leila here for some R and R one day. A camping trip with none of the distractions of home sounded wonderful right about now.

But they had other things to think about. A lot of them, in fact, and foremost was finding, then killing the animal they were tracking. Bawb's shimmer cloak was utterly useless in this place, its magical invisibility rendered completely non-functional like every other spell they attempted. Fortunately, the cloak was only a tool, and one the Ghalian assassin could easily function without.

In fact, despite the situation, both of the men were rather enjoying the primal method of their hunt. It was invigorating, stretching their legs, getting the blood pumping as they worked in tandem, and if not for the circumstances, they'd have been enjoying it as much as a pleasant jaunt in the hills above their homes. But this was not Malibu, and whatever was out there could very well be far more dangerous than any wildlife back home.

Bawb and Charlie's ears were straining to find any sound of their prey when Bawb abruptly stopped. Charlie knew better than to move a muscle when something caught his friend's attention. After a few seconds, his hand slowly drifted toward the pulse pistol on his hip. Bawb looked around, his senses on high alert, but did not draw a weapon—not as if doing so would take him more than a fraction of a second if need be. A moment later he crouched down.

Now Charlie saw what had caught his attention. Carefully, he brushed aside the dirt to expose a bit of shiny metal. More than just that, it was clearly a fragment of some sort of advanced construction, possibly even from a spaceship, given the look of it.

Bawb lifted it up and shook free the last of the dirt. Yes, it was almost certainly taken from a ship, but it had been worked by hand and formed into something quite different than a spacecraft. What Bawb was holding was a familiar sight, even this far from home. Something used by primitive races since the earliest times.

It was an arrowhead.

Judging by the look of it, this particular one had been fired from a rather large bow. Not quite spear length, but definitely longer than Earth standard. Whatever it had been embedded in had clearly not been killed by the shot, rather running off into the woods at speed, fleeing its attacker and breaking free the arrow in the process.

That fact made Charlie wonder if the local fauna might have some sort of plating or scales akin to a Zomoki or other tough-hided creature. If that was the case, their space cow could very well be more akin to a space bull, and as much of a handful as such a beast could be.

It was a two-part threat, however. The animal could prove troublesome, of course, but now they had definite confirmation of intelligent life here. And they were *armed*, no matter how primitively. Worse, without magic at their disposal, Charlie and Bawb would be forced to defend themselves in entirely conventional ways. And against unexpected arrows, *that* could be something of a challenge, even for a Ghalian.

Bawb nodded to Charlie. Even without their silent communication in play, they still knew what the other meant. It was nice being able to talk silently with their magical connection, but they'd grown close enough that their unspoken shorthand and body language would more than suffice.

"Eyes open" was what Bawb's signal meant as he slowly drew his Vespus blade from its sheath. Charlie nodded his understanding, drawing a pair of wicked daggers. Weapons fire would draw attention, and that was unwanted, given this new wrinkle in their situation.

When Kip came to pick them up there would be no avoiding making their presence known, but until then, the quieter they could be, the better, and not only for the hunt.

CHAPTER FIFTEEN

Bawb's nose twitched. There it was, the scent of *something*. His pale hand signaled for Charlie to move to the left flank just off the trail. They were getting close now, and any minute they would be upon it, whatever it was.

Charlie stepped to the side and took three paces then froze in place, his foot still in the air. Bawb noticed the movement, or, more accurately, the cessation of movement at once.

"What is it?" his eyes asked.

Charlie gingerly stepped back, placing his raised foot in the print of where he'd previously tread. He pointed to the ground in front of him. Bawb drew closer and leaned in for a better look. He nodded his head appreciatively. It was a snare-type trap designed for animals by the look of it. They were not the only ones hunting.

The pair placed the hunt on hold a moment to investigate the trap. It was skillfully made, and with a clever blend of organic components one would find in the woods as well as a few metal and composite pieces at stress points, all of them tied together to form a simple and efficient snare.

"Look," Bawb whispered. "The connection point."

Charlie examined the knots closer. Anyone less skilled than the Geist would have missed the signs, but not Bawb. His sharp eyes picked them out immediately.

"This was made by a caster," Charlie gasped.

Bawb nodded. Indeed it had been, and that meant someone else was a power user on this world. And if they were crafting non-magical snares in the woods, it seemed they had lost their power as well. But even without that flowing through them, some habits were muscle memory. Habits such as forming certain knots and bindings with the intention of bolstering them with a spell to increase their efficacy.

But there was no trace of magic on the snare. Not one iota. Yet the person who had crafted it was undoubtedly of a particular skill set. One the two men also shared.

A twig snapped nearby.

Charlie spun and looked in the direction it came from but saw nothing. He turned back with a questioning look, but Bawb had already vanished without a sound. Even minus his shimmer cloak the master assassin could blend into the environment as easily as some people breathed. Or ceased breathing as was often the case when Bawb was involved.

Charlie had a good idea of where the sound had come from deep in the brush off the trail, and that meant the poor beast they had been hunting was not long for this world. He moved forward, his feet carefully avoiding twigs that might give away his position and send the creature scurrying off.

Here, little space cow, he thought with amusement. Pretty soon, Ara would be enjoying space burgers, albeit minus the bun and condiments.

Charlie pushed aside a low branch and crept to the right, making his way around the dense copse of greenery blocking his way. He shifted his grip on his knives. He'd make it quick and painless, the whole thing over in an instant.

A growling roar burst from the grove, followed a moment

later by an enormous animal that one would have to be on a serious quantity of drugs to ever confuse with a cow. It was larger than any bovine, for starters, and its body was covered with thick plates of fibrous, dense skin as tough as a lizard's scales.

Rust-colored tufts of wiry fur sprouted up from the gaps where they overlapped. From what Charlie could see of it as the creature charged him, those small areas were the only vulnerable places on its body. It was no wonder the alien arrow had been unable to find its target. Even the most skilled archer would have a difficult time with this one.

Charlie dove to the side, rolling behind a stout tree, narrowly avoiding the slashing claws that whistled through the air where he had just been standing. Despite its size, this thing was apparently quite agile. It was also nowhere near as easy a target as a cow.

Charlie's hands flew up, and he rattled off a stunning spell on pure instinct, but the beast kept charging.

"Shit. No magic," he blurted as he lunged out of the way.

The animal seemed determined to turn the tables, and the hunter was entirely on the defensive, dodging behind trees while long claws gouged deep gashes in their bark. With the benefit of a few trees providing him cover, Charlie got a better look at the animal. He was not heartened by what he saw.

If its claws were terrifying, the mouthful of teeth it sported was even worse. In fact, its bristling chompers made a shark look like a damn puppy.

Charlie swung his knives, hoping to gain purchase in one of the vulnerable gaps. He drew a tiny bit of blood, but it was only a glancing blow and didn't slow the animal one bit. He kept at it, though, stabbing and slashing, trying desperately to land a solid blow.

It had become abundantly clear that without his magic he was outmatched by the giant creature. What he had initially thought would be an easy kill now appeared to be just as likely to inflict that same fate upon him.

Running and retreating, a desperate plan formed in Charlie's mind. He turned and sprinted toward a cluster of trees, their trunks growing upward in a V pattern. He dove high, passing the crux of their trunks and landing in a rough roll on the other side. The beast lunged after him, leaping surprisingly high for its size but nevertheless finding its head stuck in the gap.

Charlie didn't wait, springing to his feet, not in a retreat but in a hasty attack straight at the snapping teeth of the thing's face. He narrowly avoided the gaping maw while driving both of his daggers into the animal's eyes. He pushed until they were hilt-deep, expecting a cry of pain from the animal. But it did not react. Not one bit. In fact, it didn't move at all.

Blood ran down his arms as he pulled his daggers free. It was then that he saw Bawb sitting above him, resting calmly atop the beast's head, his Vespus blade driven straight into the creature's skull.

"I had it!" Charlie exclaimed.

"I am sure you did," Bawb replied with a wry grin. "And I very much enjoyed your improvised tactics. They proved to be as effective as they were entertaining."

"Oh, shut up," Charlie grumbled. "At least we've got food for Ara."

"That we do," Bawb said as he pulled his sword free with a wet slurping sound. He wiped the blood on a tuft of hair before resheathing it. "It would also appear to be much larger than the space cow you had hoped to find."

"And a whole lot more bitey," Charlie added. "But there's just one problem we hadn't thought of."

"Oh?"

"Yeah. I tried to cast against it on sheer instinct."

"I saw. A most unsatisfying outcome, that was."

"Well, it's not that spell that I'm worried about," Charlie said. "What troubles me is something far more basic than that."

"Such as?"

"Dude, magic didn't work. *Doesn't* work."

"Yes, as we have already established."

"Precisely," Charlie said. "So, riddle me this. Without any magic, how the hell are we supposed to move this thing all the way back to Ara?"

Bawb's grin faltered then fell entirely. "Damn," he said.

"Yeah," Charlie agreed. "You said it."

CHAPTER SIXTEEN

Charlie and Bawb were dripping sweat as they heaved and strained, dragging their makeshift sledge through the smoother sections of undergrowth.

Kip was not quite ready to fly to pick them up yet, and even if he was, he would require a clearing to land in to retrieve them. That meant somehow getting their prize to the nearest acceptable area. And there was only one they'd come across that fit the bill. The crash landing site.

Gustavo's impact had flattened a decent swath of trees, creating a clearing in the woods where there had previously been none. And the angle at which he'd impacted wound up acting like a bowling ball knocking down pins, only these pins were trees. The result was an area large enough for Kip to land quite easily. Additionally, it had left behind something they could use for their current dilemma.

Gus's craft had been equipped with all of the standard loading gear one would expect, from floating sledges to anti-grav jacks, but with the entirety of the ship having lost power it was the lowest tech item that was now proving its worth, even in the most futuristic of times.

"This is maddening," Bawb murmured as they strained against the cordage tied to the large piece of salvaged ceramisteel they had eventually levered the carcass onto. "We require a more level surface."

He was referring to the way the wheels they had scavenged from the pair of roller carts that were folded up into storage for the rare occasion such an old-school piece of gear might come in handy. Whoever had loaded it aboard had certainly never thought they would be used for *this* sort of thing.

They had managed to separate the wheels from their ruined carts, fastening them to a sturdy section of hull that seemed just about right for their needs. The ceramisteel was far lighter than normal metal while being capable of supporting the mass of the dead animal. And once the wheels had been affixed, they had a means of moving it, albeit with great effort.

"It beats the alternative," Charlie said. "I mean, do you want to chop it up and carry this thing piece by piece?"

"That would not be ideal."

"No, it would not. So buck up, little camper, and keep moving. Things could always be worse."

"Have you not often spoken of the foolishness of tempting your friend Murphy?"

Charlie's mirth lessened slightly. "Point taken. But seeing as we've been sucked through a portal—"

"You really should work on your phrasing."

"Fine. *Pulled* through a portal to some random planet in some random part of the galaxy, lost one of our ships for sure, and have no idea where Rika and Griggalt are, not to mention being utterly devoid of any magic whatsoever, I really think this is one of those rare occasions that Murphy has already paid us quite a visit."

"Though we did not come under fire once through the portal," Bawb noted. "That is an interesting wrinkle to this puzzle."

Charlie had been thinking very much the same thing. "The fact there was nobody sitting around when we got *pulled* into the portal would seem to mean that whoever we were after had already gone through. Odds are, they're stuck here just like we are, though where they might have crashed I have no idea."

"*If* they crashed."

"Bob, you saw what it did to Ara. She's powerless. And the attack on our fleet used incredibly powerful magic. Hell, that's the whole reason we were the ones who flew out to deal with it in the first place."

"True. And logic would dictate that the same phenomenon that has affected the Wise One and us would have also disrupted our adversary's power."

"Exactly. Whatever they did when they cast and opened that portal, they totally shat the bed. I tell ya, people really need to stop playing with powerful magic or more mishaps like this are bound to happen."

"At least they will be at the same disadvantage that we are," Bawb noted.

"Yeah. But if we can help Ara regain her strength, she could be our ace in the hole. Speaking of which," Charlie said as he keyed on his comms. "Hunze, how's Ara doing?"

There was a long pause. Far too long for Bawb's comfort.

"Hunze, are you all right?" the Ghalian asked, ready to drop their load and take off at a sprint all the way back to her if needed. Fortunately, that was not required.

"I am here," she said a moment later. "My apologies. I was rather covered in mud, and I had to clean my hands before keying my communication device."

"Mud?" Bawb replied. "What were you doing that would cause you to be muddied?"

"I noted the high mineral content of the clay here and determined that it may very well have restorative properties. It would seem I was correct in that assumption. I have been applying it to Ara's burns to soothe the damage."

Charlie whistled appreciatively. "Damn, nice thinking, Hunze. I'm glad to hear some of Ara's injuries are being treated."

"Oh, I have applied it to more than just a few areas. She is quite covered, from head to tail. At least, the portions not in the water."

Charlie and Bawb looked at one another. They hadn't been gone *that* long. Hunze had apparently put in yeoman's work in caring for their friend.

"Is she awake?" Charlie asked.

"She still slumbers, but she does appear to be resting more comfortably now."

"Good. Bob and I have something for her when she wakes up. We caught her a meal, and boy is it a doozy. Speaking of which, Dukaan, you got your ears on?"

"Yes, Charlie, I am listening."

"How come the repairs? You guys gonna be able to fly and pick us up anytime soon? I swear this thing is getting heavier with every step."

"Soon, I hope," he replied. "But there is another issue; however you may have addressed it unknowingly. Did you happen to capture enough food for the rest of us?"

"Oh, yeah. This thing's huge. But why? We've got all the food we could want."

"Well, yes and no."

Bawb looked at Charlie and mouthed the word, "Murphy."

Charlie stuck out his tongue in response. "What happened, Dukaan?"

"The replicator appears to have been knocked out of alignment during the, uh, *event*. I am afraid it is not good for producing much beyond a basic nutrient sludge. It is perfectly edible, but not exactly what one would call appetizing."

They had all experienced a food replicator's default setting at least once, and Dukaan was quite right in his assessment. It would produce something that could sustain them so long as its power supply was not interrupted, but it would be the stuff of necessity, not pleasure.

"We'll carve off a few steaks before we hand it over to Ara," he said. "There's more than enough to go around. Refrigeration still works, right?"

"Yes, that is unaffected. At least so far, though power fluctuations have been an issue. Less so since I have removed the strange devices stuck to Kip's hull, but nevertheless, some irregularities remain."

Charlie let out a little sigh. "Finally, some good news. I tell ya, I was beginning to worry Murphy really had—"

Bawb spun, dropping to a crouch. He had drawn his blade so quickly Charlie hadn't even seen it leave its sheath. A moment later the sound reached Charlie's ears. Footfall. And it was coming closer.

"We'll call you back," he transmitted, then moved into position with Bawb. Whoever was coming, they were going to be in for a big surprise.

CHAPTER SEVENTEEN

Charlie and Bawb watched from the bushes a good distance away from their kill. Away, and downwind. One never knew what abilities the approaching beings possessed, and having sweated a fair amount, they would no doubt be easier to pick out from the smell alone if the newcomers had sensitive olfactory apparatus.

They would have normally just cast the simplest of masking spells to cover any odors that might be wafting off of them after hard work or battle, but, as they were constantly being reminded, that was simply not an option they could currently rely on.

The alien group that stepped into view did not seem to smell them, fortunately, though it was also likely that the coppery smell of blood and musk from their kill was providing a distraction where their magic could not. The aliens were bipedal, as they'd expected, and mostly humanoid in shape.

Their feet, however, were exceptionally wide and round, almost like an elephant's, and quite a bit larger than Charlie or Bawb's. Additionally, their ears seemed to possess the ability to pivot to better focus in on sounds from varying directions. As for their attire, they wore what were clearly space crew uniforms, though of a variety neither Charlie or Bawb had ever seen.

Their skin appeared to be somewhat leathery in texture and a deep, reddish-brown color with no body hair they could see. Their heads, however, sported jet-black, close-cropped wiry hair. They looked somewhat military in that regard, but they were clearly not a hunting party, nor were they a recon team. These people, all nine of them, were carrying baskets laden with fruits and vegetables. Though armed, they were gatherers, not hunters. At least not at the moment.

The carcass had come into view now, and the foraging party froze in their tracks, stunned by the sight. They moved closer, timid. This was a threat they had clearly encountered in the past, and they were taking no chances with it. The apparent leader of the group stepped forward and nudged the animal with his boot, quickly hurrying back. Satisfied it truly was deceased, he moved closer, chattering some unintelligible language with the others.

Charlie and Bawb shared a look. This didn't seem like it would be a fight. And these people did not appear to be armed for one if there was. Their tools and weapons were somewhat primitive, though they did carry knives on their belts that seemed far more advanced than the rest of their gear. And more importantly, neither could sense so much as a trace of magic between them.

Charlie made a decision. It was a gut feeling and nothing more, but something told him these were not the people they were seeking. The ones who had attacked their friends. *That* group possessed incredible power, and even stripped of it, they would undoubtedly have not reverted to primitive means so quickly.

"Watch my back," he said, then stood up from his cover. "Hey, over here."

The aliens spun, their blades drawn and arrows nocked on

bowstrings in an instant. Charlie kept his hands held up and open, moving slowly out of the bush and onto the trail. "We're not your enemy," he said in as soothing a tone as he could manage while he moved closer to them. "Come on out, Bob. I don't think they're going to attack."

The pale assassin rustled the bushes conspicuously as he rose, the noise utterly uncharacteristic for a man whose very survival depended on absolute stealth. But if another person suddenly appeared out of nowhere, the odds were one of the startled aliens would let loose with an arrow, if only out of pure surprise. And then Bawb would likely have no choice but to kill them all.

"Tormada! Arriskuan!" the leader said, followed by a verbal barrage of what was clearly an interrogatory aimed at the newcomers, and a hostile one at that. No one attacked, but not one person lowered their weapon.

"What was that?" Charlie asked, instinctively casting a translation spell.

Another flurry of questions peppered him. At least he thought they were questions.

"Shit, the translation spell is toast," Charlie groaned. "I'm so used to casting it—what the hell do we do?"

"Something, and quickly. Our new friends do not appear to be understanding of our dilemma. I believe they think we are hostiles," Bawb noted, nodding slightly toward the arrows pointed at them, which had not budged an inch while the chatter became more heated.

Without a spell to handle the communication issues they were screwed. Something Charlie was acutely aware of when fortuitous moment of inspiration hit him.

"Hey, Kip, can you hear these guys over my comms?"

"I'll amplify the receiving settings to pick up ambient sounds better."

"So, is that a yes?"

"Yes."

"Great. Then here's what I need from you. These guys speak some language we've never heard before. I want you to do as best a translation as you can and send it to me simultaneously in real-time. You think you can do that?"

"I'll do my best. But I need to hear them speaking for it to work."

"Right. I'm on it," Charlie said, turning to the leader as he tapped his own chest. "My name is Charlie. *Charlie.* This is Bob. We mean you no harm. What is your name?"

The man clearly understood this pantomime and touched his own chest. "Nakk," he said, following that with a stream of gibberish.

"Nakk, nice to meet you," Charlie said. "Can you say more words?" He motioned a talking gesture with his hand next to his mouth. "We need more words to understand your language."

Nakk seemed to get the basic idea and chattered on a bit more. He turned to his people and said something else. Slowly, their weapons lowered. "Grivaa, arriskuan Brixxax amada," the leader said, gesturing to the dead animal. He gave an appreciative nod then followed with something that even without a translation spell Charlie felt sure must have meant something along the lines of, "How the hell did you kill that?"

Apparently, taking down this thing was an impressive feat.

Charlie took the hint and pointed at the daggers on his hips. "Bob, show 'em your sword."

"I do not think that would be wise," he replied. "The coloration of the blade would make its nature clear, and without its normal power, it could become a source of conflict if one of them should covet it."

"Fine. But we need to keep these guys talking."

"I have a feeling they will, especially if we take them to the crash site. I would wager they will become quite chatty once they see the wreckage."

"Likely," Charlie agreed. "We're taking this to our friend," Charlie said, pointing at the beast.

"Brixxax," Nakk said.

"It's called a Brixxax?"

Nakk nodded.

"Okay, now we're getting somewhere," he replied. "Bob, check it out. Now that they know we killed this Brixxax these guys are looking at us like a couple of badass hunters."

"I would remind you that, in fact, we *are*, as you say, a couple of badass hunters."

"Valid point. But one we can leverage to our advantage. Better to have them in awe of us and wanting to join up than thinking about jumping us for our gear."

"That would *not* go well for them."

"No, it certainly would not," Charlie said, holding back his chuckle. He turned to Nakk once more. "Hey, Nakk, what do you call this?" he asked, pointing to a bow.

"Sittalk," the man replied.

"Okay, that's bow." He redirected his gesture to an arrow. "And this?"

"Hooshta."

"Arrow. You getting this, Kip?"

"Of course. And listening to their chatter amongst themselves, it seems the basic structure of their language is actually a rather logical pattern of consonants and vowels, though with alien tonal structure, sounds, and inflection points, naturally."

"Naturally. So, this is working, then?"

"Yeah, but I need you to get a lot more names of things. Adjectives too. Basically, I need them to talk."

Charlie pondered a moment. "You know what? I have an idea."

CHAPTER EIGHTEEN

"Maruktin ashka ne poma arriskuan hargoh," Nakk said as they walked, all of them pulling the lines attached to the oversized sled.

"Yeah, arriskuan, you keep saying that," Charlie replied. "Kip, you getting any closer on that translation?"

"Slowly but surely, yeah," the AI replied. "I'm just not really as set up for that kind of processing as the bigger-brain AIs, ya know? I'm more specialized for flight ops, blasting bad guys, and that sort of thing. Sorry."

"Not a problem. I know you're doing your best. Just keep working at it."

The alien group had all fallen in to help pull the Brixxax once Charlie and Nakk's pantomime performance had finally sunk in. It seemed the formidable newcomers were asking for their help, and seeing as these strange new arrivals managed to take down a full-grown Brixxax, they were happy to oblige.

It was actually a relatively pleasant walk now that they had enough hands to move the load without so much effort. And as they did, the group talked quietly among themselves, which Kip listened in on to help further bolster his initial Rosetta Stone to begin a proper translation of their language.

The smoke from the downed ship had lessened significantly since their initial pass of the crash site, but the location was still easy to find regardless now that they had their bearings. Nakk, however, seemed reluctant to head that way, pointing and rambling off a stream of alien chatter.

Without their translation spells, Charlie and Bawb were at the mercy of their ship's computing power for now, so all they could do was nod and gesture, ensuring they moved ahead. Once Nakk and his people saw the wreckage and realized what sort of visitors the newcomers were, it was their hope the alien tribe would have any lingering doubts about them allayed.

Originally, Charlie and Bawb had planned on playing good cop/bad cop with the lesser-armed group, but now it was clear the archers were no longer feeling as threatened by them. Of course, the duo still kept their guard up, watching one another's back, just in case.

Thanks to Bawb's training, not to mention Charlie's gladiator and pirate skills, even without any magic they could take every last one of them down in short order if it came to that. But given the turn things had taken, they really hoped that would not be necessary.

"You know, it looks like they're all wearing variants of a crew uniform," Charlie said. "Nothing crude like you'd expect from an indigenous people."

"Yes, I would say with a degree of confidence that these people are survivors of a crash, much as we are."

"But a long time ago."

"So it would seem given their current state of attire and weaponry."

They walked on, Charlie pointing to things, naming them, then having Nakk say the word in his own tongue. It was a bit tedious, given their habitual use of translation spells, but Kip actually seemed to be making decent progress.

"Try saying this," Kip said. "Ngoro amatza harruk yakkta."

Charlie obliged, though his pronunciation was somewhat shit by comparison. Nakk cocked his head, a confused look on his face.

"Okay, that was obviously crap. Let me try that again. Repeat it to me one more time, Kip."

The AI did, and the second time around Nakk smiled and nodded, correcting his pronunciation but clearly understanding his meaning.

"That went better. What did I just say, Kip?"

"You just said 'thank you for your help.' At least, I think that's what you said. I'm still fine-tuning a few things."

Nakk looked at Charlie with an odd expression as the newcomer talked to himself. With the bone-conduction comms patch, of course it looked that way, but this also gave Charlie an idea.

"Hey, Bob. Lemme borrow your comms patch."

"What do you wish to do with it?" he asked, peeling it from behind his ear.

"I think we can establish a better chain of communication if we dial Nakk here in with Kip. You know, cut out the middle man and let him translate directly. It's too hard to do a real-time translation in my head with Kip and him talking."

"Hmm, interesting," Bawb said, handing him the patch. "This may very well work."

"Thanks for the vote of confidence," Charlie chuckled.

He motioned to Nakk, pointing to the patch in his hand and the one attached behind his own ear, gesturing for Nakk to stick it on his own head. The alien took the patch, gave it a quick once-over, then put it in place behind his own far larger ear.

"It's in place, Kip. Try saying something."

"Hello, can you understand me?" Kip asked, speaking slowly in the new language.

Nakk's expression barely shifted. The novel tech was apparently not as much a surprise as Charlie had anticipated.

"Yes, I understand," he replied. "Your accent very better than friend's."

"He'll get there. It take time with new language. My name Kip, by the way. Pleasure meeting you."

"Same, same," Nakk replied.

Charlie watched the exchange with great interest. "So, we good?"

"Yes, we are good," Kip replied. "It's still a bit shaky, but we're figuring it out."

Nakk nodded. Apparently, Kip was already doing the real-time translation thing. Being an AI had its advantages, that was for sure. Like being able to multitask far better than a mere meat brain ever could.

Charlie turned to Nakk. "So, we can talk now."

"Yes, we talk now," Kip translated over his comms as Nakk spoke.

"Thank you for helping pull this," Charlie said, gesturing to the Brixxax. "We have a friend who will be very grateful."

"We happy to help," Nakk said. "But tell, how does your communication work? Allpower no work here."

"Allpower?"

"Force what make things go. Power flow in galaxy. Allpower."

"You mean *magic*."

"No magic. *Allpower*."

"Call it what you will, I think we're still talking about the same thing," Charlie said.

"But whycome this device work?" Nakk asked.

"Ah, that's *technology*," Charlie said. "Not magi—I mean, Allpower."

"I can see is technology. Is obvious. But energy supply is some sort battery?"

"I thought you were just talking about Allpower."

"Not for technology," Nakk said as if it was something only a fool would suggest. "What kind world you from use Allpower for technology?"

"Uh, we aren't. But the way you were talking, I just figured—"

"So, this use battery of some sort. You still power have. Almost no devices here still have. You indeed fortunate."

Charlie mulled over what he had just heard. "You say devices here don't work? So you have tech?"

"Of course."

"And ships? You have ships?"

"A great many ships stranded on this world. But no can power to fly."

"They say they have ships but no power," Charlie told his friend.

Bawb took great interest in that comment, wondering exactly how many other spaceworthy vessels might be strewn about the planet's surface. Charlie was thinking the same thing. If this place was a power vortex for both technology as well as magic, or Allpower, or whatever you wanted to call it, there could very well be dozens, if not hundreds, of stranded ships.

Suddenly, taking Nakk and his crew to the crash site seemed like far less of an impressive undertaking. They'd seen plenty of wrecks, most likely, and Gustavo's remains would be nothing new. But they were nearly there, so that revelation was a bit late in coming.

"Hey," Charlie said as they approached the final bend in the trail that would take them into the crash site. "You kept saying a word back there. *Arriskuan*, or something like that. What does that mean?"

Nakk's expression shifted slightly, a look of concern in his eyes. "It mean danger."

"Uh, danger?" Charlie said. "Oh, the crash. You saw that. Don't worry, it was our ship."

"No crash. *Danger*."

The repetition was a little confusing, but they'd be in sight soon enough and would put that to rest. "No, you'll see. It was one of ours. Just around this—"

They turned the bend and saw a pair of ships parked beside the wreckage. *Functional* ships. And standing there in the clearing was a large group of armed troops.

Charlie swallowed hard. "Oh, shit."

"Shit?" Nakk said. "Is bad?"

"Yes, is bad."

"But you strong fight. They no have Allpower. Evens odds."

"There have to be twenty of them," Charlie said just as the nearest guards took note and began raising their rifles.

Rifles, yes, but if these people were used to casting, or whatever they called it in this part of the galaxy, lacking that ability just might put them off their game. Out of their comfort zone. Their ships and rifles were obviously running on tech, and functional tech at that, but beyond that, if they were magic users they were at as much a disadvantage as the rest of them. And that just might even the odds.

Charlie hoped he was right. Judging by the menacing looks being thrown their way and the speed at which Nakk's people scattered, it seemed they'd need every bit of help that might come their way.

CHAPTER NINETEEN

The hostiles, which Charlie and Bawb had determined them to be before a single weapon had even been raised, were tall in stature, clad in deep gray uniforms with integrated padding at key areas. Clearly tactical, but of the most basic variety.

For a skilled killer there were myriad weak points in which to drive home a blade.

They possessed gray-green skin and had somewhat oversized heads with elongated chins and ears, a pair of thin lips covering dual rows of pointed teeth. Carnivores, no doubt, their thick neck and jaw muscles apparently developed to rip flesh from bone. They looked almost like some burly bastardization of Tslavars. Maybe a distant cousin.

It appeared they were used to being the top of the food chain, and on this world where they were the only ones with functioning technology, that sense of superiority was only reinforced. They were cocky in their posturing. Almost laughing at the sight of the poor saps who had stumbled upon their reconnaissance team.

Overconfident.

It would be their demise.

The apparent leader of the troops lackadaisically raised his rifle, as if taunting the helpless victims he was about to make an example of. What he didn't count on was that in so doing he identified himself as a key player. The head of this particular group. And that made him target number one.

What he also did not expect was that Charlie and Bawb were armed not only with blades, but also fully functional pulse pistols, weapons they put to immediate and efficient use.

The first shots killed the team leader outright, Charlie and Bawb both hitting him center mass before turning their guns on the other troops. Four more fell in rapid succession before the flight part of their fight-or-flight instinct kicked in. It was followed moments later by the fight part. But the tone had been set. The newcomers had put the alien guards on their heels, and Nakk's people took note.

Return fire blasted out into the trees, utterly missing its target as the soldiers fired in haste. It was that adrenaline-fueled sloppiness that set the assassin and his friend into high gear.

Bawb was a blur of deadly motion, his daggers slashing and stabbing as he raced into the fray. Charlie was right behind him, attacking on the opposite flank, pistol in one hand and dagger in the other.

While Bawb was much more of a fan of the up-close-and-personal nature of blade work, Charlie was from Earth and perfectly happy relying on his pistol to help even the odds. And against a numerically superior enemy sporting unknown weapons, he'd take whatever he could get.

The duo moved and dodged, almost vanishing from sight as they used tricks of angles and shadows rather than magical camouflage to advance into the enemy's reach. Screams rang out into the air and blood flowed freely onto the soil as Charlie and Bawb engaged more of the troops. The first batch had fallen easily, but now that they were aware of their adversary's true skills, those still upright adjusted tactics accordingly.

Quickly pulling together into groups of three, the soldiers placed their backs to each other, creating a firing solution in all directions while protecting themselves on all sides. It was a clever maneuver, and one that, while by no means impenetrable, nevertheless made penetrating that perimeter a good deal more difficult, even if they were minimally skilled individually.

"Bob!" Charlie called out, not worrying about their enemy understanding them. "We need to pair up!"

"On my left," the assassin called back.

Charlie immediately fell into position, just as they'd trained together countless times. Now it was time to get serious. Bawb twirled the daggers in his hands and smiled, his fangs sliding into place even though there would be no magical feast. At the very least, he could strike a healthy bit of fear into the hearts of these adversaries.

As for support, Nakk's people were nowhere to be seen, vanishing into the trees and brush, leaving the two newcomers to fend for themselves. And what a show they were putting on.

A master class in death and bloodshed.

"Now," Bawb stated quietly.

The two men raced ahead, Bawb's daggers flying from his hands in a flash, a replacement set taking their place from his hidden sheaths before the hurled weapons had even landed. His target let out a gurgling cry as his throat was pierced.

One of the three was down, and their defenses were broken. Charlie followed close behind, letting off pulse fire at the other groups of three, keeping them from gaining a firing solution on them.

Bawb, in the meantime, made quick, bloody work of the two remaining men as they so desperately attempted to shift position to defend themselves. It was futile. Both were dead before they knew what hit them.

Even so, it was an uphill battle, figuratively, but Charlie and

Bawb were doing their best, slowly but surely making their way through the enemy.

"Six more to go," Charlie said as another group fell.

"Are you so sure about that?" Bawb replied, nodding slightly to the parked ships.

Charlie glanced briefly and saw what he was referring to. A dozen more troops were streaming out of each of the ships, rushing headlong into the battle. This group was not taken by surprise, nor were they unprepared. This was the backup, waiting for their moment to attack.

Charlie and Bawb had no choice but to advance. The trio they had engaged had to fall before they could even entertain the idea of fleeing. But something unexpected happened. Suddenly, with no warning, arrows began raining down on the advancing reinforcements from the cover of the trees.

In their haste, the troops were singularly focused on the two men slaying all of their comrades directly in front of them. It was a classic blunder, and one for which they were now paying the price. With their attention aimed at Charlie and Bawb, they didn't even notice as their men were being expertly picked off one by one from behind. It wasn't until their number had been halved that they realized something was amiss.

By that point, Nakk's men were streaming from the trees, groups boarding the ships to finish off the flight crew while the others engaged the foot soldiers at close range.

"I appear to have been mistaken about their cowardice," Bawb said.

"Yeah? Well, we're not out of the woods yet. There's still a ton of them, and these are dug in and better armed," Charlie replied.

The blasts of weapons fire all around him served as punctuation for his statement. They had made quite a showing, but without magic at their disposal they were still woefully outnumbered, even with Nakk's people.

"We could really use Ara right about now," Charlie grumbled as he drove his dagger into the gap in a soldier's armor.

The man did not drop as expected but instead seemed to take the attack personally, increasing his aggression rather than falling to the ground. It was decidedly inconvenient to say the least, if not outright unsettling.

Charlie instinctively reached for a killing spell before remembering his handicap. This had to be done the old-school way. But he was a space pirate and gladiator before he was a caster, and he had been well trained in a great many deadly arts, and that was before he and Bawb had begun sparring together.

Shifting his center of balance, Charlie flowed around the enraged man's attacks, bending at the hips even as he dug in to push off harder and land a killing blow. A glancing shot grazed his shoulder, but Charlie ignored the flash of pain, his arm and blade acting as a single unit, pistoning forward and up with singular intent and strength.

The dagger plunged into the tiniest gap between the protective plates and slid up into the man's torso. Charlie's hope that his physiology included having his heart in that location proved correct when the soldier dropped at his feet like a marionette with its strings abruptly cut.

He turned and looked around. Nakk's people were pinned down by the remaining troopers who were laying down heavy fire all around them. There was nowhere for them to go. No escape route. And there was no way for Charlie or Bawb to help them.

Massive pulse blasts suddenly rained down from above, blowing the alien goons to bits in a dazzling show of force and death. A moment later, the air fell silent and the dust began to settle.

What had been a strong line of enemy forces was now no

more than a scattered pile of limbs and meat smoldering in the sun.

Kip dropped down from above and settled into a hover, his railguns targeting the two parked craft.

"Sorry it took me so long. I was having more glitches than expected."

Charlie let out a sigh of relief. "Nothing to be sorry about, Kip. We are damn glad to see you. And just in the nick of time."

"Yeah, that didn't look too good. But those ships? You want me to blast 'em?"

"No, hold off. Nakk's people were trying to take them."

"Ah, that would explain it."

"Explain what?"

"They were transmitting a little while ago. Trying to send an outgoing transmission. I blocked them, of course. But the signals abruptly stopped. Nakk, did your people take those ships?" Kip asked.

"Yes. We taking ships," he replied.

"That's amazing," Charlie said. "And now you've got not one but *two* working ships."

"Oh, we have ships," Nakk replied. "Every time killing the Urvalin we take ships."

"You've done this before?"

"You no think we just sit and wait dying, do you? We fight back."

Charlie let out a little laugh. "That you do," he said. "Goddamn right, that you sure as hell do."

CHAPTER TWENTY

Kip set down in a relatively open area close to the battleground. It had been a horrific crash landing, but one that had created a rather clear swath of land in its wake. He powered down to low but didn't drop into a true landing mode. His weapons stayed hot, and he was ready to leap up into the sky at a moment's notice if needed.

They may have won this fight, but there was no telling if more were coming.

The airlock hatch cycled open, and Dukaan stepped out, a very healthy quantity of weapons strapped to his body. Four pistols—one for each hand—as well as several knives and even a stun baton. He also had a pulse rifle slung across his back.

Nakk's men took great interest in this new arrival, though not so much because of his flashy arrival and weaponry, but rather they hadn't seen a four-armed alien before. Between Charlie, Bawb, and Dukaan, it was a trifecta of previously unseen races.

Charlie saw the look on their faces. "Nakk, this is Dukaan. Our pilot."

"Pleased to meet," he said, unsure which hand to shake.

"Likewise," Dukaan replied. He noted Charlie's look. "Don't be surprised. Of course Kip told me about his translation protocol. I put on a comms patch some time ago and have been monitoring alongside him."

"Of course you have," Charlie said. "The poster child for competence, as always."

"Thank you."

Charlie turned back to their new friend. "Don't worry, we're new to you, but you're all new to us as well. It's a big galaxy, and I'm sure there are countless races just waiting to be discovered."

"True, there are. We know many. Galaxy *very* big place," Nakk replied. "Glad to meet new friends."

"New *allies*," Charlie said.

"Yes, allies."

Nakk's people were stripping the bodies of any equipment they could salvage. There were weapons as well, but they ignored them, opting for the knives and other gear.

"Nakk, why aren't they taking the guns?" Charlie asked.

"Ah, is tied to user. We take in past, but can no make work."

"I can probably help with that," Kip said. "Might as well bring 'em with and give it a try, right?"

"I'm with Kip on this one," Charlie agreed. "We should take absolutely everything that might prove helpful."

Bawb was examining several of the bodies nearest them, removing items and scrutinizing them with great interest. Especially the belts they were wearing. The material was pliant but appeared to be made of a woven metal. Only it was lighter than any ordinary metal and possessed great flexibility. Additionally, symbols were an integral part of the design. Almost like runes of some sort. Almost like some konuses he had used in the past.

"Nakk," he said, "what are these? They appear to be more than just belts."

"The *banda*? Is a banda. You no have these?"

"I have never encountered one before."

"But you say you use Allpower, yes?"

"We use magic. Power of a sort, that is correct."

"This store Allpower. Amplify and let people use more than they naturally possess."

"Naturally possess?" Charlie asked. "Is that a common thing here?"

"Of course. Most people have at least a little Allpower in them," Nakk replied.

The implications were huge. This was a part of the galaxy in which magic was apparently commonplace. It was not unheard of, Charlie supposed. Rika had tapped into their galaxy's magic once she was saved by the Kalamani people, after all, though that had required bonding magical pigment directly to her flesh. But that power flowed through the plants and animals of their world, so it only made sense that in other realms it could be in people as well.

The banda was another thing altogether. Apparently, it served the same purpose as a konus or slaap, more or less. A device used to store magic for later use. He was most interested in examining these bandas once they were able to access power once again.

"Take them, Bob," Charlie said. "If not now, eventually they may be of use to us. And I want to know how they work. What makes these suckers tick."

"I agree. Dukaan, would you assist me, please?"

"I would be glad to," their pilot said.

"But there is no Allpower in them," Nakk said. "There is no point."

"For now, no. But I'm hopeful that eventually we'll be able to change that," Charlie replied.

"Excuse me," Kip interjected. "I don't mean to be a downer, but aren't these guys going to be missed?"

"I'd assume so," Charlie said. "Why? You got something on your scans?"

"No, but if weapons don't work here, I was just thinking this mess we just made might be an issue."

Charlie saw where he was going with this. "Of course. Nakk's people have taken ships in the past, but with primitive weapons. If they catch wind of what we've got they'll probably ramp up their searches dramatically. And heavily armed at that."

"Precisely," Kip said.

Bawb pondered this new twist in their plans a moment then began violently stabbing one of the bodies at his feet. A moment later he hacked at the charred end of a blasted-off arm before moving on to the next corpse.

"Dude, what are you doing?" Charlie hissed. "Not cool!"

Bawb shrugged. "We must disguise our actions here. And that means making the bodies not so obviously blasted with pulse weapons appear to have been the victims of bladed weapons. The other bodies too burned for that will need to be disposed of. We can leave no trace of our pulse fire."

"You mean hide them?" Nakk asked. "We have done this in the past."

He called out to his people, and moments later they all leapt into action, mutilating the deceased when they could, dragging the more charred corpses onto the captured ships for later disposal at another location.

"We will get rid of these bodies when we land at the hiding areas. It is a large network of caverns that we discovered some time ago," Nakk said. "There is an area nearby that is frequented by some of the larger animals that will serve that purpose quite well. Hopefully some of the predators will develop a taste for our enemy in the process."

"Hey, Kip, his English sounds much better," Charlie noted.

"Yeah, I've heard a lot more chatter now between Nakk and his guys, so my translation is getting refined," Kip replied.

"Hopefully you sound as clear to him when I translate the other way."

Nakk nodded his approval. "It is greatly improved, yes. Far easier to understand."

"Excellent," Charlie said. "Now, tell me more about these ships you say you've previously captured. This isn't the first run-in you've had with these, what did you call them?"

"Urvalin."

"Right. *Urvalin*. Exactly how many other ships of theirs have you managed to snag?"

"At present we have eleven other ships, all of them secreted away in our hiding places around the region. We do not dare store them all in one location in case they discover one of them. We also do not keep them near our stranded vessels. We still have hopes of restoring their power one day."

"And drawing additional attention to your downed fleet would be tempting them to strike even if the ships are powerless," Bawb noted.

"Exactly," Nakk said. "It is the same reason we do not fly the captured craft at all. Once detected in use, we stand a great likelihood of losing that portion of our fleet as well as the possible attack on the rest of our craft. We simply do not possess the numbers required to rise up. Not yet, anyway. But one day? Oh, one day we shall rise up and take our revenge on the Urvalin."

"Here's to hoping that happens sooner than later," Charlie said.

A commotion broke out nearby. The others had been gathering up the dead who were obvious pulse weapons victims and mutilating the others to leave in place, but, apparently, one of them was still breathing.

Charlie, Bawb, and the others rushed over to see what they could make of their lone prisoner. He was a tough one, clearly. Thick in the neck and resolute in his gaze. He had suffered a superficial stab wound, it seemed, as well as a blow to the head, which had rendered him unconscious. When he awoke, he found himself bound and a prisoner of the wretched castaways stranded on this planet.

"Do they speak the same language as you?" Bawb asked, staring, unblinking, at the survivor as he applied a new comms patch.

"Yes, they do. It is not their native tongue, but they all know our language," Nakk replied. "It makes it easier for them to track and kill us in this place."

"I see." Bawb leaned in closer, his fangs sliding into place as he smiled. Interestingly, the man did not react. At least, not as he'd expected. There was no fear in his eyes. Just a look of resignation.

"Where are your leaders?" Charlie asked. "How many ships do you have in orbit?"

The man simply smiled at him, remaining mute.

"Look, man, we're going to get answers the hard way or the easy way. And trust me, you want to go with the easy way."

At that the prisoner began laughing. Not just a little chuckle, but a full-on belly laugh. Apparently, he did not take Charlie's threat seriously. Not one bit.

"Okay," Charlie said. "But don't say I didn't warn you."

"It is you who should heed the warning," the man growled.

"What was that?"

But the prisoner did not reply. Rather, his head fell to one side, a faint wisp of green gas leaking from his lips.

"Back!" Nakk yelled.

Everyone jumped away immediately. A moment later the plume faded away into the air.

"What the hell was that?" Charlie gasped. "Did he just go all poison pill on us? Tell me he didn't just pull the fake tooth trick."

"It appears he did," Bawb said, examining his mouth. "Not a poison pill, though. It seems his tooth contains a concealed injection apparatus. Very advanced design, clearly made so as to not accidentally deploy in a fight."

"Well, shit. That's seriously unexpected."

"Indeed. And there is more to it than mere inconvenience," Bawb noted.

"I know," Charlie said. "It's not normal."

"No, it is not."

"Worse than that, it tells us something very important about our enemy."

Nakk watched the two men assessing the scene with great curiosity but didn't entirely follow them. "What is it you are talking about?" he asked. "This is what they do sometimes when captured."

"And that's not normal," Bawb replied. "Ordinary soldiers do not do that. This sort of commitment to a cause requires great strength of will. Conviction. A willingness to die for one's cause. These are no mere foot soldiers, I fear."

Charlie stared a long moment at the dead prisoner before finally speaking. "Bob? What the hell have we stumbled into?"

CHAPTER TWENTY-ONE

While Nakk's people quickly piled into the captured ships, loading them up with their rather substantial foraging haul as well as the spoils of battle, Charlie, Bawb, Nakk, and Dukaan managed to drag Ara's soon-to-be meal into the little ship's cargo hold.

It was a tight hatch when it came to oversized alien beasts, and the creature's hind legs had to be broken and bent out of the way to make it fit. With a bit of sweat and elbow grease, they ultimately managed to get it aboard.

"Try not to make too much of a mess with that thing," Kip said. "You know what a bitch it is getting Brixxax blood out of my carpeting."

"You do not *have* carpeting," Dukaan quipped.

Kip let out a little sigh, which was all the more notable as he was a computer and didn't have any lungs. "Why do you hate me, Dookie?" he joked.

Charlie chuckled. "You two are like an old married couple."

"I have far better taste in mates," Dukaan quipped. "Now, come. Let us get back. We have been away too long already, and Hunze is waiting for us."

A little smile creased Bawb's lips, but he said nothing. While he was concerned for his mate's health and well-being, as he always was, he also had the utmost confidence that she could more than take care of herself should any be foolish enough to test her mettle.

"Nakk, I would like to introduce you to the largest member of our little family," Charlie said. "Would you fly with us to where the others are waiting?"

Any doubts about the newcomers Nakk had previously had were gone. They had fought together, and the bond of battle had forged a degree of friendship. Something he hoped would strengthen into a true alliance given time.

"I would very much like to meet them," he replied. "Skohla will join me. She is a skilled warrior and was a talented pilot when our ships still flew. The rest of my people will return on foot while a lone pilot flies each of the captured craft close to the surface until it is safely hidden."

"Map of the Earth," Kip said. "Though this isn't Earth. But the idea's the same. Hug the terrain so close you avoid being picked up on scanning apparatus. Solid move."

"What is Earth?"

"Home for some of us, and a second home for the rest," Charlie said. "A long way from here, I'd wager, though we still don't know exactly where in the galaxy we are."

Nakk nodded. "We too do not know where we have been imprisoned. But this world appears to be blocked off from the Allpower entirely, though how that is even possible none of us have been able to discern. And the others who have been here far longer than we have are no more informed than we are."

"Others?" Dukaan asked.

"We are not the only ships to have been trapped here. From what we know, the other people who came before us have been stranded here for a very long time. They are known as the Horka."

"Fascinating," Bawb mused, the gears beginning to turn faster in his head.

"Well, we can figure all of this out while we're feeding Ara," Charlie said. "If Hunze's right and the mud's helping her heal, she's going to be one hungry girl."

"Your friend is a girl?" Nakk asked. "This is far more meat than a girl could possibly ingest."

Charlie grinned. "You'll see."

The flight back to the shoreline was brief, and Kip showed off his own low-flying prowess, hugging the terrain for their brief time airborne. He spun a quick loop over the landing site, making sure there were no hostiles in the area, then dropped down to the water's edge.

Nakk and Skohla followed Charlie from the ship. The sight that first greeted them was a stunning woman. A woman with impossibly golden hair, tied in a long braid wrapped around her body. She was sporting a sword on her back and daggers on each hip, they noted. Not just a pretty face by any means. Something Skohla approved of. She was considered something of a looker by her own people's standards and had more than once dealt with the unwanted advances of males who valued only her looks while underestimating her other attributes.

Bawb stepped out of the ship and strode directly to her. The brightening shift in her radiance was immediate. The visitors knew at once she was his, just as the man who had barely spoken since they had witnessed him meting out death with frightening efficiency was entirely hers. Among their people, such a bond was a sacred thing, and a rarity. Something to be treated with the utmost of respect and deference.

"You fought without me, love," Hunze said, noting the blood spattered on Bawb's clothing.

"It was not by choice, I assure you," he replied. "But our new friends here made a proper show of it and proved themselves worthy allies." Bawb turned to the alien pair. "Nakk, Skohla, I wish to introduce you to Hunze."

"It is our honor," Nakk said.

Skohla did not yet have the luxury of a comms patch translating for her, but knew of the device Nakk was now wearing, and when she heard what her leader said she spoke with confidence, knowing their new friends would understand even if she did not.

"It is a pleasure to meet you," she said. "Your man is a formidable warrior."

Hunze blushed slightly. "Thank you," she said.

"It is good meeting new friends," Nakk said. "Though she is not as large as you had me believing."

Charlie let out a laugh. "Oh, *she's* not the big one. Look behind you, at the water's edge."

Nakk and Skohla turned and nearly tumbled over themselves at what they saw.

"What is *that*?" Nakk gasped.

Ara, covered in mud from head to tail, opened her enormous golden eyes and stared at him with a calm gaze. "*Who*, would be more appropriate."

"Hey, you understand them?" Charlie asked.

Hunze stepped forward. "I had Dukaan leave an extra comms patch behind when he and Kip left. I placed it on Ara as I was working. I wasn't entirely sure it would work, though."

"It worked just fine," Ara said, her exhaustion and pain clear in her voice to those who knew her. "I have been listening in on your adventures, though I am sorry I have been in no condition to provide assistance."

Charlie walked up to her and rested his forehead against her cheek, the drying mud leaving a little smear on his skin. "You need to rest, Ara. We can take care of ourselves for a little while."

She seemed okay with that, though they all knew how truly

drained she must have been for her to give in so easily. But even the toughest of men and Zomoki sometimes had to let others take up the slack. The wisest knew not to fight when that time arrived.

"We've got something for you!" Kip chirped.

"Yes, I heard a comment about your carpeting, though I thought perhaps I misheard you."

"You did not mishear him," Dukaan said. "Kip was being Kip."

"That was my second guess," she said with a soft chuckle.

Charlie headed back to the ship. "Back in a minute. Guys, give me a hand?"

All of those present helped pull the dead Brixxax from the hold and drag it over to Ara, depositing it on the shore in front of her. What had seemed like such a massive animal when they were hauling it now looked comically small when compared to the sheer mass of their Zomoki friend.

"You'll want to step back," Charlie said.

He led the others to a safe distance. Once they were clear, Ara slowly lifted her head, wincing from the pain, then blew out a plume of flame. Only this fire was not magically charged as it normally was. It was just regular fire. The Brixxax, however, burned just the same.

Ara leaned in, her hunger apparently setting in now that there was the smell of fresh meat, but she stopped abruptly.

"What is she doing?" Dukaan asked.

Charlie couldn't believe his eyes, but he knew the answer full well. "She's letting it cool," he said.

Dukaan may have found that a bit odd, but Bawb and Hunze looked at Charlie with great concern. They were from her realm and knew how seriously a Zomoki had to be injured for it to be vulnerable to harm from heat and flame.

After a long minute the flames extinguished entirely. The meal was still hot, no doubt, but Ara's weakened body would wait no longer. She snatched it up in a single gulp, downing it in a flash. She swallowed hard then settled back down onto the shore. Fortunately, while her outside was burned and raw, at least her insides were relatively unscathed from her fiery descent.

"Thank you," she said, then looked at Nakk and Skohla. "It was very nice meeting you. Now, if you'll forgive me, I think I need to nap for a spell."

She then closed her golden eyes and drifted off to sleep.

CHAPTER TWENTY-TWO

Ara slept for several hours after her meal, breathing deep, the mud on her flanks crackling slightly as it dried in the sun. Her rest seemed far more peaceful than upon their arrival, though she was clearly still in a great deal of pain.

It would take more than a snack to truly fire up her healing process, but it was a start. And if her strength returned, Charlie and Bawb hoped she would be able to hunt for a proper meal.

The two men had been waiting for their friend to wake, Hunze quietly stepping away from the rather interesting discussion with their guests periodically to check in on her as their silent connection was nonfunctional. At long last, she roused.

"Hey, we need to go have a little chat with Ara. We'll leave you in Dukaan and Kip's capable hands for a moment," Charlie said.

"Of course," Nakk replied. "I have found discourse with your ship most fascinating. A mind inside a vessel? It is an amazing trick of Allpower."

"Science, technically," Kip said. "But whatever works for you. And I'll have Dukaan get a comms patch for your friend so she can participate. Not much fun if you don't know what's going on, am I right?"

Charlie and Bawb left them to their discussion on the finer points of artificial intelligence and made their way to the shore. The water seemed to have receded slightly, but Ara was still partially submerged in it, a line of mud-free scales showing where the water level had dropped.

They could see clearly how hurt she actually was and knew for her scales to have sustained that degree of damage, she must have entered the atmosphere without any magical protection whatsoever.

"I am glad to see you have rested," Hunze said as she scooped up fresh mud and began applying it to the exposed areas.

Ara shifted her gaze. "Thanks to your help. This mud has greatly eased my pain."

"I am pleased to hear it."

Ara looked at Charlie and Bawb. "And that animal you brought me was of great benefit as well. And rather large for two men with no magical means of transport."

"We made do," Charlie said.

"It is fortunate Kip was able to provide assistance," Bawb added. "Though I believe Nakk and his people would have helped us pull it all the way back here if we had asked it of them."

"Yes, your new friends. I am most curious to hear how you encountered them. Are they a local race?"

"Actually, not so much. In fact, they're pretty much like we are. Namely, screwed and stuck here," Charlie said.

"So, they also suffered a failure to their ships?"

"Yeah. And apparently it was that same portal that stranded us here. It looks like these people use a mix of technology and magic sort of how we do now that we've connected with your galaxy. But they don't call it magic. They call it 'Allpower.'

"Hmm," Ara said. "And what of the others? I failed to sense them when we arrived. It was such a chaotic incident it was hard to keep track. I noted Gustavo and Griggalt were pulled through before we were, and I have no sense of Rika. Beyond that I am afraid I remain in the dark."

Charlie and the others shared a look. Ara may have been exhausted, but her senses were still quite sharp.

"Ah, I see," she said. "How bad?"

"No sign of Rika and Jo whatsoever. On top of that, Griggalt is missing," Charlie said. "As for Gustavo, we found his wreckage several miles away. He didn't make it, I'm afraid."

"And his crew?"

"From what we could tell, some of the escape pods had been launched, but whether or not their mechanical fail-safes were able to bring them in for a landing is anyone's guess. They could be anywhere. We've been hoping when Kip was finally airworthy again he could do a survey for them. Maybe he'd be able to find the pods and the others."

"I sense a but."

"But after we met Nakk's people we found something else back at Gustavo's wreckage."

"Let me guess," Ara said. "A hostile force."

"Yep. With our luck, how did you ever guess?" Charlie said with a grim chuckle. "It's a group Nakk called the Urvalin. Nasty pieces of work. Kind of remind me of Tslavars in an asshole distant cousin sort of way."

Bawb nodded his agreement. "I do see the similarity, though their morphology could also signify a relation to any number of other races."

"Yeah, I know," Charlie said. "But you know my history with Tslavars. In any case, they still have power to their ships."

"Interesting. So, if they can operate machines, it would seem they must have something to do with the technological power loss in this place."

"It looks like it," Charlie agreed. "I don't think there'd be any other way they could operate their ships otherwise."

"There is more," Bawb interjected. "These Urvalin also possess devices called bandas. A belt-like unit that would appear to function much in the manner of a konus, storing their magic for later deployment. But it appears their use of what they call Allpower is blocked here as well. In that regard, at least, we are on a level playing field."

"We captured several of those devices," Charlie added. "I figured that they may have no juice at the moment, but maybe one day we'll find a way to make them work. Some mechanism to tap back into magic again. And if that happens, it can't hurt to have a stockpile of 'em on hand in addition to our own gear."

"A wise decision," Ara said, lifting her head a bit higher as she reached out to the power normally coursing through her body. "There is no connection to the galaxy's soul whatsoever. No power, not even from the sun," she said, glancing up at the strangely distorted rays. "This should be impossible. We should be able to connect to it. To sense it at the very least."

Charlie nodded. "Like I said, their bandas are useless, just like our konuses."

"But it is more than that, Charlie. We possess our own power. We generate magic from within."

"I feel nothing," Hunze noted. "No new magic created and none stored. Even all that was in my hair seems to be gone." She hesitated a moment, reaching within. "It was not taken from me, though. I can just no longer sense it."

"As with Ara and me as well," Charlie said. "It's downright creepy, missing something you've gotten so used to being there. It's like when an ache finally goes away and you didn't even realize you were in pain until there was none."

"But if these new adversaries suffer the same loss that we do, that would mean they create their own power," Hunze mused.

"Yes. Nakk said that power is common here. Most people

have at least a minor amount of their own. They use a triad system of joining forces, quite literally, to help amplify and focus their efforts," Charlie said. "Pretty cool if you ask me."

Bawb's demeanor grew more serious. "But there is still the issue of the nature of our foe to be discussed. These are no ordinary soldiers or minions. The one survivor we captured ended himself without a second thought. These are believers. Disciplined followers of whoever it is that leads them. To so blithely take one's own life speaks to the seriousness of their belief in their cause."

"Or fear of their leaders," Charlie added.

Ara's interest was most certainly piqued. "You say they commit suicide rather than be captured? That makes them a dangerous foe indeed. One to be taken most seriously."

"That we will, Ara. That we will. But right about now, we need to figure out how to heal you up and get our asses off of this rock," Charlie said. "Hopefully we'll find Rika in one piece, and maybe even those escape pods. And then we work on a hasty departure."

"But how can we do so?" Hunze asked.

"I don't know. But first things first, we need to pick our new friend's brains."

CHAPTER TWENTY-THREE

Ara had continued to rally, her strength slowly returning while the fog of exhaustion lifted as her body began to heal. She still had quite a long way to go, but she was out of the woods, her survival no longer in question. That is, unless the Urvalin sent ships along this stretch of shoreline.

It was a risk there was little they could do about.

Kip and Dukaan had given their guests the grand tour of the ship, discussing the differences between their worlds' technologies with great interest. It seemed that Nakk was more than just a leader of his little band of survivors. In his previous life, before becoming a castaway, he commanded a fleet of his own. And many of those ships had come down on this world.

"I can see you appreciate the finer points of airframe engineering," Kip said as Nakk commented on the beautiful quality of his construction.

"Your welds are perfect," Nakk marveled. "I see no flaws."

"I'd hope not. Our best AI engineers designed this ship for me."

"You were not always in this body?"

"Uh, no. But that's a long story. I'm sure there's a lot of other stuff far more interesting we can get into."

"Just be sure not to ask him for any heated bread products," Dukaan said with a snicker. "He is rather fixated."

"Shut up, Dookie. I am not."

The Chithiid merely grinned.

"Hey, guys, Ara's up and wants to talk to Nakk," Charlie said over the ship's comms link. "You mind sending him and Skohla out?"

"Straightaway," Kip said. "If you will step outside, it seems Ara's feeling up for a chat."

"Of course. We look forward to it," Nakk said.

Dukaan could feel the ship's AI sigh of relief. "Saved by the bell, my friend," he said with a laugh.

"Oh, bite me."

His Chithiid friend laughed. "You are made of metal. I most certainly know better," he replied. "I will, however, accompany our friends. I, too, wish to hear what Ara has to say."

Nakk and Skohla's awe at Ara's mass had not diminished during their absence from her presence. In fact, now that her vigor was somewhat restored, she was even more impressive a specimen than they had initially realized. Dragons, it seemed, were not commonplace in this part of the galaxy. And one who spoke was even more of a marvel.

"I apologize for my earlier brevity," Ara said. "As I am sure you have learned, I suffered some injuries upon our arrival here, and recovery has proven a bit burdensome."

Nakk stepped closer. "We understand completely and are pleased to see you feeling better."

"Thank you, your concern appreciated." She shifted slightly, the mud on her body cracking and falling off in places.

Hunze quietly began gently reapplying it while Ara spoke. The absolute trust and comfort they had with one another struck Nakk and Skohla. A creature that could devour her in a single gulp was a trusted friend and ally. Family to all of them, it seemed. Today had proven a most unusual one indeed.

"I understand that your people are familiar with both technology as well as magic. An energy called Allpower, is that correct?" Ara asked.

"Yes," Nakk replied. "Though we do not call Allpower magic. It is simply Allpower. The power that flows through all things."

"As does the magic bonding every corner of the galaxy. And you use this Allpower to drive some of your ships, yes?"

"Sometimes. We typically use engines for that purpose, but those strong enough in Allpower have been known to power their ships in that manner."

"One person's magic is another's science," Charlie said.

"Very much so," Ara agreed. "And your people, they often operate in a cooperative of threes, like a triumvirate of energy, keeping a constant flow, each caster spelling out the other as they focus on the next round, if I understand correctly."

"Yes, we very often work in trios. It is the most useful conjoining of power and allows a constant power utilization," he agreed.

"So," she mused, "it is essentially magic as we know it, but you have a different name for it. And more interestingly, your part of the galaxy uses it and technology interchangeably as a fact of everyday life. Most fascinating. Up until now I thought Charlie and our friends were the only ones who operated in this manner."

"Well, the galaxy is a big place," Charlie noted. "I mean, out of billions of solar systems, we've only explored a tiny fraction of them. Who knows what else is out there?"

"A valid point. There are many variations in my own galaxy, and just as is the case here, we have only explored a tiny portion of it. There could very well be similar cultures we have simply not encountered yet."

Hunze looked up from her mud-smearing task. "Like the

Kalamani," she said. "Theirs is an utterly novel use of indigenous plant life bursting with magic. And look at the results when brought into our midst."

"The Kalamani?" Skohla asked. "We have not heard of these people."

"No, you wouldn't have," Charlie said. "They're a very remote group. No space travel. No technology, just a tribal culture. One that is attuned to the naturally occurring magi—Allpower on their world."

Nakk and Skohla shared a surprised look. "A people with power but no technology? How fascinating. But it is a big galaxy, as you have noted. We are familiar with dozens of races, but we have never seen any of your kind for that matter."

"And no Ra'az either, so you definitely got lucky in that regard."

"Ra'az?" Skohla asked, her curiosity clearly piqued by Charlie's tone.

"Planet killers. A horrible race we fought to their extinction alongside our Chithiid allies. Be glad you never had to deal with them."

"We have the Urvalin Conglomerate," Nakk said grimly. "I suspect it is a similar menace. We are part of an alliance that has been battling them for many, many years. But look what that got us. Pulled into a portal trap and stranded here, impotent and separated from the fight. So many ships lost, so many others unable to power up and fly. Why, we have an entire fleet here, gathering dust as vines grow onto their hulls."

"Wait, you have an actual fleet?"

"With no power. We have repaired them all as best we can, and they are in flying condition. But without a means to launch them, they are no more than housing for the masses. A few maintained power upon arrival, but as soon as they were shut down for repairs their systems went cold. Once power is lost, it is not regained."

Kip did not like the sound of that one bit. It was at that moment he made the decision that no matter what, he would not power down. To do so, so far as he could tell, meant falling into a forced slumber or worse.

"So, you just live here, stranded?" Charlie said. "That sucks. Especially if you've got Urvalin overseeing things."

"It is worse than that. They pick us off for sport since we have no means to properly defend ourselves."

"And you don't dare launch the few ships you've captured from them lest they realize what you have and launch a full-on attack," Charlie said. "Bastards."

Skohla nodded her agreement. "Precisely. They are always expanding their reach, conquering any planet they can, claiming entire systems as their own and installing their loyal minions to rule in their absence."

"Much like the Council of Twenty," Bawb mused. "There is an organization in my home galaxy that is quite similar. We have beaten them back and slowed their plans for expansion, but they still remain a lingering threat to deal with."

"Except when Malalia whooped them all into line," Charlie noted.

"Yes, there was that."

"Malalia?" Nakk asked.

"An *extremely* powerful woman with whom we have a long, long history. She fashioned herself a ruler of galaxies, and while she was amassing her forces, she actually managed to put the Council of Twenty in check."

"I sense a but," Skohla said.

"But we defeated her, draining all of her power and imprisoning her on a distant planet with no means to regain it. Much like this place in that respect, I suppose."

"You are a great warrior, then," she said.

"Actually, it was Rika who had the honor of delivering the

final beat-down. And she didn't even use the power the Kalamani imbued her with."

Nakk stroked his chin in thought. "A race with such gifts in the realm of the Allpower, yet technologically they are but infants who have not yet learned to walk? It is most unusual."

"Yes," Skohla agreed. "I have to wonder how they ever learned to harness the Allpower."

Charlie understood where they were coming from. It had startled him a bit at first as well.

"You see, the Kalamani are kinda unique in that. It's a nature-based thing, the way they incorporate the pigment into power symbols tattooed directly into the skin. It gives the person receiving them a varying range of powers depending on the symbols themselves, as well as the compound used. It's how our friend Rika wound up becoming an even more badass bitch than she was to begin with."

"And she was indeed quite formidable in that regard already," Bawb noted.

"Yeah, she was not one to be messed with. But now the mixture of magic in her body from two different galaxies has made her something unique. And that's why we need to find her. If she managed to land safely, that unique kind of power just might be the one thing that actually still works in this place."

"If she survived," Dukaan said quietly.

"Right," Charlie said, his grin faltering. "If she survived."

CHAPTER TWENTY-FOUR

"I tell you, they were just gone. Poof. There one second, gone the next."

Rika was pacing a rut in the floor of Cal's command center, magic crackling faintly from her tattoos. She was agitated. *Very* agitated. And for someone who had recently visited a black sun system and supercharged her power in the process, that could be a disconcerting occurrence.

Jo, on the other hand, was calm and cool, patiently watching as her friend burned off a little of that energy. Of course, as a cyborg, standing still was as easy as breathing. Or not breathing, as the case may be.

Zed, Joshua, and Sid were all tied into the conversation, the greatest AI minds of the galaxy all working in unison on the dilemma of what exactly had happened to Charlie and his friends. When Rika had come back to Earth after she was supposed to rendezvous with the intercept team going after the magical assailants, they had known something was wrong. She did not run from a fight. If she was back early, and alone at that, things must have been very bad indeed.

"*Tell us again how exactly you avoided the anomaly,*" Cal requested.

"I told you, it was just a little navigational correction due to solar wind," she replied.

"*But your ship possesses top-notch equipment. And you have rather significant magic within you to boot. So how is it you were unable to compensate?*"

"Because it wasn't a big deviation. Just enough to drop us out of warp on the far edge of the portal. It was a long series of warps, and the location was way out there. Some navigational tweaks were bound to occur, and this one just so happened to play in our favor."

"I was with her, obviously," Jo said. "She's spot-on in her assessment. For a warp of that distance, it really wasn't so unusual a variance."

"Yeah, exactly," Rika said, her feet sparking with agitation.

Jo eyed her friend. "Hey, you need to slow your roll a little."

"I'm fine."

"No, you're not."

"I *am*."

"Rika, you're *burning* the floor."

Rika looked at the little char marks in the deck where a trickle of power had escaped her. "Oh, crap. Sorry, Cal."

"*Not to worry. I'll have one of Habby's people buff it out. They seem to really enjoy that sort of labor, strange as it may seem.*"

Joshua, ever calculating the odds and outcomes of countless scenarios, chimed in. "About their disappearance. You're certain it was a magical portal and not a wormhole?"

"Oh yeah. I could feel it as soon as we arrived. It's hard to describe, but let's just say it felt very *wrong*, if that makes sense."

"I think I know what you're getting at," Joshua replied. "Now, as one with your abilities, were you able to gauge where exactly this portal took them?"

"No. And that's why it took us so long to report back," she

said. "We ran hard and did recon in as many of the nearby systems as we could, expanding out in all directions in a spherical search."

"But there are a lot of systems," Zed noted.

"And we did our damnedest to visit them all," Jo added. "That's part of the reason we had to take a pause out there. The *Fujin*'s warp system was starting to overheat."

"Overheat?"

"Yeah. That's how hard we were pushing. But we didn't locate them."

"Not so much as a trace," Rika added. "Zip. Zilch. Nada. Wherever that thing took them, it was farther than a few simple warps away. Believe me, we looked."

"Interesting," Joshua said, his strategic gears turning as pieces of the puzzle began to align. "And you weren't able to even discern the basic direction the portal took them?"

"I told you, not a clue. We looked in *every* direction, and it was a no-go."

"And the portal, it is still open?"

"Open? Yeah. And almost impossible to see. That thing's hidden out there, and for a reason. I'm thinking it's probably not the best idea to go chasing after them blindly. Whoever lured them out there did this for a reason."

"*You think this was a trap?*" Cal asked.

"Oh, no doubt."

"*What makes you so sure?*"

"Well, for starters, there were no warships in the area when we got there. Not any kind of ship for that matter. Just this massive, hidden portal."

"We got out of there immediately," Jo noted. "But not before I pulled data and ran a threat assessment for the surrounding area. There were no vessels anywhere near enough for that localized scan."

Rika nodded her agreement. "But there *was* something that *I* was able to pick up. Namely, jump magic residue in the area. A decent amount of it. And let me tell you, whoever the hell it was, they have some seriously strong magic powering their ships. Like, we're talking Council of Twenty level juju."

"But the Council is on its heels, and in a different galaxy, no less," Zed noted. "After Malalia's defeat, they were in disarray and lacking any real focused leadership, not to mention after seeing what she was capable of, their casters kind of paled by comparison."

The door to the command center burst open, followed by the echo of a pair of heavy boots stomping into the room.

"What happened? Whose head do I need to separate from their neck?" Marban bellowed.

He was breathing hard. From the looks of him he'd run all the way to command from the landing pad. And judging by the dark red flush to the scar running from his head to his collar, he was not in a trifling mood. Someone had attacked his friends, and that was a smiting offense.

Rika rushed over to him, her own agitation diminishing as she shifted her focus to calming the gregarious pirate. "Hey, it's okay," she said, not thinking of the irony of her using the very same words that had so recently had absolutely no impact on her own raised ire.

"Charlie's gone," he said. "And Ara. Bawb. Hunze. It's not right."

"I know."

"Leila's pregnant, Rika. And now Charlie's missing. He has to be here for the birth of his—have they determined the kid's bits yet?"

"Not yet. They want it to be a surprise."

"Well, whatever it is. He should be here when it comes into this world."

Rika was not a maternal type by a long shot, but seeing the salty pirate's display of papa bear protectiveness, even if by association, was more than a little endearing. He may have looked like a brutal pirate, and he played the part often enough, but Marban was a man of great depth and emotion and more layers than an onion. Or an ogre, for that matter.

"We're working on a plan, Marban. And we *will* find them. But something nasty is in play, and we can't just go blindly barreling into Lord knows what. Not without a plan. Not without knowing what we're dealing with. It was a trap, and whoever set it was a powerful caster."

"We have dealt with powerful casters before."

"And they lured them into a camouflaged portal, so we don't even know where they are to go help them. So take a breath and slow down."

Jo cracked a little grin but kept her mouth shut. It was a serious matter, after all. And besides, there was plenty of time later to call Rika out. Plus, this was calming her down, so it was a two-birds-one-stone kind of situation.

Marban processed what Rika said, but the vast majority simply didn't stick. His big brother gene was expressing itself, and something fierce at that.

"If it truly was a portal trap, and they are in need, we should send a ship at once," he said. "They could need our help." He rolled his shoulders back and stood a little taller. "I volunteer to take the *Coratta* and go after them. This is no time for half-measures."

"I just told you, it was a trap. You don't just go barreling into a trap."

"Why not?"

"Because it's a *trap*."

"Ah, but we now *know* it's a trap, which renders it something else entirely."

Rika rolled her eyes and sighed. "I don't care what you call it, charging in there is simply peak foolishness."

"Would you simply wait and do nothing?"

"Of course not!"

"Then what? We cannot—"

"You know, we could send a probe," Jo interrupted.

Rika turned. "What was that?"

"A probe. One of the automated survey units should work. Just a few modifications from our magic-using friends to boost its transmission profile and we should be able to set it to fly through, gather all the data it can, then hurry back to relay the information."

Rika nodded her head. "I like this. Yeah. I like it a lot."

Jo winked at her. "Of course you do. It's *my* idea."

The AIs seemed to be in agreement on the plan as well, each of them chiming in their thoughts on the prospect. Zed ultimately offered up one of his high-tech system mapping probes to be retrofitted for the job. It wasn't an AI—they didn't want to risk a sentient mind on such an uncertain mission, but it possessed a robust processing array and was as close to AI as a computer could get without actually having consciousness and self-awareness.

"I will have the unit ready in two hours," Zed informed them. "At that point we will send a small force to the edge of the system containing the portal to send it through."

Rika nodded, a vengeful smile on her face as thoughts of battle filled her head. "And then, when we know how many ships are on the other side, we send whatever size fleet we have to in order to kick their asses all the way back to whatever part of the galaxy they crawled out of," she said. "Jo, warm up the *Fujin*. We're getting our friends back."

CHAPTER TWENTY-FIVE

Orgalius and Nixxus sat perched atop Cal's command center, the two dragons bright in the full afternoon sun. Occupying Ara's usual spot in front of her own set of display monitors, the deep, cobalt blue of Orgalius's scales were a stark contrast to the red of Ara's. Nixxus, a fair bit smaller than the sheer mass of her friend, sported a mix of violet on her back and green across her belly.

Gazz, younger, muscular, and more gregarious, was a somewhat ochre brown in color, and would be joining them shortly. He was visiting his human friends out on the shores of Malibu but had said he would fly to them straightaway. A meeting had been called by the AIs, and the dragons with the strongest magic had been requested. Gazz, youthful though he was, most definitely fit the bill.

"What do you mean they called you in?" Ripley asked.

Her AI ship was sitting nearby, equally curious. "Yeah, what she said," Eddie chimed in. "I'm an AI, why didn't they call me too?"

"Or me, for that matter," Marty added. "Not like we haven't pulled our weight, right?"

"I do not know," Gazz replied. "I was just told there had been an incident and those of us with the strongest magic were requested."

"You hear that, Arlo? Magic stuff. Maybe your girlfriend can help," Ripley teased.

"She's not my girlfriend."

"Might as well be."

"We're in different galaxies, Rip."

"So?"

"It's *complicated*."

"Well, I like Kara," Ripley said. "She's cool. And Vee's a lot of fun too. We really should fly out to see them again soon. Before the trip to Taangaar, I mean."

Arlo shrugged. "I know, but she's been helping her dad and her uncle clean up after all the mess Malalia made. She's busy."

"We can help!" Ripley said. "And come on, it's not that far of a flight. Just pop through the portal and a few warps and we're there."

Ripley watched him squirm. Arlo seemed uneasy. Unsure of himself. That was not normal for him at all. Yep, he still liked Kara, all right.

"Yeah, but I'm not a magic user," he finally said. "And she's like some super powerful wizard now. I'm just a regular guy."

Ripley smacked him playfully. "She likes you regardless, dork. Don't screw it up."

"I rather like Karasalia as well," Gazz said. "We visited her and her uncle with Ara when she was showing us around her home galaxy. A good group of people, that family. And exceptionally powerful."

"Hey, how was it for you over there?" Eddie asked. "I mean, Ara was the last talking dragon in the galaxy, but now with you guys showing up, I bet a bunch of people kinda freaked out."

"Surprisingly, it went smoother than I'd have anticipated,"

Gazz said. "Of course, with Ara as our host, I suppose that would be expected."

It had been something of a miracle in her home galaxy, the shocking revelation of the existence of one of the Wise Ones thought long dead. But after the battle with Visla Dominus, it was simply no longer possible to hide her presence. And after their victory, she had been seen as something of a good omen. A kind-spirited return to the old ways before the Council of Twenty darkened so many systems.

Her travel to and from another galaxy of all places, and with these distant cousins of the Zomoki at her side, was a cause for celebration. A sign that things were finally looking up. A return of the articulate, wise creatures who had helped keep the peace so many centuries before.

"So, it all went well?" Ripley asked.

"For the most part, yes. We did, however, have a little run-in with some of our lesser relatives," Gazz said with a deep sigh. "It was a shock, encountering the mindless, wild Zomoki populating that realm. It's sad, really. They're relatives, yes, but they are also such a far cry from what we are that we might as well be different species. But that galaxy? It is truly astounding. I look forward to my next visit."

"I'm sure the portal's proximity to the sun didn't hurt," Marty said. "I mean, I know how it supercharges Ara's magic, so I assume you guys are similar in that way."

"Yes, we draw significant power from this system's sun. Not as much as Ara, but being from another galaxy, it seems certain things have different effects on us in each realm. But the transit being so close to the sun is definitely a rather nice bonus."

A figure down the beach was growing closer, and quickly. A woman, running. Even from a distance they could see the nanite arm contrasting her own skin tone.

"Hey, your mom's coming," Arlo said.

Ripley turned and watched as Sarah ran toward them. She

wasn't armed, though, so this was just a recreational outing. Sarah had long ago adopted the habit of running pretty much everywhere. The nanite-repaired lungs she sported could convert air into concentrated oxygen and shuttle it to her cells at a far more efficient rate than her original damaged ones. Cardio, for her, was effortless. And so she ran. A *lot*.

"Hey, Aunt Sarah," Arlo called out as she drew near.

Ripley gave a little wave. "What's up, Mom?"

"I'm here for Gazz."

"Carrying a goody bag?"

"And I'm also stopping by to check in on Leila. Your father baked again."

Arlo's interest was suddenly piqued. "Ooh, what did he make?"

"It's for Leila, Arlo."

"Aww."

"You know your uncle. There's always more if you want to stop by later," Sarah said. Then she did the spooky thing she sometimes did, shifting focus like flipping a switch. "Gazz, Cal and the others are waiting on you, didn't you get the call?"

"I did. I was just finishing up a conversation. I was about to depart."

"Well, get on it, Mister. We've got magical strangeness afoot, and it looks like you get to be a part of it."

"Ooh, strangeness!" Ripley chirped, grabbing her things and heading to her ship. "C'mon, Eddie. Let's visit Uncle Cal."

"Ripley, you are *not* going to crash Cal's meeting. This is important stuff here. And Eddie's supposed to fly up to see Joshua about those upgrades."

"*Moooom*, I'm an adult!"

"And a veteran," Arlo added.

"Yeah, and a veteran. A *combat* veteran. I am totally not missing this meeting. And Uncle Joshua can wait, right, Eddie?"

"It's no rush. I'll just be trying out some new add-ons he's come up with," the ship replied.

Sarah sighed. She saw the look in her daughter's eye and knew this was one battle she would not win. "Fine. But behave yourself. And I expect you back in time for dinner."

"I'll be there," Ripley said as she shook the sand off her feet and stepped aboard Eddie. "Arlo, you coming?"

"Nah. I told my dad I'd help out with some stuff. But let me know if there's anything cool, okay?"

"Will do," Ripley said as the hatch shut.

Moments later the little ship lifted off, falling in beside the large dragon flying inland to Downtown. Sarah and Arlo watched them grow smaller in the distance.

"Tell your dad Finn wants to barbecue this weekend," Sarah said, then dug a scone out of the bag. "Don't say I never do anything for you."

Arlo accepted the treat with a grin. "Thanks, Aunt Sarah."

She ruffled his hair, which she knew he hated, then continued her run.

Arlo's best AI friend lifted into a low hover. "You think there's anything serious going on?" Marty asked.

Arlo shrugged. "I doubt it. If there was, I'm sure they'd have called *everyone* in, ya know."

"Yeah. But your mom's out of town, and we all know calling *her* is the real *things-are-bad* litmus test."

"True that," Arlo chuckled. "All right, I'm gonna head home, I guess."

"Dad duty?"

"Yep. I just hope it's not gardening again," Arlo said, wondering if, perhaps, he should have played hooky and gone with Ripley and Gazz.

Meanwhile, that pair had already landed at Cal's command center, Gazz taking up his place on the rooftop with the other dragons, looking like a trio of massive gargoyles, while Ripley made her way to the heart of the building.

Eddie could have tied her in from the outside since he was connected for the meeting and had already informed Joshua he would be late arriving at his moon hangar, but Ripley enjoyed visiting Cal "in person" even if he didn't have a physical body.

Surprisingly, Rika and Jo were sitting in command when she got there.

"Hey, guys! What's up?"

"*Hello, Ripley. I had a feeling you might be joining us for this meeting,*" Cal said with a warm chuckle.

"Hey, Rip," Zed chimed in.

"Where's your cousin?" Rika asked.

"He's helping Uncle Vince. But me and Eddie are here. And Gazz, of course."

"Good. We'll need all of the magical help we can get," Jo grumbled.

This wasn't good. Jo could be surly at times, but she was typically a pretty darn chipper cyborg. Something serious was going on.

"Uh, guys? What's the deal?" Ripley asked.

"*We are all here, so let's get to it,*" Cal said. "*At issue is a disconcerting event. One that Rika and Jo witnessed first-hand and were very nearly caught up in. Namely, a hidden portal. Charlie, Ara, Kip, Gustavo, and Griggalt, all flew in pursuit of a magic-based attacker, chasing them quite a distance from this system. But when they exited warp at the final destination, they were pulled into a portal.*"

"A trap, then," Orgalius said. "And an expertly laid one if it caught that group off guard."

"That it was," Rika agreed. "And I have no idea where they were sent."

"*And that is where you come in, my new friends. With Ara gone,*" *we are incredibly limited in our ability to track this new enemy. Or our missing friends, for that matter. But your kind can smell magic."*

"Ah, I see your need," Orgalius said. "I would be happy to assist in any way possible."

"Joshua, you want to chime in?" Zed asked.

"Of course. Tactically, it makes the most sense to deploy our resources in multiple areas, limiting risk to our assets while increasing efficacy. With that in mind, I propose one of you accompany Rika and Jo in their search for Ara and Charlie, as well as their assailants. The others will take up positions on Earth, standing by for deployment should another attack occur."

"Sound reasoning," Orgalius said. "Given the nature of this threat, I agree that I should travel with Rika and Jo. Once their ship and my magic are in tune we will be able to warp and jump in close unison."

"Yeah, we've done it plenty with Ara, so the konus adjustment shouldn't be difficult," Jo said. "But what about Daisy and Freya? They're not magic users, per se, but Freya has really gotten a knack for it since her nanites learned to recreate that magic power."

"Don't get me started on that," Joshua said with a laugh. "She is constantly trying new things with those nanites. But so far, a lot of her more lofty attempts are still hit or miss. But in any case, she and Daisy are out of town at the moment on a little peacekeeping mission."

"Where'd they go? Taangaar? We can send a message for them to come back," Rika said.

"I'm afraid that won't do," Joshua replied. "They've gone quite a bit farther than that."

CHAPTER TWENTY-SIX

The mist hung low to the ground, adding a particularly eerie vibe in the dim light thrown by the storehouse windows. The other buildings in the area were long dark, their occupants having called it a day and gone home hours ago. But not this one.

Booted feet stalked as quietly around the perimeter as they could, drawing close to the windows to assess exactly what was going on inside. This was unheard of. Here? On this planet? They were under the protection of Emmik Parvin, a vital part of the Council of Twenty's weapons fabrication apparatus.

Or, he *was*, until a certain spaceman from Earth and his friends put the kibosh on all of that. And it was likely that shift in the power structure that had made the crazy redheaded woman inside think she could get away with this.

That woman was not from this galaxy, but her great-great-great-great ancestor was. The woman who would eventually be known as Dominus. Malalia Maktan. A distant relative from her brief stay on Earth all of those years ago.

And at the moment, Daisy's brutality would have actually made her proud.

"I told you, no selling this crap to ignorant kids," she said, bitch-slapping the red-faced man on his knees before her.

"I don't sell them. I just facilitate the transfers."

"Which then winds up in the hands of kids." Another sharp slap rang out, his face jerking to the side from the blow. "I mean, smuggling konuses is one thing, but *faulty* ones? Those things are a loaded gun just waiting to go off."

"What is a *gun*?"

"Never mind that. The point is, kids have no idea how to control them, even if they weren't busted. But these? Not acceptable. Not one bit."

The man tensed, expecting another blow, but was spared this once.

"What is it to you?" he asked. "It's just a job, lady. That's all. Don't take it so personally."

Her palm cracked across his face. "I *have* kids," she growled. "So yes, I do take it personally. *Very* personally. Children have been hurt by your goods."

The man just shrugged. He knew he couldn't appease this woman. He just had to hold out until his magical alarm was responded to. The door burst open right on cue, and a handful of very large bruisers pushed their way inside.

"You having some kind of trouble, Boss?" the largest of them asked.

A wicked grin replaced his look of fear. "Not anymore," he said, glaring at Daisy. "Get her!"

"Six, Daze," Sarah counted. *"No major weapons, but I think at least one of them might have a little power."*

Yeah, Stabby senses it, she silently replied. *I've gotta keep him in check. The poor guy's feeling power hungry.*

"In the literal sense," Sarah joked.

Exactly, Daisy replied. *Look sharp, it's time to dance.*

Daisy left her sword sheathed as the thugs moved on her. There was no need to kill these henchmen. She felt quite confident they would underestimate her. She was just a woman, after all. What could she possibly do against the six of them?

Sharp elbows and viciously thrown knees quickly answered that question for them as Daisy launched herself into the fray, all of the myriad martial styles she'd learned over the years flowing from her in a dizzying display of empty-handed violence.

The nearest goon dropped in a heap before he could cry out in surprise and pain. Another dropped to his knees as her kick connected with a very sensitive area. The remaining men realized the error of their thinking and were just reaching for their weapons when they all fell, bowled over by a blast of magic. Daisy nearly fell as well, but the defensive konus she was wearing absorbed and redirected the spell.

She turned to look at the new arrival. He was tall, with deep blue skin and bright red eyes. His hair was an inky blue-black, and so far as she could tell, it ran from his head down the length of his back, though one couldn't be entirely sure what was inside his tunic.

"Emmik Parvin," the beaten smuggler said with clear relief.

The emmik surveyed the room with a cool eye. An eye he soon turned toward his unwanted visitor. "Roughing up my men? Don't you know under whose protection they fall?"

"Obviously not yours," she said with a laugh. "If they do, well, it's kinda shit protection, wouldn't you agree?"

The blue man's face darkened. "Who the hell do you think you are, talking to me that way?"

"Daisy's the name, and kicking henchman ass is the game."

"Daisy? An unusual name."

"I'm fond of it."

"And one that is familiar," Emmik Parvin continued. "You're that bitch who fights alongside the traitor Charlie and his ilk."

She raised her hand faux-sheepishly. "Guilty as charged."

"I lost a great deal of business because of that man," the emmik growled. "And you're one of his lackeys."

Daisy bowed with a flourish. "At your service."

"Well, you've just stepped in it, haven't you? I know of you and your strange craft. But you are alone and on foot. And from what we've all heard, you are not a magic user."

"No, I'm not," she said with a grin. "But *you* are."

She did not seem concerned. Not one bit. It was more than a little disconcerting.

"Yes, I am. And I am not just a mere magic user. I am Emmik Parvin."

"You say that like I should give a shit," she shot back. "But hey, thanks for showing up at least. It was getting really hard finding excuses to drag things out with your underlings here."

"You do not scare me, *girl*. I am more powerful than you think."

"We'll see."

"And I have a dozen of my finest guards just outside."

Daisy flashed an unsettling grin. "Oh, do you now?"

The emmik suddenly felt a twinge of something he was unaccustomed to. A pang of concern. He kept his poker face strong, hiding his worries as he called out to his men. There was no reply. He called again, ordering them to come inside. Again, nothing.

Daisy's grin grew even wider. Something was afoot, and whatever it was, the emmik had to act, and decisively.

He began casting fast and furious, hurling magic at Daisy while urging his men to attack. And this time, they armed themselves with blades and konuses.

"Oh, fine," Daisy said as Stabby casually deflected the magical attacks. "I guess you get to play after all."

The bloodthirsty sword nearly sang out in joy at being unleashed to wreak destruction upon those who dared oppose them. His edge was beyond razor-sharp, and limbs separated from bodies with such ease the goons didn't realize they'd even been cut for a good several seconds after their appendages dropped to the ground.

But for Stabby it wasn't enough. He wanted the emmik, sensing his power as he fought off the man's attack. The sword began physically pulling Daisy toward the caster.

"No, Stabby, we need him alive."

The sword understood but was not happy with the situation. He wanted to drink blood. Power user blood. Fortunately, one of the goons did in fact possess a tiny bit of his own, and Stabby greedily took it from him as he snuffed out his life.

The emmik was pulling upon his deepest well of magic, casting the most powerful spells he could muster at his troublesome opponent, when icy-cold fangs sank into his neck, draining him of his power in an instant. His eyes drooped closed before he could even see who had gotten the better of him. Had he been awake, he'd have been surprised to see a kindly older woman at his side.

Farmatta drained him of his magic, taking the power for her own, but stopped short of killing him. This one had information. This one got to live.

"Nice one, Farmatta. Thanks for the assist," Daisy said, driving Stabby into the dying guard to satiate his thirst for magic at least a little bit. "Poor Stabby, though. He was hoping to feast." She pulled the sword free, wiped it clean, and slid it back into its sheath. "But thanks."

"It is my pleasure," the Ghalian master replied. "Your cause is a just one, and I am glad to be of assistance. We simply cannot have dangerously crafted konuses spread about the systems. Several dozen innocents have already suffered injury because of them."

"And I'm hoping this guy helps stop it there," Daisy said. "And if he coughs up the name of who he actually works for then that will be that."

"One would hope," the assassin said. "Now, what are your plans?"

"Me? I've just got a couple of things to wrap up, then it's back to the beach. I promised my family we'd take a little vacation once I get back. Somewhere warm, ideally. With no drama."

"It sounds like a delightful use of time," Farmatta said, hauling the unconscious man up effortlessly.

It was amazing just how strong the woman was despite her appearance. But that was how the Ghalian were. Deceptively powerful and damn near indestructible.

"I think it will be," Daisy replied. "It's been far too long since we took a proper vacation."

"You do have a lovely family," Farmatta noted.

"Thanks," Daisy said as she stripped the dead and wounded of any valuables, magical or not. "I really can't wait to get home and see the boys. I just hope they didn't get into too much trouble while I was away."

CHAPTER TWENTY-SEVEN

Far away, across a magical portal in a distant galaxy, Daisy's son was doing what boys his age so often did when their parents requested some of their precious time.

Namely, he griped.

It was sunny out on the bluffs overlooking the pristine shores of Malibu, and Vince had strong-armed his son into some good old-fashioned manual labor. Arlo was not exactly what one might call thrilled with the task.

They'd been pulling weeds and pressing new seedlings into the freshly tilled soil for a few hours, transforming another patch of ground into a seasonal vegetable garden. It was something many of the survivors of the Great War had taken up as a hobby. Replicated food was fine—better than that, even— but there was something about fresh produce that bolstered one's spirits.

That all commercial farming had vanished hundreds of years earlier made the task all the easier to get involved with. When there was no convenient supermarket or produce shop at which to grab whatever was fresh, growing your own just made sense.

The AIs had fired up the old farming equipment once more and had begun producing crops in slowly increasing quantities, but nothing at all on the scale of the planet's former industrial farming operations.

"If it was something serious they would have told us," Vince said as he set wire cones around his tomato seedlings. "Besides, you know Ripley will relay whatever it was as soon as she gets back."

Arlo poured a slow stream of carrot seeds from the funnel in his hand then gently covered them with moist soil before moving on to the next row.

"I know. It's just weird, is all. They wanted the dragons, and not just Orgalius. Why would they want them?"

"You did say it was a magic-related stuff—"

"Magic-related *strangeness*, Dad."

"Right. Strangeness. Well, whatever it is, I'm sure we'll know soon enough."

Arlo was about to posit another conspiracy theory when something down below on the shoreline caught his eye. A very large, very alien form was slowly walking their direction along the coastal trail, an enormous Graizenhund padding quietly at his side.

"Hey, Dad, Grundsch is heading this way," Arlo said.

"Yeah, I spotted him way up the coast when I was out for a paddle earlier," Vince replied. "That guy sure does love his long walks. Beats the alternative, I suppose."

"What alternative?"

"Going back to his old ways. I like him; it'd be a shame to see him back slide."

The Ra'az Hok soldier was the last of his race, at least that they knew of, and he was all alone. But what he lacked in hivemates, he had made up for with new friendships of the most unlikely sort. Friendships with those he and his people had very nearly driven to extinction.

But he had been thrust into a new life, thrown into another galaxy where he spent time bound in the service of Visla Palmarian, helping raise the man's daughter into a fine young woman. And much to his surprise, he had actually bonded with her, filling with a deep affection that his kind should not have been able to feel.

From that point it was a slippery slope, and Grundsch eventually found himself not only befriending magic-wielding aliens and humans, but also fighting alongside them in defense of their homeworlds. And now, with no one left to fight, he had settled into a tranquil life of relative quiet along the coastline with his four-legged friend, often visiting Charlie and Leila for a playdate for Bahnjoh and Baloo.

"Hey, Grundsch!" Arlo called out as the enormous Ra'az grew within earshot.

Grundsch looked up at the bluffs and waved to Arlo and Vince then continued on his way.

"I still can't get over being friends with a Ra'az," Vince said.

"He's a good guy," Arlo said.

"Oh, I know. But you weren't born yet when we were fighting his kind to the death."

"People change, Dad."

"They do, and his actions most definitely spoke louder than words. He more than proved himself fighting off Malalia and her horde. Why, hell, your mom even likes him, and *that* is really saying something."

"She *can* be a little harsh at times," Arlo said with a laugh. "But don't tell her I said that."

Vince drew his fingers across his lips. "Not a word. Now come on, I want to get the rest of this done before sunset."

The two set back to work while Grundsch continued on his stroll, trudging along through the sands, then shifting course from the coastline to the trail up to the bluffs. Soon he arrived at a familiar destination. One that made his companion begin to bounce with excitement.

"Soon, Bahnjoh," he said with a chuckle. "We are nearly there."

The unlikely duo walked another few minutes until they arrived at Charlie and Leila's home. Grundsch headed around the side to the expansive yard overlooking the ocean. Baloo bounded over, thrilled to see them, but also hesitant. The massive canine looked back at his mama.

"It's okay, Baloo, you go play," she said with a contented grin.

That was all he needed to hear. Baloo and Bahnjoh took off in a flash, racing off to tear through the trails surrounding the bluff-top home. But his wanderings were curtailed this time. Now that Leila was so far along, he never strayed too far, always ready to protect her at a moment's notice.

Leila patted the large seat next to her. A reinforced chair they had acquired specially to accommodate their Ra'az friend's substantial mass when he visited.

"Come, Grundsch, sit with me."

"Thank you," he said, taking a seat. "Are you well? Do you need anything?"

"I'm fine, thank you. I've been well taken care of, and my food supplies are bordering on comical."

"Ah, Finnegan has been cooking again, I take it."

"You would be correct. Can I offer you anything? A drink? A snack? A five-course meal? Finn has been busy, after all."

Grundsch chuckled. "No, I am well-hydrated and ate before I came, thank you."

Leila reclined back in her seat. "So, what brings you this way? Another long stroll, I take it?"

"Yes, a stroll," he replied. "And you are with child and alone. I will keep an eye on you in Charlie's absence."

"I'm fine, Grundsch."

"I know you are. But you are pregnant, and near term from what I can tell. For Charlie's sake, as well as your own, I will watch over you. I would not have you alone in this condition while he is gone."

"Sarah and the others are close by."

"Yes. And now I am as well," Grundsch said, reclining in his seat, staring out at the vast expanse of the Pacific. "It really is quite beautiful here," he said, then fell silent.

Leila looked at her friend as he soaked up the tranquility that she had come to call home. He wasn't going anywhere, and Leila knew better than to argue.

"Thanks, Grundsch," she said, then joined him in his silent reverie as the sun dropped across the western sky.

CHAPTER TWENTY-EIGHT

Kip's systems were mostly functional thanks to a lot of elbow grease from Dukaan. To be fair, he hadn't been so much *damaged* when they went down as he had elements simply lose power.

Now that he realized just how close he had come to being rendered comatose, or worse, he was grateful the problems had been localized and non-critical. And he was itching to get back into the fight, so to speak.

Part of that was making an inventory of the captured gear in addition to their own equipment brought with on the mission. They had been prepared for a conflict, but they had expected it to be both in space, and largely magical in nature. As such, most of their weapons were konuses to bolster their own casting as well as a few slaaps should they really need the boost.

But Charlie and his friends possessed more than enough internal magic to handle just about any situation. That is, any situation but the one they currently found themselves facing.

"We've got a lot of very pretty paperweights," Charlie grumbled as they went over the list of inert magical weapons. "Fortunately, we did also load up with a hefty assortment of pulse rifles and pistols out of habit."

"A fortunate occurrence," Bawb said. "When fighting starts, one is often not presented with the battle they had expected. It is wise to be prepared for the unlikely."

"Well, this sure as hell counts as that."

"On that we are most certainly in agreement," Bawb replied. "We were not planning on a land-based fight or we would have brought more conventional weapons. But for whatever reason, Kip's arrival seemed to have missed the power suck almost entirely. And as such, the equipment we do have aboard was spared as well."

"There were those leech things on his hull, though."

"*Remoras*," Kip corrected. "They were more like remoras. Power-sucking little bastards."

Charlie shrugged. "Okay, *remoras*, though that sounds more like leeches."

"He just likes the comparison to a shark," Dukaan interjected.

"I am totally more like a shark. You know how I—"

"Kids, please," Charlie groaned. "We're trying to assess our available assets here. We've got enough for our own crew, but if we can help arm Nakk's people as well we'll be magnifying the impact our forces will have on these Urvalin pricks."

Bawb looked at the gear spread out before them. "I am hopeful we will have reinforcements arrive long before we need them."

Charlie had been of the same mind for some time. "Yeah, we haven't been gone that long. With none of us checking in with any of the relay satellites, I have to think they'll have noted us going off-radar by now. Hopefully they'll find us soon."

"Perhaps," Bawb mused. "But as no magic reaches or leaves this place, one would have to assume it would be a difficult location to pinpoint."

"And Kip's distress calls have likely been blocked as well," Dukaan added. "And even if the transmission did make it out, we do not know how far from our own system we have been pulled by this portal. For all we know it could take centuries for a conventional signal to reach our people."

"We have had this discussion as well," Nakk said. "And in the end, none of our people came to our rescue, though quite a few more were eventually drawn into this place."

Charlie didn't want to admit it, but the writing was on the wall. They were quite possibly on their own. And for all they knew it was only a matter of time before more of their friends fell victim to the same hidden portal if they came looking for them. They needed to get back to warn the others, but they simply had no means. At least, not yet.

Worse, there was no sign whatsoever of Rika. Kip had been transmitting on their encrypted channel ever since his comms systems regained full functionality but to no avail. They had no idea where she was or if they could even reach her.

The one bright spot in all of this was they had made new allies. And though Kip was the only functional ship that had crashed here, the captured ones hidden away were a wildcard they had up their sleeve. For what, he wasn't sure, but Charlie had little doubt they'd need to play it sooner than later. But first, they had to find their friend.

"Kip, is your active camouflage working?"

"Yeah. Dookie and I thought that should be one of the first things we got back online."

"Good call," Charlie agreed. "Rika's out there somewhere, so I'm thinking, maybe you can pop up and do a low-altitude survey. You know, something to keep you out of sight of any scans as well as any visual spottings, know what I mean?"

"Oh, totally," the ship replied. "We can do that."

"Then everyone grab a gun and offload. We'll stay here while Kip and Dukaan do their thing. I don't want to leave Ara alone in her condition, especially now that we know exactly what kind of baddies are lurking around out there."

They quickly began arming themselves with conventional weapons, leaving the inert magical items where they sat. Within minutes they were offloaded and ready to face the enemy.

"See ya soon," Kip said, then he and Dukaan quietly lifted off and began flying their search grid.

"Okay, listen up," Charlie said to the group. "In case the Urvalin are running active tech, if we should have a run-in with them we will want to keep any pulse fire to a bare minimum. The less tech-related events, the less likely we are to get noticed by something larger than a recon team."

"Stealth is the best option," Bawb agreed. "However, we do still have the matter of our rather large friend. The Wise One is currently lacking the ability to properly conceal herself in her weakened condition. This will need to be addressed, if at all possible."

"The mud should work as a basic camouflage," Charlie said. "But you're right. We'll need to think up something better. If Kip finds Rika, maybe she'll be able to do something about it."

"If she still possesses her power."

"Yeah, and that's a big if," Charlie agreed. "Let's just hope she's okay."

A short while later a gentle breeze stirred the air above them. The sky was growing darker, but there was still ample daylight to see there was nothing there. Or so it seemed.

"Impossible," Skohla gasped when Kip turned off his active camouflage just as he settled down on the ground. "He was *invisible*."

"Specialized nanite camouflage," Kip said. "Pretty cool stuff, right?"

"I would call it far more than that," Skohla replied. "It is the sort of thing that could give us a great advantage over the Urvalin."

"Yeah, about that..."

Charlie knew that tone. "What is it, Kip? What's the matter?"

"Well, me and Dukaan, we decided to fly high for a minute to get some readings, and what we saw was kinda nuts."

"Define nuts."

"Nuts as in there appears to be a two-layer micro-sat system surrounding this entire planet. And the way they interlink, it forms a sort of honeycomb pattern of that weird power suck we experienced. It drains anything that passes through it."

"And those remora things are just a redundancy to finish the job," Dukaan added.

"The metal discs," Nakk said, knowingly. "Yes, we have pried a great many of those from our vessels' hulls in the repair process. Remnants of an older mechanism, it seems. Unfortunately, our ships were already devoid of power by then, so it would seem the old and new systems both did their jobs admirably."

This raised questions, and more than a few. "So how did you make it through?" Charlie asked. "Not that I'm complaining or anything."

"It looks like Gustavo pulled out all the stops trying to compensate when he was hit by the power-suck field. We came in just behind him and must have lucked into a brief weak spot. It probably used a great deal of energy to handle him. Really, I'd be willing to bet that's the only reason we made it through."

The team felt a wave of sadness as well as gratitude to their companion for his sacrifice. Gus's death had meant their survival.

"Good work, Kip," Charlie said. "Any sign of Rika while you were out?"

"Not that I could detect. But this place is big and overgrown. If the *Fujin* is down and without power, there'd be little way to find it short of it being on fire or something."

"Which we most certainly do not want."

"No, definitely not," Kip agreed. "Oh, and there's something else weird going on."

"Weird?"

"Yeah. There appear to be periodic gaps in the energy barrier."

"Gaps?"

"It looked like an anomaly at first, but when we took a closer look it seemed like it was the Urvalin dropping tiny segments when their ships entered or exited the atmosphere."

Charlie's mind began to race. If the Urvalin had a means to operate in this arena that meant there *was* a way out. And it looked like Kip may have just stumbled upon a key element to it.

"You realize what this means, right?"

It was Bawb who replied, his tactical brain charging ahead in lock-step with Charlie's. Great minds think alike, even without a magical bond linking them, it seemed.

"They would have to possess a terrestrial base of operations," he said. "And regardless of the possession or lack of active magic, that is a weakness to exploit."

"I was thinking the same thing," Charlie agreed. "If we can take down their planetary hub, we may very well be able to disrupt the orbiting micro-sat blockade."

Nakk's eyes widened. "And if you do that, our ships may very possibly regain power."

Charlie grinned. *This* was more like it. This was a plan. No sitting around waiting for fate to present an option. They would take the reins and make it do their bidding.

"Okay," he said. "New course of action. We start planning how to track their base, then infiltrate and take it down."

"And seize control of the planet in so doing," Dukaan said. "I like it."

"Yeah," Charlie agreed. "And if Lady Luck is with us, our friends will have found us by then and we'll have reinforcements aplenty."

CHAPTER TWENTY-NINE

Orgalius had spent much of the past several months with Ara, the two forming something of a bond between the oldest and strongest members of their respective species of both galaxies. But aside from simply enjoying one another's company, an additional benefit was that Orgalius had quickly become attuned to the intricacies of magic from another realm, as well as how Ara integrated her own power with her friends and their ships.

It was a novel idea, interlinking warp technology with magic —his kind had never had the sort of close interaction with other races the way the Zomoki had in Ara's galaxy. But he was a fast learner, and in no time Orgalius was able to tie in his magical jump with a technological warp with little effort.

Of course, that had been with Ara at his side, but with her out of the picture and quite possibly in distress, it now fell to him to utilize only his own magic.

As it turned out, he was more than up for the task.

"I have received the location from Cal," he said over his new comms setup, shifting his wings, acclimating to the unfamiliar sensation of a tech harness. "I sense the *Fujin's* konus and am connected. Are you prepared to warp?"

"Yeah, we're looking good here. Green across the board," Jo replied.

"Green across the board? I have not seen any shift in the *Fujin's* external coloration."

Rika chuckled as she keyed her comms. "It's a technology saying," she said. "It refers to the systems readiness lights. Red means not ready, green is good to go."

"Ah, I see. Well then, while I lack lights on my new harness, I too am green across the board."

"Copy that."

"Why would you copy me? You said your lights were already—"

"Radio communications slang," Rika said. "It just means we hear you and understand."

"So, I should say copy that?"

"Yeah, you've got it now."

"Very well. Copy that."

The blue dragon surveyed the few electronic items housed in his new harness with interest. What they did was not terribly thrilling in the grand scheme of things, but this was his first time ever *operating* technology. For an entirely magical being, it was something of a fascinating novelty.

Rika and Jo had given all of their equipment the once-over, twice, confirming their weapons and drive systems were operating at peak capacity. They had also loaded up the railgun ammunition housing with a few thousand rounds of modified sabots, magically charged to provide an extra "oomph" when used against magical defenses. Or so they hoped.

It was an entirely new blending of technology and magic that had been the end result of many months of experimentation, the magical power courtesy of a variety of casters contributing their own particular flavor of power.

Ara and Charlie's was the same. Hunze's was quite different, but it was still originating from the same galaxy. But Rika had her own unique blend, and while it took some doing to figure out how to not only release her magical energy at a trickle rate, but also do so in a way that would bind it and its spell to an inanimate piece of metal, she had eventually succeeded.

It was those particular rounds she had put aside in their own storage bin for last resort use, given her comfort with her own magic. She was confident the others would work, though to what degree she couldn't say, but hers just felt right once she'd dialed them in.

"Jo, you good on the guns?" she asked.

"You know I am."

"And is the probe good to go?"

"Yeah, it's running at peak levels and holding strong. It should have no problem powering through the portal and making its survey. The automatic return sequence is triple-redundancy protected, so even if there's a failure in one or two of the systems it will be able to report back without any issues."

Rika liked what she heard. There were no guarantees, of course, but this was as close to ideal as one could get, given the circumstances. And now it was time to shit or get off the pot. Fortunately, she was not a fan of obsessive procrastination. Rika was more of a "kick ass first, ask questions later" type of woman. And if her friends had been hurt, oh, the amount of ass that would be kicked.

"All right, then. It's time to start the process. Orgalius, we'll do a short warp to start to make sure we're dialed in, then we will increase the length as we progress. The coordinates are a pretty long way out there, and we need to make sure we arrive at a good distance from the portal."

"Of course. And while we have technology shielding from your ship and my harness, I will also provide additional magical protection for us when we arrive, both to keep us from notice as well as shield us from any traps that may have been laid."

"Perfect," Rika said, shifting in her seat and tightening her harness, just in case. "Okay, here we go."

She powered up the *Fujin*'s warp system then waited a few seconds for Orgalius to link with them. She sensed when her onboard konus had connected and engaged. The warp-jump went smoothly, depositing them at the far edge of the solar system. A tiny distance, but a logical baby step.

"Looking good so far," she said. "Let's do this."

This time she powered up the warp drive much higher and set a course for the first of their distant waypoints. In a flash the joined ship and dragon popped out of existence, leaving the solar system in a burst of magical and warp energy. It took them several more times before they reached the second to last location. From there they would make the final jump to the dangerous portal's location.

"Jo, be ready to launch the probe," she said.

"All set. And before you ask, yes, weapons are hot and ready."

"You read my mind."

Jo flashed a knowing grin. "Not such a hard thing to do," she replied.

"Bite me."

"Is this another Earth term?" Orgalius asked.

"Sorry, didn't mean to transmit that. Just talking shit with my copilot."

"Ah, talking shit. *This* is something I have heard of. Charlie introduced me to the concept."

"Of course he did," Rika chuckled. "Okay. Here we go."

She powered up the warp drive and engaged.

The pair arrived at the far edge of the intended solar system, right on target. They were far enough away that an enemy's system-wide scan would almost certainly miss them, yet not so far as to hamper their own survey of the region. There were several planets there, along with an unimpressive sun of moderate power, but they found no signs of hostile vessels.

"Could they be using shimmer ships?" Jo wondered.

"If they are, I should still be able to sense them," Rika replied. "And I don't see anything. In fact, if I didn't know the portal was there, I wouldn't have noticed it either. Orgalius, you got anything?"

He sniffed the solar winds, taking in this new place. "Nothing," he said. "This system does not appear to have any active magic beyond the portal you described. It is a very unusual type of magic, though. One I am unfamiliar with."

"Yeah, new fun for all of us," Rika said. "I'm going to take us in closer. Everyone keep your head on a swivel. No telling what other surprises they may have in store out there."

She piloted her ship around the system, running a circuit of the planets from the outermost to the inner. Each appeared devoid of any craft, hostile or otherwise. She finally pulled up to a stop a good distance from the portal.

"You see it?"

"Barely, but I do," Orgalius replied. "Most unusual."

"Yeah, that's a word for it. Keep your eyes open, we don't know what's going to happen when the probe pops back out." She did one more quick scan of the area. There was nothing. "Okay, looks like we're clear. Jo, you're up."

"Copy that," the cyborg said. "Deploying the probe."

The small craft released from the *Fujin* and immediately flew off toward the hidden portal, circling it twice, sending back reams of data before diving straight into the center. It vanished in a rather unimpressive little flash.

"Okay, this shouldn't take long," Jo said. "Now we just wait. Once it gives us the star chart readings from the other side, we'll know where Charlie and the others have been sent."

They all stared at the portal, its blackness blending in with the surrounding space in a disconcerting way. Minutes ticked by, but the probe did not return.

"Must be a lot of data to gather," Rika said, hoping she was right but fearing she wasn't.

"Yeah, it should pop back out any minute now," Jo said.

An hour later the two women turned to one another.

"It's not supposed to take this long, is it?" Rika asked, knowing the answer full well.

"No, it's not," Jo replied. "Something is wrong."

There were multiple fail-safes and backups powering the probe, and it was fast and maneuverable to boot. Even in a worst-case scenario, it should have been able to avoid any dangers and make its way back through to report its findings. This was not good. Not at all.

Rika powered up the warp drive, but held off engaging it. Finally, she powered it down, instead setting a course a fair distance from the portal but still within the system.

"New plan," she said. "We're pulling back and going dark. Something's not right."

"No, clearly," Orgalius agreed. "But the new plan?"

"We watch and wait. Something's gotta happen."

"And if not? If nothing comes through?"

Rika didn't like that possibility, but it was increasingly looking like that was the case. "Then we head back to base and try to figure out what the hell went wrong."

CHAPTER THIRTY

Charlie and his new friends were sitting quietly, enjoying a meal of both replicated food from Kip's galley as well as local vegetables and even a large roasted piece of the Brixxax that they had carved off before Ara made a meal of the animal.

The exchange of information between the new arrivals and the castaways had been enlightening, and it was looking more and more like these Urvalin who had trapped them all here were indeed very similar to the Council of Twenty in their power-hungry machinations.

Nakk and Skohla had also noted the parallels, marveling how no matter what part of the galaxy one was in, there seemed to always be some variant of the same thing. Namely, a group intent on claiming as much of it for themselves as possible.

They were just getting into the geopolitical intricacies of the Urvalin's reign when Ara raised her head, sniffing the air. "Someone is coming," she said.

"I'm picking up a single heat signature moving toward us," Kip added. "Can't tell much more than that, but it's not very large. Person-sized, from what I can tell. Just the one."

Ara sniffed again. "It is the same race as Nakk and Skohla."

"Not an Urvalin, then," Nakk said, his shoulders relaxing. Sure enough, one of Nakk's men came rushing through the trees a moment later.

"We flew here. How did he know where we were?" Charlie asked.

"My people knew the direction we were heading and the rough distance."

"But that's a long run."

"Yes, but we are accustomed to speed in the trees," Nakk replied. "You have already met the Brixxax. I am sure you understand the motivation."

"Yeah, no doubt."

The man leaned in and spoke into his leader's ear, unaware the newcomers could actually understand his speech.

Nakk nodded and told the man to eat, drink, and recover his wind. "Charlie, your tribe's presence has been requested," he said. "One of the hunting parties found something they think you should see."

"Far?" Charlie asked.

"Not terribly."

"Then we'll go on foot. The less Kip flies the better, given what we've seen of the Urvalin so far. Plus, I want him to keep an eye on Ara."

"I would protest," Ara said, "but one does not reach my age without learning the value of accepting help when it is needed. Thank you, Kip."

"Happy to help," the ship replied.

Hunze rose to her feet and adjusted the sword strapped to her back. "I am coming with."

Bawb stepped close and spoke in a hushed tone. "But given your condition?"

"I am pregnant, not incapacitated," she replied, squeezing his hand. "But your concern is appreciated."

Bawb knew better than to push the matter any farther. There

was no sense arguing. Hunze may once have been a mild-mannered Ootaki slave, but since bonding with the master assassin she had developed an impressively strong will, not to mention the skills only a handful of elite killers possessed.

She was still Hunze, however, sweet and loving almost to a fault. But she was also self-assured, and heaven help any who threatened her loved ones.

"She is with child?" Skohla asked.

"Yeah, but it's still early, clearly," Charlie replied.

"Clearly. She is not showing."

"Well, to be fair, with the way she and Bob train, their fitness kind of puts most people to shame."

"Apparently," the woman said, sizing up the Ootaki with newfound appreciation.

Charlie turned to Dukaan. "Hey, could you stay with Kip and Ara? I'd like to have boots on the ground, so to speak, just in case."

"Of course," the Chithiid replied. "Should you need us, do not hesitate to call."

Charlie patted his shoulder with a grateful nod. "Thanks, man. We'll keep comms open. I'll call if things go sour." He turned to their alien guide. "All right, Nakk, lead the way."

The trek through the trees had gone quite fast given the path was being laid by the people who had lived here for years. Charlie, Bawb, and Hunze each noted the snares, pitfalls, and other traps they sidestepped on the way. They'd have found them on their own, but having Nakk guiding them around the obstacles just made it all the easier.

Finally, they arrived at a tiny gap in the trees. Light shone down from above, illuminating the little clearing. From the looks of it, something had punched right through the canopy, but not like the way Gustavo had ripped through them on impact. This was different. A more localized impact. And as they grew closer, they could see why.

"Oh, poor Griggalt," Hunze said, her heart going out to the charred dragon.

One look and it was clear what had happened here. Their friend had hit the atmosphere unprotected, much as Ara had, but there had been no one there to stop his fall. Burned and likely unconscious, he had fallen to his death. They all hoped he didn't suffer.

"You found Griggalt?" Ara asked, listening in over Kip's open comms line.

Charlie hated to be the bearer of bad news, but there was no sugarcoating this.

"Yeah, Ara, we did. Unfortunately, he didn't fare as well as you did."

"He is severely hurt, then?"

"I'm sorry, Ara, but I'm afraid Griggalt is dead."

A long silence hung in the air before she spoke again. "Now we know where he disappeared to," she said. "He was the first through the portal. It is no wonder we lost track of him."

"Wise One, I am sorry for your loss," Bawb said.

"It is the way of life, Geist," she replied. "We live and we die. And it is knowing there is an end that makes living worthwhile. And oh, how Griggalt did live. He made the most of his time."

Bawb nodded his somber agreement. "Well said. He was a good ally. I will call upon Nakk's people and provide him the burial he deserves."

"No," she replied. "Save your energy. There is no need for the exertion, though the intention is well appreciated."

Charlie seemed perplexed. "Ara, are you sure?"

"Yes, Charlie. You have not dealt with this part of Zomoki existence, having so recently come into our world. But it is our way to contribute to the circle of life. Just as we eat to survive, so too must other creatures. And while Griggalt was our friend, that which made him who he was is no longer within that mortal shell."

"Are you saying to just leave him here?"

"Yes. And perhaps in death he can now provide life for other creatures on this world. I am confident it is what he would have wanted."

Bawb glanced at Charlie, the two nodding to one another.

"As you wish, Wise One," Bawb said.

Nakk observed the interaction with great interest. This wounded beast contained far more depth than he had realized, and he found his respect for her growing.

"You know," he said, "there were once similar beings to your kind. The Borzalik, they were called. Strong in their Allpower and fearless in their flight."

"What happened to them?" Ara asked. "Where have they flown to? I would like very much to meet another distant relative once we are free of this world, if possible."

"Unfortunately, the Urvalin would not allow so powerful a being to exist within their sphere of operations. As their reach expanded, they set out to slaughter any they encountered. So far as I am aware, the last of the Borzalik were killed off hundreds of years ago. But their legend remains, and though you are of a different place, your dignity and wisdom does them justice."

"I have long thought it a great shame that these sage, flying creatures should be extinct," Skohla said. "Their presence would be of great comfort to those oppressed by the Urvalin."

Ara considered what she and Nakk had said and found herself even more anxious to heal and rejoin the fight against these Urvalin.

"There is one thing," she said, a renewed vigor in her voice. Vigor, and a coloring of anger. "Despite what the Urvalin may believe, we are not all deceased. And should I regain my strength—"

"*When*," Charlie corrected.

"*When* I regain my strength," she said, "the Urvalin will find they have more of a fight on their hands than they bargained for. They think us extinct. I look forward to proving them wrong."

Ara was interrupted when a bright flash abruptly streaked across the sky above, visible and most certainly drawing the attention of any with a clear view overhead.

"What the hell was that?" Charlie wondered, oblivious to the origin of the ill-fated probe burning up in the atmosphere above, fragments tumbling down to the ground, though where they would impact was anyone's guess.

"I do not know what that is," Bawb said. "But I feel this will almost certainly draw further attention to the goings-on upon the surface, and not only where the debris lands."

A faint rumbling shook the air.

"Urvalin ships have launched from their base tower," Nakk said. "We should move deeper into the trees."

The team did not hesitate, and it was a good thing, as several Urvalin craft buzzed the surface in all directions. They flew right by in their haste, giving Charlie a momentary sense of relief that perhaps they'd been overlooked. That, however, was short lived. One of the ships peeled off and looped back in their direction, moving in a slow scanning path.

The downed dragon, it seemed, had been spotted.

CHAPTER THIRTY-ONE

Ara was in no condition for battle when the Urvalin troops rappelled down from their hovering ship not terribly far from her location. The trees were simply too dense to land, and the only open space was currently occupied by a massive dead beast.

The reason for their arrival.

Much as she would have enjoyed taking flight and roasting them from above, it would take a long, long time for her to heal at this rate, and there was no telling when she would be able to spit fire for any length of time without harming herself in the process.

So it was she had to sit quietly and listen to Charlie's updates while not participating herself. Inaction of that type was difficult for her, to say the least.

The Urvalin had deployed a dozen troops to the surface, and this lot appeared to be much more disciplined and skilled than the last group they had encountered. There would be no easy ambushing of these soldiers. At least, not without risking bloodshed from their own numbers, and that was not in the cards, especially as the dragon lying before them was already dead. It was not worth the risk, and no amount of protection could help it now.

Two-thirds of the men formed a perimeter, backs toward the downed dragon, while the others set to work examining the charred animal. Charlie noted with great interest that their scanning technology appeared to be working just fine, though one of them did appear to be trying to cast out of force of habit. Clearly, the lack of magic here was something of an inconvenience to them as well, regardless of rank. It wasn't much, but it did bolster his spirits ever so slightly.

"We have found the beast," the team leader said into what was apparently a comms unit mounted on the shoulder of his armor. "It did not survive re-entry."

He appeared to be listening to an earpiece, nodding along to whatever was being said.

"Yes, that is correct. It has perished," he replied to whoever was on the other end of that call. "Very well, we will do as you command." He then turned to his comrades and gestured toward Griggalt's corpse.

The others powered up their weapons and stepped back, then opened fire on the most damaged parts of the dragon's body where the scales were weakened from the fiery crash. The weapons appeared to be similar to pulse rifles, though exactly what manner of energy they shot was something they could not determine without a close scan. Given the circumstances, no one would be approaching to do so.

The blasts tore into the seared flesh, but the great dragon did not move. This one was not playing possum. Charred from head to tail, the former apex predator was most definitely deceased.

"It is confirmed," the man transmitted. "The magic-wielding beast known as Ara is no more. We have not yet seen signs of her companions, but our teams are searching. It is only a matter of time."

Charlie looked at Bawb with a startled expression. "How the hell do they know Ara's name?" he whispered.

"I do not know," Bawb quietly replied. "But it seems clear there is far more at play here than we originally assumed. This was not a mere trap of opportunity as it appeared. We were the intended targets."

The Urvalin continued to walk around the carcass, surveying the size of the dead animal as he spoke to his commander. "I have seen no trace of additional bodies at this crash location, but if its rider was thrown clear during the descent, it is very possible he was either burned up upon entry or torn to bits by the force of impact." He paused, listening. "Yes. Yes, we will continue to search. The downed ship launched several escape pods before it broke apart. We have the survivors and are holding them pending your interrogation."

Charlie felt a surge of hope. Someone had survived. More than one of them, it seemed. And they were being held by the Urvalin. While that in itself was bad, at least some were still alive, and that was a hell of a lot better than they'd thought up until now.

The hard part would be finding out *where* they were being held. Once they knew that vital factoid, the gladiator, the assassin, and his bonded mate would rain down havoc on those who stood in their way. And if they were fortunate, their new friends would join them in the hunt.

"Okay, you lot. Back to the ship," the Urvalin called out. "We still have a search to do. The one called Charlie is nowhere to be found, and his beast is no more. And the pale assassin and his bitch were not among the retrieved escape pods."

"This is good news," one of the troops said. "Their strongest casters are dead. Without them to oppose us, we cannot help but prevail."

"I hope you are right," the leader said. "But do not count your victories before their blood coats your blade. The fates

177

have a funny way of shifting against those who take them for granted."

"Of course, you are right," he replied with a respectful bow of his head.

The lines dangling from the ship hovering above began reeling in the men as they grabbed ahold, pulling them back into the belly of their ship to carry on with their mission. A few moments later the ship flew off, leaving the survivors in an eerie silence.

Charlie's head was spinning. These people had attacked from nowhere. Using magic, no less. It seemed so totally random. And yet here they were, searching for his body and assuming the only dragon they had come across was Ara's. It seemed that as much as they knew about Charlie and Ara and their friends, the dragons were something of a wild card. One that was now playing to their advantage.

"They were targeting us, Bob."

"I realize this."

"They know who we are. Our powers. What we are capable of."

"It would appear that is the case, yes."

Charlie felt his anger swell. "I'm going to kill them all."

Bawb rested his hand on his friend's shoulder and looked calmly into his eyes. "Charlie, you simply must not. Not yet."

"I want them to pay."

"And they shall. But put aside your anger and think. We now hold the upper hand."

"No magic, an injured Zomoki, and half our team dead or captured?"

"They believe *we* are dead, my friend. And *that* is an advantage the likes of which we shall put to good use. But in order to do so we must be *very* careful not to reveal that we yet draw breath." He turned to Nakk and Skohla. "No one can know who we are. Can we trust your people to keep silent if so instructed?"

"Against the Urvalin? You may rest assured, not a word will be said."

"Good. But now we have another task ahead of us. The Wise One must remain hidden, and yet she is vulnerable and unable to fly as of yet."

"The mud will mask her from thermal scans pretty well," Charlie said. "And strange as it may be, with her magic drained, so long as she stays by the water I would think she'll remain pretty invisible to their scans, though I don't even know if their tech could detect magic in the first place."

"It is possible, but we believe in other regions where our Allpower flows, they use that to search for our energy signatures, not mere technology," Nakk said.

Charlie nodded, ideas churning through his brain. "All right, then. We've just got to figure out some way to not only make her hidden from their scans, but also from visual detection as well. She's kind of blending in with all of that mud, but she's still a pretty damn big Zomoki."

Skohla nudged Nakk and said something beneath her breath. He seemed to agree, nodding his agreement.

"My friends," he said. "Skohla has made a suggestion."

"To hide Ara?" Hunze asked.

"Yes. I believe my people can help."

CHAPTER THIRTY-TWO

Nakk's runners were swift of foot, and in only a few hours a stream of able-bodied men and women appeared out of the trees back at the water's edge. Bawb, Hunze, and Dukaan were working with Skohla to help direct them according to her plan, their comm patches handling the translation as fast as Kip could manage.

He was an AI, and a very clever one at that, but his proficiency was at flight-related tasks, and the concern was if they had too many individual conversations going at once, he might have some trouble keeping all of the simultaneous translations straight. As the first arrivals were sent off to their tasks, a new batch would appear from the tree line.

"Impressive," Charlie said. "They move fast, and they're quiet too."

Nakk nodded approvingly. "It is a skill born of necessity, for the Urvalin are not the only hostiles out there on this world."

"Yeah, we met the Brixxax up close and personal-like."

"Not the Brixxax. The Horka."

"Horka?" Charlie asked.

"Yes. Others who have been stranded here far longer than we

have. Those who have forgotten their roots, or willingly given them up, and now live in a tribal culture. A violent one at that."

"Whoa, Lord of the Flies," Charlie said.

"The Lord of the *what*?"

"Nothing. Just an old tale from my world. A cautionary one."

"Not a happy one, from the way you say its name."

"I definitely wouldn't call it that," Charlie replied. "But tell me more about these other survivors. Are they from your people? Your race?"

"Some are, but other races are also trapped here on this world, and some of them have gone down that dark path with them."

Charlie sighed. Here they were, making alien contact and expanding their alliance, but they were doing so with no support from their fleet. No might of the combined forces to back them up. No one to call for help if their new friends needed assistance.

Of course, as it was, Charlie and his team were the ones who needed help just as much as Nakk's people did.

Bawb stepped away from the buzzing crew of workers as they all scattered off into the woods and rejoined his friend.

"All is going well," he said with an approving nod. "Nakk, your people are fast and efficient."

"Thank you. We try to maintain peak fitness and operational readiness, though trapped here as we are, what that even means anymore is questionable."

"They listen to your leadership and function well as a unit. It is all a commander can ask for."

"I suppose you are right. We *have* fared better than the others in that regard."

"Others?"

"Yeah, about that," Charlie said. "Apparently, there are other people down here. Not Nakk's group and not the Urvalin, but survivors of a different type. Tribal."

"Hostile, I take it?" the assassin asked, clearly already knowing the answer.

"With our luck, is there ever any other kind?"

"It would appear not. But are they an immediate threat?"

"We have not seen any of their hunting parties in the area in recent days, but with a new ship crashing to the surface and the Urvalin searching the area, it seems likely they will head this way."

"They are not of a fixed location, then?" Bawb asked.

"They are somewhat nomadic. Typically, they stay clear of my people and we stay clear of them, but there are nevertheless occasional skirmishes."

"Then let us hope they do not feel up for an attack while Ara is healing. She can handle herself, but in her weakened condition her scales will not protect her as they normally would."

"Bob's right. We need to make sure Ara's off their radar, so to speak," Charlie said. "And along those lines, how's the plan going?"

"See for yourself," Nakk said, pointing to the tree line.

At first it looked almost as if the woods had come to life, the branches moving along as if giant Ents were marching to battle. But moments later Nakk's people began streaming out to the shoreline carrying massive limbs hewn from deep in the woods in their arms.

They moved to Ara, who calmly watched them with her golden eyes, nodding her thanks as they began positioning the branches around her. It would be time consuming this way, making the cut trees look like a smaller copse along the shoreline, but it would hide Ara's outline from aerial surveys far better than merely laying the branches against her.

"That's some good work," Charlie said as he watched their progress. "And once Ara is safe, then we can plan our next steps."

"Next steps?" Nakk asked.

"Yeah. You said the Urvalin had taken some of your people."

"Poor souls. Yes, they do not only kill, but they also capture, though to what ends we do not know."

"Well, we're going to find out. And we're going to stop it."

"What do you mean? In small numbers we can stand up to the Urvalin, but not in any significant amounts."

Charlie shook his head. "You're not understanding what I'm getting at. They took your people, but we know they took ours as well. Now, I don't know who they have or what shape they're in, but we do not leave our people behind."

Nakk shook his head in disbelief. "A single, small ship from time to time is perhaps an achievable goal, but more than that? It is madness. Without adequate weapons I simply do not see how we would stand a chance."

Charlie and Bawb both smiled. The armory housed within Kip's walls was not particularly large, and the additional konuses and slaaps they had thought to bring along on this magical battle were currently of no use.

However, just because they were heading into a magic-based conflict did not mean they had not also loaded up with a respectable assortment of conventional weapons. And while they were by no means kitted up for a full-on military-scale conflict, the weapons they had with them possessed one thing that would provide them that most valuable of assets.

The element of surprise.

These weapons, unlike all of the technology on the planet, still had power.

"You've seen our pulse weapons," Charlie said.

"Yes, and you are fortunate to possess functional technology."

"Well, we kinda have *more* of them."

Now he had Nakk's attention. "More, you say? How many more?"

"Between pistols, rifles, and stun batons, I'd say we have enough to kit up at least a dozen of your people. I know it's not as much as you would like, but it does give us an advantage against the Urvalin."

"Yes, surprise," Nakk said.

"I was thinking the same thing. But we still need more intel about their base of operations down here."

"An elevated platform with a landing pad, internal hangars, and an unknown number of Urvalin within."

Bawb considered this bit of news. "Elevated, you say? It will add an element of difficulty."

"They designed it to prevent anyone from making any sort of assault on the facility. Without a ship there is no way we could ever access them."

"But you have the stolen ships."

"And they are small and few in number. If we used them we would have faced extermination. With no weapons we would be flying in with technology only to enter into combat armed with sticks and rocks."

"But now?"

"Now? I see a possibility. But we still need more information. We have only ever observed the tower from the ground."

Charlie grinned. "How far is it?"

"Perhaps three days' travel. But the path leads through hostile territory. It is an area we avoid if at all possible."

"Well, we have a ship. And he has active camouflage, as you've seen."

"An impressive technological feat," Skohla said. "But I share Nakk's concern. They will scan with more than just their eyes near their base of operations."

"Oh, didn't I say? I've got a basic stealth package as well," Kip chimed in. "Never really have to use it, but from the signals I picked up on my last flight, I'm pretty confident I'll be able to avoid detection. At least, I think so. I'm not really sure what sort of tech we're trying to defeat, after all."

"Well then, I think it's time to fire up the engines and find out. We need to gather more intel," Charlie said. "Kip, you up for it?"

"You know I am."

"I thought as much. We'll fly as low a pattern as we safely can. Get a lay of the land, so to speak. And once we've got the area mapped, we'll pop up a bit and grab as much data as we can, as fast as we can, then scarper the hell out of there before they even know we were there. Nakk, you up for a little flyover?"

"I would very much like that."

"Okay then, let's load up."

Charlie, Bawb, Nakk, and Skohla climbed aboard and took a seat behind Dukaan's pilot's chair. "Strap in. You never know if it might get bumpy," the pilot said. "Kip, lifting off. Activate your camouflage."

"Already did," the ship replied. "We should be invisible for all intents and purposes."

Dukaan grunted his acknowledgment and set off on the heading Nakk had given them. It was a several-day trip all right, but that was on foot. The terrain was wildly varying as it passed beneath them, and Charlie took great interest in the pockets of thermal activity.

There were hot springs, bubbling pits of sulfur, and even a few active magma flows. This planet was a churning mass of energy just below the surface, likely millions of years old, but still a baby in the celestial scheme of things.

Something else caught his eye. A lot of somethings, actually. Outlines nestled into the terrain, some seeming to have had the trees themselves grow up around their forms.

"Are those all ships down there?" Charlie asked.

"Yes. A great many crashed down in this part of the globe," Nakk replied. "There was something about the gravitational pull of the planet and the strength of the technology negating field that sent most of us in this general heading. Not all arrived here, of course, but a lot did."

"Your people?"

"Yes, for the most part. But the others as well."

Charlie's mind reeled. He knew Nakk was a commander of a portion of a rebel fleet, but he had no idea it was a force as substantial as this. Of course, they had been captured over time —this was not the result of a single event, and the Urvalin had been trapping people on this world for a long time. But whatever the chain of events may have been, an honest-to-God fleet lay dormant on the surface of this planet.

It also struck him that there were a *lot* of alien races out there, and it had only been blind luck and the sheer size of the galaxy that had kept them from bumping into one another. But the expanse between the stars was a very big place.

They flew on, covering a lot of ground, distancing themselves from Nakk's sphere of influence. As they did, other signs of life passed beneath them. Settlements built in the ruins of crashed ships, moving lines of animals being herded to a new pasture. And fires. Many small fires dotting the landscape.

"Dangerous people," Nakk said. "The ones we avoid."

"They've got camps set up all over the place."

"But those are mere offshoots. A central group controls them. The lesser ones pay tribute for continued survival."

"Like the mob," Charlie mused. "You know, it looks like some of them were heading toward your territory."

"Likely investigating the newest arrivals," Nakk said.

"Well, let's just make a point to avoid them, then."

"A sentiment I share," Nakk said.

"Hey," Kip chimed in. "We're getting closer to what looks like a dead spot on my scanners. I'd wager that's the Urvalin base."

Charlie looked at the scan readouts. "Dukaan, fly a loop. Low, slow, and wide. It may take a while, but let's plot out absolutely everything around it in all directions before we make our pass of the facility itself. Kip, ramp up your countermeasures to eleven and see what chatter you can pick up."

"On it," the AI replied.

The dangerous part of their little adventure was about to begin, and there was a very real possibility the day might end with shooting. Hopefully not, but they had to be prepared for anything.

Charlie looked at the initial images from the long-range cameras. It was a tower, all right. Maybe eighty feet tall, starting out relatively narrow then flaring out the higher it went.

Periodic gaps in the structure seemed to be small craft landing bays—the ships they'd seen earlier, most likely—but it also appeared to have a large, flat area on the uppermost reaches. A landing pad, Charlie guessed. They would find out soon enough.

Once they knew the ins and outs of the facility, they would be able to properly plan their assault. And *then* they would get their friends back.

CHAPTER THIRTY-THREE

A lot had happened since the incident with the portal. For one, both Charlie and his friends still on the other side had independently come to the realization the phenomenon was a trap. This was no coincidental event. The portal was meant to pull away Earth's most accomplished casters. *Someone* was out there stirring up trouble, and that person possessed magic. *Strong* magic.

What's more, it seemed that whoever that was had done a vanishing act of their own, leaving virtually no trace of themselves in either system. Of course, Charlie and his friends caught in the trap had proved far more difficult to sideline than likely expected.

As for Rika, Jo, and their dragon escort, the disappearance of the probe through the portal made one thing abundantly clear. The trap was anything but benign. Whatever was on the other side, it had been enough to keep their probe from making the return trip, leaving them with a dearth of much-needed intelligence.

One thing was certain. Whichever side of the portal they were on, the comrades in arms had been made aware they were most certainly facing a new threat.

They didn't know the half of it.

Casually strolling the bridge of his command ship, a glowing Vikann stone dangling around his neck, Torgus surveyed the tactical readouts surrounding his central casting podium. The reinforced seat at the center was imbued with a massive charge of stored Allpower on top of what he already possessed and generated within himself.

What's more, so long as he and the others possessed the Allpower-charged stones, set in their mechanized bezels, the Vikann stones would heed their wishes and serve as a power-channeling link between himself, Commander Fraxxis, and Commander Prin, the other two master-level casters who comprised their command triumvirate.

Each of them possessed a similarly powerful craft with an equally powerful casting podium, the device connecting the three of them across impossibly vast distances thanks to a particularly tricky bit of magic, and a hefty amount of it at that. The end result was their ability to communicate and even share power from just about anywhere.

Their three command ships were each leading their own massive fleet, and every one of their loyal ships was ready to act on their orders, even if it meant death. Such was the way of the Urvalin, and it was how they had gradually conquered the dozens of systems they called home.

But they had far bigger plans than that.

"Prin," Torgus messaged his partner. "Are your forces ready to strike?"

"We have been awaiting the word," she replied, casually reclining in her seat atop her casting podium. "All we are waiting on is Fraxxis."

"Yes, I know you await me. And I have news," the third in

their trio said. "Our teams have performed a survey of the crashed ship and the beast. The latter is dead. Burned terribly upon entry before smashing into the ground below."

"So, the mighty Ara is no more. Excellent. And their ship?" Prin asked.

"Broken up when it hit the atmosphere," he replied. "Several of its escape pods did manage to launch, but we rounded up those survivors as soon as they hit the ground."

"Were you able to confirm the demise of Charlie and his assassin friend?"

"Those who did not manage to reach an escape pod were either reduced to ash as they passed into the atmosphere, or had their bodies scattered when they plummeted from the sky. We have not located the bodies, but as they are not with the survivors, and the launched escape pods are all accounted for, it seems there is little doubt as to their fate."

"But you are not sure," Torgus said. "We still need confirmation."

"Are we not going to proceed?" Fraxxis asked, exasperated. "We have come so far. Spent so much time on this plan."

"And it will succeed because of it," Torgus replied. "No, brother, do not fear. We proceed. We have waited a long, long time, and have spent countless years and resources establishing our agents in the right places. And now our patience is about to pay off. Are our people ready?"

"Situated at the seats of power, ready and eager to do our bidding," Prin said, her eagerness almost palpable even over the magical communication.

Torgus smiled as the game pieces presented themselves to him on the board he and his predecessors had spent so many years arranging. And now, at last, it was finally time for the game to commence.

"Then we begin," he said. "The moment is upon us."

Torgus, Prin, and Fraxxis, linked as they were, gave the

command to the various arms of their fleets as one, setting into motion the grand attack the likes of which the denizens of both Earth's galaxy as well as the magical one had never before seen.

A fighting force of extraordinary magnitude.

Thousands of ships began warping and jumping to their destinations, using magic as well as technology in the process. The majority arrived at slightly distant waypoints to their final targets, but a few began immediately engaging their foe.

Olo and Tym just so happened to be engaged in a particularly lucrative piece of business that may have been a bit on the gray side of legal when their little smuggling operation was rudely interrupted by the arrival of a dozen ships. But these weren't Council ships. These were something else.

"What the hell?" Tym blurted as he raced for the airlock connecting his craft to the larger vessel he had been offloading his illicit cargo onto as the bombardment commenced. "Olo, who's firing on us?"

Olo hadn't even completed the docking procedure when the attack began. It was twelve against five, and two of those five were merely smugglers making their delivery runs. The others, however, were a bit on edge, given the nature of their business, and they had bolstered their shielding spells and begun casting as soon as the intruders switched to a hostile footing.

They may have been outnumbered, but they were not going to roll over so easily.

"Tym, can you disengage your umbilical spell? There are more smaller ships launching from those people's baseships," Olo sent.

"Already sealing the hatch," Tym replied. "I'll be clear in ten seconds." His ship rocked as the magical shielding bumped his hull. "Hey, there's a ship out here!" he angrily sent to the captain of the vessel. "Watch it with your shield spell."

"We're under attack," the captain shot back. "If you want out, you'd better do it fast. I'm enacting our maximum defensive protocol in thirty seconds."

Tym's hands flew over his controls, and he cast the flight spells at high speed by rote. "I'll be out of your hair in twenty."

Olo circled around him from a safe distance, ready to engage the increasing numbers of enemy ships. "Hurry up, Tym."

"Shut up and let me cast."

At last, Tym pushed free of the larger vessel just as its shielding ramped up, quickly pairing with Olo and making a break for a patch of more open space from which to assess the situation. What they saw shocked them.

Magical attacks were buffeting the larger ships, testing their shielding spells with every impact. The defensive spells were robust, however, deflecting the incoming barrage as one would expect of well-funded smugglers. They had not skimped on their armaments. Not one bit.

But then the unexpected happened.

Metal projectiles were fired from the invading craft, and those were able to pierce not only the magical defenses, but the hull beneath them as well. The large ships staggered and lurched from the impacts. Olo and Tym, however, were flying smaller craft and were able to maneuver out of the line of fire, but only just.

The larger ships may have been damaged, but they still had plenty of fight in them. But their commanders had clearly decided this was *not* a fight they wanted to be in. The craft cast their jump spells in unison.

Nothing happened.

Something was blocking their jumps. They were trapped.

At that moment Olo and Tym read the writing on the wall, and it was written in enormous flashing block letters. The message was clear. This was a losing fight. And worse, it was an adversary they'd never encountered before and had no idea how to deal with.

"We need to get word out," Tym said.

"Agreed. Spread the word, then rendezvous at our usual spot," Olo replied.

The swarm of smaller ships the intruders had deployed was racing toward them, like a school of eager piranha rushing to devour their prey.

Olo warped away first, the new tech systems his friends in the other galaxy had provided him after Malalia's defeat having been already primed and ready for use in case of a problem with their smuggling transaction before the Urvalin even arrived.

No sooner had he warped than Tym saw twenty more ships jump into the space his friend had just been occupying.

"Nuts to this," Tym said, engaging his ship's backup drive system and warping away as well even before his final coordinates were locked in.

It was a simple calculus. Stay those extra seconds to fully plot the course and die, or risk the incomplete jump coordinates dumping him into a sun but at least have a possibility of living.

For Tym the choice had been easy. His little ship flashed out of existence as he jumped away just moments before the enemy craft swarmed his location.

"Commander, the smaller vessels somehow evaded our jump blockade," Prin's number one said. "The larger craft, however, are ours."

On her command bridge's casting podium, Prin watched the two small ships escape with great frustration. "Where *are* they?" she hissed, a slight wave of Allpower swelling around her.

She forced herself to calm. Losing her temper while connected with the others on the casting podium could be dangerous.

Billus, her right hand, continued with no fear. He'd served her loyally for many years, and while she might lash out in anger on rare occasion, she had never once harmed him.

"They appeared to have utilized warp technology to make their escape," he said.

"Those ships were from *this* galaxy," she growled. "They do not use warps here."

"I am aware, Commander. But, apparently, we were mistaken about these two."

Prin took a deep breath then silently relayed that information to the others. They would have to accelerate things if those ships could not be stopped. She turned to Billus. "Track them."

"I have already so ordered. In this galaxy where technology is so rarely used, it is only a matter of time before we trace the warp residue."

"I hope you are correct," she replied. "Because if they manage to alert others before our forces arrive at their assigned targets it will become a far more costly battle. The goal here is to conquer them as fast and cleanly as possible."

"Of course, Commander. I will have my men pour all resources available to them into the task."

Commander Prin nodded her approval then slid down into her seat. She would need to strategize with the others, which would require a significant amount of power from this distance.

Communication was a far different thing than sharing their Allpower in battle, and it could be a bit of a drain. But plans were underway, the dice cast. After so many years the invasion had begun. Soon enough, the outcome would be known.

CHAPTER THIRTY-FOUR

A blast of magic drove the hurled dagger home with so much force it slammed through the thick wooden target and straight out the back, embedding in the magically shielded training structure's wall. It was a new addition to Amazara's grounds, quietly built by her lover over the past months as his niece grew in strength.

Apparently, it had been a wise safeguard.

Korbin wanted her to have a safe place to train. One where she could go to work on her casting without the pressure of her father's loving, but overly protective, eye. Sometimes a novice just needed a safe place to make mistakes and work out the kinks without fear of judgment. Here, where no one knew her, was perfect.

"Again," Korbin said. "Stronger. Trust your power."

Kara nodded, fine beads of sweat gleaming on her brow from the hours of effort. Amazara had come and invited them both to take a break for some refreshing tea, but Kara was deep in her training, opting to power on through until dinnertime.

It had been quite a shift in her character since she had discovered her stepmother was stealing her power all of those years. With the realization that she had power—*real* power that might one day rival even her father's—Karasalia Palmarian had plunged head-first into her studies.

And she had excelled.

Kara felt the power within her holding strong despite the hours of work. She had been casting without the aid of a konus for several months now, relying entirely on her own internal magic to power her spells. At first, she had tired quickly, her magic waning. But now she had learned to control the expenditures and feel her own power levels instinctively, as Korbin had taught her.

She eyed the target and channeled her power, quietly casting her spell simultaneously as she drew and hurled the blade tucked in the sheath hidden in the small of her back. The weapon flew in a blur, a faint magical glow trailing in its path. No sooner had it impacted than the entire target burst into flames.

"Kara," Korbin chided.

She laughed then cast the extinguishing spell, but rather than merely putting out the flames she encased the entire thing in a layer of ice.

"Better, Uncle Korbin?" she said with a wry grin.

Korbin's eyes crinkled with amusement. "Yes, Kara, that was better," he said. "You're really coming into your own."

"Having a kickass teacher doesn't hurt."

"*Kickass*? You've been spending time with Arlo and Ripley, I see."

"Not for a few months. But it's been too long. Me and Vee are going to hop back over to Earth in a couple of weeks to meet them for a trip to Taangaar."

"The Chithiid homeworld? I went with Zara not too long ago. It was a surprisingly beautiful place."

"I know. And that's why we decided we should see it for ourselves. And who better to take us?"

"Aside from a Chithiid."

"Well, duh. But I think we'll have more fun with Rip."

"And Arlo. You two are still seeing one another, are you not?"

Kara hemmed and hawed, her violet skin darkening slightly. "Well, uh. It's complicated."

Korbin knew not to press the matter. "I know complicated," he said. "I wish you nothing but happiness, whatever form that may be, and whichever galaxy it may reside in."

"Thanks, Uncle Korbin."

"Of course. Now, what say you we head inside and clean up? I know Amazara would love your company in the kitchen."

Kara perked up even more. Aside from working on her casting skills, she and Amazara had grown close in her time visiting, and the joys of cooking together was one of her favorite pastimes.

Aside from destroying her uncle's new targets, that is.

She had spent an increasing amount of time with the couple of late. Her father had healed fully from the damage his treacherous ex-wife had inflicted upon him, his powers finally restored to their full capacity. But she had caused a lot of harm, and now that he was whole again, the mighty Visla Palmarian spent every free moment making up for the damage done in his absence.

Malalia's acts had hurt the people of his world. The people who depended on him and looked up to him for leadership and protection. His top priority now was restoring the faith his people once had in him.

The doors to his tower estate were opened to the public, and many of his floating gardens were likewise now accessible to all for public use. As a result, a great many had taken to picnicking with their families there when the weather was right. But that was not all he had done.

Visla Palmarian had also become an even greater patron of the arts than before, sponsoring countless exhibitions, plays, and musical performances all around the region. A soothing balm of art and beauty to feed and restore the spirits of his people. And in the process, he found himself becoming a truly benevolent leader. Benevolent and kind, but also so crazy powerful no one in their right mind would ever mess with him or his people again.

But that sort of drive meant he was often swamped with his self-imposed duties. And while he dedicated himself to spending as much time with his daughter as possible, Karasalia knew that he felt a visceral need to make amends to his people for what had happened. He wasn't always around, but he was her father, and he loved her, and that was enough.

"I was thinking," Korbin said as they walked back to Amazara's hilltop home. "It has been ten days."

"Ten fantastic days," she said.

"Yes, they have been. And you've made a huge amount of progress this visit. But don't you think your father will be missing you?"

"Nah, we're good. I make sure to go with him on a bunch of his social outings when I'm home, so he gets his fill of me, I'm sure. Plus, we have some pretty intense training sessions, and I may have neglected to tell him that my visits here were a bit heavier on the casting than the rest and relaxation bit."

"Kara—"

"What? C'mon, Uncle Korbin, you know how he is. You've been friends since forever."

"That is certainly true," he said. "Though I would be hesitant to call it *forever*. I may be older, but I'm not *that* old."

Kara laughed brightly. "Oh, you know what I mean."

"Just pulling your leg."

Kara flashed a surprised look. "Well, now look who's been spending some time with Earth folk."

"Daisy and Freya have visited recently," he admitted. "That woman is quite impressive. And her ship? Amazing."

"Yeah, I know."

"And, I suppose, perhaps, I have picked up a few bits of Earth slang in the process. But Amazara thinks it's charming."

"Then that's all that counts, right?"

"Very much so."

The pair stepped up onto the porch and into the warmth of Amazara's kitchen. The smell of fresh-baked bread still hung in the air as the loaves cooled on a rack. Almost everything in this house had been grown on her property, and those that hadn't been were acquired from the local vendors she knew so well down in town.

It was a bit of a trek getting there, but her Malooki were always happy to be taken out for a proper ride, and their powerful haunches could easily support the weight of their passengers as well as whatever produce they may have acquired.

"You two have a good time?" she asked. "I could have sworn I felt a tremor of power all the way out here at the house."

Korbin cocked his head. "Really?"

"Really."

They both looked at the young violet-skinned woman with curiosity.

"Well, then," Korbin said. "I had best amplify the dampening spells. It would seem our dear Kara has been progressing even more than I realized."

"I could have told you that," Amazara said.

"Yes, dear, you could have. But what's the fun in that?" he said, leaning in for a quick kiss.

"Oh, you. Why don't you both get cleaned up. And then, if you're still up for it, Kara, I could use your help preparing dinner."

"I don't get to help too?" Korbin asked.

"Much as I appreciate your culinary talents, my dear, sometimes us women enjoy a little girl time to ourselves."

"As you wish," he said, strolling from the kitchen with a contented grin.

Amazara blushed as he left. It hadn't been long ago that Daisy showed them the ancient entertainment images from Earth's olden days. The one about the six-fingered man and a pirate called Roberts. Both had enjoyed it immensely, glad that someone had the foresight to preserve the delightful film despite the fall of mankind.

"You two are so cute," Kara said with a chuckle.

"I don't know what you're talking about," Amazara replied with a wry grin.

"Uh-huh. Well, I'd better wash up. Back in a flash."

"I'll be here," Amazara said. And here she would be indeed, enjoying something she never thought she would.

A family life.

CHAPTER THIRTY-FIVE

The air was quiet in the dark of night, the Malooki sleeping tranquilly in their pens, the wildlife surrounding Amazara's compound all tucked away safely in their dens until daybreak. It was one of the things Korbin had found so restful about this place. The simplicity of a life in nature.

Yes, the planet had cities bustling with activity, and the nearby town was run by a rather gregarious visla of moderate power named Kwinnius. It was somewhat unusual for someone of his strength to oversee so small a region, but after the Council of Twenty had their operations thwarted, he had left his old homeworld for a less conflicted one.

Fighting the Council, albeit quietly and with tact rather than overt force, had been exhausting, and thus, a new home had been settled on. Fortunately, he did not seem to notice Korbin's power on the occasions they crossed paths, thanks to the visla's considerable skill at masking it, so he and Amazara were able to remain perceived as no more than that sweet couple up the hill.

When she visited, Kara spent her time almost exclusively with them, training and cooking, mostly, and the rare occasions she did go to town were utterly uneventful. It really did seem the three of them were living their best lives.

It was enough to almost make Korbin let his guard down.

Almost.

His eyes opened, a killing spell forming on his tongue as he reached out with his senses. Amazara felt him wake and turned toward him, her own level of alertness passing from comfortable and sleepy to sharp and awake as soon as she intuitively felt his power ready to deploy.

She looked at him questioningly but remained silent. After a long moment he let the spell go and turned to her.

"Did you feel that?"

"Feel what?" She was naturally attuned to fluctuations in power, but whatever had woken him had not roused her from her slumber. "There's nothing, Korbin. And we're so far out, no one will bother us."

"I don't know," he said, getting out of bed. "It was unusual. *Something* is out there."

Amazara propped herself up on her elbow and cocked her head slightly.

"I still don't feel anything."

"It's faint now, barely there. But I know something is off."

Korbin and Amazara turned toward the bedroom door. *This* presence they could both feel growing closer.

"Come in, Kara," Amazara called out.

Kara entered the room a moment later, not a trace of sleep in her eyes despite sunrise still being at least an hour away.

"You felt that, right?" she asked, pumped full of adrenaline. "It wasn't just me."

"I did," Korbin replied. "A disturbance of some sort. But tell me, what do *you* sense?"

"It's kinda hard to describe. Like, there's some kind of magic out there in this system. I mean, it seems like it's all around us, but it's not normal. And whatever it is, it's growing closer to the planet."

Korbin was already out of bed and putting on the stash of fighting gear he kept stowed in a small chest in the corner of Amazara's bedroom. Ever since their fight with Malalia, he had resolved her home would never be unprotected, and the amply charged konuses and enchanted blades stored there would do the job admirably even if he wasn't there to use his own power.

"What is it, Uncle Korbin?" Kara asked, a tinge of growing concern coloring her tone.

"Whatever is happening, I don't like it," he said. "I want you two to get dressed and gather your things. I'm going to take a Malooki down to my ship. Be ready when I'm back."

Amazara held him by the arm. "What are you going to do, Korbin? How serious is this?"

"I can't say for certain. But I am going to cast additional shimmer spells on my ship while you two pack up to leave. It might be nothing, but I don't like this. That craft is our escape, should we need it, and I want to be quite sure it remains uncompromised and unnoted."

Amazara nodded stoically, but her eyes said far more. Kara rushed close and hugged him hard.

"Be careful," she said.

"I always am," he replied, then headed out to the stables.

Amazara pulled a mid-sized pack as well as an empty larger bag from their storage space and began loading every additional weapon Korbin had brought. Kara opened the smaller of the two, intending to stow some of the weapons there. What she saw made her gasp.

The pack was filled to the brim with pulse weapons, explosive devices, and even a few old-timey combustion weapons, all of which were utterly unheard of in this galaxy.

"Holy crap! Where did you get all of these?"

"We have friends in high places, do we not?" Amazara

replied. "Our allies on Earth thought they might serve us well one day, so they supplied Korbin, myself, and select others with their technology weapons. They also upgraded a few ships, including your uncle's, with their warp drive systems."

"I didn't get a goody bag full of guns," Kara griped.

"You are still a child."

"Hey!"

"An amazing, talented, brave child, but, nevertheless, they did not feel it would be appropriate arming you to the teeth."

Much as she hated the logic being used, Karasalia understood where the rationale would make sense when applied to just about any other person her age.

But she wasn't like them. Nor were her friends. Not after their contribution in the intergalactic battle less than a year ago. But the cards had been dealt, and she had no choice but to play her hand.

"And my father?"

"He has a few items locked away as well, though with his power restored I doubt he would even bother with them. Now, come. We must be prepared when Korbin returns. Help me fill a larder bag in the kitchen."

A little over an hour later, Korbin returned from his hasty ride to the bottom of the hill. The women heard him coming and hurried outside to greet him. The Malooki's mood-changing hair, they noted with concern, was shifting color in the dark purple range. The animal was spooked, and not just a little.

"What did you find?" Amazara asked.

"Nothing so far, but I sensed a disturbance in the direction of town, and so did my Malooki." He looked at his niece. "Kara, did you sense it as well?"

Kara had been so busy helping Amazara that she'd almost ignored the feelings of strange energy growing closer by the minute. But now that Korbin mentioned it, she *did* feel something stronger in that general direction.

"I-I'm not sure what I sense."

Amazara shouldered her bags. "We are ready to go. Is the ship safe?"

"It is. Come, we should waste no time."

The trio quickly loaded up their steeds, then Amazara locked up her home and cast protective wards over the sensitive areas where she had hidden her valuables. They then set out down the winding trail. It was a somewhat difficult path in the dark, but the sky had begun brightening. In any case, the Malooki knew the route by heart, and in short order they reached the landing clearing.

Korbin lowered a sliver of the shimmer spell hiding his ship.

"Load everything onto my ship."

"You expect trouble?" Kara asked.

"You know your uncle," Amazara said. "He may not expect it, but he always prepares for it."

A troubled smile curved the corners of Korbin's lips. "You know me so well, Zara."

"By now I would hope so."

"Valid point. Now, you two load up and lie low. There's something I need to do."

Kara's magic crackled slightly. "Wait, where are you going?"

"Don't worry, Kara, you will be safe here. But I have to know what's going on out there."

"What do you mean? What are you going to do?"

"I'm going to head into town."

This time Amazara was the one who reacted, though a bit more violently. She punched him in the arm.

"Ow! Hey!"

"Don't *ow, hey* me. This is *my* home, Korb. My friends. And if there's going to be a recon to town, *I'm* damn sure going with."

"Me too," Kara said, sliding a belt with a pair of enchanted daggers around her waist.

Korbin looked at the women in his life and felt pride. They

were right. Who was he to keep them from harm's way? Especially as they were far more competent than most seasoned guards. He reluctantly nodded.

"Very well. But, Kara, don't bring those daggers, only unenchanted ones. We need to travel free of external power that might be noticed. Something is strange about whatever is going on, and if we can sense it, there's a good possibility that works the other way. The less of a magical signature we present the better."

"We will take the Malooki," Amazara said. "They are sensitive creatures, and their coloration will warn of hidden dangers before we might sense them."

"A good plan," he agreed. "And we take the long way. The less frequented paths. It will take us longer, yes, but I fear it may be wisest to be overly cautious in our approach. I have a bad feeling about what we might find."

"As do I," Amazara said, dropping the last of her gear and sliding back onto her Malooki's back. "And there's no time to waste."

CHAPTER THIRTY-SIX

Far, far away in a distant galaxy, Kip had completed his stealthy circuit of the area surrounding the Urvalin base. He and Dukaan had agreed it would be best to extend the perimeter survey an additional hundred or so miles beyond their originally planned flight path.

It would take a lot longer, but that distance was enough to give them a much more detailed idea of what exactly was out there besides the Urvalin.

Not much, it turned out. Aside from assorted pockets of downed ships spread around the landscape, there were just a few geologically active areas and even a lava flow.

As Charlie watched the pool of molten rock swirl, occasionally spewing up a gusher of fresh lava from within the planet's core, a crazy idea flashed through his mind. It lingered a moment. Long enough that the tiniest seed of an idea was planted.

They flew on, noting activity on the surface below. People. There were evidently pockets of tribal groups living in these distant areas. Groups even Nakk was unfamiliar with.

"None of those are mine," he said as they took note of the

downed ships nestled in the trees. "A few of the craft appear to be from other rebel groups, but we have not been in contact with them. Obviously, with our communications out and no Allpower, there has been no way to even know they were here."

"Until now," Charlie said.

"Yes. Until now. Your ship friend's camouflage system is most impressive. Even if our craft had remained functional, we would not have been able to fly this sort of reconnaissance without being noted."

"Speaking of stealth and whatnot," Kip chimed in. "Is it time?"

Charlie and Bawb glanced at one another. "Yeah, it's time," Charlie replied. "Set a course for the Urvalin base. Countermeasures cranked to full, weapons hot, and scanners going full-tilt. We need to record as much data as possible in as short a period as we can."

"Gotcha," Kip said. "I suggest everyone tighten their harnesses. If we have to do evasive maneuvers, my gravity dampers won't help much down here in atmosphere."

"Meaning it could be a *very* rough ride," Bawb said.

"Yep indeedy," Kip agreed. "So, if you all are ready, please keep your arms and legs inside the vehicle at all times."

"We do not have a choice," Skohla said, a bit confused.

Charlie chuckled. "He's just making obscure Earth references. Ignore him and strap in."

Skohla did so, shaking her head at the oddball ship's personality quirks. He may have been an incredible feat of technological wonder, but he was also quite strange.

"All righty, then. Dookie's got the course plotted, and I'll be making the approach below their scans where possible. We should be there in ten minutes. Once we're in their visual range we'll divert more power to the active camouflage and take us in."

The minutes ticked by painfully slowly. Knowing they could

very well come under fire at any moment made them feel every jolt and turbulence bump acutely. But updrafts and thermals were all they encountered, and Kip's alarms did not activate once.

"We're coming up on the tower," Dukaan informed them. "We will slow, then make a gradually upward spiral around the structure from a distance. We will capture as much data as possible on the way up, then will add to it on the way down."

"Then we boogie the hell out of here," Charlie added. "We'll have plenty of time to review the footage and readings once we're safely far away from here."

"Precisely," the pilot replied. "Beginning ascent in twenty seconds."

Charlie and Bawb leaned in close to their displays, searching for any weakness that might make itself readily apparent to them. They would do a detailed review later, but the sooner they had a basic understanding of this facility, the sooner they could start to formulate a plan.

The base was unremarkable. Solid metal that rose up into the sky, tapering outward, making it impossible to scale from the ground. Up and up they went until the first of several openings presented itself.

As they had suspected on their initial long-distance pass, these seemed to be launch bays for small Urvalin ships the likes of which they had captured with Nakk and his people. Charlie felt his sphincter clench as they passed in front of them, ready for a wave of enemy craft to spew out toward them in an attack formation. But none came. So far, Kip's camouflage was working.

Flying slowly undoubtedly helped. The active camouflage could be a bit wonky in the sky, occasionally showing an imperfect image that an astute observer could notice. But the Urvalin had ruled here unopposed for so long it was almost impossible that they would be maintaining the degree of operational readiness and vigilance that would be required to spot them.

"The top. Over to the side between the elevated sections. Do you see it?" Bawb asked.

Charlie scanned the structure, immediately seeing what his friend had noted. "A barracks, it looks like," he replied. "And that would mean a guard stationed there."

"Exactly."

"You know, any attempt on that landing area would require the guard being addressed first, otherwise we could find ourselves facing an unknown number of unfriendlies."

Bawb smiled. Charlie knew that look. The Ghalian had something particularly wicked up his sleeve.

"But if we chose to *not* incapacitate their guard?"

"Let them see us, you mean?"

"Yes. We could utilize those nearby structures to stage our own forces. Forces they would be aware of."

Charlie saw where he was going with this, and it was, for lack of a better word, awesome.

"And then we can have a small group arrive on the other side while we're drawing them out and focusing all of their attention on the *wrong* threat."

"Exactly. And then we strike them down with no mercy before they realize what has happened."

"Damn, that's cold, Bob," Charlie said. "I love it."

"I thought you might."

Nakk and Skohla nodded their appreciation. "An inspired deception," Nakk said. "But we must first gather our people to prepare for such an attempt."

"Which we'll do," Charlie said. "But now we need to get back."

"Already on it," Kip said. "Finishing the descent run and plotting a course back to Ara, with a few random turns thrown in, just in case we've got bogies."

"Thanks, Kip. Better safe than sorry."

"Ain't that the truth?" the ship replied.

They made fair time heading back on the circuitous route, but as they drew closer to their camouflaged friend where she lay hidden on the water's edge, something unusual stood out in the trees below. Namely, torches.

"Nakk, are those yours?" Bawb asked.

Nakk looked at the display, enhancing the image just as Dukaan had shown him. His proficiency with new technology was admirable, Charlie thought. The ability to adapt and learn so quickly was a fantastic trait. He'd be a great ally indeed if they could ever get off this rock.

"These are not mine," Nakk replied. "They are yet far off, but this appears to be the Horka."

"That's not good," Charlie muttered. "Hopefully they'll miss her entirely, but with Ara's condition, we'll have to do everything we can to protect her."

"The Wise One shall come to no harm so long as I draw breath," Bawb said plainly.

Nakk and Skohla noted the way the pale man spoke. This wasn't a blustery show of machismo, it was a simple statement of fact. And looking at Bawb they thought his odds against so many were actually quite good.

"Ara, how long until you are well enough to fight?" Charlie asked over their comms link.

The Zomoki sounded quite tired when she answered. "At the rate I am healing, weeks at the least. I believe flight may be an option soon, however, but not for any great distance."

"Flee rather than fight?"

"If need be."

"Well, let's hope it doesn't come to that. We'll be touching down in a minute, and we can discuss it properly once we're on the ground."

"You know where I will be," she said, mustering the smallest chuckle.

It was pained and weak, but hearing Ara's laugh brightened both Charlie and Bawb's spirits immeasurably. Their friend was hurt, yes, but she would be okay.

CHAPTER THIRTY-SEVEN

Charlie rose from his seat and began digging in the supplies Leila had packed for him.

"I bet she did," he muttered to himself. "She always seems to find just the right—there it is!" he said, pulling out a silver canister and accompanying metal pot. "Aw, babe. Thank you!"

"Coffee?" Bawb asked, recognizing the item.

"What can I say? Leila knows my vices," he replied, yet again thinking just how lucky he had been to meet her, and a bazillion miles from home in an entirely different galaxy, no less. Fate, it seemed, worked in mysterious ways indeed. He opened the canister and took a whiff. "*Real* beans, not from a replicator. I don't know why, but the replicated stuff just lacks that *oomph*, ya know?"

Bawb chuckled. "It is a good thing your vices are so benign."

"She wouldn't be with me if they weren't."

Kip set down, killed the engines, and popped his hatch. "Would you like me to boil some water?" he asked.

"Nah, I kinda feel like doing it like my dad used to when I was a kid," Charlie said as he stepped out of the ship.

"Your father?" Bawb asked. "You have not spoken much of him."

"Yeah, we didn't always get along. But the good times were when we would go camping when I was a kid. I mean, I was no Boy Scout, but I've been known to spend some time in the woods."

"And you will boil water without magic?"

"Just watch me," Charlie said, gathering up dry twigs as he walked.

By the time they settled down near Ara he had enough for a small fire. More than enough to boil the water and make a strong pot of coffee. Bawb, Hunze, and Dukaan were familiar with the process, but for Nakk and Skohla this was something of a novelty.

Starting the fire was actually quite easy as flint stones were abundant, and just a few strikes with the back of a knife was enough to spark the kindling aflame. In no time the water was boiling and ready for the ground beans.

"Trust me, you'll love it," Charlie said when his brew was ready. "Or hate it, I guess. It's hit or miss."

He poured each of them a small mug of the hot beverage then took a sip of his own. He looked at the others, a shocked expression on his face.

"Holy crap, Bob, did you feel that?"

"Feel what?"

"You didn't feel it?"

"Again, feel what?"

"Wait, you don't generate your own power. Right. Hunze? How about you?"

Hunze took a sip and sat up a bit straighter. "A tingle. Tiny. Faint. But yes, it was there."

"What are you talking about?" Dukaan asked, sipping his mug. "It is coffee."

"Yeah, but you know how it works on magic users."

"But there is no magic here."

"Or so we thought. But this? I felt something."

Hunze nodded her agreement. "As did I."

Charlie looked at Nakk and Skohla. "Hey, I know you use your magi—I mean, Allpower. But are you generating your own, or is it pulled from a banda?"

"We both possess a small amount of our own power," Nakk said. "But the banda greatly increases its potency, as does linking with our triumvirate."

"Hmm. Try this and let me know if you feel anything."

Nakk and Skohla each sniffed the brew, then took a sip. Each of them cocked their heads slightly at the taste as well as their physical reaction.

"I felt *something*," Nakk said. "Minute, but it was there."

"As did I," Skohla added. "What is this beverage?"

"Coffee. It boosts the magic of some people. And, apparently, it still works, even here."

Dukaan's interest was piqued. "If it can restore power, perhaps it can cure Ara. How much coffee do you have?"

"Not enough to make a dent in someone Ara's size. Her mass is just too great, no offense."

"None taken," the Zomoki replied with a chuckle.

Dukaan crossed his arms as he pondered the development. "Then if not Ara, perhaps it can at least restore your and Hunze's power."

Now it was Charlie's turn to laugh. "Dude, the amount we would need to drink, we'd be shitting our brains out long before any real power kicked in."

Bawb shook his head. "Charming, Charlie."

"Hey, the guy asked a question."

"And you provided a colorful response, as expected."

"Just stating a fact." He turned to Nakk and Skohla. "You see, it's tasty, and it boosts magic, but it's also a diuretic in moderate amounts, and a laxative in larger ones."

The pair lowered their cups.

"No, not one cup," Charlie said. "Don't worry. But if you drink a lot of it, well, yeah."

He pondered just what this could mean. Magic didn't seem to function here, but what if they'd found proof that it *could*? That meant there was more at play here than a black-and-white absence of power.

"Ara, what do you make of this?" he asked.

The Zomoki sniffed the air, her senses sharpening as she slowly recovered from her wounds. "As I heal, I do sense power here," she said. "It is incredibly faint, as though very distant, but not through the skies."

"What do you mean?"

"The sun's energy. You have seen how the rays are distorted on this world. Whatever power they might once have possessed never reaches the surface. What I am sensing is a different type of power. Old. Slow. Deep. There is power within this planet, the core of whirling molten rock seems to be its own source."

"Then why can't I feel it?"

"In time you will. Our power is linked, and as mine restores, so will yours."

Charlie considered what this might mean. If what she was saying was correct, then there *was* a source of magic here after all. And if they could actually generate a bit of power, they'd have a little surprise up their sleeves when they finally dealt with the Urvalin. There was magic in the planet's core. The big question now was how to tie into it.

A big circuit to connect them would be ideal, Charlie mused, his engineer's brain kicking into high gear. But there wasn't much they could do to reach the core. Not even geothermal tech would suffice. Even if they had all of the tools and resources of home at their disposal, it would still be a Herculean feat.

"I'm racking my brain here, but I can't think of any way to access that power," he grumbled. "Sorry, Ara."

"It is not something to be sorry about. Even for my kind, this would be a near impossible task."

"I hear ya. It's not like there's some convenient circuit to tie into, after all. Nothing runs all the way down to the—" He stopped in his tracks as a realization hit him. "Hang on a minute. We just need something connected to the core, right?"

"Yes. But—"

"And that connection wouldn't have to be a solid link," he added, his excitement growing. "So a conduit of any sort would be a way to connect."

"I am wondering where you are going with this," Ara said, worried her friend was perhaps losing it a tad.

But Charlie was on a roll, the ideas gelling into the beginnings of an actual plan. "A volcano," he said.

"A volcano?" Bawb asked. "I fail to see how—"

"Lava, Bob. Get it? Ara? Anyone?"

"Damn, that's actually pretty clever," Kip said. "Using molten rock and ore as a giant circuit? Way to go, meat brain."

"Gee, don't sound so surprised."

"No, I don't mean it like that. Just it's pretty outside-the-box thinking is all."

Bawb and Hunze shared a laugh. "Oh, but that describes Charlie perfectly," Hunze said.

Ara refrained from joining the merriment, her great mind weighing the possibility. It might actually be possible, she realized, but in her condition the odds of success were incredibly decreased.

"Kip, I need to fly to those volcanic areas we passed over. The fissures and lava flows. Can you be ready to fly in five?"

"I can be ready to fly now, if you like."

Charlie was already moving toward the little ship. "Then let's go. I want to do a proper survey of all areas that might have deep connections to the core's main body of magma."

"We'll have to fly close," Kip said. "And it'll be risky."

"Worth it," Charlie said. "We need options, and this just might be our best one."

CHAPTER THIRTY-EIGHT

Kip had made a very basic topographical map of the surrounding areas during the survey passes, but nothing of any great detail. They were enough, however, to make tracking down the largest of the areas of geothermal activity relatively easy.

The first several seemed promising, but upon arrival they proved to be no more than bubbling geysers and hot springs. It was a phenomenon tied to geologic activity below the surface, but for their needs it wouldn't suffice. Lava was required. A liquid form of the same rock and ore running all the way to the core of the planet.

"We're going to need to refine this search," Charlie said after another flyover turned into a bust.

"I see some open fissures that looked promising," Kip said. "They're down in a kinda hairy spot, though. Lots of rocks and not a terribly inviting location."

"If it has a decent lava flow it might work, so let's give it a try," Charlie said.

Kip shifted their course, remaining low and with his active camouflage engaged, but also flying high enough to allow them to survey a wider area from their bird's-eye vantage point.

It was also a hell of a lot safer up there.

Smoke in the air signaled their arrival at the next site on the list. And this time it actually did seem to be volcanic.

"Hey, Kip, is that lava?"

"It appears so, but the angles of the rock outcroppings are really making it hard to get a proper look."

"You think this spot's got potential?"

"It seems so. There's definitely a good amount of geological activity in the area, and that does look like lava down there. Whether or not it ties into a larger pool remains to be seen."

Charlie considered their options a moment. "Well, howzabout you take us down closer?"

"Closer?" the ship asked. "Uh, how much closer were you thinking?"

"Don't worry, I'm not talking *crazy* close. Just close enough to get a real feel for how much lava there actually is."

"So, you *do* actually mean crazy close, then."

Charlie chuckled. "Yeah, I guess I do."

"Well, all right then," the ship said as he began a quick descent. "Hang on. Here goes nothing."

As the ground drew near, the lines of slow-moving black and orange that marked the path of the lava flows weaving through the jagged stones grew clearer. This was definitely what they were looking for.

It was a very harsh and uninviting environment to most, but to Charlie, the lava made it a most welcome sight. More than just a welcome sight, but also a sought-after sensation. For here, this close to the lava, Charlie could actually feel the slightest hint of what Ara had been talking about.

There *was* power beneath the planet's crust, and here at the break point he could sense it. He smiled to himself and eagerly scanned the area below.

What looked like a solid piece of land jutting out into the flow caught Charlie's eye. It didn't seem to be made of volcanic rock, but of regular soil. A little remnant of the ground that had been there before the molten rock overtook it. That meant they could land there if need be. It wasn't perfect by any means, and the approach would be dangerous, but it would be cool enough for what Charlie had in mind.

"You know what?" he said. "I think we can—"

The ship jerked to the side, Kip's AI reflexes barely saving them from a direct hit from the unexpected geyser of orange-hot lava that splashed up into the air.

"Hold on!" Kip exclaimed as he accelerated into evasive maneuvers. Whatever was feeding this flow had chosen the most inopportune time to surge to the surface, and the result had very nearly covered them in molten rock.

"There! On the right!"

"I see it," Kip said, spinning into a roll. "And we call it *starboard*, thank you very much."

"Pardon my foregoing nautical terminology in favor of brevity," Charlie shot back. "Look out, look out!"

"I see it," Kip said as a massive spray of rocks burst into the air.

The next twenty seconds were a master class in precision flying by the AI. Kip may have had a rather unorthodox origin, and his expanded intellect and abilities since then were anything but normal, but one thing was for sure. The ship sure could fly.

Once they were safely hovering outside the danger zone, Charlie reached out, trying once more to sense the power. Only the faintest tickle reached him.

"Damn," he grumbled.

"What is it?"

"I can't really get a good fix on the power."

"So, it is there."

"Oh, that it is. But I don't think I have the ability to tap into it."

"But if you can't, we're all kind of screwed here," Kip said.

"Yeah, maybe. But you know what? I think Ara just might be up for it. Get us back. I need to talk with her."

Kip flew them directly to the shore and set down beside Ara, his landing gear sinking slightly into the damp soil. Charlie was out of the hatch before the engines had even cycled down. Ara watched him approach with her curious gaze.

"I can tell by your excitement you found what you were looking for," she said. "I take it there is a suitable flow?"

"There is," Charlie said. "And I felt the traces of power there. I'm not as attuned to it as you are, but it was definitely there."

Ara nodded her massive head. "As I had expected. This is good news."

"Yeah, but just one hitch."

She raised a brow. "Oh?"

"I can't tap into it," Charlie said with a groan. "I tried, but I just can't."

"I see," Ara sighed.

Charlie looked at the others. Bawb and Hunze were stoic as always, and Dukaan was pretty much unflappable, but there was a tinge of frustration that only someone who knew them as well as Charlie did could discern.

Nakk and Skohla, on the other hand, wore their disappointment more openly. The hope of actually being able to use their Allpower again had been a tempting carrot dangled before them, only to be snatched back by a pernicious Lady Fate.

Or had it?

Charlie looked at Ara a long moment in thought. Yes, it was possible, he mused. If she could fly, then maybe she could make it to the lava herself. Ara could surely tap into that power if anyone could.

"Ara, I have an idea," Charlie said.

Bawb snickered. "I do not know why, Charlie, but whenever you say that I get that funny, worried feeling in my gut."

"I understand the sentiment," Ara added. "But tell me, Charlie, what is this thought of yours?"

"Okay," he said, "hear me out. Now, I know you're hurt, but your wings are intact."

"And tender," she noted.

"Yes, and tender. But I was thinking that if you could manage to get aloft, we could have Kip and maybe one of the captured Urvalin ships help partially carry you."

"Carry me? Carry me where?"

"To the lava flow."

Bawb's back straightened slightly. "The Wise One is injured, Charlie. The lava would be dangerous to her in her state."

"I know, man, but even hurt, Ara's a Zomoki. If anyone could handle the ambient heat there, she could. And she's our best shot of getting a magical advantage on our side." He turned to Ara. "You know I wouldn't suggest this if I didn't think it could actually work. But it's your call, Ara."

The Zomoki thought on it a long moment, weighing her injuries against the possible benefits. And on top of that, the likelihood that she could actually remain undiscovered if the Urvalin truly came searching.

"Very well," she finally said. "I shall attempt the flight. But we must remain low. I do not think it would be wise to venture too high in my condition."

Charlie broke into a grin. "Thank you, Ara. We'll do everything we can to make sure you get there safely." He turned to Nakk. "Can you have one of your captured ships aloft to help us?" he asked. "I don't know if Kip can handle the assist on his own."

"It will be here shortly," Nakk replied. "I have already sent a runner with the request."

"Excellent. Then let's prepare what we can. It's a short flight, but anything can happen."

An hour later the commandeered Urvalin ship dropped in low, hovering just above the trees.

"That was fast," Charlie said. "I guess your hiding spot was closer than you initially let on."

Nakk smiled. "One does not part with tactical secrets lightly, my friend."

"Words of a leader," Bawb agreed. "Wise One, are you ready?"

Ara sat up and stretched out her wings, the mud cracking and falling away. The wings beneath bore clear signs of burn trauma, but were intact. Ara shook her body, and the rest of the mud crumbled.

"As ready as I can be," she said. "Shall we?"

"Everyone load up," Charlie called out. "Ara, we'll fly right below you, leading the way. At any time if you need a rest, just settle down atop the ships, okay?"

"Believe me, I will take you up on that offer should the need arise."

They loaded aboard Kip and took to the air, settling in beside the Urvalin ship. Ara flapped her wings and surged up into the sky. Charlie and Bawb could see her wincing at the pain, but she powered through it and stayed aloft.

"You okay?" Charlie asked over comms. It was still weird using technology to talk to his bonded friend rather than their magic-powered link, but he was thankful at least the tech was working.

Ara turned her head, clearly in pain, and nodded to them once.

"Okay then," Charlie said. "Let's make this quick. Away we go."

CHAPTER THIRTY-NINE

The lava flow they had discovered was not terribly far away. In fact, on any other occasion it would have been an utterly trivial flight for the Zomoki. But in her weakened condition, Charlie could see Ara was struggling to stay aloft.

"Stay close, you guys," he said, wishing they could hurry up and get there faster.

Bawb and Hunze were also watching their friend as she taxed herself to maintain her airspeed. The couple shared a deep concern for Ara, each wishing there was some way they could contribute at least a little power to helping her. But with magic non-functional on this world, even Hunze's powerful locks were useless to her as well as her friends.

"Only another hundred miles or so," Charlie said. "Hang in there."

"I am trying," Ara replied, the strain clear in her voice.

It was clear to everyone aboard that she was using all of her strength to make this flight. If Charlie's plan didn't work, she'd lack the ability to fly clear of the lava field. But there was another more pressing concern to deal with.

"Uh, Kip? Guys? Do you see that?" Charlie said as he

watched the lightning and dark clouds in the distance grow closer.

"There's no way around it," the ship replied. "Dookie and me have already tried plotting alternate courses. It's a localized storm, but too wide to circumvent."

"Ara, you hear that?"

"I did."

"Do you want to land?"

"No. We must press on," she replied.

Charlie didn't like it, but looking down at the hostile terrain below, he knew there was no alternative. They were far from Nakk's territory, and setting down here would be an unacceptable risk for them all.

Rain began to spatter all around them. It wasn't much, fortunately, and Ara actually found the water soothing on her burned wings. But the winds were picking up, and the skies grew darker as they flew on.

"Distance?" Charlie asked.

"Eighty miles," Dukaan replied.

"She is not going to make it," Bawb said. "We must land."

"She can't land. She'll be vulnerable."

"And we shall do all we can to protect her."

"We've got to make it, Bob," Charlie said. "Kip, contact the other ship and prepare to give her a—"

A blast of lightning crackled through the sky. It was close enough to shake Kip, and the smallest tendril of electricity arced over Ara's body. She was normally impervious to such things, but not here. Not in this condition.

Her wings locked up from the shock, and she began to fall from the sky.

"Kip, get under her!" Charlie shouted.

The ship was already in motion, closing the gap in an instant. The craft dipped sharply when her mass impacted it.

"We're dropping fast," Kip said. "She's too heavy."

"Where the hell is the other—"

Abruptly, they lurched upward. Nakk's people had taken a few moments longer to get into position, but now there were two ships carrying the struggling Zomoki.

"Can you both maintain the rest of the way?" Hunze asked, concern furrowing her brow.

"I've linked up with their pilot," Kip said. "Yeah, we can make it, but the landing's gonna be a bitch."

Charlie didn't like the sound of that. "It's lava, Kip. We need precision."

"We'll do the best we can. But Ara's going to have to help us out on the final descent."

He wanted to argue, to tell the AI he had to do better, but he knew if there was anything more the ship could do, he would. Ara was his friend too, after all. He switched his attention to Ara.

"Ara, we're getting close, but we're going to need you to help us get you down. If we slow the descent, can you land?"

"I shall try," she replied.

It was the best he could hope for.

Ten minutes later they had passed the storm and were making their descent to the area Charlie and Kip had found on their prior visit. There was lava flowing all around, but the spit of dirt was still untouched.

Normally, it wouldn't have been a problem for the Zomoki to make a precision landing there, but now? It would be close. And a painful demise awaited if she missed.

The two ships had dialed in their tandem flight at least, and as they dropped down toward the smoking terrain they were synched up and right on course. All Ara would need to do was slip off and control her last twenty meters of descent. That would give the ships the room to clear out of her way while getting her as close to the ground as they were able without risking taking a plunge into the lava themselves.

"We're almost there," Charlie called out. "You ready?"

"As ready as I can be," Ara replied. "And, Charlie, should this not work, know how greatly I have valued our bond."

He felt emotions welling up, but there was no time for that. "You know I feel the same, Ara. But this is going to work. You can do this. Just one last effort and you'll be down safely."

"I shall do all I can."

"Okay. Kip, count us down."

"We're there in ten," the ship replied. "Five. Four. Three. Two. Go, go, go!"

The two craft peeled away, one heading to either side, leaving Ara a clear shot straight to her landing site. She strained hard, flapping her wings and ignoring the pain and exhaustion. All eyes were on her as her feet hit the soil hard. But she was moving too fast.

"Come on, Ara!" Charlie growled. "Come on!"

With all of her remaining strength Ara flapped hard, arresting her slide. At last, she settled to a stop a bit closer to the lava's edge than they'd planned. But she was down. And despite the heat of the place, she was safe. Injured as she was, Ara was a Zomoki, and her tolerance was still far greater than other creatures.

"She did it!" Charlie shouted, hugging his friends with unbridled joy. "Hell, yeah!"

Ara settled into the dirt and lay her head down, her giant eyelids sliding shut. She was utterly drained from the effort. Charlie rushed to the airlock.

"Kip, you sure the air's safe for humans?"

"Yes, it'll stink a bit, but it's safe. Hot, but safe."

"Good enough for me," he said, popping the hatch and hurrying to his friend's side.

Kip had perhaps understated both the smell as well as the heat. It was miserable out there, but, at this moment, he didn't care. Ara was okay, and that was all that mattered. Charlie leaned in and rested his forehead against her cheek, a wave of relief washing over him as he felt her body shift as she slowly breathed. And there was something else here. Something he hadn't felt during the flyover. There was magic here.

"Ara, can you feel that?"

The Zomoki slowly opened her eyes, exhausted but alert. "Yes, there is a tangible power here," she replied.

Charlie was beside himself with joy. "And now you can get better."

Ara, however, was not so upbeat. "There is power, Charlie, but I cannot draw from it. It is contained within the flow. We can sense it, but there is no way to touch it."

He knew it might be an issue when they flew there, but he'd not expected it to be this bad. Normally, Ara would have no problem with the molten stone and ore of the planet's core flowing around them. She could fly into a sun, after all. But now, hurt as she was and without power, the lava would consume her.

Or would it? A cautious smile crept onto Charlie's lips.

"Hang on," he said. "I have an idea." Charlie reached into his innermost pocket and withdrew a small metal cylinder. "You need to connect with the planet's core itself, right?"

"Yes."

"And the lava will act like a conduit, just like a wire would connect to a battery."

"I suppose it does, yes."

"Right. So, what I was thinking is, if you can dip just one talon into the lava flow, that should forge a link, and from that, if I'm not mistaken, then you should be able to draw directly from it, though we don't know how strong the flow will be, of course."

Nakk looked at Charlie like he was mad. "Your friend will burn," he said. "What kind of man would even suggest such a thing?"

"No, it's not like that—"

Bawb slowly shook his head. "I have to agree with Nakk. In

her condition, Ara would not be able to withstand the heat. Unless I am mistaken. Wise One?"

"No, you are not," Ara replied. "Tough as they are, my talons would burn in the attempt."

"Ah," Charlie said. "Normally, yeah, they would. But also, no, they wouldn't."

"What do you mean?"

"I mean, if you can handle the pain and are willing to give it a try, I have a pretty radical idea. I'm pretty sure it will hurt. A *lot*. At least until you begin to replenish your power. But once your magic is finally restored, you can protect yourself from the heat while drawing more power." He unscrewed the lid of the container.

"What do you have there?" she asked.

Charlie moved it closer for her to smell. Ara's head jerked slightly, her eyes widening with surprise. "Balamar waters? You brought Balamar waters on this mission?"

"Just a little 'oh shit' precaution," he replied. "Just enough for emergency use but not enough to give anyone an advantage if they should somehow take it from me."

"But I am far too large."

"We don't need to heal all of you. We just need to heal enough to survive the contact with the lava. One talon, to be precise. Knowing how strongly you react to the waters, I'm willing to bet it'll be enough to keep it intact long enough to draw in the planet's magic."

"*You're* willing to bet?" Hunze asked. "It is not *your* appendage you wager."

"Obviously. But I think this is our best option. Our *only* option."

Ara pondered the suggestion. She knew her own physiology, and Charlie was correct about her reaction to the waters. More than most, they had a particularly powerful reaction where she was involved. He was also correct in his assessment that this was their best option. Short of her regaining at least some power, they were out of others.

"Very well," she said. "I will attempt it."

Charlie felt his emotions swell. "It'll work, Ara. I have faith in you."

"And I have hope. Hope your plan works. We are stranded here if not, and losing a talon in the attempt is worth the risk. But I am weakened now. The flight drained what little energy I had restored. Even with the Balamar waters, I do not know if I will be able to endure."

Bawb stood tall, full of purpose and drive. "We will procure sustenance for you, Wise One." He turned to the others. "Ara requires our aid. We must hunt. And we must do so at once."

Hunze nodded her agreement. "You are correct, love. And we are best served by spreading out. Flying to surrounding areas where the land is more fertile and verdant and deploying in hunting parties."

Bawb smiled. "Of course, you are correct. I would think four teams, two from each ship, would be the most logical use of our assets. You, Charlie, Nakk, and myself will each lead a small group. Nakk, call your people. We will provide weapons from the armory for the endeavor. In this, we cannot afford the leisure of a silent hunt."

CHAPTER FORTY

Countless light years away, a trio moved through the trails on the outskirts of town. Their Malooki had been spooked the entire ride, skittish, reacting to something none of them could see. At least, not at first.

"There," Korbin said in a hush. "Through the trees."

Amazara and Kara looked where he was pointing. There was a small clearing near the narrow trail they were riding on, and a break in the foliage afforded them a good look at the clearing, as well as the strange alien ship parked in it.

"What are they?" Amazara asked. "I've never seen the likes of them before."

"I don't know," Korbin replied, careful to keep his urge to go storming into the landing area to demand answers in check. "They appear to be some distant relative of Tslavars, or Altsavs, maybe. But there's more to them than that. Do you feel it?"

Indeed she did. Kara as well. All three of them were power users, and there was a persistent sensation of wrongness in the air. A power that grated with their own. These intruders were in possession of something new it seemed.

Korbin's feeling of alarm grew exponentially. "If we can

sense them, they can likely sense us. Take care to use no power whatsoever. We must blend in. Melt into the woods."

"As I already do," Amazara said.

Kara, on the other hand, was not so experienced as her uncle and his partner. A look of concern flashed across her face.

"We will help you," Amazara said. "Just focus on the Malooki's breathing. Feel its heartbeat through your legs as we ride. Relax into that, and your own power should calm on its own."

Kara did as she suggested, and while it was a little difficult at first, after a minute she began to feel her tension slip away. The Malooki's breathing became clearer, and its powerful heartbeat felt stronger and stronger now that she knew what to look for.

"Good," Zara said. "That's it."

She flashed Korbin a look, their silent shorthand from years of friendship conveying thoughts almost as clearly as speaking. These were no ordinary intruders, and they would have to be *extremely* cautious.

Five minutes later they had cleared the landing area, and the sensation of the strange power had left. The ride to town would take a little while longer now that they were avoiding *this* kind of a threat. But there was nothing to do for it. They simply had no choice.

Kara rode in silence, but it was clear the focusing trick had grown old. Her agitation was palpable, though she was at least not crackling with power as her father sometimes did when he was truly upset.

"Kara, we will protect you," Amazara said.

She shrugged. A teenage response if ever there was one, but it was clear she was upset.

"Zara is right," Korbin said. "So long as we are with you, we will keep you safe."

The teen sighed dramatically. "If you can. I mean, what are those people, anyway? They feel wrong."

Korbin rode his Malooki closer to her and leaned in close. "It is not just us. You have power as well. Significant power. And if it comes down to it, I have every confidence your training will serve you well."

"But that's the thing," she said, her emotions welling up. "I don't want to fight anymore. I mean, training is fun and all, but we nearly died last time, and Vee isn't even here."

"Perhaps that is for the best. As an Ootaki, I don't think she would be able to mask her power the way we can."

"*I* have her hair," Kara said, opening her jacket to show the long braid wrapped around her body. "I have her power. And I should be with her to keep her safe. She's my best friend."

"She will be safe with her parents. And remember, your father protects the area. He is one of the most powerful vislas I've ever seen."

"This sucks," she grumbled. "I just wish I was home."

Korbin said nothing, but it was his opinion that perhaps it was for the best she wasn't. If these invaders were here, on a relatively unimportant world, there was a good likelihood they would be visiting other planets as well. And Karasalia Palmarian's home was a tempting target indeed.

Little did Korbin know just how accurate his concern would prove to be. When Torgus commanded the attack begin, he unleashed a massive fleet of power-wielding forces, all of them moving in a carefully planned sequence, pressing the advantage Malalia/Dominus had unintentionally given them.

When she forced the Council of Twenty to the shadows, commandeering its strongest casters for her own purposes, she had made a powerful entity, indeed. But her defeat had splintered the remaining casters, and a power vacuum had been left in their absence. And separated and working on their own, the casters were vulnerable.

Torgus's comrades in arms swooped in, in a flash, bombarding the vislas and emmiks with a dizzying array of attacks, cornering them and overpowering them when possible, killing them outright when not, until a great many casters were in captivity.

All of their strengths were negated and their weaknesses exploited in the endeavor, for this had been an attack many, many years in the making.

Mighty houses toppled as deeply planted operatives received the signal to activate. The Urvalin had been patient in their plans, as well as very, *very* generous with coin. But often it was not as much of an issue as they'd have expected. In fact, it was downright shocking to the Urvalin leaders just how little it took to tempt someone to betray all they held dear.

Pocket change for the wealthy was enough to make men burn decades of friendship and sell their relatives into servitude. To sever ties with those once held dear and to betray those who had treated them with nothing but care and respect.

One such victim was particularly powerful. A visla of exceptional power rarely encountered. The Urvalin had done their research and targeted such people very specifically, sparing no expense to place their people close for when the moment arose.

Those power users could be a great asset if they could be turned. And from captivity, where their Allpower was neutered, pressure would be applied. All of the years of research put to use to convince them to join the Urvalin cause.

It was much like the Council of Twenty had done, in a way. Only rather than creating a network of lower-level servants operating beneath the twenty rulers, the Urvalin would introduce these men and women to the ways of triumvirate casting, linking them in groups of three to do their bidding.

But first came their capture.

Some were taken by force, but the majority were strong

enough to cause great losses in the process as well as unacceptable delays. For that reason a much simpler method was used.

Gomallin extract was a particularly difficult substance to acquire. One the Urvalin had cornered the market on and stockpiled. Even so, quantities were extremely limited.

It was technically a poison, and deadly at that, but only to non-power users. Those who possessed their own internal source would merely be incapacitated by it. Sent into a deep slumber for anything from hours to days.

This was how the mighty Visla Palmarian was taken. Kara's father was captured not with a fight, but without a struggle at all.

He was in his estate tower, the safest of inner sanctums. None could bypass his wards and reach him there. But his enemy was already inside his walls. A cook named Mozza and several of his guards had been paid handsomely for their services.

The only bloodshed was from his loyal staff who saw their unconscious patron being whisked to the landing pad where a ship was waiting, its crew already overpowered and its course set.

It was quick, and it was brutal, but the visla slept through it all. By the time the ship took to the sky, he was already fitted with a control collar and locked into his room. The Urvalin had come to appreciate that particular bit of magic and had adopted the use of the collars themselves. One more thing to ease the transition. A means of control that those from this galaxy were familiar with.

When word of the unusual activity at the visla's estate spread through the city, Vee's parents bolted the doors tight, keeping their daughter locked away and out of sight.

They didn't know what was happening, but as the visla's daughter's best friend, she would be a target of opportunity if caught on the street. And while her Ootaki hair had been shorn, the manner in which she had done so, and the situation in which it had occurred, had caused a most unusual thing to happen.

As her power-storing hair began to grow back, it no longer accumulated magic as it used to. But she wasn't neutered of her gift. Rather, hers had mutated into something entirely different. Unique. For Vee had become the unlikeliest of Ootaki. She was one who stored the power she absorbed within herself.

It had never happened, at least not that anyone knew of. But in a distant galaxy where that world's sun's rays fed into her, somehow, amazingly, she had become something new. She was a magic user.

She wasn't powerful. Not yet, at least. But for the first time in her life, Vee could cast. And with that change had come another. Gone was the timid girl who had spent her life hiding who she was. In her place was a confident young woman. One who felt the need to act.

"I have to find Kara," she said as her parents physically blocked the door.

"You will do no such thing," her mother chided. "It's not safe out there."

"But there's something going on. She has to know."

"And she will," her mother said, nodding to her husband.

With a grim look on his face, he slid his most powerful konus onto his wrist, strapped a dagger to his hip, and pulled on his most inconspicuous cloak. His wife stepped aside, letting him out the door.

"Where's Father going?" Vee asked.

"Metzin owes your father," she said. "He has gone to call in that favor."

"Metzin? The old junker captain?"

Her mother allowed herself a little smile. "He was more than that, back in the day. If anyone can get word to Karasalia and her uncle, he can."

Vee hugged her mother tight and felt her anger drain away. "Thank you. Thank you so much."

"You are our daughter. We would do anything for you. And right now, that means helping you while keeping you safe. Now, come. It does us no good to stand at the door waiting. Metzin will do as requested. The rest is up to the fates."

CHAPTER FORTY-ONE

The hunt was on.

Nakk had sent his stolen Urvalin ship back to its hiding place once Kip and Dukaan had outfitted it with a basic comms unit so they could communicate without cluing in the enemy as to their whereabouts.

Once that was done, the group had flown a fair distance away to a lush bit of woodland where game of the large variety would be plentiful.

The four hunt leaders had each taken one of Nakk's people with them as they set out in different directions. North, south, east, and west, roughly, as if that had any meaning on this alien world. What mattered was they were moving fast and quiet in very mobile and adaptable teams. Each team leader wore a bone-conduction comms patch, and all were well armed for a hunt and ready to take down whatever they could find.

Once they had acquired enough animals they would return to Ara so she could feed and regain her strength. But as they made their way through the unfamiliar woods, Nakk and the others noted something very quickly. There were tracks here, and not the animal variety. It seemed they were not alone.

The question was whether the local survivors were friendly or not. Civilized or tribal. There was no time to be delicate about the matter and make tentative contact, however. Time was of the essence, and flying to another location might not yield any better results. So, it was here they would hunt. Charlie, Bawb, Hunze, and Nakk each led their partner in different directions. The hunt was underway.

The area was apparently more populated than expected, as each team soon came across more signs of inhabitants. One, however, discovered something a bit more.

Hunze held up her hand, signaling her hunting partner to stop. "People," she said in a whisper.

Even without his own translation patch, the man understood, nodding and remaining silent. Hunze hid her weapons under her clothing and motioned for him to do the same. She was on the hunt, but they were about to encounter a different kind of beast. The smart kind that walked on two legs. Given the circumstances, she decided their inevitable introduction should at least be made on her terms.

Without further ado, she stepped on a small branch, the noise alerting the people that someone was near. She talked in a normal voice, even though no one would understand her, presenting herself as a person, not an animal, to make sure no arrows would be mistakenly fired in her direction. Without her magic at her disposal, even with her Ghalian skills, an unseen arrow could have fatal consequences.

As they stepped into view, she saw that the people were the same race as Nakk and his group. If nothing else, at least her associate could hopefully communicate with them if it came down to it.

They were a hunting party, it seemed. Looking at the way the men stared at her, however, Hunze decided this was not a group they wanted to interact with any more than absolutely necessary.

She was used to people in her home galaxy seeing her as an object and not a person. A thing of value. A mere financial calculation in coin and the power her hair contained. But this was different. More primal. Unsavory. The men had taken note of her golden hair and fair complexion, no doubt, but not because she was an Ootaki.

She nodded once, a curt greeting, then motioned for her hunting partner to follow as they hurried off into the trees, hoping these miscreants would be smart enough not to follow.

"We have encountered the local tribe," she transmitted quietly. "A hunting party by the looks of them. They do not appear friendly."

Despite his utmost confidence in her martial abilities, Bawb's protective instinct flared to life.

"Where are you? I can be to you quickly."

"It is all right, love. We are moving past them."

"How many are there? We are not geared for battle. Your vespus blade is aboard the ship."

"We are hunting game, not rushing into combat," she said.

A slight twinge in her belly made her wince. Pregnancy, even early on, could be particularly uncomfortable for Ootaki. It seemed she had finally reached that point. She was glad her mate was not with her at that moment. Perceptive as he was, even with her masking the discomfort, he would see her distress and be concerned, and that wouldn't help anyone right now.

"You should abandon your efforts in that direction at once," Bawb said. "We have taken down a large herbivore already. And even if there is game where you are, taking it in a tribal group's territory could very likely lead to an entirely new conflict over the spoils of the hunt."

He was right, of course. And though they were both more than adequately trained in the deadly arts, avoiding needless conflict was as much a part of their skill set as the spilling of blood.

"Of course," she agreed. "We will adjust our path to loop back toward your trajectory. At the pace we have been maintaining, I would estimate we will join you in perhaps twenty minutes. Less if we ignore signs of game in the process."

"Do not stalk, dearest. We can find suitable game elsewhere. Move with haste."

"Very well, we will be with you short—"

A rustling in the brush on either side of them told Hunze that she and her companion had apparently not skirted past the hunting party as effectively as she had hoped. They had company, and if they were flanking them, that meant one thing. The two hunters were now their prey.

"They are coming for us," she quietly said over her comms.

Bawb felt his adrenaline spike, which for one as controlled as him was unusual indeed. "Run," he said. "Run now."

Hunze turned to her partner to relay their new plan when another sharp twinge hit her belly. It wouldn't have mattered, though, an arrow had already struck him in the neck, dropping him to the ground, where he lay twitching as he bled out. Hunze forced the pain to the back of her mind and focused on the sounds around her.

She was seriously regretting not bringing her vespus blade, even if it was the totally wrong weapon for hunting. But even without it, here was at least still a possibility she could defend herself from the incoming attack if she timed it right.

But the arrows never came.

She tensed her legs, ready to fight or flee when the enemy finally presented themselves, but again, her condition chose the most inopportune moment to make itself known, nearly doubling her over from the sharp pain. Ootaki pregnancy was a tricky thing at times, and its effects left Hunze uncharacteristically disadvantaged.

She realized this was the time for flight, not a fight, and it was at that moment she saw the men creeping toward her from the tree line. And they weren't coming at her with weapons drawn. They were coming with open hands.

They intended to capture her.

She forced the pain aside and turned to run, her feet shifting to propel her in her flight. Hunze only managed to take a half dozen steps before she ran headlong into a net, the trap dropping all around her and yanking her off her feet. Had she been in possession of her full abilities she would possibly have noted the two hiding in the trees above and taken them out with ease, but the situation had been fluid and her pain acute.

The tribesmen, it seemed, had driven her right into their trap, just as they would have done with whatever it was they were hunting. And now, Hunze was their prize.

Hunze's first instinct was to fight back. If she wasn't pregnant and was in possession of her magic she would lay waste to the lot of them without breaking a sweat. But she was incapacitated, trussed up, and vulnerable. And given her condition, the prospect of enduring a severe beating for attempting to flee was not in the cards for more than one reason. So she went limp, playing the victim. An overconfident enemy was quite often a soon-to-be-dead one.

Rough hands bound her and took her blades as well as those of her dead companion. She felt fortunate in this moment that she had foregone bringing a pulse weapon with on the hunt, favoring the clean and quiet way of the blade. She could have taken down many from a distance, but then the arrows *would* fly, regardless of how valued a prize she might be.

There was no gun, but she did possess one bit of technology on her person, and her captors had not a clue it was there. She had her bone-conduction comms patch, hidden beneath her hair.

"I am captured," she said quietly then went silent, making sure not to draw any attention to her comms.

The others would have heard. More importantly, *Bawb*

would have heard. And he would be coming. And heaven help her captors when he did.

CHAPTER FORTY-TWO

Bawb had been reluctant at first to accompany the game they had taken back to Ara. His woman was out there and she was in danger. But Charlie cared for Hunze as well. Perhaps not as much or as fiercely as Bawb, but she was still like family to him, and the Ghalian knew it.

Charlie hated that they had to fly back while Hunze was in harm's way, but there was no other choice.

"It sucks, but we have to. It is vital that Ara eats soon. And you need to clear your head before going after Hunze," he said. "As soon as we land we'll offload these things out of here, and Kip will haul ass back to the area she was taken. He's flying as fast as he can. We'll have this to Ara in under five minutes."

Bawb seemed calm, as usual, but Charlie knew the assassin well enough by now to feel the deadly undercurrent of rage even without any magic in play. Bawb was pissed. Angry to a degree that anyone in their right mind would be scared by. The five-minute flight was more than enough time for him to arm to the teeth. When he set out to recover his woman he would be loaded for bear.

Nakk rose from his seat and walked to his new comrade,

resting his hand on his shoulder in sympathy.

"I know this is a difficult moment for you," he said. "But she will not be harmed. The crews that have been stranded here the longest were mostly crewed by men—a tradition of a long-gone era. As such, she is undoubtedly seen as a valuable prize."

"Hunze is no one's prize," Bawb said coolly.

"I mean no offense. I am merely pointing out that she will be treated as something important and therefore will not be damaged. She is a woman in her prime child-bearing years."

Bawb's temper flared. "She is already *with* child," he growled. "*Mine.*"

Nakk saw the scary look in his eye and quickly backed away. Bawb would never harm an ally, even in a fit of pique, but Charlie could totally understand the man's reaction. Frankly, Bawb could be one seriously scary fucker at times. And as for the men who took Hunze? As enraged as Bawb was, Charlie almost felt sorry for them.

Almost.

"Hey, Nakk. How about you and Skohla help me and Dukaan get these animals out to Ara?"

"Of course. We are glad to help," he said, happy for an excuse to do something. Something a little bit farther away from the vengeful killer in their midst.

They moved quickly, hauling Ara's food out of the craft to the waiting Zomoki. It was more food than the lone Brixxax had provided, and for what was planned, she'd need every bite of it.

Ara blasted the carcasses with fire then waited for them to extinguish and cool sufficiently for her to eat. Having seen her devour flaming enemies like so much popcorn, Charlie found it a truly strange thing to observe. But she was hurt, and this was how it had to be. For now, at least. Once she was healed, all bets were off.

"Where was she heading, Kip?" Bawb asked as he dug into his cache of weapons. Knives, cudgels, and both his and Hunze's vespus blades quickly found themselves strapped to his body. He left his wand and konuses in their containers. Deadly anywhere else, they would do him no good here. But even without them, Bawb was arming himself for more than just battle. He was kitting up for outright slaughter.

Kip thought it best not to mention the sheer quantity of deadly implements he was planning to carry. It was a wise choice.

"She was moving at a roughly ninety-degree course to yours no more than two miles out," the AI said. "But then she ran, and that all changed pretty quick."

"I will require a starting point. A location from which to pick up her trail. I understand terrain may play a role, but the closer to her position the better."

"That's doable. I can try to get you a better pin-point based on her transmissions, but she's got her comms off for some reason."

The Ghalian nodded. "Preserving her tactical advantage, in all likelihood."

"But if she could give us intel—"

"To do so would likely give away that she was utilizing a piece of functional technology. So long as her captors do not realize she is in possession of the comms patch it shall remain an asset we may yet utilize when the time is right."

"I guess that makes sense. But what if—"

"Focus, Kip. Take me as close as you can to where you lost her signal. I shall take it from there."

Dukaan boarded and took his pilot's seat, ready for their mission, as expected. Then Skohla strode back aboard the ship, her hands freshly washed of the blood from the spoils of their hunt. But Bawb still smelled it on her. He could always sense death. And this woman was clearly familiar with it, and not just the animal variety. She was carrying a pulse pistol, he saw, as well as a few blades and a bow and quiver of arrows. The way she handled herself, he had little doubt she knew full well how to use them.

She then took a seat beside him. *That* Bawb was not expecting.

"What are you doing?"

"I am coming with you," she said plainly. "Only a fool rushes into the unknown against a numerically superior enemy alone."

Bawb chuckled. He was actually thankful for the moment of levity, albeit mostly internal.

"I am no fool, I assure you. And I work alone."

"Yes, your friend Charlie said as much."

"Then you know I appreciate your offer, but your services are not—"

"You didn't let me finish," Skohla said. "He told me, and then I informed him that while perhaps that was the case where you are from, *here* it is foolishness. Speed and efficiency is required, and two can achieve that better than one."

Bawb hesitated a moment, gauging this unusual woman. He was about to inform her that he was not some ordinary killer, but a Wampeh Ghalian, the most elite assassins in the galaxy, but as he studied her posturing, it was rather clear she was not planning on going anywhere.

"Very well," he said, accepting his unexpected partner. "But we move fast, and you do not question my methods."

Something about the way he said that was a little too intense, but she held her tongue. His woman had been taken, so a bit of leeway was to be given.

"As you wish," she replied.

"Then we go. Charlie, we are departing. Skohla is accompanying me," he transmitted.

"Okay," he replied. "I'm still helping Ara feed. You two be safe out there. I'm going to stay here with Ara until we've made our attempt with the lava. Once that happens I'll have Kip bring me to you as soon as possible."

"No, you should remain with the Wise One in this difficult time. She will need your support and protection more than I."

Charlie knew he was right, but it pained him letting his best friend go rushing headlong into harm's way on his own. But there was little choice in the matter.

"All right. Good hunting, amigo."

"Thank you, my friend."

Dukaan recognized his cue and lifted off without further ado, quickly skimming low as he and Kip carefully navigated the terrain as they rushed to Hunze's last trackable location. Bawb and Skohla would have to jump into the treetops and climb down if they wanted to be dropped right at the exact coordinates, but Bawb had decided that time was of the essence and the climb would be fast and relatively safe.

He and Skohla moved to the hatch and stood ready.

"Twenty seconds," Dukaan informed them.

Bawb cycled the inner airlock door and stepped through. Skohla followed close behind, fearless and ready. He had to admit, he admired her confidence, even if he would have preferred to do this alone. But perhaps his time fighting side by side with Hunze had made him grow to appreciate foregoing the normal Ghalian ways. Sometimes a partner *was* a good thing. He hoped this would prove to be one such occasion.

"Five seconds," Dukaan called out as the ship slowed and dropped into the treetops, bending the uppermost branches as it lowered to where the limbs were thick enough to support a man's weight. "We're here," Dukaan said.

Bawb opened the door and stepped out into the treetops without hesitation, expertly grabbing branches as he quickly made his way to the ground below. Skohla was right behind him, equally confident in her climbing, dropping down beside him silently a moment later.

Kip and Dukaan didn't wait, flying off the moment the pair were out of the hatch in case they were observed. A momentary pause would not give away their friends, but a lengthy hover most certainly would.

Bawb gestured to Skohla to follow. To his pleasure, she understood and nodded, silently falling in behind him, a soot-darkened blade already in her hand ready for action. Again, Bawb approved. Her time on this world had been well spent, it seemed, and a very particular skill set had been developed.

They walked quickly, staying low and to the shadows. Bawb pointed and signaled for her to flank to the left as they approached an area of disturbed soil. Skohla peeled off and moved around while Bawb made his way to the site of whatever had gone down.

He sniffed the air, straining his every sense as he listened and searched for any sign of hostiles. There was nothing. They were alone.

He knelt down at the most churned-up bit of ground, studying it intensely. Skohla made her way out of the trees just as he stood back up, a strand of golden hair in his fingers. Hair, and a drop of blood.

There had been a struggle, and Hunze had sustained a minor injury. Nothing serious judging by the lack of blood, but Bawb did not seem to care. He was no longer just a man on a mission. He was *pissed*.

"Orxalt is through the trees," Skohla said. "Slain by an arrow to the neck. Stripped of his weapons and clothing."

Bawb nodded once, the muscles in his jaw flexing as he scanned the ground with expert eyes. "This way," he said, a knife somehow appearing in his hand though Skohla hadn't even seen him reach for it.

He was *very* skilled, it seemed, and at that moment she was particularly glad he was on her side. She also realized perhaps she had been a bit hasty in her assumption he needed her help. But the die had been cast, and the game was afoot. And soon, it seemed inevitable blood would be shed.

CHAPTER FORTY-THREE

Charlie sat as close to his friend as he could endure while she ate her cooling meal. He'd have stayed right at her side under any other circumstances, but without his normal magical protections, he was simply not able to spend more than a few minutes so close to the lava flow.

When it came to getting right up close to it, only Ara, whose kind even without their magic still naturally thrived in hot environments, was able to stand the heat.

She downed her food while it was still smoldering, he noted. That was a good sign she was beginning to heal even without the Balamar waters or magic. It was not long ago at all that she could barely move, let alone eat.

Her scales had also seen the return of a tiny bit of their normal deep-red coloring where the burns had been less severe. Her wings were still suffering the effects of her flaming entry into the atmosphere, but even they were regaining some of their strength and elasticity.

Even so, at this rate she would still not be ready to combat the Urvalin, let alone achieve even proper flight. Not for weeks, if not months. And while they had avoided detection for now, the odds of staying unseen that long for a creature her size were slim.

They truly had no choice but the dangerous, molten lava option, and they both knew it.

Ara lay her head down and napped for a short while after finishing the last of her meal, her belly not necessarily full, but her hunger sated enough for the time being. Charlie simply sat and watched over his friend, sweating as he protected the protector as she had done for him on so many occasions.

At long last Ara's golden eyes fluttered open. She slowly sat up and stretched, careful not to put too much tension on her damaged bits in the process. She was moving cautiously, but it was clear the meal had given her at least a modicum of the energy she so desperately needed.

She locked eyes with Charlie and nodded. "I am ready."

There was no point in lengthy discussions at this point. They had gone over the plan and what might go wrong enough times already. The most fluid portion of the lava had been selected, as it felt like it had a stronger connection to the molten ore swirling deep within the planet's core below. Charlie would coat her talon with the Balamar waters then step back, leaving Ara space to settle in to endure the significant pain this was sure to cause.

She might not burn if this worked as he hoped, but it would hurt like hell no matter what. They both rose to get into position, but when she moved, Charlie could see her discomfort. He winced at his friend's clear pain. Even with their magical connection blocked, there was the faintest of connections between them trying to reconnect. The finest thread of an unraveled sweater that might be lost if tugged too hard.

Ara flinched as the lava sputtered nearby as she settled down onto her haunches.

"You sure about this?" he asked, stepping close beside her, the metal container ready to be deployed.

Ara's mass partially blocked the blast furnace heat from the flow, but nothing could reduce it to a level he could tolerate for long.

"I am sure," she said with resolve. "Our situation demands nothing less. And the worst that may happen is I burn off an appendage in the process. Given our predicament, I do not think that is the worst of possible outcomes should this fail to work."

"Okay, then. Here goes. Which talon?"

Ara extended her massive left index digit. "I am right side-dominant," she said. "I may as well risk the left."

Charlie unsealed the small cylinder. It was already growing hot from being so close to the lava flow, but while normal water would evaporate in a flash, the Balamar waters still possessed their unique properties even in this place.

They had no idea why, but Ara had posited it might be because so many centuries of condensation as well as cross-galaxy transit had imbued it with an even stronger inner power. And sealed within the magically protected cylinder when they crossed the portal, that vessel had likely been the only thing that kept it from losing its potency.

Of course, it was all conjecture, but so long as it worked that was all that mattered.

Charlie carefully dripped out the first bit of the waters onto Ara's talon, his hand cupped beneath to ensure they would not waste a single precious drop. It hurt this close to the lava, and he would almost certainly suffer a minor burn from it, but there was no other way. It had to be close. With the possibility that the waters would lose power as soon as they were poured, the window between application and submersion could not be longer than a few seconds for all they knew.

The water absorbed into the cracked talon immediately, her body sucking it in like a parched wanderer at a limpid pool upon exiting an arid desert. Ara shuddered from the sudden feeling of strength in the farthest end of her limb. It was working.

Charlie's hands were beginning to blister, but he held the cylinder steady. They had this one chance only.

A lone drop slid from Ara's talon and spattered onto his skin. The blistering ceased at once, and the pain faded away. He still felt the heat, but it was nowhere near as intense as before. He looked at Ara's healing talon with renewed hope. This plan might actually work.

Charlie poured more of the waters onto her talon, working his way up from the tip, then back down again. But when the container was nearly empty he stopped, reserving a few drops for his friend to at least ease her pain just in case this didn't work.

"That's it," he said. "Are you ready?"

"As I will ever be," she replied.

Charlie looked at her talon, healed and pristine. But the healing had covered far less than he had hoped. Ara was simply too big, and her body had absorbed too much of the waters to address her other ailments as he applied it.

Of course, he realized. It made sense her body would try to heal everything at once. He just hoped the talon had absorbed enough for itself to survive the lava.

"Step clear, Charlie," she said, and for just a moment, Charlie thought he could feel their silent bond struggling to connect.

"Good luck," he said as he backed away to a safe distance. It was still hot where he was, but there was no way he would leave her out there on her own. Not now.

Ara took a deep breath then extended her talon out toward the lava. Her body's natural instinct to avoid damage kicked in fiercely, nearly causing her to jerk it back away from the danger, but she forced it to steady. With one last pause she submerged it up to the knuckle in one fluid motion.

Charlie felt her shock of pain even as faintly connected as

they were. It was as if his hand had suddenly burst aflame while being hit repeatedly with a white-hot baseball bat.

With spikes.

And acid.

In short, it was unbridled agony. Charlie swayed on his feet from the sudden flash of sensation but stayed upright, steadying himself as he watched his friend power through the pain. If it felt this bad to him, he could only imagine how much this must be hurting the Zomoki.

Ara twitched slightly but otherwise held herself steady, forcing herself to override her self-preservation instinct and keep her talon submerged in the flaming lava. But the digit had thus far remained intact. It hadn't burned off into a charred stump. The Balamar waters, it appeared, were working.

The pain, however, was far worse than she'd ever anticipated.

"Ara, do you want to stop?" Charlie called out. It felt as if their silent connection was strengthening, albeit slowly.

"No," she said through clenched teeth. "I can sense the power."

"But the pain. The damage. The effort it requires to overcome it—"

"I am taking in more power than I am losing," she said. "But only just."

Charlie's own power gave a little tickle deep inside. His power was drawn from his bond with Ara, and a tiny fraction had returned. It wasn't much, but it was enough for him to cast the smallest of spells to at least minimize the pain he was sharing with the Zomoki.

The pain lessened but did not cease. However, he could feel Ara doing the same, protecting herself as best she could. But her mass was so much greater, she did not have enough strength to achieve nearly the same degree as he had.

Ara focused hard, then abruptly passed out, her head sliding to the ground. Her talon remained in the lava, but when Charlie moved to try to help pull it free what he saw was amazing. Her talon had not only remained intact. It was healing. And more than that, the healing was slowly spreading up her limb. It was incredibly slow, but there was no mistaking what he saw. The plan was working. All they needed now was time.

He hoped they had it.

CHAPTER FORTY-FOUR

Bawb was also connected with Charlie and Ara, though not nearly as powerfully as that pair's bond. Even so, as he trekked he felt the slightest twinge of resurgent power as the Zomoki slowly began to absorb the planet's deeply hidden magic.

They were reconnecting, although when it would kick in for real he had no idea.

He noted the sensation but put it aside. It was something to perhaps call upon at a later time if it became potent enough to be of use, but not now.

For the moment the assassin was on a very specific mission, and *nothing* would distract him from his goal. He wove through the trees, never slowing, never tiring. A man driven by something deeper than a mere mission.

Skohla had been following closely behind him as he relentlessly pursued the men who had taken his mate, and she was impressed. More than impressed, actually. Frankly, she was rather in awe of Bawb's skills.

It was really saying something, considering she and Nakk had been on this world for a considerable length of time, in which she felt she and her comrades had become quite talented at hunting and tracking prey. They were good. Better than good, even. They were excellent.

This man, however, moved with a speed not even their finest scout could match, picking up on the faintest signs of their quarry without breaking stride. Even knowing there were traces of their prey to be seen, courtesy of the Ghalian leading the way, Skohla could only detect perhaps half of the markings, instead hurrying along after Bawb as he had already shifted course to follow the next clue.

This strange pale man was clearly a far better tracker than any of her people could ever hope to be, even without the benefit of Allpower, or the thing his kind called magic. And she suspected that this was quite possibly the lesser of his skills, judging by how fluidly he moved through the trees, like a silent apex predator on the hunt.

She was considering what his other abilities might be when Bawb abruptly slowed his pace, sniffing the air, his head slightly cocked to one side as he listened to what sounded like nothing to Skohla. But when he drew one of the blue metal swords strapped across his back, she took his cue without question, pulling the pistol they had provided her and holding it ready.

Bawb heard the sound of her holster and turned and looked at her, shaking his head, holding a lone finger to his lips. They had to be silent, and pulse weapon fire, while not exactly cacophonous, was certainly still significantly louder than a blade. Skohla signaled her understanding, holstered the gun, and drew her longest knife. Bawb nodded his approval and continued on, hunching slightly lower to stay below the brush line.

They had progressed onward for only a minute or so when Skohla's ears finally heard what it was the Ghalian had picked up on. Voices. Faint. Perhaps four or five of them in the distance. Males by the sound of it.

Bawb was already moving faster, closing the distance with

the stealth of a deadly animal, his footfall silent as they made their way through the trees and brush. There was no need to ask what the plan was. His intentions were abundantly clear. He was going to engage.

They moved toward a rocky incline and padded up to an elevated position to better see what they were approaching. He may have been on a mission, but even driven as he was, he was not so reckless as to rush headlong into a fight without first gathering a bit of intel. He crouched down and observed the men no more than fifty meters away. His nose twitched as he calculated his next steps.

They were cleaning the carcass of some sort of mid-sized game animal, its entrails pulled free already as they prepared it for transport to their camp. Skohla suddenly realized the man had smelled the blood before he heard their voices. And for reasons that she couldn't put her finger on, that made her a little uneasy.

Bawb pointed to the far end of their worksite then took off in the other direction. Apparently, he wanted her to flank them from the other side. Skohla moved at once as fast as she could without making any noise. Fortunately, the men were loud enough to mask her steps even if she wasn't completely silent.

She reached her position a few minutes later and crouched down. She was close enough to smell the stink of the hunters' sweat, but there was no sign of Bawb. Or so she thought.

A pale blur streaked from the trees, fists, knees, elbows, and the pommel of his deadly sword bowling the men over before they knew what hit them. He was incredibly fast, and the way his blows landed, it was almost as if he were a machine rather than a person.

The precision derived from decades of practice and repetition was paying off, for as the saying went, the more one sweats in training, the less one bleeds in combat. At the moment, the only blood spilled was that of the hunters.

Skohla emerged from her hiding place and surveyed the fallen men. Bawb had already trussed their hands and feet and was binding them to individual trees set a little distance apart. An interrogation setup, from the looks of it. And it seemed he had more than a little experience in this sort of thing. Still, she wasn't sure if this group would actually be of any use, and time was an issue when following a trail. Dally too long and it might go cold.

"We have no way of knowing if these men were traveling with those who took your woman. Clearly, these men are merely hunters and do not have her in their possession," she said. "And I doubt the four of them would have been her match, from what I gather of her skills. What is your plan?"

"They do not have her, no," he replied. "But they may have seen her. And they likely know where a prisoner of her sort would be taken."

Skohla considered his words. "Perhaps, but how can we tell?"

"We shall *ask* them."

Skohla couldn't tell if he was joking or serious. With this one it was sometimes hard to say.

"And you believe they will tell us if they have?" she asked.

"Oh, I do," Bawb said.

He smiled wide, and at that moment Skohla found herself wondering how she had never noticed his fangs before. It was a smile, yes, but the expression behind it was anything but friendly.

CHAPTER FORTY-FIVE

The shifting colors of Amazara's Malooki had cycled through a range of unhappy tones during the ride to town, darkening when they passed closer to the strange invaders before finally settling on a deep purple with occasional flashes of gray. Something was in the air. Something not normal. And it was spooking the massive animals with every passing minute.

They had taken an extremely roundabout path into town, avoiding the more traveled areas where the intruders appeared to have set down. It took a very long time, and the initial look of the situation was disconcerting to say the least.

Visla Kwinnius might not have been a very powerful visla, but he was not one to roll over when his people were threatened. For the unexpected ships to have not already been booted off the planet meant something serious was afoot.

It became far more clear just what that was when the riders drew closer to town.

"Do you feel that?" Korbin asked.

Even a non-power user would have noticed the crackle of magic in the air. Magic, and something else. Something very few people in this galaxy had ever experienced. There was tech at work as well. And judging by the sounds of fighting and the surge in power in the air, it seemed Visla Kwinnius was in the thick of it.

"The visla," Amazara said. "He must be defending the town."

Kara's control over her power slipped a moment at the thought of battle, but with so much magic in the air, the odds of her being noticed were slim to none. Korbin sensed her, of course, but didn't comment. Soon enough, he feared, she would be using her full unshielded power anyway.

"The central square," he said. "The main fighting feels like it is coming from there."

"It makes sense," Amazara noted. "The visla would have selected a visible location from which to make a stand."

"But if he's still fighting them, and if they're using technology weapons against him as well, it's only a matter of time before his magic fails him."

They all knew Korbin was right, just as they knew what their next steps would be, like it or not. The three of them were going to get their hands dirty, it seemed. Amazara pointed to a side avenue that would take them around the combat for the moment, giving them an opportunity to gauge the strengths, weaknesses, and assets the invaders possessed.

Their magic was a strange flavor, for certain. Some element of it just felt wrong, but none of them could put their finger on why. The tech was also a bit unusual, but the basic gist was something they had experienced plenty before. Pulse weaponry of some sort, though not quite like their friends from Earth utilized. And the poor visla was doing all he could to stop it.

They rounded the corner to the plaza and saw Visla Kwinnius surrounded by three groups of attackers. At the center of each group stood what was clearly a caster, their magical glow visible even in the heat of battle. Flanking each of them were foot soldiers armed with pulse rifles. All were bombarding the visla without pause.

Korbin realized at once that only the massive konus on the visla's wrist was keeping him from being overpowered. Clearly, he had the device set to automatically deploy pre-cast defensive spells should he need them. It was likely a simple habit he'd undertaken every day out of habit as so many older casters did. Pouring their power into a konus for later use, often with a specific spell in mind.

No one would dream of taking on a visla, though, and for that reason alone the konus had the time to accumulate quite a depth of defensive spells. And it was a good thing. The three attackers were casting in an overlapping manner, never pausing to give poor Kwinnius a moment's respite.

"His shielding spells will fail soon," Korbin observed. "We cannot wait."

A look of alarm flashed across Kara's face. "But we don't know how to fight them. They're using magic and technology."

"And?" Korbin replied. "If you will recall, so have I, and on more than one occasion."

"With your ship, maybe. But this is different."

"Not so different as you might think. Now, you stay put, and don't let them see you. He pulled Amazara close. "Keep her safe. I'll take care of this."

Without further ado he cast a series of powerful defensive spells, spacing them around himself at varying distances, the layering done in such a manner as to prevent any single attack from activating more than one defense. If he was on the offensive he would certainly employ that tactic to wear down his adversary's spells, and he was not about to underestimate this enemy.

Ensconced in spells, he strode out into the battlefield. It was his first clear look at the attack underway, and it wasn't a pretty one. The visla was actually injured, a few small blooms of red on his tunic showing where some sort of shrapnel attack had managed to pierce his defenses. Korbin could sense his power wavering, both from the injuries as well as the sheer effort of maintaining this degree of casting for so long.

The attackers, however, were fresh and strong, their overlapping attacks providing each of them the opportunity to recover between spells without lessening the intensity of the barrage. He had to admit, it was an admirable offensive technique. And coupled with pulse weapons it was a force to be reckoned with.

But Korbin wasn't just another visla. Perhaps not as strong as his friend Visla Palmarian, but he was a particularly powerful caster in his own right. And more than that, he had fought more than his share of unconventional battles and come out victorious.

"Hey! Leave him alone," he shouted as he strode into the open.

Amazingly, they actually did seem to ease their attack, but more from the pause required to assess this new threat than anything else. The apparent leader of this group focused their attention on the newcomer.

"Who the hell are you?" he asked with an overconfident sneer.

"Me? I'm the man telling you to leave this place."

"Leave?" the caster said with a laugh.

"I won't ask again."

There was something about this man's voice that made it clear he was going to be trouble. And for this lot, the best way to handle trouble was quickly and decisively. Without warning the caster hurled a furious barrage of spells at Korbin while his accompanying guards opened up with their pulse rifles simultaneously.

Korbin batted his magic aside with ease. It felt very wrong when it contacted his own casting, but that wasn't the important part. What was, was that he was stronger than this man. *Much* stronger.

The other two realized this and began casting at him as well, splitting their offense between the two vislas. Kwinnius almost fell over from the renewed assault, but Korbin redirected some defensive spells to help him recover. On a purely magical level, it seemed this duo could probably win.

The pulse blasts, however, proved more difficult to stop, and more than one blew through multiple layers of magical defenses. This was a different type of pulse weapon than he'd dealt with before it seemed, and Korbin actually felt a pang of fear as another barrage smashed through his spells.

The tech was different enough from what he was accustomed to so as to make his casting only partially effective. This was a problem, and it was only getting worse.

Korbin dove aside as another volley zeroed in on his position. It was a good thing he did. The spells he'd cast shattered under the intensity of the attack. Had he still been standing there, he would have taken the brunt of it.

Now it was becoming a game of tech vs magic whack-a-mole, with Korbin on his heels. He had struck the casters hard, knocking one of them out of the fight, which allowed Visla Kwinnius to regain a footing for retaliation. But these pulse weapons had evened the playing field, and quickly at that. Korbin was on the run.

He was just about to launch another desperate counterattack to buy himself the time to cast more protective spells when a pinpoint wave of magic flashed past him. But it wasn't just magic, he realized. There was also something within. It was a spell all right, but one propelling a dagger. A dagger that embedded itself hilt-deep in the forehead of the nearest Urvalin gunner.

Korbin glanced behind himself. What he saw was both surprising, yet a little bit expected. Kara had stepped out from hiding to join him, Vee's braid wrapped around her body, her own power crackling slightly across her violet skin, her orange hair flowing menacingly in a breeze that wasn't there. Kara, it seemed, had begun to believe in herself.

"Leave my uncle alone!" she growled, casting as she threw daggers with both hands.

It wasn't something she had practiced yet, attacking two targets at once, but caught up in the flow of things, it just came to her naturally and without a second thought. Both blades flew true, one taking down a pulse rifle gunner, the other deflected away from a caster, but only barely. Her power was *strong*, and she was no longer holding back.

Korbin and Visla Kwinnius quickly layered their spells atop one another, joining forces as Karasalia distracted the enemy with her combined practical and magical attack. This time it was too much. With one of the three alien casters down, the tide had turned. A tsunami of power came crashing down upon caster and pulse rifle gunner alike, throwing them aside like rag dolls.

The enemy still fought back, and hard at that, emptying their rifles of charge as they desperately tried to overcome the sudden surge in magic bearing down on them. But Kara and Korbin were powerful. Exceptionally so, in fact. And when Visla Kwinnius had regained his equilibrium, they had simply proven too much to overcome.

But the Urvalin would not surrender. It wasn't their way. They would fight to the death, and in short order that wish was granted. The Urvalin lay dead and dying on the ground, their spells and weapons fallen silent.

"What sort of attackers were those?" the visla asked as Amazara rushed from cover to help tend his wounds. "That was not like anything I've ever fought before. Magic, but something else. Something *horrible*."

"I've encountered it before," Korbin said. "A thing called technology. Weaponry and more that functions without the aid of magic."

"Without it? How is that possible?"

"Those who use it often ask the same of our use of power," Korbin replied. "If you'll excuse me, Zara will tend to your wounds."

Korbin walked over to Kara. She was staring at the dead body the strange alien caster. The one with her dagger still embedded in its head. He bent down and pried it free, wiping it clean on the dead man's clothes before handing it back to his niece.

"Impressive casting," he said. "Your diligence with your lessons paid off. You may have very well saved my life just now. Thank you."

Kara nodded, but she was clearly thinking about something else. The dead body at her feet, for one.

"You had no choice, Kara," Korbin said. "It was us or them."

"What?"

"The man you killed."

"Oh, him," she said, apparently not as distraught as he'd first believed. "I'm fine with that. It's the way they fought that has me concerned."

"Me as well. But tell me, what aspect is it that troubles you?"

"It's just not something you ever see. Not here, not even in the other galaxy. I mean, tech and magic combined? Only a few of us and our friends even know how to do such a thing, but to these people it seemed perfectly normal. As if it was something that comes naturally to them."

"Yes, it is very disconcerting," Korbin agreed. "And if they have pulse weaponry, it begs the question, is there a traitor in our ranks? One sharing technology with the enemy?"

Kara thought long and hard. "I doubt it," she finally said. "But it can't be ruled out. There's only one thing to do now."

"Just one?"

"Yeah. We need to warn everyone we can," Kara said. "And we need to find my father."

CHAPTER FORTY-SIX

"What do you mean, attacking *everyone*?" Daisy asked, pacing the chamber with nervous energy.

"Cool your jets, Daze. They're just relaying information," Sarah said quietly inside her head. *"And while they may like you, it's generally not a great idea to go pissing off the leaders of a clan of elite assassins."*

Gee, thanks, Sis. Great pep talk, Daisy silently replied. *And they're an 'Order,' not a clan.*

"Bite me."

Sarah was right, though. The Wampeh Ghalian had broken millennia of tradition after the war against Malalia Maktan and her Council of Twenty lackeys, establishing formal ties with counterparts in the newly discovered galaxy.

They all had a common foe and had fought together on an intergalactic scale. Not to mention they had discovered that the Geist, one of their most storied masters of the order, was not only miraculously alive, but had bonded with an Ootaki, of all things. And, incredibly, she now possessed the knowledge and skills of her mate.

It was unheard of, putting it lightly, but one thing was clear. The world had changed. The galaxy had. And it was time the Wampeh Ghalian evolved yet again.

Daisy had intrigued them. A woman who carried the mind of another within her? It should have been impossible, even in their realm of magic. And Daisy was brash and mouthy at times, no doubt, but her skill and drive were undeniable. In addition, her ship was a truly impressive craft, and they were fiercely protective of one another.

Then there was the blade she called Stabby. Her sword was a marvel, drinking in power just like the Ghalian did. Not a thinking consciousness exactly, but definitely a living, feeling thing. A blade that had more than a bit of bloodlust.

The assassins couldn't help but like him, though *they*, at least, kept their proclivities under wraps.

Master Zilara waited until Daisy had calmed herself before responding.

"These unknown forces have appeared out of nowhere, attacking strategic points across the galaxy. So far, they have succeeded in every attempt we have been informed of."

"So, you're saying someone has just been invading the whole damn galaxy and no one saw it coming? Come on! You don't mobilize those kinds of resources without someone somewhere noticing."

"What did we just say about pissing off the deadly assassins?"

"Sorry, I just find it hard to believe a massive attack on this scale could somehow sneak up on everyone."

Zilara's expression had not changed to one of anger. In fact, if anything, she seemed slightly amused.

"You certainly are full of fire, Daisy. While it is not the Ghalian way, I nevertheless respect your passion. You clearly possess a great deal of concern for your friends and allies."

"Who are all on the other side of the portal," Daisy noted.

"And I'll do whatever it takes to make sure the fighting stays on this side."

"A reasonable desire," Zilara replied. "And to that end, an opportunity has presented itself. We have identified a portion of the enemy force that will be cut off from their other ships for a short while when the system they've attacked experiences a solar eclipse."

"How does an eclipse block them? It's just sunlight."

"Ah, but in our galaxy, quite often a sun emits far more than just light, Daisy. And when an eclipse occurs, the distortion of power can sometimes have a disruptive effect on all things within the solar system. In this instance, the invaders' unusual variety of magic as well as their technology-based communications systems. If you check with your ship friend I am sure she will confirm what I have told you."

Daisy spoke into her comms knowing Freya had been listening the entire time. "Hey, Freya, is what Zilara said accurate?"

"I'd need to know the specific system, but from what I've seen in this galaxy so far, it does track with the way the suns affect everything anywhere near them. I mean, there's some really cool stuff spewing out of those things. Like the one that Rika soaked up? Black suns are really, really out there in terms of radiation signatures. And then—"

"Okay, we get the picture," Daisy chuckled. "What you're saying is it's a possibility."

"Solar flares wreak havoc, so it makes sense something smaller like an eclipse could do what she said."

Daisy wondered exactly what trick the assassin had up her sleeve. That the little grin on the woman's face was carefully placed for her benefit, she was sure.

"*I was thinking the same thing,*" Sarah said, reading her sister's mind quite literally.

"So, you said there was some kind of opportunity?"

Zilara's grin widened. "Oh, there is, indeed. And our people have already been tracking the forces on the ground. If we act quickly, we can take them without the body of their fleet knowing until it is far too late."

"And then we get some answers," Daisy said.

"Precisely. So, my new friend, are you up for a little excursion?"

Daisy wasn't a bloodthirsty sort, but this sort of action was right up her alley.

"Ready?" she said. "I was born ready."

"Cheesy, Daze."

Oh, blow me, Sarah.

Freya had no problem tying in with the Ghalian shimmer ships and their jump spells. She'd been playing with magic for almost a year now, and her nanites were becoming quite adept at pulling the energy from the galaxy for her to direct. And in this moment that meant a warp-jump to the Vaxxal system.

The blue sun threw off a considerable amount of power normally, and the brief eclipse when one of the nearer planets crossed between it and their destination would provide them nearly twenty minutes in which to operate. A little less than a half hour to incapacitate an unknown number of hostiles, take the survivors prisoner, and vanish without a trace.

Daisy was positively giddy looking forward to it.

The team consisted of Daisy and Freya and five Ghalian assassins, including Master Zilara herself. Only a year prior having Ghalian working in tandem, let alone a group of five, would have been unheard of. They were solo operators, and for good reason.

That is, until faced with not just another contract, but an actual enemy threatening the order itself. That was different.

That called for drastic measures. And so the Ghalian engaged in force in the conflict with Visla Dominus.

In the aftermath it was clear that the old ways were outdated. They would work in teams if needed from now on, and it looked as though the Wampeh Ghalian might never be able to go back to their impartial ways. And not all of them thought that was a bad thing.

Having a cause beyond coin and code actually felt good. And now they were partnered with a strange woman, her dead-not-dead sister, and their living ship. Times were changing indeed.

They exited their warp-jump a full two hours before the eclipse was to occur. Plenty of time for the shimmer-cloaked ships and the strange nanite-skinned craft to sneak down to the nearby planet's surface near the enemy occupiers. And more than enough time for the masters of subterfuge and disguise to take up their positions as scouted out by their formidable network of spies.

"We will focus on this one group," Zilara said to her team as they looked at the topographical map of the city. "You each have your deployment area. Be stealthy, leave no trace. And above all, take the highest ranking alive. We are here for information, and the dead tell no tales."

The pale killers nodded and vanished in an instant. Daisy, however, was not a Ghalian, nor did she possess a shimmer cloak or any other useful magic. But what she lacked in this galaxy's toys, she made up for with her own unique skill set.

"I'll cause a distraction here," she said, jabbing the map with her finger. "I figure while they're looking for me, it'll give you and your people an easier time snatching the leadership."

"And if you should be forced to fight?" Zilara asked.

"Oh, I'm planning on it," Daisy said with a grin.

"Good. I am looking forward to seeing what you and your pointed friend are capable of."

With that Zilara turned and disappeared in the blink of an eye.

"I really need to learn how to do that."

Sarah laughed. "*You really do. Now get moving. When the sun blacks out, all hell's going to break loose.*"

"Yep," Daisy said with a grin. "And we're gonna be the cause of it."

CHAPTER FORTY-SEVEN

The denizens of the entire planet had grown accustomed to the difficulties their system's sun could pose during eclipses and solar flares, and as such were largely shutting down their businesses and getting off the streets well in advance of the pending event. The newcomers, however, appeared to be lacking in that one particularly valuable bit of intel.

It genuinely seemed like they had no idea what was coming.

Darkness would descend upon the planet, yes, but also five of the deadliest killers the galaxy had ever seen, along with their somewhat unpredictable new ally. It promised to be a most interesting engagement, indeed.

The Ghalian had deployed to their target sites silently and quickly. Daisy was also relatively quiet, but nowhere near that of the Ghalian. And that worked to her advantage at the moment, for she was to be the distraction. And what could be more distracting than a woman from another galaxy casually strolling through the recently occupied streets? A woman seemingly talking to herself while brandishing a strange, white sword, no less.

Yes, Daisy would serve their purpose wonderfully.

The Urvalin troops patrolling the region were following the pattern the Ghalian spies had previously observed, so getting herself to the right place to catch their attention and lead them to the kill box shouldn't be too difficult.

Of course, the goal wasn't an actual kill box this time, but more of a catch-the-boss box. And now it was Daisy's turn to shine.

"*First group at ten o'clock,*" Sarah said.

"Yep, I see 'em."

"Hey, you!" the forwardmost soldier called out.

Daisy pretended not to hear or understand, though the translation spell bound to the konus she wore these days worked just fine. Rather than react, she continued to walk, carefully changing course to plot an intercept of group number two.

Hopefully, by the time the groups caught up with her all five patrols would have been picked off by the waiting Ghalian. And if not, well, then she would have to get creative. But the clock was ticking.

Daisy turned down the next street, the course memorized in the planning stages. She knew somewhere close by an assassin was shadowing her and the men she was leading into this trap, even if she couldn't see them. The comforting warmth of Stabby in her hand put her even more at ease. *He* was tangible, and she was very well acquainted with what he could do.

"*We need to move faster,*" Sarah said.

"I know, but if I go too fast we might shake the ones we already have following us," she replied. "These guys are kinda crap at this whole chasing people down thing."

Regardless, she picked up her pace. Sarah was right, they were on a tight schedule, and even if the invaders weren't exactly cooperating in terms of their speed of pursuit, she had to draw the attention of the other groups nearby, and fast. Daisy hustled into a wide intersection, where she saw another group passing at the far end of the road.

She had to find some way to get their attention, but they just weren't looking her way, so Daisy decided to do the one thing she could think of. She started yelling profanities as she kicked over a vendor's stall, left empty in anticipation of the solar event.

That got their attention, and with a growing number moving toward her position, it seemed clear they were in communication with one another, either by tech or magic. She really didn't care which so long as they followed.

"*Hurry, Daze.*"

"I *am* hurrying."

"*Faster, then.*"

She heard footsteps rushing her way from two adjacent streets. It was looking like her ploy had worked. Perhaps a little too well.

"I think that's all of them. At least I hope so. Too many footsteps not to be."

"*That would mean their groups met up already.*"

"Looks that way."

"*The eclipse should kick off any minute now,*" Sarah said.

"Yeah, I know. Freya, what's the countdown?"

"One minute seven seconds, give or take."

"Give or take? You're a state-of-the art super AI, what do you mean give or take?"

"I didn't want to get into the whole millisecond thing, so I rounded."

"Jesus, Freya, seriously?" Daisy chuckled.

"What? You said it. I'm a super awesome AI. Thinking in terms of mere seconds is kind of a step down for me."

"*Both of you, focus. Shit's about to get real,*" Sarah interjected. "*You'd better put on your game face, Daze. Our friends are growing curious, and we've still got a full minute before the eclipse.*"

"Well, shit."

She didn't have the chance to pontificate any further on the interesting twist in their situation. She had been afraid of being late, but instead was a bit early. Early, and severely outnumbered.

"You, there! Drop that strange sword. Your Urvalin conquerors have banned all forms of weapons, magical and otherwise. Your sword is contraband. You must hand it over at once!"

Daisy looked at the growing mass of troops and estimated there were forty at the minimum. No trouble once the Ghalian stepped in, but it was looking like she was on her own until things got dark.

Well, it looks like Stabby's going to get to have a little fun after all, she mused.

The man who had demanded she disarm strode to her, overconfident in his support, especially against just one lone woman armed with nothing more than a sword. He reached out to grab the blade, again, cocky in his surety his armored gauntlet could grip the blade with no ill effect.

He didn't know Stabby.

His digits hit the ground before he had even felt a thing. Stabby wasn't just sharp, he make a surgeon's scalpel seem dull. Before the man could react, Daisy twitched her wrist, sending the blade in a small arc. A limb fell to the ground, and now it was the Urvalin who was disarmed.

Literally.

Stabby sucked the power from the man's blood greedily. He was excited now. These weren't powerful casters, but they nevertheless contained some degree of magic, and it was a flavor he hadn't tasted before. His lust for more of it was palpable.

Sarah, linked as she was with her sister, felt the draw from the blade. "*Oh, shit.*"

She didn't get to say more as combat awareness took priority. Troops rushed in from all sides at the location of their comrade's injury, casting stun spells to take this foul woman prisoner and teach her what happens to those who oppose the Urvalin. But

Stabby was already full of magic, and now that he knew what manner the Urvalin possessed, blocking their lower level attacks was child's play for him.

"On your left!"

I see them.

Daisy spun into action as the men moved on her, startling them with not only her unexpected martial skills, but also the unparalleled sharpness of her sword, slicing off legs and arms with singular purpose as she tore into the closing ranks.

"We need them alive, Sis," Sarah pointed out.

Why do you think I'm only taking their arms and legs? Daisy shot back as she delivered a spinning kick to the jaw of the nearest attacker.

In twenty seconds at least a dozen men lay bleeding on the ground, and yet the strange woman had somehow managed to avoid all of their magical attacks. The Urvalin attackers paused, giving her a moment of space to catch her breath as they reached for conventional pulse weapons instead of magical ones. *Those* Stabby couldn't do much about, but just then the sky began to darken.

"What the *hell* are you?" the nearest man growled as the sun dimmed.

Daisy grinned, and it was not a pretty sight.

"Not the worst you'll be facing today, I'm afraid," she replied.

Her unsettling smile was the last thing the man saw before the lights went out.

Daisy quickly escaped the area when the Ghalian set to work. She had focused all of the aggressors' attention on her, leaving the rear of their ranks ripe for the picking. Or picking off, as the case happened to be. By the time the eclipse ended Daisy was aboard Freya and headed for their rendezvous point, a small planet a short warp away.

As for the Urvalin, several dozen of their men wound up slain, and many mysteriously went missing entirely that day, though no one knew how or why. When Daisy walked into the Ghalian holding facility they had given her directions to, an unexpected sight met her eyes.

Urvalin soldiers, most of them higher ranking and even a few officers by the look of their uniforms. And all but one of them dead on the ground. One, however, was still drawing breath, albeit through a bloody mouth.

"What the hell happened? I thought we were supposed to question them?" she blurted.

Master Zilara merely shrugged. The kindly, deadly old woman known as Master Farmatta, however, smiled that disconcerting pointy-toothed grin. For someone who looked, for all intents and purposes, like a sweet old lady, it was more than a little unsettling.

"This was not our doing, dear," she said.

"What are you talking about? That guy didn't bust his teeth out on his own."

"*Tone, Daisy.*"

Screw tone. I just put my ass on the line to capture them, and these guys just off them? Daisy silently replied.

Zilara walked over to the nearest body and rolled him over. His eyes were wide open, a slight frothing at his mouth.

"You see, Daisy, he killed himself rather than talk. All of them did."

Daisy felt her stomach flip. "Hang on. You're saying they committed suicide?"

"Yes."

"*All* of them? But that's crazy. No one does that. Not even seasoned soldiers."

"Indeed. And that is why we had to go to somewhat extreme measures to ensure our last captive did not follow in his comrades' footsteps."

"So you beat the shit out of him?"

"No, that is not the Ghalian way."

"But look at his—"

"But we *did* remove all of his teeth to ensure he could not bite down on a poisoned tooth. We need information, after all. And we also numbed his tongue until we secured a powerful control collar around his neck. One cannot cast a suicide spell if one cannot speak, after all, and the collar will prevent him from casting once sensation returns."

Daisy saw their attackers in a whole new light after that bit of information. Ordinary people didn't kill themselves. Not for their military, and certainly not lower-level troops. But these were not elite officers they'd captured. They had selected men who were more than just foot soldiers, but these were not the kind to drink the Kool-Aid and die for a cause. At least, not normally.

"You think you'll be able to get answers out of him?" she asked. "If they're willing to die, I don't know what good torture would be."

This time it was Farmatta's turn to shrug. Zilara, however, began to smile.

"Oh, trust me, Daisy. We have our ways."

CHAPTER FORTY-EIGHT

"I'm sorry, say that again?"

Daisy was pacing. *Angry* pacing. The master assassin wasn't afraid of her, not by a long shot, but she was, however, glad that Daisy was not a power user. A temper like that could be a liability when internal magic was involved.

Zilara rose from her seat and walked to the nearby table upon which a frosted pitcher of sorgus nectar sat and casually poured herself a glass. She slowly sipped it, enjoying the complex flavors while also allowing, or rather, forcing, Daisy to slow her roll and calm down, at least a little.

"What I said was our operatives have reported that these invaders, these *Urvalin* as they are called, have made simultaneous coordinated attacks at power centers across the galaxy."

"Not that part. The *other* part."

"Ah, you mean what we extracted from our unwilling guest," the pale killer replied, glancing over at the bloody mess of a man strapped to a pole across the room.

It was something that Daisy found interesting in the brief moment where she transitioned from her initial concern that full-on torture was underway to an almost tangible bloodlust of her own. As soon as the man—Gallus was his name, they learned surprisingly easily once the experts had begun working on him—revealed the other part of their plan, Daisy felt red-hot rage flare up in her belly.

The Urvalin, it seemed, had plans beyond this galaxy. Aspirations of domination on a multi-galactic level. These cheeky bastards were going to attack Daisy's home as well. Everyone she loved was at risk, and Daisy's mama bear instincts reared their head in an instant.

Unfortunately, the prisoner had a moment of clarity and realized what he'd done. His own loose lips were informing the enemy of their plans, and he was trapped without access to poison, weapons, or suicide spells. Limited as he was, he took the opportunity a brief interlude in his questioning provided to smash his own head into the pole he was tied to.

The Ghalian were actually surprised, which was not something that happened often. Surprised, and grudgingly respectful of the man's willpower.

To crack his own head hard enough to cause cerebral hemorrhage was no simple task, and even most Ghalian would be hard pressed to accomplish the feat without losing consciousness before its success. These Urvalin were proving a most difficult adversary indeed.

Daisy glared at the dead man, wishing he was still alive so she could kill him herself. "Yeah, what he said," she growled. "My kid's back home. Vince. Hell, my entire extended family."

"And they are safe," Zilara replied. "The monitoring ships stationed at the portal have reported that no Urvalin have come anywhere near it. And believe me, Daisy, they would have seen. Your people are still safe."

Daisy felt the slightest sense of relief, but it was minuscule and short lived. What if they made a run for the portal? What if they regrouped and tried to cross over?

"*Joshua and Marty won't let anything happen to Arlo,*" Sarah said. "*And you know Zed and Sid have got a rapid response team stationed on Dark Side ready to fight if anything comes through the portal.*"

I know. But I still don't like it. And what about Vince? Or Rip and the others?

"*I'm confident that corporeal me is more than up to looking out for our family,*" Sarah replied. "*And Cal also has a seriously robust defensive fleet ready to launch at a moment's notice if need be.*"

Daisy cut her silent discussion short and focused her attention on the perpetually calm woman idly studying the corpse who had proven such a difficult prisoner.

"Okay, let's say no one makes it past the portal guardians. What does that mean for *this* galaxy? From what you've said, the Council of Twenty seems to have been a primary target, and many of its surviving members have already gone missing in the midst of the Urvalin attack."

"Those who did not perish, yes."

"Are you hearing what you're saying? These guys are killing off the Council of Twenty. Supposedly the biggest, baddest wizard dudes in your galaxy."

"As an organization, yes, they are formidable," Zilara said. "And indeed some of the members are extraordinarily powerful. But it is the strength of their ranks as a group that has always afforded the Council such dominance. And you saw what happened when Malalia Maktan took over under the guise of Visla Dominus. The Council was fractured, and only those loyal to her escaped destruction."

"Right. Sure. But that's my point. These powerful casters are being picked off."

"Which, as I said, is far easier when they are not acting as a group but rather individually. Ever since Visla Dominus fell, the remaining Council members have found themselves in a difficult situation, diminished in numbers and reputation and quite unable to thrive as they had in prior times."

Daisy pondered the woman's words a long moment. *Tactics, Daze,* she reminded herself. *Planning over emotion.* She was right on that count. This may have started out as a chess game, but it had evolved into some sort of multi-dimensional mayhem that even Joshua in all his tactical might would have found challenging.

But the Ghalian had a vast spy network and could provide intel that reached all corners of the galaxy. The question was, what were they to do with that information?

"Freya? Your take on this?" Daisy asked.

"Me? Uh, I don't want to step on toes here," the AI replied.

Zilara cracked a little grin. That this thinking, living ship was worried about impropriety and feelings was a novelty that she did not think would get old any time soon.

"Please, I would also like to hear your thoughts," she said.

"Well, in that case," Freya said. "First off, I don't know that they're actually trying to *take out* the Council's casters. I mean, yeah, some fight back hard and make it so there's no choice. But if they're also trying to take them without a struggle, I'd think they're maybe gathering up potential ammo for their cause."

"An enslaved visla? I suppose it could be possible," Zilara said. "But it would take an exceptional amount of power to do so."

"Which, if they're so well established that they can attack this many targets at once, I'd assume they have," Freya replied. "Anyway, second, I think that maybe things aren't going quite as the Urvalin had expected. War's funny like that, right, Daisy?"

"You know it, kiddo."

"And if they're finding a fly in that ointment, their plans for further conquest might be on hold. If these guys are as good at this as it seems, I'd think they'd also know not to spread themselves thin on multiple fronts until they'd achieved a solid foothold."

"So, the Council really aren't a threat," Daisy said. "At least for the time being. Hell, it sounds like they're as much a target as anyone from what you're saying. Maybe even more so seeing as they're power users."

"You are correct. And Freya's assessment is accurate. In addition to those killed, the Urvalin do appear to be rounding up any with the strength to disrupt their plans, including those not in the Council of Twenty."

Daisy mulled over what the two had said. Pieces were falling into place. "It makes sense," she said. "And that means these bastards are vulnerable."

"And powerful," Freya said.

Zilara nodded her agreement. "We have forces of our own, but if these Urvalin have done their homework about the capabilities of the wielders of power, as we believe they have, I think we will need reinforcements. The kind an enemy would not expect the Ghalian to align themselves with. Those who have no affiliation and a reputation to match."

"Oh, I think I know just who to call," Daisy said. "Unconventional, but I've seen 'em in action."

"You're not thinking of who I think you're thinking of, are you? Please tell me you're not," Sarah groaned inside her head.

Daisy chuckled. *You know it, Sis.* She leveled an amused gaze on the Ghalian. "I know a guy. We just have to find him."

Olosnah and Tym were flying in an unlikely group formation, combating wave after wave of these new intruders' ships. Marban had flown the *Coratta* to the other galaxy, but the rest of his trusted pirate associates had remained behind, using their recently captured Council ships on all manner of adventures rich in Council coin and booty.

It had turned out to be a profitable venture, and, as they were arriving at their targets in what were very clearly Council ships, it had been a relatively incident-free one. A little subterfuge saved a lot of bloodshed.

That is, until a new adversary appeared out of nowhere and began targeting the Council vessels in their flotilla.

It was unheard of. Specifically going after only the most powerful and retribution-happy people in the galaxy? These newcomers were mad. Mad and startlingly effective. Of course, the pirate band had spun off and engaged from all sides, swarming the Urvalin ships, but these craft were devilishly difficult to fight. *These* ships used technology as well as magic.

Fortunately, Olo and his associates had fought in the intergalactic conflict against Visla Dominus and were now well acquainted with quite a few of the marvelous tricks of technology the other galaxy had to offer. They had also already encountered these newcomers and were instrumental in organizing this hastily gathered fleet to combat them. As such, they proved a much harder target than the Urvalin had expected.

These were not your ordinary Council ships and attending vessels, it seemed. These were crafty.

"Aim for the rear of their ships," Olo skreed to his counterparts from his smaller smuggling craft, which also happened to be outfitted with some lovely tech-based firepower, courtesy of Cal and the appreciative people of Earth. "The tech portion uses a thing called engines."

"Engaging," Tym replied, sending the sleek attack ship he'd swapped out of his smuggling ship for into a spiral as he cast a wicked barrage of impact spells at the nearest of the enemy vessels.

The other pirate craft followed the cue and made their attempts on the Urvalin ships, but they were armed only with their magical weaponry, tied into the massive konuses bonded to their vessels. It was an impressive array, no doubt, but these new adversaries seemed more than prepared to counter their spells.

"It's not working!" one of the other captains transmitted. "They're blocking our attacks!"

"Mine too," another chimed in.

Only Olo and Tym seemed to have any luck at all, but they were merely two little ships taking on a small fleet of far larger ones. They were working on some sort of solution to the problem when the Urvalin abruptly shifted to a new formation. But rather than focusing on all of the craft buzzing around them, they directed all of their firepower on the Council ships.

It only took a moment for it to become clear this was not a normal engagement to the death. These ships with their strange magic and even stranger technology were fighting, as expected, but were also incapacitating the Council ships, not aiming to destroy them. This wasn't a regular battle. This was something else entirely.

Olo read the writing on the wall immediately, his years of self-preservation in the smuggling game blazing to life and screaming at him to flee. It was a message he reluctantly shared with his comrades.

"They're after the Council ships," he informed them. "Those were our most powerful assets. There's no way we can take them on and win without those."

"But the others need us," Tym said. "We can't just turn and—"

"Go," the captain of one of their embattled Council ships interrupted. "We will do what we can to buy the rest of you time to escape."

It was a somber moment, but these were all men and women of action, and they knew the cards they'd been dealt were a bad hand. The newcomers were already moving in on the immobilized vessels, and they simply could not reach their friends to help them abandon their ships. There was only one option. Leave. Leave and live to fight another day.

"We will avenge you," Olo said as he powered his warp drive rather than his drookonus, just in case. "Whatever it takes."

Without any further attempts on the Urvalin armada, the rest of the pirate fleet jumped away to their safe rendezvous spot, reluctantly leaving their comrades behind. One day, and hopefully soon, they would honor that pledge. One day these bastards would pay in blood.

CHAPTER FORTY-NINE

Korbin had flown as fast as he could from the carnage he and his friends had left bleeding out on the ground. He felt bad leaving Visla Kwinnius to deal with the messy aftermath, but at least now that he knew what he was up against, and with a little time to prepare for any pending retaliation, he hopefully stood a better chance.

They had jumped and warped, utilizing both modes of travel and taking a circuitous path to confuse any potential trackers. Arriving as quickly as they could at their destination was of vital importance, but so, too, was being smart about it no matter how much they wanted to just take the direct route.

Prudence dictated they watch their step, and with where they were heading, it was the only choice. They weren't just going to any old magic user's world. They were heading to Kara's home. They were heading back to Palmar.

Karasalia Palmarian's father was not just a ruler. He was a power user of exceptional strength. With Visla Palmarian fighting with them, Korbin, Kara, and Amazara would have the power on their side to become pretty much impervious to whatever attacks these invaders might throw at them. But as they set down quietly at the outskirts of town, it was clear something was amiss.

There was an odd feel in the air, for one. Something not quite right. As they raced through the city, careful to hide Kara's orange hair beneath a hooded cloak, it became apparent what it was.

"My home," Kara gasped.

Korbin and Amazara could clearly see the problem, though to any not familiar with the Palmarian estate it might take a bit of observation to note the issue.

Parked atop one of the floating gardens beside the estate tower was an alien ship, and three more were located at ground level. Visla Palmarian's city had been occupied.

"How?" Kara wondered. "He's too strong for them."

"I don't know," Korbin said, scanning the streets around them. "But it's clear you can't go home."

"But my father—"

Amazara shook her head. "He's right, Kara. Your home is now occupied territory. It's not safe for you here."

Korbin watched the comings and goings of the Urvalin forces with great interest. They were in control of the building, and the city as well. And that meant that these invaders had almost certainly taken the entire planet in the process. How they'd managed to best the mighty Visla Palmarian wasn't the question. More pressing at the moment was finding out their ultimate purpose.

The visla would have been a very, very difficult opponent, but the guards around the Palmarian estate seemed relaxed, casual even. Mere occupiers. It was then Korbin realized they were not looking for Karasalia. The visla had been captured, and they did not need any leverage over him. As such, his daughter was of no interest to them. And they likely didn't know about her blossoming power.

"Amazara is right," he said. "It is not safe here. But I believe you were not a target of this attack."

"But if they're looking to stop the Palmarian line, I'm his only heir. And my power has grown so much in the last year."

"That is true, you have developed into a very formidable caster. But your training has taken place in secrecy. Away from here. Far from prying eyes who know your face. Here, for all these people know, you're still just the same girl as before. Weak compared to her father, and not a threat."

"It wasn't intentional. I just think people who flaunt their power are kind of lame."

"*Lame*?" Korbin said. "You have adopted some amusing slang habits, but I think the amount of time you spend with Arlo and Ripley so far from home may also have played a role."

Amazara nodded her agreement. "It's a good thing you did not choose to flaunt your newfound skills upon your return to this galaxy. That has surely kept you from scrutiny."

"But what about you, Uncle Korbin? You're one of the strongest casters I've ever seen."

"Only those who knew me in my youth would remember that. I've lived a life out of the public eye, far away from all of that, for a reason, Kara. And it has afforded me a great deal of peace. And, much like yourself, I think I may have been spared scrutiny because of it. These people are looking for power, and we are not of interest to them."

Kara's eyes widened. "Vee! She's not coloring her hair anymore. If they know she's an Ootaki—"

"But she is shorn," Amazara noted. "And *you* possess that powerful braid."

Kara didn't have to be reminded. She had taken it from its storage bin and wrapped it around her body for this journey. Vee had made an enormous gift to her, giving her hair to her best friend in an act of friendship and love. She hadn't known if it would work in that distant galaxy, but fortune had smiled upon them.

"We've gotta get Vee," Kara said.

Korbin and Amazara knew there would be no dissuading her, so they simply followed close as she changed course for her best friend's home. Kara did, however, take side streets and alleyways to avoid scrutiny. She may have been in a hurry, but she was no fool.

Vee's door opened just a crack when she knocked, then opened wider to allow the visitors entry. Kara immediately found herself wrapped up in a strong embrace.

"You got the message!" Vee blurted with relief.

"What message?"

"We sent Captain Metzin to tell you what was happening. He didn't find you?"

"No, we never saw him," Kara said.

"But you're here."

"Just good fortune, I guess. But listen, you need to come with us. Uncle Korbin says these people are looking for power users. And you're an Ootaki."

"A *shorn* Ootaki," Vee corrected.

"Yeah, whatever. You know what I mean."

Vee's parents watched the discussion with concern.

"You're safe here with us, Visanya," her mother said. "We will keep you from harm."

Korbin gave a sympathetic look to the woman. He understood what it was to protect your loved ones. But he knew that if the enemy came for her, there would be little her parents could do about it.

"I'm sure you would," he said. "But if they should discover what your daughter is now capable of, I fear she would become a target. However, if Visanya was to leave this place, go far from where they might find her, I'm sure you would agree she would then be in an even safer environment. And you have my word, we will not allow any harm to come to her."

The woman looked at her husband, torn. But they were not only protective, they were also smart people. They were not warriors, and they had no power to speak of. They knew Korbin was right. And more than that, they knew just how powerful he actually was. Vee would be safer with him, moving quickly and quietly, and they had little doubt he would protect her with his life.

Vee's mother pulled her in tight, her husband joining her in a family embrace. "Be safe, Visanya. We love you."

"I love you guys too," Vee replied, her eyes glistening. She turned to Korbin. "I just need to grab a few things."

"Of course. Get what you need."

Five minutes later they were on the streets, quickly and stealthily making their way back to the outskirts where Korbin's ship was tucked away. There were Urvalin troops on patrol, as well as periodic guard outposts utilizing both magical sensing spells as well as technological scanning apparatus. It was disconcerting to say the least.

"What are they doing?" Vee asked.

"Looking for anyone with power, I think," Korbin replied. "And scanning for advanced technological devices, such as Daisy's ship."

"They'll never see Freya," Kara said with the utmost confidence. "Even with sensing spells it won't work. She's incorporated magic into herself, thanks to those nanite thingies. From what Ripley told me, she can blend in and evade detection from both tech and magic now, and easily at that." A tiny flicker of power flashed across her body at the happy thought.

Korbin's lips curled up slightly. "Amazing. I never get tired of that ship. Truly a marvel."

A small group of Urvalin turned their way as they tucked

into a small alley. Korbin glanced back. They were being followed.

"I fear we may have been detected. Quickly, this way."

They turned down the next street. It was a narrow roadway and not often frequented. The sound of rushing footsteps behind them told them that would change momentarily.

"You, there! Stop!" an Urvalin trooper called out.

"What's the problem?" Korbin asked, holding back all traces of power.

"Identification."

"Gentlemen, we are merely out for a pleasant stroll. I don't see why—"

A spell formed around the Urvalin, ready to be deployed. A painful one, from what they could tell.

"I said show me your identification."

"Of course," Korbin said. "I do not see the need for this—"

A violent stun spell flew from his lips, slamming the invader into the wall. Kara's own power flared strong, tossing two of the others to the ground. Amazara was in motion the moment the first spell was cast, binding the downed men as soon as they'd hit the cobblestones.

The remaining guard attempted to call out for help, but Vee stepped forward and cast the spell Kara had taught her, though she had no idea if she could actually make it work in a moment of duress.

The Urvalin was violently flipped backward, the force spell pushing only the top half of his body, forcing him off his feet in a most brutal way. He crumpled to the ground in a heap.

Kara, Amazara, and Korbin looked at her with amused disbelief.

"Vee, that was amazing!" Kara squealed. "Did you see what you just did?"

"I-I actually did it."

Korbin looked at the man folded on the ground and adjusted

his body to a more natural-looking position while the girls were distracted.

"Very nicely done, Visanya. We will work on your aim once we are clear of this place."

"I didn't kill him, did I?" she asked, her joy tempered.

Korbin flashed the quickest of looks at Amazara. She crouched over the dead man and began binding his hands, slipping a gag in his mouth.

"He's fine, dear," she said. "You did well. Now hurry along, we need to get clear of this place."

Korbin heaved the unconscious men into an alcove and set them as though they were sleeping, courtesy of a discarded alcohol bottle. His subterfuge wouldn't stand up to any real scrutiny, but most tended to avoid looking directly at scenes like this. With any luck they would be long gone before the trussed-up troops were noted.

They rushed away from the scene as quickly as was feasible without raising attention and managed to make good time back to Korbin's ship. Once aboard, *then* they could all let out a sigh of relief. They weren't out of the woods just yet, but they were well on their way.

"We need to connect with the others," Amazara said. "Contact our network on both sides of the portal."

"Agreed," Korbin said. "And Charlie and Ara most certainly need to be made aware of this situation. Rika as well. We will need the strongest casters we can muster."

CHAPTER FIFTY

Earth seemed tranquil and quiet when viewed from space, a bright blue-green marble orbiting a particularly powerful sun of rather novel energy. Hanging there in the inky black, it looked beautiful from a distance. Peaceful. No sign of conflict or turmoil of any kind.

That was about to change.

The Urvalin command ship had been watching from a safe distance far beyond the edge of the solar system. The images and data were all being relayed through an ingenious Allpower and tech-driven network of small booster relays disguised as mere floating space rocks. Shielded and operating with both magic and electronics not familiar to this world, the odds of being detected were minimal. And that was the point.

A tall Urvalin officer strode to the casting podium and bowed his head.

"All of our operatives have been contacted, Torgus. The network is fully operational."

The commander eased his connection with the leaders of the other two command ships to better focus on what his right hand had to say.

"The sleeper agents have all received their first bonus payment?" he asked, still maintaining his link with Prin and Fraxxis, sharing their power as well as communicating his situation update in real time.

"They have, sir. Both here on Earth, as well as the forces on Taangaar. They are in place and ready to execute their mission goals."

"And the others? The alliance's lesser partners, and those of minimal individual potency?"

"The non-allied races we had determined to be potentially problematic have been invaded, rolled over, and occupied, all without a word of warning escaping their atmospheres. As for those in close alliance with the humans, the Kathiri will pose no significant problem. Our agents have managed to infiltrate the heart of their command hierarchy and await the go signal. As for the Urok, while they do not allow outsiders into their inner ranks, they have permitted an exchange of staff as part of their truce."

"Still not willing to form an alliance even if it is to their benefit?"

"They are an *extremely* stubborn people."

"And rather hostile as well," Torgus added.

"Indeed. While their leadership conceded defeat at the hands of the human and Chithiid alliance, they refused to do more than that. Now they merely prowl and sulk in their part of the galaxy."

"Childish fools," Torgus said with a grin. "How *wonderful*. We will use that to our fullest advantage. A few carefully placed rumors in the right paranoid ears should keep them quite busy while we handle the real threats to our plans."

"Of course, sir. All are ready and await your command."

Torgus rolled his shoulders and called upon the deep magic welling within not only himself, but his two connected partners. A triumvirate of Allpower, drawing from their shared strength as well as the stored Allpower within their ships. At long last, it was time.

"Begin."

The signal was sent in a flash, received on Earth and Taangaar's surfaces by the traitorous natives who were so willing to sell out their own kind for a mere pittance. They would receive coin, yes, but also the promise of being in the Urvalin's good graces.

Almost like familiars were for their vampiric lords and ladies, these underlings desired more than just wealth. They wanted to be made part of the elite. And who knew? Perhaps when Earth had been conquered, if he felt particularly generous, a few might actually be allowed to fulfill that dream. But first they would have to prove their worth.

At the moment Torgun's command was received, many hundreds of traitors set to work on their tasks while the forward attack wings warped into close range of their targets.

Between Earth and Taangaar, the Urvalin had managed to sway enough to their cause to identify and efficiently target all crucial systems as well as those individuals who might be the most problematic when it came to their defense.

It was how they had known to lure Charlie and his closest friends and allies into their clever trap. Anything less than an overt show of massive magical power would have only warranted a warship. But they needed to take the most powerful casters in this galaxy out of the equation. And their plan had worked perfectly.

Or, so they thought.

At that very moment one caster was warp-jumping her way back to Earth, and when she got there, the Urvalin would have one *very* angry magic user to deal with, not to mention her powerful dragon friend.

But what Torgus didn't know would not slow down his attack. Rather, he pushed his Allpower outward, triggering the myriad spells he and the others had been preparing for years and years, quietly awaiting their activation.

This world was a technologically advanced one, as was the Chithiid homeworld of Taangaar, so all energy would be devoted to negating this adversary's use of it. Once that had been achieved, they could regroup and complete the invasion using their Allpower, overwhelming the pathetic, non-magical beings who inhabited both worlds.

"Someone is attempting to take control of transit hubs and communications," Cal transmitted to Sid and Zed.

Something was wrong. One of the moles set to work implementing hardware overrides in one of his command nodes, but Cal had noticed immediately. Unfortunately, he was not alone in his worries.

"We've got dozens of attack ships warping into the area," Zed replied. "Came out of nowhere. I've got my teams on it, but this is a full-scale assault."

"Sid, are you secure at Dark Side base?"

"So far, yes. Ground cannons are aimed skyward," the AI replied. "I'm observing and strategizing with Joshua. Once we know the enemy's nature we'll be better able to—"

The comms connection went silent, but not abruptly as in a catastrophic attack, but with effort, as though it was being intentionally jammed.

"Cal, you hear that?" Zed asked. "Sid was blocked. I'm reading some really strange power signatures. Several ships already made atmosphere, more are now in orbit."

"I've seen. I'm tracking them, but something is interfering with my systems."

"There has to be a breach somewhere. Be prepared to fall back to your—"

Zed's signal cut out as well, as the fighters under his command engaged the enemy all across the solar system. He didn't know it, but the defensive ships stationed at Taangaar were experiencing the same thing as Earth and were doing their best to respond.

Meanwhile, Urvalin shock troops were rocketing toward the surface of both worlds, acting on intel from their spies, ready to take out the remaining high-value targets.

One of those ships landed on the shores of Malibu, its teams dispersing quickly and quietly, armed to the teeth and ready to engage this unusual pocket of likely resistance. The one called Daisy lived here, as did her sister. Two very formidable adversaries, they had been informed. And, of course, there were also the nearby magic users.

The assassin and his woman had been taken out of the equation by Torgus's trap, but Charlie's mate had unexpectedly stayed behind. The informant relayed that she was pregnant, so she'd likely not be much of a problem.

Nevertheless, he had heard talks of her possessing some sort of powered artifact, though none had been able to discern what it was. They did know, however, that Charlie possessed a hidden vault of very powerful magical weapons. The spy didn't know where, exactly—no one did, as that would have negated the whole 'secret cache' element of it—but they did know his home could be a difficult target, even with a pregnant woman as its only occupant.

Three teams fanned out, the largest and most well-armed heading toward Charlie and Leila's place while the other two diverted in the direction of Daisy and Sarah's homes. The trails were frequented only by the families that lived in the area, so the Urvalin forces progressed quickly and without fear of any unexpected resistance.

That is, until the unexpected paid them a visit.

Snarling fangs belonging to a pair of utterly terrifying beasts were the last thing two of the rear troops saw. Their teammates spun at the sound, shocked by the sight of the massive animals hauling the thrashing men into the bushes.

It was their distraction that allowed the huge alien killer lurking just ahead to tear through three more of them before they realized they had inadvertently walked right into one of the wildcards they'd heard about.

The last of the Ra'az Hok. He roamed the hills and beaches, living a quiet life. That is, until his new home and friends found themselves in harm's way.

Grundsch was spending a lot of time around Leila's home as he watched over her while Charlie was away, but he did take the animals out for short walks a few times a day. They would hunt and play, their konus collars allowing him to keep better track of them and help them find and corner their prey. But now they had a different sort of game afoot, and it was a bloody one.

The three of them had spent so much time hunting together that this was as natural as breathing at this point. The poor Urvalin didn't know what hit them.

One managed to cast a deadly spell at Grundsch before the animals returned. The Allpower flew true, a killing spell of extraordinary strength cast for an enemy of extraordinary size. But Grundsch had learned plenty about magical fighting not so long ago and grabbed one of the man's teammates, pulling him in front of himself while casting a defensive spell from the powerful konus Charlie had gifted him.

The Ra'az wasn't really what you'd call a magic-using kind of man, preferring to fight with his hands and familiar technology. But Charlie had convinced him that even someone as big and strong as he was should learn at least a few key spells. And given his size, the defensive one he'd been taught was a doozy.

The Urvalin's spell smashed into his comrade, breaking his body into a bloody pulp before the weakened remains of the magic deflected off of the unexpected defense. The man's eyes widened with the realization that this Ra'az, incredibly, was using magic. That wasn't supposed to happen. He would have to contact his—

Baloo's jaws snapped shut around his neck, crushing the lightweight armor that would have protected him from lesser attacks. The remaining men spun, but Bahnjoh leapt at them from behind, having circled around while his friend distracted them. A deadlier hunting pair would be hard to find, and with Grundsch laying waste to those his four-legged friends had not yet dispatched, the fight was over before a warning could even be sent to their commander, let alone the other teams.

At the same time, all across the globe, Urvalin troops were engaging strategic targets on the ground, sometimes with human and Chithiid traitors taking up arms alongside them. It wasn't all-out warfare, but rather a series of strategic, pinpoint strikes unleashed at once.

Leila was resting outside on a recliner, her pale green skin soaking up the sun's warming rays, when the large group sent to capture her stormed into her yard, pulse weapons aimed and magic ready to be cast.

"You are the one called Leila," their team leader said, his weapon ready to discharge as he looked her over. She was unarmed, though. No konus, no firearm. Not even jewelry, save the lone pendant around her neck.

Leila sat upright, adrenaline spiking. These men looked a lot like her unsavory Tslavar cousins, but there was something different to them. More sinister.

"What are you doing in my yard? Get out of here!"

"You will—"

"I said, get out! You are trespassing," she said, lurching to her feet, a slight angry tremor in her voice. "And you can't go startling people like that. I'm pregnant."

The man was taken aback at this woman's reaction. There was a tiny hint of fear, yes, but that seemed to be more from surprise than actual worry. But she was Charlie's mate. She was leverage. One way or another, he would bring her to his commander.

"You will come with us," he said. "Resist us and your unborn child will suffer the consequences."

Now Leila was alarmed, he noted, smiling to himself with malevolent amusement. This was one of the perks of his job, taking pleasure in the little things. And if it got rough, all the better.

The flare of green from the stone hanging around her neck seemed like a trick of the light at first, just a ray of sun caught in the stone's facet. But it was growing brighter, and quickly.

Leila gave him an almost pitying look.

"I warned you."

For what it was worth, the men realized something very bad was about to happen and they tried to fire on the woman responsible before it was too late.

It already was.

All their attack did was hasten their horrible demise. It wasn't Leila's doing, though. Not exactly. It was her Magus stone going full-on mama bear, all of its incredible power currently focused on one thing alone. Until her child was born, it would defend her at all costs. She might not have been able to direct its magic, but so long as it rested around her neck, nothing would touch her.

The men were already reduced to piles of steaming meat when Grundsch came storming out of the brush.

"Stop!" she called out.

He saw the slowly dimming stone and the carnage it had caused and froze in place. He had already been warned previously that he should move a little slower around her these days, just in case.

"Is it safe to approach?" he asked as Baloo and Bahnjoh padded out of the tree line.

Baloo walked right up to her, the stone knowing that this fur baby was as much her child as the one she was carrying. Anyone else, however, would have to tread more carefully.

Interestingly, the stone quickly fell silent. Far faster than she'd expected.

"I think it knows you're a friend, Grundsch. It has judged you a worthy companion."

The Ra'az nodded once, stoic, but she could see emotion coursing just beneath his rugged surface. For one who had been reviled by pretty much everyone on the planet to have come so far and even be accepted by the purest, most unbiased judge of character he knew of, was quite a testament to who he had become.

"There may be more of them," he said, a faint crack in his voice. "We must go."

"But this is my home."

"And that is why they knew to find you here. Whatever is happening, you were not an unintentional target."

Leila knew he was right, but it made no sense. But one thing she'd learned from her time with Charlie, sometimes you had to act, not ask.

"I'll get my bag," she said, hurrying into the house to get the backpack she'd planned on taking to the hospital when it was time to give birth. "Grab that large pack over by the fireplace," she added.

"More clothing?"

Leila grinned. "Weapons. Lots of them. I'll be right back."

Grundsch looked in the bag and smiled. Of course Charlie had left her with ample defenses. Not just ample, some of the biggest toys in his arsenal were in there. Little did he know she wouldn't need them. Leila was protected, but for Grundsch and any others they might join up with, they would come in quite handy.

Leila dressed quickly and met him outside three minutes later. She may have been pregnant, and a former queen, no less, but high-maintenance was not in her wheelhouse.

"We should go to Sarah and Finn's place," she said, heading for the well-used trail.

"Not that way. There are likely additional forces on those trails. From what I can tell they landed on the beach."

"So?"

"So, we should take the inland route," he replied, slinging the bag over one shoulder then taking the one in her hands and throwing it over the other. "Bahnjoh, out front," he said. "Baloo, the rear."

The two animals knew what he wanted even without their konus collars and set out to form a razor-fanged perimeter.

"Now, we go," Grundsch said. "Stay close."

Leila took one final look at her home then turned to follow him, wondering exactly where fate would lead them.

CHAPTER FIFTY-ONE

Finnegan loved to cook. Like, he *really* loved to cook. Anyone who knew him would say that, aside from his family, it was his true love. He'd made do with limited resources flying through deep space, relying on whatever the food replicator in the galley had been outfitted to generate for the journey. But once the Great War had ended and he and Sarah selected an expansive estate to settle down on, he had set to work making upgrades.

The kitchen, while already impressive, was brought up to Finn's demanding standards, and all of their friends were now the beneficiaries of his culinary largess. He cooked, he baked, he barbecued and fried. The kitchen was his happy place.

Four Urvalin troops now lay dead on the tile floor of that happy place, pools of blood slowly spreading from the many high-end chef's knives they had found themselves unexpectedly sheathing in their chests and necks.

Finn didn't just use knives to cook. He was also a very experienced knife fighter, as those foolish enough to threaten his family had just learned the hard way.

Jovial, friendly Finn was also a deadly killer. His wife, however, was even more dangerous.

Sarah's nanite arm shifted form into a wicked blade the moment the first of the Urvalin came crashing into their living room. She leapt to her feet backwards over the couch and removed his head clean from his body before the magical stun blasts from his associates had even begun to fire. The war may have been long done, but her killer instincts were as sharp as ever.

She took a shot to the chest, the force blasting her across the room and into the wall. It would have killed a normal person, but Sarah was anything but normal. The swarm of nanites that had saved her life and rebuilt the damaged parts of her body also made her exceptionally resilient. Nevertheless, the impact stunned her a moment, and that gave the Urvalin the time they needed to storm into the house.

The floor plan of that area was open, and Finn was fixing them a charcuterie board in the nearby kitchen. Had the man who just blasted his wife with a magical attack survived more than a few seconds, he'd have likely wondered why the knife jutting from his neck smelled like cheese and hot salsiccia, but he was dead on his feet before he hit the floor.

Ripley and Arlo had been up in the nearby hills when the Urvalin ship had come in hot, and they'd hurried back to see what their parents had heard, if anything. Ripley's house was closest, so that was their first stop. What they found was a chaotic free-for-all.

"Mom!" Ripley shouted as she saw Sarah slowly climbing to her feet.

The cousins did the opposite of what most do in dangerous situations. They grabbed whatever was near that could be used as a weapon and ran straight toward the conflict, rather than away from it. They were teenagers, yes, but they'd also played important roles in the recent war, and they were anything but children.

Also, given who their parents were, they had learned the use of all sorts of weapons since their childhood and could improvise with just about anything, though in this case, there were plenty of actual ones in both of their households.

"Kids, stay back!" Finn shouted as he wrestled with a particularly difficult goon.

Ripley was having none of that. "Mom's hurt!"

"She'll be fine. Look out!"

Rip and Arlo knew better than to question his warning, both spinning away and casting defensive spells from the konuses they'd been habitually wearing since they learned about magic actually being real.

The spells they cast were advanced ones, but then, their teachers were some of the toughest fighters in either galaxy and didn't waste time on training wheels. Not for this pair.

The Urvalin saw his magical attack fail and immediately switched to his pulse pistol, knowing the weapon would be more effective than magic against that defense. Fortunately, the cousins had also learned to blend their spells and had thought to protect themselves against conventional arms as well. Regardless, the blasts still shook them, knocking them to the ground.

A growling yell echoed in the chaos, and even in the middle of an attack all heads turned.

Sarah was on her feet, her damaged areas rebuilding before their eyes as her nanites did their work. But she wasn't waiting for full healing. Someone had just tried to hurt her baby, and that, more than anything in the world sent Sarah into a rage.

"Oh, shit," Finn said, knowing what was coming next.

He pushed himself free of his opponent and moved clear. The man he'd been fighting was confused at the strange tactic. Finn had been gaining the advantage, albeit slowly. But now he gave it up so easily? It made no sense. The logic became clear when he found his body pierced over and over by Sarah's nanite arm, which was shifting state from a stabbing implement to a slicing one to a cudgel as fast as it could.

She was a whirling dervish of death and destruction, and no one was safe from her attack. The remaining troops realized they were in way over their heads and tried to fall back, but it was far, far too late.

By the time she finally slowed down, all that remained of them was a pile of corpses on her living room floor.

Sarah stood still, barely breathing hard thanks to her rebuilt lungs, blood dripping from her body, though none of it her own. She looked down at the dead intruders and heaved a big sigh.

"Babe, you okay?" Finn asked.

"I'm good," she sighed, eyeing the mess. "Ripley, get a mop, would you?"

Finn surveyed the carnage. "Magic *and* tech? Who the hell are these guys?" He keyed on a comms panel accessing a direct line to the most powerful AI on the planet. It was good to have friends in high places. "Hey, Cal. We just had an encounter here at the house. Some weird alien commandos came after us at home. You know anything about this?"

"There is an all-out invasion underway," Cal replied. *"They seem to be targeting our top military assets. Any key players in our defense. They've already blocked communication beyond the planet."*

"It's global?"

"Yes. Reports are coming in from all over, but with the comms issues there are still some knowledge gaps."

"How the hell did this happen?"

"I can't say for certain, but it looks like there may have been a mole. Many, to be exact. My systems are under attack, as are the other AIs running major systems. Someone has inside knowledge."

"Should we—?"

"Use the backup protocol. Yes. We implemented it for exactly this kind of emergency. Get safe and we'll be in touch."

Arlo's eyes widened.

"Shit! My dad!" Arlo blurted, then took off running.

"Arlo, wait!" Finn called after him, but he was long gone. "Gear up, we're going after him."

Sarah, Finn, and Ripley quickly grabbed weapons from the numerous hidey spots within reach. To any visitor it might have been shocking seeing the arsenal they had casually stored around their home. But they had survived all manner of adversaries so far, and for a good reason.

"Let's move!" Sarah said when they were loaded to bear just twenty seconds later.

The three of them rushed out of the house, splitting up and taking parallel paths to approach Daisy and Vince's place from two sides. Sarah went with Ripley toward the back while Finn looped around to the front. When they arrived, they found body parts strewn about the yard and the door blown in. The dead, they noted, were all alien.

Sarah gestured to Ripley to move to her right flank. Holding her pulse rifle tight to her shoulder, she then spun into the doorway, dropping to a knee as she swept the barrel left to right. She rose, quickly moving deeper into the house. There was more damage. More blood. Dead bodies. Ripley came in from the side door and met up with her.

"Up here!" Finn called from the front of the house.

"I guess we're clear," Ripley said.

They rushed ahead and found Arlo kneeling next to his father.

Finn was standing over them, his gun ready, but lowered. "All of them are dead," he said. "I didn't see any active threats, but we don't know if more are coming."

"Same out back," Sarah replied. "I'm heading to check on Leila."

Finn nodded. There was no sense trying to talk her out of it. "Hurry back, babe."

She gave him a quick kiss then bolted out the back door.

Finn looked down at his friend where he lay on the ground. He'd taken a beating and was bleeding from his left side. Whether it was a blade, shrapnel, or something else, he'd been hurt, but not before successfully defending his home.

"Damn, Vince. You made one hell of a showing of it," she said.

"Never attack a man while he's cleaning his guns," he replied, forcing a pained smile.

"Looks like they picked the wrong rec room," Finn said with a chuckle.

"You said it. Help me up."

"You sure you're good to move?"

"Do I have a choice?"

"Good point," Finn said, reaching out his hand.

Vince was clearly in pain and would need to be patched up better than they could do here, but first things first. They had to figure out what the hell was going on. Vince hobbled toward the kitchen and grabbed a towel, the white quickly blossoming red as he pressed it into his side.

Arlo shared a look with his cousin and slowly shook his head. "Man, Mom's gonna be *pissed*."

CHAPTER FIFTY-TWO

Sid's comms arrays were among the most powerful in the solar system. Being a formerly secret military base restored to more than its former glory after the Great War, it only made sense.

That, and as Freya and Joshua's fabrication hangar and defacto home was nestled in a hidden facility there, it meant access to all of the nifty upgrades two of the greatest AI minds to ever live could come up with.

Naturally, they would want a guinea pig.

But now Sid was cut off. Dark Side base, despite the far side of the moon not actually being dark, was in this instance, aptly named. Comms were silent, and there was nothing they could do about it.

Once the communications were disrupted, the Urvalin fleet sent a sortie of attack ships to engage the base's defensive craft. Most circled the moon at high speed while a few dove toward the base hoping to get a clear shot.

What they hadn't counted on was the new battery of cannons aimed skyward. It was a nasty surprise.

On Earth, their spies had room to be approached and converted, but up on the moon there was no such casual means to do so. And as every member of the team was serving long deployments, there were virtually no opportunities to sway them during brief times away.

Also, the Dark Side crew were a particularly stoic bunch. You had to be selected to serve there. And that meant a far smaller likelihood of bribing one to betray their own people. So, when upgrades were made to the base's defenses, the Urvalin were unaware. And now their ships were paying the price.

"Two more down," Sid announced as the cannons blasted a pair of approaching ships. "How are things on your end, Joshua?"

The AI had been in the middle of upgrading a few systems on his latest ship design, and as such was unable to immediately launch into the battle. He had been monitoring it, though, and he was plotting out the best courses of action even as he rushed to have his craft made ready for combat.

"The attack is rudimentary," he said. "This fleet seems sizable, but they are spread out in an unusual formation. Some have moved toward Earth while others toward Dark Side. I see another contingent heading sunward."

"Options?"

"We hit them and hit them hard. Our pilots are the best. We should be able to flank them and cut off the ones closest from the main body of their fleet with no significant problems."

"Copy that," Sid replied. "Attention all captains. Defensive waves A and B launch at once. You will form two wings and engage the hostiles. Joshua will send you coordinates. Comms are jammed outside of the immediate area. Once you're out there we won't be able to communicate, so stay sharp. Good luck."

The ships housed at Dark Side were fast and tough, their crews hardened combat vets who knew the ins and outs of zero-G combat like the back of their hands. And with a new enemy on their doorstep, they were itching for a fight.

Both waves launched at once, sixteen ships burning hard into space, ready for whatever might be thrown their way. Or so they thought.

"What's going on?" Sid asked as ship after ship abruptly went dark.

He could see them clearly even if he couldn't communicate with them. Each and every ship had suffered the same catastrophic systems failure at two miles above the surface. From what he could tell they'd lost power in an instant, but there was no visible attack.

Worse than merely powering down, some of the craft seemed to have had airlocks lose their seals, voiding the ship of its atmosphere. As for the others, if they maintained an atmosphere, it wouldn't last long with life support knocked out. They'd either suffocate or freeze to death. It was just a matter of time.

"Do *not* launch any more ships. I repeat, no ships are to launch," Joshua said.

"But the others are already out there. They need help."

"It's too late to recall anyone. Look at the scans."

The AIs both fell silent, studying the data they had recorded up until the incident. Visuals confirmed what the datastreams told them. The ships had their weapons hot and engines engaged when suddenly everything cut off. All electronic systems seemed to cease at once.

"It's an energy-dampening array of some sort," Joshua said. "The first attack wave, it circled the moon. They weren't doing recon, they were depositing some sort of power-kill devices. It's the only explanation."

Sid saw what he was talking about. The ships all had momentum when their power was cut off, so they were still drifting at speed, but the enemy wasn't even bothering firing on them. Why waste the ammo when the crews were as good as dead already?

He shifted his focus to his other apparatus, namely, one of the long-range telescopes positioned around the moon normally used to scan deep space.

"What are you doing?" Joshua asked.

"We don't have comms, but we can still see what is happening," Sid replied. "I'm aiming the far side telescopes at Earth."

Joshua saw what he was trying to do. Gather information and see if the planet was also under attack. It wasn't much, but it beat nothing.

Sid repositioned the array and began sweeping the skies above planet Earth. What he saw was horrifying.

"Those ships are heading right toward the atmosphere," Joshua said. "They lost comms and enacted the recall protocol to protect the planet."

"No! They'll crash! Look," Sid said, dialing in the array on what seemed to be a series of tiny microsatellites encircling the globe.

"So, that's how they do it. Ingenious."

"The surface is attempting to launch ships as well. They must have lost their comms as well. No one knows what they're flying into."

Joshua and Sid watched helplessly as the gung-ho defenders of Earth either blasted into space only to lose power, drifting to their demise, or enter the atmosphere then plummet to their death below.

"Look. Fires on the ground. Some have already crashed on the surface. Hopefully terrestrial comms are working and they're able to recall anyone still pushing upward toward space."

Indeed, ships had begun turning around, some flying back to the surface, others remaining in space. But the damage had been done. The Earth and the moon were cut off, and without comms to their leadership, the ships in space were left wondering what to do.

"Sid, there's another wave of enemy ships heading toward us."

"But they'll crash."

Joshua wasn't so sure about that. He dialed in his readings and confirmed his assumption. They weren't operating with regular engines. These ships were now flying with magic.

"Change of plans, I'm afraid," he said. "If I'm right, then this energy-dampening array knocks out tech but doesn't affect magic. And that's what they're using right now."

Sid saw what he was talking about. There were no energy signatures like normal ships. They'd had them originally, but now they were only giving off the faintly visible traces of magic. And that meant in all likelihood they could pass through the barricade unscathed.

They were coming in for another attack.

"Power up all remaining ships. Have them hover just above the surface, aiming upward," Joshua transmitted. "They'll be expecting our cannons now, but we've still got more firepower. Once they get within the bubble they created, engage. Set a hard ceiling at one point seven five miles. Any higher and you risk losing power. Sid, target wide with the cannons and drive them into a closer grouping."

"An aerial kill box."

"Exactly. The others can take it from there."

"And then what?"

"I've got a few ideas, but I need time."

"On it," Sid replied, then opened fire, funneling the invading craft gradually closer.

It was an audacious plan, and Joshua didn't know if it would work, but if they could just hold them off long enough he might be able to install himself into his old standby ship and join the battle. It was an impressive craft, and it could separate into many smaller pieces, each of them armed to the teeth. It would level the playing field significantly.

If they could keep the invaders in check long enough. And his diminutive companion could help.

"You ready for a fight, Eddie?" Joshua asked.

"Itching for one," the little ship replied.

"Good, because you're going to get a bit more upgraded than we'd planned."

The machinery in the fabrication hangar fired up as Joshua sent every available device at his disposal to work. It would be a race against time. For everyone's sake, he hoped he'd make it.

CHAPTER FIFTY-THREE

Earth was deceivingly quiet once the ships had ceased falling from the sky. The Urvalin ground troops had swept through many of their primary objectives quickly while the traitorous saboteurs spread across the globe enacted their plans.

Skyports were shut down, ships disabled, and ground defenses neutralized. But not all of them. Not yet, at least. There were robust backups in place and protocols to protect them only the most trusted had access to. And it was now that those were being enacted.

The inside men and women attempting to isolate or even disable the AIs overseeing the planet moved with speed and precision, managing to take several of their targets offline either through electronic or violent means, the latter costing more than a few innocent lives caught up in the process.

Cal, however, was very, very paranoid, and it looked like that was now paying off in spades. He and many of his upper tier AI brethren had shifted their minds to secondary and tertiary locations to thwart the saboteurs' efforts. A secret network of massive processing arrays that had been kept off pretty much everyone's radar since the Great War. A little secret only the AI elite and their closest, most trusted allies knew about.

As such, several major cities went dark, but their overseers had not been disabled as the attackers believed, but rather were playing possum, allowing them to think they had been successful in their endeavor. But they didn't roll over without a fight. That would raise suspicions, and there was one very good way to eliminate that risk.

In Los Angeles, Sergeant Franklin and his team of cyborg commandos took up heavily fortified defensive positions and had been laying waste to anyone who so much as tried to enter Cal's main facilities. The ones pretty much everyone believed held his processors.

There had been a robust guard there for years and years, and at this point the building's top-secret contents were pretty much common knowledge.

Only it was a lie.

A ruse.

A very, very long con set up as a decoy for precisely this sort of unforeseeable event. Something would likely happen, but they didn't know what or when. Apparently, that day had come.

The Urvalin ground forces were bolstered by their air support, provided by a pair of their ships, hovering and attacking using magical energy rather than tech. It was a blistering barrage, and after a valiant defense the commandos were finally forced to fall back.

"This way! Protect the core!" Sergeant Franklin called out loudly to his men in a fearful voice before turning and running into the structure.

His team followed close behind at a full run and slammed the door shut as soon as they were inside. The Urvalin had them on the ropes. All they needed was to move in for the kill.

"Advance!" their leader called to his men. "No prisoners!"

The hovering ship fired a concentrated barrage of

thundering force spells at the door, smashing it over and over until the reinforced metal finally buckled and gave way. The soldiers didn't hesitate, storming in through the opening, weapons at the ready. But there was no one there to defend that choke point. Apparently, the defenders had retreated all the way to the core of the building.

It was perfect. They were trapped and didn't even know it.

The commanding officer surveyed the area then saw what he was looking for. The route to the core, just as their spies had described it.

"All teams, follow me!"

The entire Urvalin force rushed through the inner sanctum of the building, but the deeper they went, the quieter it became. Something was off. They reached the processor core and had not encountered any resistance. It was extremely unusual.

Had they known the men defending the facility were actually cyborgs and capable of taking quite a beating, not to mention being impervious to fear, they might have realized they were walking right into a trap.

That, and the fact that Sergeant Franklin had no need to yell instructions to his men. They were AIs and communicated silently. The panicked retreat had all been a show. But that tidbit was lost in the mix, and the sergeant and his men were long gone, safely whisked away deep underground in an unused loop tube branch.

The Urvalin didn't stop to think, instead seizing the moment and battering the door to the processor core with both magical and conventional means.

"That was a mistake," Cal said, his voice booming in the hallways. *"Goodbye."*

The Urvalin didn't have the opportunity to reply as a massive burst of high-test rocket fuel sprayed into the building and ignited, engulfing the entire facility in an instant, blowing out all of its doors and windows in a massive blaze of glory.

So far as the Urvalin ships knew, something had gone wrong in the destruction of the AI and they had lost many men in the process. But the objective had been achieved. The one called Cal was dead, reduced to ash in the inferno right alongside them.

And that was precisely what Cal wanted them to think.

Unlike the Ra'az, this wasn't an extermination. This was an invasion, and this time humanity would not hide. They would fight to the end. And that meant it was time for stealth and planning.

Cal reached out to his associates and apprised them of the situation. That from what he could tell from satellite data before comms went dead, these invaders were trying to take not only Earth but the entire system. And they had inside help.

"Cal, look at the Mt. Washington telescope feed," the AI overseeing the survey facility said.

He pulled up the stream in a flash and parsed the data.

"That's Orgalius and the Fujin," he said. *"Rika has returned."*

"And she is heading right for us."

This was bad. This was worse than bad. She had no idea there was a blockade sapping power from any craft who passed the exosphere, and Cal had no way to warn her. Worse, it seemed the others were experiencing the same comms blackout.

Rika saw there were several things wrong with her homeworld immediately. Alien ships flying to the surface for one. And a large group of them in orbit attempting to cast some kind of weird spell, blocking anyone else's magic from functioning.

There was a strange, off feeling to their power. Something about it made her tattoos itch. Spells blocking out magic? This was far more than it had initially appeared. This was *serious*. And seeing as she was fully powered up from both galaxies, Rika decided to do something about it.

"What are you up to?" Jo asked when her captain began to glow.

"Just making our presence known," she replied. "Orgalius, hang tight. I'm going to give these assholes something to think about."

She unleashed a massive wave of power, not sure how the spell would affect the aliens, but hoping it would flip their spells back on them and knock out *their* magic instead of everyone else's. The spell burst forth, shaking the enemy ships hard as their magical drive systems konked out. All through the system Urvalin ships found themselves abruptly forced to switch to warp drive engines.

A brief, static-filled burst of comms chatter blasted over the internal speakers.

"Cannot function...tech blocked...atmospheric entry impossible."

She straightened up in her seat, a look of fierce resolve in her eyes. "Oh, we'll see about that." She began glowing again, her power reaching out to her ship, latching on to every inch of it. "Hang on."

With that she spun and dove the *Fujin* straight into the exosphere, powering toward the surface. The ship hit the barrier, and everything went haywire, everything failing in a flash despite the amount of magic Rika was flooding its systems with. Like it or not, she was falling.

"Jo, see if the backup can reboot."

No response.

"Jo?"

She turned to see her friend staring blankly, her body limp in her harness.

"Shit! Jo!"

The *Fujin* flipped and spun, driving her into her seat, the G-forces making her wonder if she might actually black out. Suddenly the ship lurched hard, its spin and downward plunge abruptly arrested.

A lurch, then another told her clearly enough what had happened. Orgalius had somehow matched her speed and latched onto her ship, his mighty wings flapping hard to slow her fall.

Rika realized there was nothing she could do about flying the ship now. It was all up to the dragon, and she had the utmost faith in his abilities. She popped her harness, safety be damned, and rushed to Jo.

"Hey! Hey! You're gonna be okay."

But she was not going to be okay. Whatever it was blocking the atmosphere, it didn't just affect ships. It affected *any* electronics, and under her flesh exterior, Jo was still a machine.

The AI big brains down below would know what to do. They'd know how to reboot her. Once they got to Cal—

She saw the smoke and flames from downtown as Orgalius guided them toward LA. Cal's command center. It was even worse than she imagined. And with today's luck, things would only go downhill.

CHAPTER FIFTY-FOUR

A slight rumble in the air alerted Arlo and the others that a ship had arrived. But this was a familiar hum. One that Arlo had known all of his life.

"Marty, what are you doing here?" he transmitted.

"Dude, there's a full-on invasion going on. What did you think I'd do?"

"I don't know. Maybe go fight off the invaders or something."

The ship chuckled. "Not a chance. Not without my best friend. But that's not why I'm here. There's an enemy ship down on the beach really close. Cal sent me to get you all to safety."

Finn and Vince looked at one another. "Safety is for *after* the fighting," Finn said. "If you can sneak us past that ship—"

"Oh, I can do that. Already made it here, didn't I?"

"Good. Then take us to the command center. We need to plan our next steps."

"Sorry, but that's not possible," the AI replied. "We're going somewhere else."

Finn's brow furrowed. "Marty, we're not kidding here. This is important."

"No, you don't get it. I'm not kidding. The command center was destroyed twenty minutes ago, didn't you hear?"

A collective gasp rose from the group.

"What do you mean?" Arlo asked. "How could it be destroyed? That place was a fortress."

"Oh, totally. But Cal says there was an insider helping them. Someone was dropping defensive systems and trying to block him out of his own networks. Of course, Cal's way too smart for that and had a plan."

"But if they blew up the command center they killed him, Marty!" Arlo said.

"No, they didn't. But they think they did. He did have to abandon that facility, though, and switch his main presence to one of his other decoy nodes."

Now it was Ripley's turn for disbelief. "Decoy nodes? What are you talking about, Marty?"

"Well, it was meant to be super-duper top-secret, but now that the shit has hit the proverbial fan, I guess it's time to spill the beans."

"Information, Marty," Vince grumbled.

"Right. Cal never actually used the processor core in that building. It was real enough, but his real mind isn't housed there. Ever since the Great War he's been ridiculously cautious, and today showed that to be a pretty smart thing. He said we all need a safe place when things go horribly wrong. Like how I've got my mom and dad's hangar on the moon. Safe haven, ya know?"

"I guess so," Vince said. "What does Cal want us to do to help?"

"Dunno. He was swamped dealing with this when his comms went silent. I'm sure I'll get ahold of him again eventually, but he's probably laying low and assessing the situation while playing dead. You know, so the bad dudes think they killed him and all. Now come on. Get outside and load up, we need to go."

More discussion could be had in the air, so the group quickly gathered up their weapons and hurried outside. Marty had set down nearby in the tight space out front of the house where two streets intersected. It was an impressive piece of flying, but then, he was an impressive ship. That, and he'd been frequenting that house pretty much as long as he'd existed.

The Urvalin, on the other hand, were both flying a larger craft, and they didn't know the lay of the land like Marty did. It was the one thing that gave him an advantage. And from the beach they couldn't get a visual on his over-land approach. At least, he didn't think they could.

"We need to wait for Sarah," Finn said as he slid into his seat and strapped in. "She's at Leila's place."

"Okay," Marty said. "I'll open a comms line to her. Connecting, hang on. She'll be on in a sec. You know, I could just fly over there. I don't think—oh, crap!"

"What is it?" Arlo asked from his pilot's seat.

"Just got a ping on my sensor drone. I left it hovering at the edge of the bluffs. The ship seems to be powering up. We need to go."

Finn began unfastening his harness. "Not without Sarah."

"Dad, this is Mom we're talking about here. She'll be okay."

"No fucking way. I'm not leaving my—"

Sarah's voice cut him off. "Jesus, Finn. You can't afford a gunfight. Get our kid out of here before they see you. I'll be okay. We'll meet up later."

"But—"

"No buts. Marty, you hear me? Go. Now!"

The line clicked as Sarah cut off her comms. Finn knew she was right. Hell, the poor saps on the ground didn't know what they had coming. Reluctantly, he gave the word.

"Get us out of here, Marty."

"On it. Hold on."

Marty took to the air and flew away at speed, hovering just above the trees until he had flown through the pass to the valley side, safely out of sight of the enemy ship.

"We can make Dark Side in no time," Arlo said as he checked the aerial scans. "I don't see any hostiles blocking the path all the way up. Let's go, Marty."

Finn, Vince, and the others held on tight, ready for the burst of speed that would accompany a run for space. For the edge of the atmosphere. And unbeknownst to them, for the deadly energy sink blocking the entire globe.

Marty's drive systems hummed with increasing power, then engaged. Everyone felt the Gs pressing them into their seats, but something was wrong. They weren't flying up, they were staying level, headed east.

"Marty, what the hell?" Arlo said. "Where are you going?"

"To a safe place. Hang on."

Marty increased his pace, pushing through the air just above the surface. Even if the enemy was watching, it would still be next to impossible to track him. A short while later a familiar site came into view. One none of them expected to be visiting ever again.

"Marty, that's Cheyenne Mountain," Vince said.

"I know."

"That's where NORAD used to be before it blew up."

"Like I said, I know. It's where my dad was born."

"Trust me, we know Joshua's history. But it's blown out. Has been for decades."

"Well, yes and no," the AI replied. "He told me if things ever went truly wrong I should go there and hide. It's the one place absolutely no one would ever think to look."

"Again, because it's blown up," Finn noted.

"While the base itself was destroyed in the Great War, Dad's had a small group of mechanoids slowly cleaning up the entry cavern and stocking it with supplies."

"Why didn't we know about this?" Arlo asked. "We're family."

"Well, yeah. But the whole point of the emergency bunker was having it ready for an emergency. Tactically speaking, he said the less people who know it exists the better. It's a somewhat tight fit, but it's large enough for me to tuck in and avoid any scans. And the mountain's granite will shield us from any fallout, should things get really serious."

The group had to admit, it was a clever plan. And Joshua had been right. No one would think to look there. The place had been abandoned as scrap decades earlier, and there would be no record of Joshua's covert repairs.

Better yet, there was still an active link to the loop tube network nearby. How long the attackers would allow that to remain operable was anyone's guess, but it was not a main artery and likely hadn't been targeted by the traitors as a vital hub to take down.

"You know, this is a smart move," Arlo said. "Aunt Sarah will be fine, and this will give us an opportunity to figure out what exactly we're up against before we go rushing headfirst toward an unknown enemy."

Vince looked at his son with a curious gaze. "Are you sure you're the same Arlo and Marty?" he said. "Caution and prudence over reckless action?"

Arlo grinned at his father. "We've learned a few things."

Vince felt a swell of pride. "Well, then. Let's see this hideout of yours."

Just under a thousand miles away, a stealthy form stalked the brush of Malibu cloaked in a makeshift ghillie suit and moving with deadly intent. A ranger of sorts, ready for violence and death.

Leila's home had been vacant when Sarah arrived, but the bloody remains of more of the Tslavar-looking aliens she'd found on her approach told her Leila was not alone. Bite marks made it quite clear that her canine friend had been hard at work. And judging by the carnage, it seemed likely Bahnjoh and Grundsch had been there as well.

The mess Leila had created also made something else clear. Judging by the sheer destructive force that had been unleashed, her Magus stone had been active, and it was not fucking around.

Sarah moved on, quickly heading for the trails to get a better view of the invaders' ship. She could track her friends later. For now, she needed to know who they were up against.

Footsteps sounded on the trail ahead. A half dozen by the sound of it. Sarah crouched beside the chaparral brush and held perfectly still as the Urvalin troopers approached. They moved fairly quietly, given their size and bulky armor. Sarah noted it seemed more suited for impact than for bladed weapons.

Perfect.

Her nanite arm shifted into a wicked point, ready to relieve the intruders of their precious blood in short order. The troops walked past her, not a word spoken as they moved along the trail in single file. Six of them, as she'd initially thought.

Sarah stood and took three rapid steps forward, driving her weapon-arm right through the gap in the rearmost Urvalin's neck protection, severing his spine in a single blow. She strained against his weight, making sure to lower him to the ground as quietly as she could. His comrades hadn't heard a thing.

One down, she thought with a vengeful grin.

These people had attacked her home. Her family. Her friends. And one by one, they would pay the price.

CHAPTER FIFTY-FIVE

There were all manner of dangerous animals stalking through the woods and scrub brush of the distant world. Predators in search of an easy meal. However, where the Geist and his associate moved, they all steered clear.

Even an apex predator could sense something more dangerous than they were. And in his current state, Bawb was all but radiating deadly intent.

Fortunately, the tribespeople he encountered had no such awareness of his presence. Their abilities were hobbled the moment their Allpower was blocked from them. Lacking an animal's keen sense of smell, they were sitting ducks for the angry assassin.

"I shall ask again," Bawb growled at the bound man at his feet. "Where did they take her?"

The man appeared to be a hunter, judging by his garb and the weapons he carried. However skilled he was at tracking down game, he had nevertheless been an easy capture for the pale killer. The younger man who had been hunting with him was not so lucky.

Bawb would have liked to question him as well, but when he

moved to draw a weapon, Skohla acted with speed and violence. He was dead before he could shout a warning, but he was also now useless as a source of information.

Bawb said nothing. These things happened, and he had slain several of this tribe already. Besides, he still had someone else to question. And when he woke, he'd see the slain body of his comrade. Oftentimes, that was enough to loosen tongues. If not, he had other methods at his disposal.

"How is your voice inside my head?" the captive asked, still mildly concussed and more than mildly confused.

Bawb didn't have any intention of explaining the bone-conduction comms patch he'd stuck behind the man's ear. Let it seem like he had magic. It would make him even more fearsome in the eyes of a captive.

"You do not ask questions. Yours is to answer them. Now, again, where is she? Where did they take her?"

"Who?"

"The one with golden hair. The woman. A newcomer. Your people captured her not far from here."

"I don't know anything about that, I swear."

Bawb stared long and hard at the trussed-up prisoner, not uttering a word. The longer he stared, the more uncomfortable the man became. That was not unintentional. Very little the master assassin did ever was.

"I *did* hear something," the terrified man finally said to break the uncomfortable silence. "But I didn't know what the elders were talking about."

"Tell me."

"I don't know details. All I heard was there was a large group of hunters passing through."

"Which hunters?"

"The Horka."

Skohla nodded grimly. "As we feared. The most aggressive of

the tribal groups," she said. "More violent than most. The largest, most feared of the tribes. Bullies of a sort."

Bawb's fangs gleamed through his frightening smile. "I hate bullies. You will point us in the direction they traveled."

"But I—"

"Or your neck will find itself wanting for your head. Am I clear?"

One look at the scarily calm man and the prisoner knew without a doubt he was deadly serious.

"Along the small river," he said. "Not far. That is where they have a large settlement."

"How far?"

"Five hours."

Bawb gauged the man's fitness at a glance and calculated that he could cover that distance in half the time if Skohla could keep up. He felt relatively confident she could.

"And you are sure they headed that way?"

"If they have a prisoner like you say, it is where they would take them."

Bawb quietly gazed at the man, watching him squirm under his scrutiny. A helpful trick in the Ghalian arsenal. Finally, he felt comfortable the prisoner was telling the truth. Whether he was accurate or not was another thing entirely, but at least he believed what he was saying was correct.

Bawb ripped the comms patch from behind the man's ear, placed a gag in his mouth, but did not kill him. "Skohla, come," he said, then turned and walked away.

Skohla was a little confused by his actions, especially given the way Bawb had so efficiently slaughtered the previous three hunting parties they'd come across. And he'd done so all without possessing even a trace of Allpower. The sheer deadly skill he possessed was unlike any she'd ever seen before, and the hunters had fallen quickly to his rage.

But for all of his ill intent, he still meant to gain intelligence.

To take prisoners. Those men, however, had been foolish enough to think stoic silence or overt aggression was the right path to take when facing the pale man.

They were quickly, and violently, proven wrong.

"Do you truly wish to leave that man as he was?" she asked once they had passed out of earshot.

"He is bound. He is gagged. And he provided what I asked for. Now he is no longer my concern."

"But if he warns—"

"He may eventually work free of his bindings, but he will not warn anyone of our presence before we reach our goal."

"A valid point. But what of the wild beasts? He might find himself becoming something's meal."

Bawb slowed his pace for a few seconds, turning to look at the impressively capable woman following his lead.

"Frankly, I do not care," he said, then picked up the pace.

In that moment Skohla saw it clear as day in his eyes. Bawb would get his woman back, and soon, or he would die trying, undoubtedly taking a *lot* of people with him in the process. It was her hope they could avoid that result.

The pair moved quickly, running through the woods and crossing the network of small creeks feeding into the larger river along whose shores the Horka had based their camp. They were making good time when something unexpected presented itself in their path. A ship. A ship and the smell of slaughter.

Bawb readied his blades and moved closer under the cover of the trees and brush. What he saw disgusted him. Not for the sheer bloodshed, but the cowardice in spilling it.

The Urvalin were there, a lone ship resting in a clearing where a tribal village stood. Or *had* stood, to be more precise. Judging by the dozens of bodies, the Urvalin, it seemed, had killed everyone. And these were not hunters or fighters. They were the weak. The harmless. Mere villagers and not a threat.

Bawb felt his anger shift to this new target and grinned.

"Wait here," he said to Skohla.

"What do you—"

He was already on the move, his blades flashing from their hidden sheaths and burying themselves in the heads and hearts of the Urvalin troops. Five had fallen before they even noticed the pale man in their midst.

"Fighter!" one yelled just before a dagger drove through his open mouth and out the back of his head.

The others spun, drawing their weapons, ready for a fight. But Bawb was not merely carrying edged weapons, and he had become more than a little proficient with the use of pulse rifles.

He pulled the butt tight against his shoulder and let off a quick succession of blasts, the intensity turned low so as to both reduce noise as well as increase the likelihood of perhaps getting a survivor out of the encounter. He dodged and weaved, expertly picking off the enemy as he moved.

The Urvalin got off a couple of shots, but nothing that would draw anyone's attention. Not after the bloodshed they'd wrought so recently. Anyone nearby would just think it was them finishing off any survivors.

Skohla, however, was not having any of this sitting on the sidelines. Not this time. Not when Urvalin were ruthlessly killing innocents, even if they weren't friendly to her group.

She opened fire, the alien pulse weapon close enough to her own technology to be easy to handle. Hers, however, was not dialed down low, and the shots flew true, blowing her targets to pieces.

Bawb charged the ship's hatch as the remaining Urvalin fell, rushing inside, knives in hand. He exited a mere two minutes later, wiping the blades clean on a piece of a uniform he'd cut from a victim.

"The ship is ours," he said. "Kip, give Nakk the location and tell him to have one of his captured craft drop a team off here. His people can come claim it to add to their ranks."

"You don't want it?" the AI asked, breaking his silent monitoring for the first time since Bawb had set out on his quest.

"If we fly in, they will hear us coming. I would maintain the element of surprise."

"Okay," Kip said. "I'll let him know. Good luck."

"Thank you, my friend," Bawb said. "Skohla, any survivors?"

She shook her head, rinsing blood from her hands in the tiny creek.

"So be it," he said. "The waters flow together. We are heading the right way, and that is what matters. Come, we have work to do."

With that he turned and headed back on their path. Skohla rose and shook her hands dry then followed.

It was interesting, she noted, Bawb had seemed to have regained a bit more of his characteristic calm after finally uncorking his rage on a deserving target. It gave her hope that their pending conflict might not end with their demise.

They would find out soon enough.

CHAPTER FIFTY-SIX

The hours spent racing toward the Horka's main encampment passed quickly. For Bawb it was much like any other rapid entry into hostile territory. He had a job to do, and that was all there was to it. He moved fast and with purpose, his every sense on edge even as he ran.

For Skohla, however, it was a terrifying experience. Not that she was afraid of combat—she'd seen more than her share of that over the years—but there were obstacles they encountered on the way, all of them handled by her pale friend, and usually before she had even clocked them.

There were pitfalls and snares, which were easy enough to spot even at a run once you knew what you were looking for, but there were also tripwires and poisoned spikes, all designed to incapacitate any unwitting fool who ventured into this territory.

Bawb pointed them out as they moved, not disarming them, as that would give any who passed behind them advance warning that an intruder was in the area. Instead, they circumvented them entirely. After the first hour, Skohla found herself reacting to Bawb's hand signals without a second thought. It was an unusual situation for one so accustomed to self-reliance, but her willingness to follow the clear expert led to them moving at a far greater speed than she'd anticipated.

The terrain following the river's path was varied, and they crossed marshy land, flat fields of waist-high reeds and grasses, and even low hills and rocky outcroppings. It was relatively smooth going, for the most part.

Relatively.

The two men they came across as they neared their goal were not simple farmers, nor were they innocent hunters out looking for their family's next meal. These men had a different air about them. Violent. Rough. Dangerous.

Bawb was upon them in a flash, disarming them both and driving their own weapons into each other's chests. He inflicted a few other slices on their bodies to make it appear as if they'd had a violent altercation, then lay them strategically as if they'd landed fatal blows upon one another.

It would look like a disagreement gone wrong to any who might stumble upon them. Bawb intended to be well clear of the area long before that could happen.

"Again," he quietly transmitted to Kip.

"*Let her go,*" the AI replied in the alien tongue.

"*Let. Her. Go,*" he repeated

Bawb formed the words in his mouth carefully, repeating them over and over, working on his pronunciation as he ran. The Horka would not have the benefit of a comms patch to translate for them. He would have to make his demands clear in their own tongue. Fortunately, he was a very quick study. And if they still didn't understand, he had other ways to make his point clear.

The smell of cooking fires reached their noses before the sounds of the settlement found their ears. They were close to the banks of the river, judging by the moisture in the air and the faint sound of running water. This was almost certainly their target.

Bawb gestured for Skohla to fall back several lengths as he moved ahead. She would protect the exit route while he made his attempt. The woman was more than brave enough to join in the fight, but she knew that sometimes *not* fighting could be as strategically important as being in the middle of the action. And if things went bad, they would need a clear path to flee.

Of course, she thought it unlikely Bawb would ever consider such a thing.

The perimeter of the settlement was unguarded and open. Apparently, no one even considered that an enemy might make an attempt on the camp itself. And with all of the booby traps and sentries protecting it farther out, it seemed highly unlikely anyone could even get close without an ample warning and call to arms.

It was a crescent-shaped layout with the shoreline providing one boundary and clear-cut trees marking the curved edge. Several pathways into the trees demarcated hunting and trading routes while a few small canoe-type boats rested on the shores for water transit. A central gathering area was visible through the rows of small yurts and lean-tos used as the primary form of housing.

It seemed there were a handful of more sturdy buildings dotting the area, made of scraps of downed ships and sturdy lengths of wood, but they were the exception rather than the rule. Likely reserved for the upper ranks or royalty, if that was how these people structured their leadership.

A shift of gold caught Bawb's eye at the central clearing. Hunze.

She was in a small pen crafted from wooden poles bound into a cage. The sides were three meters high and pointed on top. By the time a captive could scale it, the guards would have no difficulty responding and stopping their attempt.

The Horka, however, had not planned on Bawb.

A pair of guards casually walked the perimeter of the

clearing. There were others present as well, though only two or three appeared to possess any sort of weapon. The others were just people going about their daily lives.

Bawb scanned the area in a flash, formulating a plan of attack in seconds. He was not waiting for more intel. Hunze appeared unharmed, but he had no way of knowing how long that would remain the case.

He bolted from the trees straight into the encampment.

The closest guard turned, his neck sliced by a knife before he could even realize what was happening, let alone shout a warning. Bawb let him drop, not slowing his movement one bit. This was not the time for hiding bodies. This was the time to get in, get Hunze, and get out.

Two more of the Horka tribesmen fell as he raced past the small structures toward the central holding pen.

Hunze may have lacked her magic, but she sensed something in the air and turned, keeping her expression neutral even as her heart soared at the sight of her love laying waste to those in his path.

The guard nearest her didn't notice her attention shift, but he did hear something unusual. He turned and saw a pale warrior steamrolling his comrades, coming right for him.

"Intruder!" he bellowed before being opened from belly to neck.

Bawb thrust the bloody knife into the lashing holding the pen closed, severing the ties easily, his adrenaline and urgency adding strength to his arm even though his enchanted blade currently lacked its magical enhancement.

He flung the gate open and wrapped his arms around Hunze, handing her a knife even as he pulled her close.

"You are safe," he said, emotion threatening to seep into his voice. There was no time for that. Not yet. Not while they were still in harm's way.

"I knew you would find me."

Bawb quickly unstrapped the second sword from his back and handed it to her along with a few smaller blades. She secured them in place in a flash just as a sound rose from the surrounding buildings. Metal clanging. Footsteps. And voices.

At least thirty armed men flowed into the clearing from all sides, a particularly large bearded man with an ugly scar across his nose and cheek leading the way. The war party's commander, if not the leader of the Horka himself. He strode forward then stopped, hands on his hips as he sized up the pale man trapped in their midst.

"Kip?" Bawb said.

"I'm ready."

"You will let this woman go," Bawb said in the Horka's tongue.

His accent was by no means perfect, but close enough for his meaning to be clear. The burly man laughed, sending the others into a raucous chorus of chortles and sneers.

"You have no power here," the man said. "And you are outnumbered."

"Let us go and we will leave you unharmed," Bawb replied.

The confidence with which he spoke confused some of the men. He was a lone man, hindered by a woman, no less. He didn't stand a chance.

The commander laughed again, drawing a crude but wicked blade from its sheath. "You fail to understand your place."

"And you fail to understand yours."

The man's eyes crinkled with amusement. "I like this one. He has spirit. He will make a fine worker." He shifted his gaze back to the pale intruder. "Yours will be to live, although briefly, working hard labor. And as you labor, we will breed the woman."

Bawb refused to be baited. Instead, he calmly looked at Hunze.

"Did they harm you?"

"Not much."

He nodded. "And the baby?"

"I am fine, love. *We* are fine," she said, assessing her condition and finding herself capable and free of her pregnancy pains. She drew her vespus blade from its sheath. "But we are *not* happy."

Bawb's own sword drew clear, a pair of legendary weapons wielded by the most elite of hands. The group around them looked at one another with both amusement and confusion. Did these two actually intend to engage such a vastly superior force?

The leader assessed them with curiosity. It was madness. And it would be a shame to lose such a prime breeding vessel. But then, she did not need her limbs for that purpose. A low laugh rumbled from his lips.

"Fools. What do you think you will do with those? Can't you see you're vastly outnumbered?"

Bawb and Hunze both smiled. Kip's translations were pretty spot-on by now, and the response was quite simple.

Hunze rolled her shoulders and swung her sword in a lazy arc. "Let us show you what we are going to do."

It was a slaughter.

Barely five minutes was all it had taken for all of the camp's warriors and hunters, as well as any others who dared take up arms against the Ghalian and his bride, to meet their demise. Only those wise enough to have steered clear of the conflict entirely were allowed to flee.

For those who dared raise so much as a finger toward Bawb's love, however, a most violent end had arrived swiftly and without mercy.

Of those, there were no survivors. That hadn't even been a consideration.

"It is done," Bawb transmitted to his friends.

Charlie received the message with a sigh of relief. "Great news, man. Now, hug Hunze for me, then get your assess back here, ASAP. We've been reviewing the recon footage Kip took and have a plan."

"Oh?"

"Oh yeah. We're gonna bust our friends out of the Urvalin station then get the hell out of this place. And we're taking Nakk's people with us."

"We shall move with haste," Bawb said, he and Hunze already in the trees where Skohla was waiting for them.

"Great. See you soon. And once we're clear of this place, we'll track these bastards down to their planet of origin, if they have one."

"What are you thinking, Charlie?" Bawb asked.

"I'm thinking that attacking our ships out in space? Dragging us down to this place and killing and capturing our friends? That shit's not acceptable. Someone's going to pay."

"I couldn't agree with you more," Bawb replied. "We will be back to you soon."

Bawb silenced his comms and ran, Hunze at his side and Skohla right behind. Charlie felt the tension he'd been holding ease a fraction. At least one of their pressing concerns had been handled. And with Ara slowly absorbing power over at the lava flow, they would likely be ready for action by the time Bawb and the others returned.

Charlie trotted toward the heat once more, heading over to the spit of land extending into the lava flow, spirits finally on the upswing.

"Hey, Ara. Good news. Bob was successful getting Hunze back. They're heading here now, so if you're feeling—"

He froze in his footsteps.

"Ara?"

She was gone.

He rushed to where she'd been lying on the ground, her limb extended into the lava.

"No. No, no, no," he gasped.

It was horrifying, but the signs were undeniable. Ara had not flown away. The marks on the ground made that abundantly clear. The edge bordering the flow had been crushed and crumbled aside. She had slid into the molten lava, and he'd not heard a thing.

"*Ara*?" he called out to her silently, straining their connection. Hoping.

But there was no reply.

CHAPTER FIFTY-SEVEN

"She's gone."

Charlie was in shock, his skin still red from the heat. It had taken Nakk and two of his men to finally pull him away from the lava's edge where his friend had perished. And if he had still possessed his power, it would have required more.

As it stood, the heat took its toll on his human body, and by the time they managed to get him clear he was more than a little dehydrated.

"Drink this," Nakk insisted.

Charlie took the cup and drained it, but without any pleasure.

"You are in need of electrolytes," Dukaan said. "I will get you a few packs from the ship."

"I'm fine."

"You are *not* fine, Charlie," Dukaan replied. "I will be right back."

Charlie sat down hard, his head spinning. As off as he was, he actually felt as if he had regained the tiniest smidgen of power from all the time he'd spent so close to the lava. That, and a decent sunburn. Or *lava*burn, to be more precise.

Dukaan returned a few minutes later with a pair of electrolyte packets.

"Drink," he said, handing them to Charlie.

With hydration in his system, Charlie felt a tangible shift in his equilibrium. That, and his body now had enough fluid to spare for tears once more.

When Bawb and Hunze returned a few hours later they found Nakk and Dukaan waiting for them outside the ship.

"Where is Charlie?" Bawb asked.

"He is inside, napping," Dukaan replied. "He needed it. This has been quite an emotional shock."

"We got back as quickly as we were able," Hunze said. "But is it true? Did Ara actually succumb to the lava flow?"

Dukaan nodded grimly. "She is gone. There are clear signs of where she slid in."

They all felt their emotions run high. Ara had been such an integral part of their lives for so long, losing her seemed impossible. But it was undeniable. She was gone, and with her, what was left of their morale.

Finally, Bawb made the call. Someone had to.

"We must continue to plan," he said.

"I'll go wake him up," Dukaan offered.

"No, let him rest. Their bond was strong. Exceptional. We can make do without Charlie, for the time being."

The others knew he was right. He wouldn't have time to properly grieve, but at least they could let him recover his strength. Even without his prolonged exposure to the lava's heat, the shock alone would have taken the fight out of him, at least for a little bit.

Kip was a relatively small ship compared to some of his other AI friends, but he had ample space for such a limited group to gather, and the images of the Urvalin base filled every display in his command center. With or without Ara, they were going to have to find a way to take out the controls of that bit of orbiting alien tech. And if they were lucky, hopefully rescue their captured friends in the process.

Of course, they didn't even know who the Urvalin had taken or what condition they might be in. The escape pods had been launched when Gus broke apart, but who their passengers were remained a mystery.

In any case, that didn't matter. *Someone* was being held in the Urvalin base, and whoever it was, they'd do their damnedest to get them out.

"I don't like the look of this place," Dukaan said as they surveyed the images. "No possible ground support, and the landing sites are all protected, save for the open one up top."

"But we do have Kip's armaments at our disposal," Bawb noted. "As well as a decent assortment of pulse rifles, pistols, and even some grenades."

"It's not a lot, though," Dukaan pointed out. "Not against an entire base that might be full of Urvalin troops."

"I would also prefer to have more weapons, but we will make do with what we have. It is the Ghalian way."

Nakk shook his head. "I have concerns. Even if we should manage to land on the top most level, and if we somehow overpower their initial defenses and gain access to the interior, we are still significantly outnumbered."

"I've seen him fight," Skohla said. "I have every confidence in his abilities."

"That may be, but we will be under attack the moment we arrive. Before, even. And with multiple landing decks, we could be facing an adversary coming at us on multiple fronts."

"Well, we might not," Kip chimed in.

"Kip, you have something for us?" Dukaan asked.

"Funny you should ask, Dookie. In fact, I *do*."

"And were you planning on sharing?"

"I'm getting to it. Jeez, how about a little patience for the reveal?"

"Kip, please," Bawb interjected. "Our time is limited."

"I know, I know. So, here's the deal. We know they've got multiple potential danger zones around that tower base, highlighted on screen."

"That's five of them, not including the top," Skohla noted.

"Yeah, I know. But you have a lot of people. Fighters. And Nakk said you have more captured Urvalin ships than that."

Bawb saw where he was going with this idea.

"And if we were to launch multiple ground attacks upon the tower while infiltrating those different landing sites, the Urvalin would be forced to direct resources to their defense, leaving those areas relatively unprotected."

"Exactly. The way I see it, even if we do nothing more than disrupt them for a few minutes, it should be enough to get a solid foothold. And with a couple of Ghalian in the mix, I'd wager we could do more than that."

Nakk stroked his chin, weighing his assets and options.

"You know, I think this could work," he said. "We have the craft, and we have the crews. It will take a little while to contact my people and have them power up and retrieve those ships from their hiding places, but once they lift off they should remain relatively unnoticed, at least during the approach."

"And I can provide you with comms to set up in each of those ships. That way we'll all be talking on our own encrypted channel and not relying on any Urvalin tech. Ya never know if they're able to track it, after all."

Hunze hunched over the image on the display table, scrutinizing one particular section of the structure.

"Kip? I may be mistaken, but this appears to be a transmission array, akin to what Cal uses on Earth. Is that correct?"

The AI had noted very much the same thing. "Yeah, it is. I would bet that's where the signal comes from."

"Signal? You had not mentioned a signal."

"Oh, crap. My bad. I thought I did. Basically, it looks like the Urvalin have a constant transmission aimed skyward. I can't say for certain, but it sure does seem like that's how they stay connected to their network of microsats."

"The ones that have sucked the power out of the ships passing through the atmosphere," Nakk mused.

"So, it should be a primary target as well," Skohla said.

"Most definitely. But just know, it's pretty heavily protected. See those doors on either side? Likely some sort of guard depot or barracks. And the indentations in the tower walls could be pop-out turrets, though I'm really not sure."

"In any case, it would be a reasonable precaution to treat them as if they were," Bawb replied.

"Yeah, totally," Kip agreed. "The big question is if we can shut off the satellites from down here."

Bawb's jaw flexed once with grim determination. "We shall most certainly try."

CHAPTER FIFTY-EIGHT

The sky above Malibu was quiet, but Leila and Grundsch both knew that meant nothing if an adversary was well-versed in stealth. For the moment they were catching their breath and letting her rest in one of the many empty homes left vacant after the Great War.

Grundsch sat quietly, listening to the ambient sounds. All seemed clear.

"Taangaar is also under full attack from what they could tell. But the ship that was relaying that news burned up entering the atmosphere. Not good," he said, peering out the window as Leila sat reclining on a dusty but relatively sound, couch.

Its cushions were faded and worn, but it was structurally intact. A marvel of modern materials when it was built, it had withstood the test of time even if the humans who'd bought it were long dead.

She shifted position uncomfortably "That won't be an easy fight. Against a population of so many billions, whoever these people are, they're going to be in for a lengthy occupation."

"Knowing the resilience of the Chithiid race, I would tend to agree with your assessment," Grundsch replied.

Leila shifted uncomfortably onto her side. Baloo moved closer, gently nuzzling his mama in her moment of duress.

"You are in pain. What can I get for you?" he asked.

"Nothing, Grundsch, but thank you. It's just a natural part of the process."

The Ra'az shrugged his massive shoulders. "Such an inefficient means of reproduction. To require so many months of vulnerability just to produce one single offspring? On my world, at the hive, the Ra'az queen could place thousands of fertilized embryos into grow colonies without slowing the workforce at all. There was no lost functionality in the process."

Leila winced in pain as a contraction hit. But a moment later it ceased. This was not the time. Not yet, anyway.

"Right about now I would welcome that process," she said as she sat up again. "But in all honesty, as difficult as this may be, I welcome the same wonder that brought me and all of my family into the universe. Even the pain of it."

Grundsch was a male, and a soldier at that. To have such feelings was simply not in his breeding. But after his time nurturing Karasalia Palmarian to adulthood, not to mention embracing his new life among the humans and Chithiid who accepted him despite his people's history, he was beginning to understand her sentiment, even if he might not agree with it.

"We will get you somewhere safe," he said. "Your child will not come to harm."

"But where, Grundsch? You heard the transmissions. Cal's command center has been destroyed, and it seems the atmosphere is impassable. I'm afraid there's no one coming to save us. We're on our own."

Bahnjoh and Baloo both sat up and cocked their heads, their ears standing up tall.

"They hear something," Grundsch said, rising to his feet and handing Leila a pulse rifle. She noted the power was set to maximum. "Stay here. If anyone but I comes through those doors, open fire."

"What are you going to do?"

"Ensure your safety," he replied. "And in the process, perhaps see if I cannot get us a few answers."

He carefully pulled power from his konus as he'd practiced and used the device to link with the two canines. He couldn't speak with them exactly, but he could urge them to follow general directions. And the current one was to flank the enemy and strike if the opportunity arose.

Baloo and Bahnjoh padded out the side door silently as Grundsch moved to the front. From what he could tell, the invaders were systematically moving from home to home in search of their prey. That meant they had found the remains of their comrades and knew Leila had escaped. And on foot, there was only so far she could have gone.

Grundsch exited the house and moved surprisingly quickly for a being his size, making it to the adjacent home in short order. He hated leaving Leila alone, but he had seen what her Magus stone had done. Of all of them, she was the only one of whose safety he was relatively sure. So long as its power held out, it would not let anything touch her.

Unfortunately, it would also make it near impossible for her to cast from within its protective shielding, even if she used a konus not connected to the Magus stone's power. It might be possible, given the power of the devices she and Charlie had stashed away at their home, but it would require an enormous amount of magic to do so.

But even protected as she was from acts of overt force, a truly clever enemy could eventually figure out a way to neutralize her as a threat, one way or another. Grundsch was going to see to it that did not happen.

The group of ground troops the animals had alerted on was growing close enough to hear. The area was open enough that vegetation and buildings did not block the telltale clicks and clanks of improperly secured gear shifting as the men moved. Judging by the sound, it seemed likely another ship had dropped down and deposited more forces once the others had been discovered.

Twenty? Thirty? He had no idea exactly how many he would be facing. But he was Ra'az Hok. A warrior. He may have embraced a peaceful life, but that could not change who he was deep inside. Not if he wanted to tap into that aggression. If he *needed* to.

The confidence of numbers made the Urvalin forces sloppy. Not overtly, but enough that a skilled adversary might gain a momentary advantage. When ten of them moved away from the others as they crossed the clear area between estates was one such time.

Grundsch leapt out from behind cover and opened fire with his pulse rifle, taking down three of the men before they knew where the attack was coming from. Soon enough they zeroed in on him, though, and the return fire was fierce, both magical and conventional.

Grundsch ducked back behind the structure he'd used as cover, hoping it was solid enough to block their weapon blasts.

While all of their focus was on him, Baloo and Bahnjoh leapt from the brush, tearing into the men still lingering in the trees. The soldiers quickly fled to the relative safety of the open space. If their comrades already had the enemy pinned down, then they could move clear of the cover the beasts were utilizing with little fear.

The two canines ended the shrieks of the men they'd taken in short order then bolted through the woods. The Urvalin fired at them in blistering salvos, but the two were moving fast.

Grundsch used the distraction to pop around the wall and open up on them once more. Two soldiers fell, but a fierce wave of return fire forced him to hide once more.

A yelp echoed out across the battlefield.

Grundsch knew that sound, and his stomach knotted. Bahnjoh had been hurt, but how badly he couldn't tell. He was able to use a konus tenuously—Ra'az weren't exactly wired for spellcasting, after all. But in the heat of battle, when they were on the hunt, it was hard to do any more than keep track of his four-legged friends, guiding them when possible.

"Bahnjoh," he growled, a rage building within.

Grundsch stepped from behind cover and began firing, but the Urvalin were ready this time. A pulse blast caught him on his left arm, sending him spinning. Grundsch could have maintained his balance, but against his naturally aggressive instincts, he let himself fall, hitting the ground and rolling to safety.

It was a good thing. If he hadn't, the follow-up shots that flew through the air where he'd just been standing would have certainly put an end to him.

Even so, the situation was becoming dire. He was pinned down, and terribly outnumbered. And with the targets out in the open, there was no way his animal friends could come to his aid without being noticed and slain.

If only he'd thought to activate the defensive spells from their konus collars. But magic was more Charlie's thing, and after a year of no conflict they had simply stopped casting that spell. The animals had no need for it.

Except for now, it seemed.

The Urvalin called out to one another and began advancing, a steady stream of fire keeping the Ra'az from even getting off a return shot. They had him pinned and moving in on his position. It was only a matter of time before—

An Urvalin trooper hit the ground, minus his head. A moment later the sound of the shot echoed in the air. The advancing troops looked around, confused.

Pop, pop, pop. Three more heads exploded, followed by the sonic reports seconds later.

"Sniper!" someone yelled, but by then it was already too late.

Their commanding officer realized his mistake. He'd chased the big alien, putting his forces out in the open in the process, assuming his prey was alone. But the woman he was with apparently had more fight in her than his intel had reported. And his men were being slaughtered for that oversight.

Twenty-three Urvalin fell as they scurried for cover, and just a few minutes later, none drew breath. Grundsch peered around the wall, in awe of the sheer carnage. How had Leila managed that when she could barely stand just a few minutes earlier? He looked to the house she'd been sheltering in and saw her peer out of the door.

It was all wrong. She was too close for that kind of delay in the gun's report. Someone else was out there. Apparently, someone with quite a grudge against the invaders.

"Leila, are you okay?" he asked.

"Are *you*?" she replied. "You're hurt."

"It is but a flesh wound."

Baloo ran up to them, bloody, but not his own. A moment later Bahnjoh walked from the trees, but with a slight limp. He was bleeding from his left haunch. Someone had managed to land a damaging shot despite his incredibly durable hide. But as he moved closer, licking Grundsch's hand, the Ra'az could see the injury was not severe. Somehow, they had both come out of this dead-end encounter wounded, but more or less intact.

"What happened?" Leila asked, looking at all of the bodies. "Who did this?"

"I did," a voice called from the trees.

A camouflaged figure was jogging toward them, decked out in tactical gear, a powerful rifle slung over her shoulder, the strap matching the camouflage of her clothes and her arm. A moment later the sniper's nanite hand shifted back to flesh tone as she pulled her balaclava off.

"Sarah!"

"Hey, Leila. Grundsch. I saw those bastards drop off a fresh load of troops and thought I'd do a little hunting. Looks like that was a bit of good fortune."

"Indeed, your arrival was very well timed," Grundsch said.

Sarah glanced up into the sky, her nanites doing their best to help her see much farther than a normal human could.

"I think there's another ship. Can't tell where it's going, but we should move, and I mean now."

"We have weapons inside. Bags of konuses and other things," Leila said.

Sarah nodded, already moving toward the house. "Then let's grab 'em and go. No time to dilly-dally, kiddies. Shit's getting real down here, and we need to be far away, and fast."

CHAPTER FIFTY-NINE

"We're in a bind, Admiral," Zed noted as he flashed tactical scenario after tactical scenario across the display consoles. "Without comms to Dark Side or Earth, we're at a tactical disadvantage. And as we've seen, ships that attempt to enter either Earth's atmosphere or the moon's airspace are having their systems shut down. It's a mess."

Admiral Harkaway paced back and forth, fidgeting anxiously with the band on her finger. Her husband was commanding one of the ships out there, and while the *Vali* had not been caught up in that disaster, it was flying at a serious disadvantage, as were the rest of the vessels in her fleet.

"But the ones closest are still in our communications network, are they not?" she asked.

"Yes, but we don't know for how much longer. Whoever these bastards are, they've been wreaking havoc on our systems."

She knew he was right even if it was hard to believe. An enemy capable of disrupting their technological systems utilizing both their own kind of technology as well as what was looking like magic? It was a worst-case scenario. Up until this point, a few ships in their alliance had been the only ones with that ability.

Now, however, it seemed clear there was another race out there who used both disparate types of power. And they were not friendly.

"Options?" the admiral asked.

"None are very good, I'm afraid," Zed replied. "We can see the enemy ships out there, but it's almost as if they're daring us to come after them. Meanwhile, Dark Side and Earth have both been attacked. Sid and Joshua were able to fend them off, but Earth has been invaded. I wasn't able to get an accurate read on the number of drop ships that hit the surface, but it seems substantial."

Admiral Harkaway hated the feeling of helplessness that accompanied this situation. Normally, she could at least charge into battle, kicking ass and taking names. But this? Without the ability to communicate or send reinforcements, she was hobbled. Cut off from most of her fleet, she couldn't effectively command them.

"How do their ships do it, Zed? How do they fly to the surface when that barrier knocks out all of our ships?"

"It looks like they're using magic rather than conventional drive systems."

"So, if we had magic-driven ships, logic dictates they would also be immune to the dampening perimeter, yes?"

"I would think so," the AI agreed. "Though we can't say for sure until we actually *have* one of our own magic-powered ships to test that hypothesis."

The admiral knew what this meant. The question was how quickly they could enact a plan.

"Zed, we need to prep a small group of our fastest ships to cross the portal to call our allies on the other side for help. It's a magic problem, and we need a magic solution."

"I'm already on it," he replied. "I've got seven small, fast ships ready to go. Once we've made contact, our allies will flood through the portal and beat these bastards down with a taste of their own medicine. Or magic. Whatever. The point is, I'm on it."

"How long?"

"Soon. It'll take a few minutes to get them into place, but they're about to— hang on, there's something happening."

Images of the magical portal floating near the sun flashed onto the command deck's displays. Emerging from warp and surrounding it were an increasingly large number of hostile craft with more coming by the minute.

"They know about the portal," Harkaway said. "Zed, deploy all forces to the sun immediately. We have to protect it at all costs."

All of the available ships that were within their limited comms range and were not trapped within the bubble on the moon or within the atmospheric perimeter of Earth immediately retasked and shifted course to the sun. They still had numerical superiority over the invaders, but the question was just how long that would last.

"Zed, prime a messenger probe as well. I want it launched during the engagement. Send it on a long arc around this whole mess. While everyone's occupied fighting, hopefully that first warning message can slip through unnoticed."

"I've got a Mark-6 ready to go. Give me ten seconds to upload the message," the AI said. "Okay, got it. Launching now."

The probe would fly off at speed, but at a different trajectory than the ships now barreling toward the sun. If Zed had calculated correctly—and seeing as he was a super-brilliant top-tier AI, that seemed pretty likely—the probe would make a wide slingshot approach, avoiding the battlefield before punching through the portal at a high rate of travel.

"Launched," Zed said. "Probe is away."

Admiral Harkaway leaned close to her displays. "Time until contact?"

"First ship should reach them in fifteen seconds."

She felt her breathing slow as she fought her body's natural instinct to tunnel vision on that one ship, that first combatant to enter the fray. But Celeste was the admiral. She was in charge of far more than just one ship, and it was resting on her shoulders to keep track of all of them.

"Five seconds," Zed announced.

Suddenly the lead ship began a slow tumble, its power drained. The enemy, who had previously been letting disabled ships merely drift helplessly, opened fire, tearing the craft to pieces.

"Zed, what the hell just happened?"

"A power drain zone," he replied. "They've set up a fucking minefield in space!"

"Recall all ships. Alert them!"

"Done," Zed replied, but three more had already fallen victim to the invisible, floating energy voids.

It was a clusterfuck. From what they could tell, the enemy had placed some sort of energy mines all over the system, and now their craft were blindly flying into them.

The enemy's whole massing of forces at the portal had been a trap. The invaders had *wanted* them to react. Celeste kicked herself for not seeing it coming. And because of it, they'd just given them exactly what they wanted.

Admiral Harkaway watched in horror as two more of her fleet lost power. The rest of the ships were aware of the problem now at least, and they were quick to steer around the dead zone they knew existed, risking their own lives to position themselves in front of the now-drifting ships.

With their power active and shields intact, they would be able to absorb whatever the enemy had to throw at them while they rescued their powerless comrades. The Urvalin seemed to realize this but rather than pressing the attack, they contented themselves with pulling back and letting the rescue unfold.

The Earth fleet was in disarray, and that was their primary objective. And in that, they had been successful beyond expectations.

Far from the battle, a small shape stealthily streaked toward the portal, coming from the darkness at a high rate of speed. The Urvalin ships realized a little too late that the probe was coming. And they'd apparently neglected to place any of their energy-sapping space mines in that direction. That, or the defensive fleet had just gotten incredibly lucky with their shot's trajectory.

Whatever the case, the probe flashed past the enemy ships and dove straight into the waiting portal. Admiral Harkaway watched as it cleared the enemy. At least it looked like it did. As fast as it was going, momentum would have carried it ahead regardless.

"You did it. The probe is through," she said. "It made it. At least, I think it did."

"I saw," he replied. "Now, let's hope our friends get the message."

CHAPTER SIXTY

The unimpressive tavern on the unnotable world was the perfect place to hold a secretive meeting between an Earth warrior, a space smuggler, and an interstellar assassin. It had taken a little doing, arranging this rendezvous, but the Ghalian network of spies and messengers was nothing if not efficient. Efficient, and very, very hard to hide from.

They'd found their men and relayed the message. It was an offer they knew better than to refuse.

"What the hell is that supposed to mean?" Daisy grumbled, pacing the dimly lit room.

Olo took a large swig from his mug. It most certainly did *not* contain a low-octane beverage, and this serving was not his first.

"It means there is something really, *really* messed up in the works," he said. "I'm telling you, whoever these people are, they were going after the Council ships. I mean *actively* seeking them out. *Council ships*! Who in their right mind does that?"

"Insane people," Tym interjected, far more inebriated than his friend at this point.

"Seriously, Tym?"

"He's drunk, but he's right," Olo said. "These people? They're nuts."

Zilara had been listening quietly as Olo and Tym spilled the details of their disastrous encounters, taking in their rambling fire hose of information and refining it into useful intelligence.

"But you said they were able to immobilize the Council ships," she noted. "If one possessed the power to do such a thing, would attacking them really be such a rash action?"

"Well, I—"

"And you said that while they were able to disarm those ships using powerful spells, they also utilized technology. The very same sort of dual-drive system that allowed you to evade them and escape."

"Sure, but—"

"So, it then tracks that these craft are likely vulnerable in the same way your ships might be. Namely, a shift between magical and technology-based bombardment to soften their shielding spells while disrupting their mechanical systems. Daisy, would you and your team agree?"

"I think she nailed it," Sarah said.

Yeah, I think you're right, Daisy silently replied. "I believe you've accurately assessed things," she said aloud. "Freya, any thoughts?"

"Yeah," the ship chimed in over Daisy's open comms. "From what Olo and Tym were saying, it sounded like these guys had spread themselves a bit thin. At least, that's the way it looked. Being in a strategically superior footing, it makes sense. Lure your target closer while they believe you to be in a weak position."

"Sound tactics," Zilara agreed.

"Yeah. But if we were to counter them with a similar sort of mélange of power, we could turn the tables and take advantage of their overconfidence."

"But how would we do that?" Daisy asked. "I mean, I know

you're up for it, and Tym and Olo's ships are modified with tech from our galaxy. But aside from them there are very few vessels on this side of the portal that have been modified."

"True," Freya agreed. "But on *our* side a lot of ships have had konuses fused with their hulls. If we were to bring reinforcements from home, we could really give these guys a run for their money."

"But only so long as they're spread thin," Daisy added. "And we don't know how big their fleet really is."

"Obviously."

The establishment they were holding their meeting in was protected on several levels, magically shielded and watched by shimmer-cloaked guards ready to slay should it be called for. Despite that, a lavender-skinned woman with deep green hair running down her back entered the tavern.

"Excuse me," Zilara said, motioning her over. She stepped away, and the two spoke quickly in hushed voices. Then, as quickly as she'd arrived, the woman left.

"News from one of our Ghalian spies," she said.

"*That* was a Ghalian?" Tym asked. "But she wasn't a Wampeh."

"Yes, she is."

"But she looked nothing like you."

Zilara grinned. "Disguise is one of the most useful tools of our kind, and some are more adept than others. Most people never learn the extent of our abilities and live," she said, the slight unspoken threat more than enough to keep even a drunkard like Tym's lips sealed.

Daisy leaned in. "You said there was news?"

"Yes. The Urvalin, they have taken Karasalia's father and many other powerful casters."

"That Palmarian guy? But he's crazy strong."

"Indeed he is, but it seems the Urvalin have been preparing for this day for a very long time. Their operatives have drugged and outright attacked the masters of countless estates across the galaxy, neutralizing their possible opposition in one very well-organized thrust. One has to admire their efficiency, if nothing else."

"*This is worse than we thought, Sis. We need to get moving, and I mean yesterday*," Sarah said.

Big time, Daisy agreed. "Freya, how many ships with the requisite upgrades from our prior encounters are within comms range?"

"Sixteen, last I counted, though that number may have changed."

"I need you to reach out to them and tell them to meet at the portal."

"What do you intend to do?" Zilara asked.

"The way I see it, we need to present as unified a front as possible. As long as we're spread out we're still vulnerable."

"On that we agree, but what then?"

"Then Freya will cross over and we'll get ahold of Cal and the others. They need to be made aware what's going on, and I'm sure they'll be able to wrangle up the ships we need in no time. And while we're there, our allies on this side will continue to gather, protecting the portal so none of these Urvalin bastards can cross over. So long as we keep them contained in just one galaxy we'll be able to put them on the ropes if we act fast."

"Their magic is extremely potent," Zilara mused. "I believe we will need to attempt something a bit drastic in addition to procuring more ships from your home."

Daisy's interest piqued. "Oh? What were you thinking?"

Zilara grinned. "The Bakana rods," she replied. "They have been separated and placed in secure locations. But if there was a time to bring them together again, I feel this is it."

"You used those against Malalia," Freya noted. "Combined your powers to drain hers."

"Yes. But this enemy has a very different type of magic.

Strange, and difficult to counter. In this instance, I believe we will require the skills of casters with an equally unique potency."

Daisy saw where this was going, and she couldn't help but agree. "You need Charlie, don't you?"

"Yes. He is bonded with a Zomoki, and a powerful one at that. A type of magic that until recently had been thought extinct. But more than that, Rika Gaspari wields an even stranger force. An amalgam of power from both our galaxies, bonded to her blood and bone, and even drawn from the extremes of black sun systems. She is a disrupter. A game changer. And with that pair linked with two of our strongest casters, we could very well overwhelm the Urvalin."

"How much time is needed to get them?" Freya asked. "We're kinda in a rush."

"We must only gather the two Bakana rods nearest our location for you to carry," Zilara replied. "While you deliver them to Charlie and Rika we will procure the other two and get them to the right hands."

Daisy rose to her feet. "Well then, we'd better get moving. Olo, is your buddy good to fly?"

"I'm always good to fly!" Tym blurted with alcohol-reeking breath that could peel paint from the walls.

Olo looked at his friend a long moment. "He'll be okay," he said. "He gets drunk fast, but his metabolism will process it out by the time we're ready to fight."

Daisy had no choice. "Okay. Then I need you guys to help round up the others. Guide them to the portal and stage there."

"I shall also send shimmer ships to help guard the perimeter as we amass our forces," Zilara said. "I will guide you to the nearest Ghalian training house. The Bakana rods will be delivered there shortly. It will be the fastest way."

Daisy headed for the door. "Meet you in space," she said.

"Olo, Tym, I'll see you two shortly. Watch your backs; these Urvalin are tricky."

"Believe me, we know," Olo replied. "Fly fast. We'll be waiting for you."

Daisy jogged to her ship and climbed aboard. Freya shot through the atmosphere in a flash then linked her warp with Zilara's drookonus for the jump.

"*I think this plan just might work*," Sarah said as the course was plotted.

"I think you're right," Daisy agreed. "As much as I want to get home to protect our own, our best bet is stopping the Urvalin before they realize there's a portal to exploit. I hate to think what would happen if they did."

Little did she know, her worst fear was already realized.

CHAPTER SIXTY-ONE

"Ya know, it's really not so bad," Arlo said. "I mean, for a bombed-out mountain base."

"Joshua did a good job fixing this part up," Ripley agreed. "Though everything past the quarter mile point heading down is a melted slag pile of rocks and busted-up stuff."

"There's nothing down there anymore anyway," Marty said. "When this place blew, the inner doors kept the majority of the destruction localized and really deep. I mean, yeah, it totally screwed up the rest of the facility, but at least the main cavern and tunnels near the surface were structurally sound enough to clean out and rebuild."

"I'll say," Arlo agreed, popping open a crate of freeze-dried rations. "I bet we could stay down here for months if we had to."

"Eight point six months given our numbers," Marty said. "But knowing how you eat, I'd round that down to an even eight."

"Oh, shut up, dude."

"As if. You know it's true."

"Boys, chill out," Finn interrupted. "I know this is how you deal with stress, but it's giving me a headache. And I'm sure your dad would appreciate a little peace and quiet for a while."

Vince lay on a memory foam cot, his body cradled in the soft material as he slept in a drug-induced nap. His injuries had been mended thanks to Marty's medical facilities, but healing tissue was exhausting no matter how it was achieved, and he needed rest to recharge his energy stores.

Fortunately, medicine had come a long way, and the sleeping aid he'd taken would process out of his system in only a few hours, the time-release stimulant kicking in just as he would begin to wake.

It was something akin to the old tradition of coffee power naps, where a person would down a cup right before drifting off, the caffeine hitting their system as they slept, leaving them alert and refreshed when they woke. But modern chemistry had improved upon that bio-hack, and now one could accomplish with a single pill what had once required a coffeepot.

Voices suddenly echoed in the tunnels, and they were not from anyone in their group. The main hangar-style doors Joshua had installed and camouflaged remained closed. Someone had come through the small pedestrian entrance hidden to the side.

Arlo, Ripley, and Finn grabbed their weapons and took cover. There was only one way in, and that led right to their hiding spot. Whoever it was, they'd get the drop on them. The question was, how the hell had they been discovered?

Cheerful conversation grew louder, quickly answering that question for them. A minute later a familiar voice called out.

"Hey, guys. I'd appreciate it if you didn't go and shoot me and the boys. It's been a long day, and loop tube rides can be damn boring," Sergeant Franklin called out. "Oh, and good tactical positioning. You're really getting the hang of this."

"Uncle George!" Ripley blurted, running out to give the cyborg a big hug.

"Heya, Rip. Good to see you. Finn, Arlo, how are you faring down here?"

Finnegan strode up and shook his hand. "We're doing quite well, actually," he said. "I've gotta tell you, it's damn good to see you. Had us worried for a minute, there."

"Yeah, how did you know we were here?" Arlo added. "Marty said Cal was lying low, and comms were all kinds of screwy."

"Oh, that's all true, but I had optics scanning toward Malibu as soon as hostilities started. Sorry I couldn't break anyone away to come get you, but I figured you could handle yourselves, which you've proven to be a correct hypothesis. I saw a few frames of Marty as he buzzed east and figured since he was staying low he'd be looking for a terrestrial hiding spot versus heading to space. Which was really, *really* fortunate, by the way."

"Why do you say that?" Marty asked.

"Because whatever these alien fucks are up to, they've blanketed the entire atmosphere with some sort of power-dampening field. Not an EMP, but it acts pretty similar. We've already lost a lot of ships both heading up to fight them in space and trying to come down to land."

Finn was horrified. "You mean they lost *all* power? Even life support?"

"Yeah, it was not a pretty thing. If you all had tried to make a break for space, you'd have been in that same boat."

"By which you mean up a particular creek without a paddle," Arlo said.

"Exactly."

"And on the way down..." Ripley quietly said.

George nodded. "Yeah. Not good. But, hey, we're here now, so let's get cracking."

Arlo gestured at the stone walls around them. "On what? It's a bombed-out cave, dude."

"You forget, I spent hundreds of years in this particular cave, albeit a lot deeper. But still, this was home for a long time. And with the repairs Joshua's been making—"

"He said he hadn't told anyone," Marty interrupted.

"Kiddo, I've known your dad since the day he was powered on. I'm not just anyone. But you're right, he did keep this little project secret from pretty much everyone else. And while we were figuring out the crucial systems to restore, we decided an old-school hardline backup would be something any advanced enemy wouldn't think to look for."

"You mean an actual *wire*?" Arlo asked. "Does anyone even do that anymore?"

"No, they don't, which is why it's perfect. It took a while to get installed, but we're good to go now. Just need to power it up."

A look of concern flashed across Finn's face. "But, George, it's a long way here, and if you didn't fly, how do you know you weren't followed?"

"No worries, my friend. The branch of the loop tube that feeds into this area has a dedicated emergency blackout protocol that keeps it entirely off tracking scans in times of emergency. Basically, we can run that pod as much as we like and everywhere in the network it'll look inert."

"A dummy system," Marty mused. "Clever."

"Yeah, I thought so. Your dad's idea, by the way. A little insurance plan, just in case. And as the feces has most definitely impacted the rotary air circulation device, it seemed like it was the right time to use it."

Sergeant Franklin's team was already fanning out to get working on making the needed connections to fire up the system. Six cybernetic commandos in total, though there had been more at Cal's command center during the attack. Once they'd lured the invaders inside to their demise, however, they had split up with different secondary objectives.

George took his group east while the others went to reinforce and rescue those they could in other parts of the greater Los Angeles area. It wasn't perfect, but the fog of war never is.

"So, Uncle Cal is all right, then?" Ripley asked.

"Yeah, he's fine. He's just lying low while we all run around in what-the-hell's-going-on mode. It looks like this is an alien occupation rather than a full-scale eradication-type assault. Either way, we really don't know what's coming next. That's why he tasked me with keeping an eye on y'all for a bit."

Arlo noted a slight discrepancy. "But I thought you said you were linking his hardline system in."

"Hey, two birds, one stone," George replied with a chuckle.

"But don't you need to be out there helping with the fighting?"

"Arlo, if anything happened to you or your family, your mom would come home and kick my shiny ass up and down the coast, and believe me, that's not something I'd be looking forward to." He glanced over at Vince, though his AI sensors had picked up the wounded man the moment he had stepped into the cavern. "And judging by your dad's condition, it seems my assistance is most certainly needed."

George walked over to the sleeping man and squatted down, giving him a more focused scan from head to toe.

"Hey, Marty. You did a good job here. I think he's gonna be just fine."

"Thanks, Sarge. So, what now?"

"We do our work, we plot and plan, and when the time comes, we strike back."

"You mentioned enemy ships in orbit. Couldn't we take them out with our hypersonic surface to air—" Finn began to say.

"You're forgetting the whole conking-out-as-soon-as-they-hit-the-edge-of-the-atmosphere thing," he replied.

"No, I was thinking the momentum might carry them on to their targets."

"And it's a good idea. But the turbulence exiting the atmosphere would throw them off course even if the momentum carried them out into space. Then we'd just have a bunch of ordnance floating around out there."

Ripley's head cocked slightly. "Hey, you said all tech stuff craps out from the dampening field, right?"

"Yeah, that about sums it up."

"Well, what about dragons? They could help."

George had to admit, it was a good idea. There was just one problem.

"Any idea how we get ahold of one?" he asked. "Charlie and Ara have gone missing, and she was our main way of contacting Orgalius and his friends."

Ripley's spirits fell, but then began to rise again. "Okay, yeah, that's a problem. But I can't help but think at least one of them will notice what's going on. And when that happens... crap, how do we contact them?"

George walked over and rested his arm around his human niece. "Don't worry, Rip, it was a good idea. And if they do show up, I'm sure we'll figure something out."

A thousand miles away on the outskirts of Los Angeles, a massive blue dragon sat with a human, her ship, and her inert cyborg friend, trying to make sense of what was going on.

"She is not dead?" he asked for the third time. "I do not sense any activity from her at all."

Magic crackled from Rika's tattoos, but she tamped it down quick. "I told you, she's got a reinforced processor system. It was a hard shutdown, but she'll wake up. She'll have a massive headache, but she'll pull through. She has to. Yeah, I'm almost sure she'll be okay."

"Almost?"

"Nothing's one hundred percent in this world."

"Or any other."

"True that. But I'll tell you what, I think Jo's going to pull through. She just needs to reboot. I just have no idea how to do that."

"Which is problematic."

"Gee, ya think?"

"I was just—"

"I know," she sighed. "Sorry for being testy. It's just my friend is comatose here and with Cal destroyed, I have no idea what the hell to do about it."

Orgalius rested on his haunches and waited while Rika figured out their next steps. This was her world, and she knew far better than he what they might be able to do in the ways of technological things. Things like Jo.

"Man, if I just had a proper comms array."

"But the *Fujin* is without power."

"Yep. And even with the konus added to its systems, I don't think flying it with my power boosting it would be the best idea. It's just too big, not to mention it would stand out like a sore thumb. No, we need something else. A safe place to store Jo while we figure this out, for one."

Rika paced, looking at her ship, her friend, and the dragon. There was no way he could carry the ship. Guide it to the ground in a controlled fall? Sure. But pick it up from a full stop and haul it around? Not a chance.

Carrying her and Jo, on the other hand, would be easy. And that gave her an idea.

"Okay, there's one thing we can try, but we'll have to leave my ship behind."

"And that plan is?"

"You're going to fly us," Rika replied. "I've got a safe place to stow her, and something that might help us in the process."

"Then we shall go at once."

"No, hang on," she replied, heading for her dark ship's open hatch. "There's one thing I need to do first."

"What's that?"

"I'm going to booby trap the ever-loving hell out of the *Fujin* before we go," she said with grim determination. "If I can't have her, no one can."

CHAPTER SIXTY-TWO

It had taken Zed's fleet's unmanned drones and probes, and a whole lot of them at that, to map out a relatively safe route to the portal where it hung just outside of the sun. Scores of the small vehicles had been sacrificed to the invisible minefield of energy-sapping tech the invaders had deployed, their deactivation pointing the way.

It was akin to the ancient Earth game of Battleship, launching strikes blindly and hoping for a hit. Only these hits were taking out their own assets one by one, though it was a small price for a clear path. In the process, a trail of signal-boosting microsats were spread, allowing for at least a slightly more stable bit of communication in the otherwise blocked space.

"Engage any hostiles, weapons free," Zed told his people. "Lock in coordinates and activate automatic proximity course adjustments. We can't have anyone accidentally blowing their power source flying into one of those dead zones."

The fleet heeded his words and swarmed to action. The larger ships, such as Zed's command craft, were unable to plot a safe way through just yet, but the mid and small-sized ones could snake their way through the path they'd identified.

The enemy saw their cautious approach, however, and opened fire long before they were through.

"Shields diverted forward," Admiral Harkaway ordered. "Power and magic combined. We need to hit these bastards with a taste of their own medicine."

Zed relayed the command in a flash, and the ships responded, all defenses shifting into a blend of tech and magic. The admiral was glad they'd had the foresight to blend konuses into the hulls of so many of the craft over the past year. It looked like the unlikely union could very well save them all.

If they first survived the day.

"Where the hell are the backups, Zed?" Harkaway growled. "I know we've got people out there who aren't stuck on Earth or the moon, and they need to get their asses here. Now."

"I agree, Admiral, but there's a ninety-three percent likelihood our comms have remained blocked past a certain distance. And even if they weren't, it looks like these dead zones are floating all around the solar system beyond our current location. I'm afraid what we have right now is likely what we'll get."

The admiral turned her gaze back to the battle unfolding on her monitors. The enemy ships were not impervious, it seemed, and several of the smaller ones had fallen to the steady barrage from her own craft. But even so, it was clear they simply didn't have the manpower to overcome them. Not without forces from the other side.

"Sound the retreat, Zed," she reluctantly ordered. "Pull everyone back."

"Admiral?"

"I know you see it too. We can't win this. Not on our own."

He did see it, of course. The AI had run simulations non-stop since before the engagement had even begun and come to the same conclusion. But sometimes data could be wrong. It was those unpredictable variables called luck and fate that sometimes put the underdog on top.

Today was not such a day.

"The order has been sent. They're pulling out," he announced.

"Let's just hope the probe reaches our people on the other side sooner than later," she replied, watching her people retreat when a sudden shift caught her eye. "What the hell is going on?" she abruptly asked. "Zed? The portal!"

The AI was watching the link between galaxies with all of his sensors on high, recording every last detail of the event. This shouldn't have been possible. Not without one of the casters from their alliance allowing it. But impossible as it was, the portal was moving.

It was dropping into the sun.

"It's not our people," Zed declared. "I don't know how, but I've picked up a massive flare of magic unlike any I've got record of in my data stores."

"But it's not possible. Only Ara and a few—" She fell silent as the portal's descent sped up.

A moment later it submerged within the sun's swirling plasma.

The portal was protected from damage; the Ootaki hair powering it and keeping it safe was also pulling its power from the sun. A perpetual motion machine of magic, as it were. But how they could ever get it back out was anyone's guess. For someone to override the powerful spells holding it in place meant magic the likes of which they'd never seen before was in play.

At the same time in another galaxy far away, Daisy and Freya were warping toward the portal as fast as they were able. With the two Bakana rods in hand, they were primed to help Zilara and the Ghalian network show these Urvalin what *real* power looked like.

Despite their rush, they flashed out of warp a safe distance from the portal, so as not to arrive on top of one of their own ships, as well as to give themselves a moment to assess the situation.

"Scanning," Freya announced. "So far, all looks good."

"Just our people, then?"

"Yep. I count seventeen including Olo and Tym. The rest must still be on their way. We should—hang on a sec. What *is* that?" the AI wondered.

"On screen."

Freya displayed what had caught her attention.

"*Is that one of our probes?*" Sarah asked.

Daisy squinted at the image. "Sure looks like it."

"It has no power signature," Freya said. "Looks like it hit one of the asteroids in the area when it crossed over. But that's really weird. Why a probe?"

"Can you access the data stream?" Daisy asked.

"No. There's, like, *zero* power in that thing."

Daisy watched the inert shape intently. "I've got a bad feeling about this. Something doesn't smell right."

"Well, if we bring the data core on board I can try to power it up on one of my auxiliary clusters. I might be able to salvage something."

"I sense a 'but' coming."

"*But* it's too big to bring aboard whole. You'll need to step outside and pull the core manually."

Daisy groaned but was already heading toward her locker. "I am in *no* mood for an EVA," she grumbled.

"I know. But it's the only way," Freya replied. "Sorry."

"It's not your fault, kiddo. I'm just being a whiny bitch."

"*So, status quo, you mean,*" Sarah snarked.

"I swear, if you weren't already dead..." Daisy shot back, then began suiting up.

Freya fired off a few blasts from her thrusters and placed the airlock door right against the probe, so it only took Daisy a minute to get what she needed and hook it up to her ship's accessory port. It wasn't exactly an EVA, it seemed. More like a zero-atmosphere retrieval minus the extra-vehicular activity. Whatever you wanted to call it, it worked for Daisy.

"Anything?" she asked as Freya worked her magic.

"Hang on a sec," she replied.

Daisy stripped off the space suit and was stowing it when Freya let out a shocked yelp.

"What is it?"

"Daisy, this is bad."

"How bad?" she asked, a knot already growing to Gordian proportions in her stomach.

"Zed sent this through," Freya replied. "Daisy, the Urvalin are on the other side, and they've attacked Earth and Dark Side!"

Daisy felt her adrenaline spike. "You said they attacked Earth? Power up your shields to full and ready all weapons systems. We're getting our asses home."

"But Zilara—"

"Her people can handle things themselves for the time being. We've got family in harm's way, Freya. There's no time to waste."

The ship hummed as the shields slammed into place around the craft, both tech-generated as well as magical, the nanites channeling their newfound magic into the defensive spell Freya directed them to implement.

"Ready," the ship said.

"Okay. Let's—"

A flash of orange filled the darkness, followed by the violent explosions of ship after ship.

"The portal! They dropped it into the sun!" Freya realized as they watched their friends flee the deadly plasma.

Olo and Tym had managed to fly clear, but only just, while several of the slower craft around them were engulfed in the blazing plasma. But it was only going to get worse.

At that moment thirty Urvalin ships jumped into the area, targeting any ships that had survived the initial event and opening fire. The shimmer-cloaked Ghalian craft were few in number, but they engaged the much larger force with zero fear or hesitation. But Daisy realized this was a hopeless battle.

"Everyone, scatter!" she transmitted over the skree she had added to her comms package. "We will lose this fight. Get the hell out of there!"

The Ghalian moved first, swarming into an offensive pattern to blast clear an egress route. Two of the small ships blew to pieces under the ferocity of the Urvalin weapons despite their defensive spells.

"They're casting continuously," Freya realized. "It's like what Olo said. There's no break."

What they couldn't know was that the Urvalin triumvirates were overlapping spells, each of the three casters aboard each ship working as a team to maintain the constant barrage while the others prepared for their next attack.

"Ocean, Sixteen," Zilara's voice called out over their skree. "Ocean, Sixteen."

The ships all began jumping away a moment later.

"You heard her," Daisy said. "Let's go!"

Freya, and the rest of their allies, all knew the coded coordinate system, memorized for just such an emergency. It could be transmitted over open communications means, but unless you had the key to decipher it, there was no way an enemy would know what it meant.

The simple fact was it provided coordinates by a mixture of numbers and letters, the length of the word as well as letter it started with providing one portion of the location while the number gave the rest. It was simple, but in the heat of battle simple was better.

"Hang on," Freya said.

A moment later they warped away, all of them left wondering exactly how their day had gone so terribly wrong.

CHAPTER SIXTY-THREE

The rendezvous site selected in the midst of battle hadn't been as random as it might have seemed. In fact, Master Zilara and Master Farmatta had selected it for its proximity to the portal but also the fact that arriving at it required jumping past it to avoid several dangerous anomalies before backtracking into the safe pocket the unremarkable trading world resided in.

The solar system was an unusual one, possessing seventeen planets, not counting the dozens of moons circling them. A perfect place to hide.

Navigation was a little bit tricky, especially for those unfamiliar with the area, and that was another reason it had been chosen. If the Urvalin somehow did manage to locate them, mounting any sort of attack would take time. Valuable time that could be used to escape.

It was at a remote estate long held for the Ghalian by one of their front organizations where the escaped ships finally met. Despite the surrounding swamps, the area possessed huge tracts of land perfect for parking the craft, as well as layer upon layer of distortion spells blocking the true nature of what might be on the ground from aerial observation.

It wasn't enough for up-close-and-personal investigation, but it didn't need to be. If that sort of thing was happening, the nosy party would be dealt with long before they could report their findings.

It was extremely unusual for more than two Ghalian to be in the same place outside of their training facilities. But this was no ordinary occasion. They were facing a threat possibly greater even than Malalia had been at her peak power as Visla Dominus.

Roly-poly bakers, jovial florists, seemingly effete aristocrats, all of whom were actually Wampeh Ghalian, ready to kill in the blink of an eye. Less than that, in most cases. Wolves among the sheep, blending in as their order had done for thousands of years. Only Master Zilara and Master Farmatta actually knew who was Ghalian and who wasn't. The others were blissfully unaware who was in their midst.

The main body of the group was chattering amongst themselves in the frontmost courtyard, foregoing drink on this particular occasion. It was not a time for celebration. It was for the licking of one's wounds.

Daisy, Olo, and the two Ghalian masters had positioned themselves a bit away from the others, letting them all deal with their emotions without being self-conscious of the commanders of their rag-tag fleet hovering nearby. But Daisy was just as worked up as they were.

"*You need to chill out, Daze,*" Sarah said, trying to soothe her sister. "*You're gonna blow a gasket at this rate.*"

"Yeah? You think I care?" she shot back in her outside voice, not caring one bit that people might stop and stare at the crazy lady talking to herself. "I mean, we just got our asses handed to us back there. And worse, our home is already under attack. Our family."

The Ghalian were privy to the ride-along inside Daisy's head and took her rants in stride. After her performance against the

Council of Twenty and Visla Dominus, she had more than proven her worth.

"Setbacks happen, Daisy," Farmatta said, flashing the warm, kindly old woman smile she had disarmed so many with.

Daisy was not having it.

"Setbacks?" she growled. "Are you fucking kidding me? This wasn't a setback. That wasn't some little mishap. It was a monumental fuckup. It was like the goddamn kiss of death, only with tongue."

"Vulgarity is the crutch of the lesser mind. Be better than that."

"Be better? Well, fuck you too!"

Farmatta shook her head, her smile never wavering, but a flash of something in her eye got Sarah's attention if not her sister's.

"Oh, shit! No you did not just do that?"

Do what?

"Daisy, even I know that you should always be particularly careful around old people who are in a profession in which they usually die young."

Daisy paused, her rage subsiding, and with it, her logic kicking back into gear along with her self-preservation drive. At her age, the amount of blood on the old woman's hands must be staggering.

"Uh, sorry, Farmatta. I didn't mean to be disrespectful."

Farmatta moved close and rested her warm hand on Daisy's arm. "That's all right, dear. Sometimes one needs to let their anger out. Do you feel better now?"

"Actually, I do, sort of."

"Good. We need you to be clear of mind."

Zilara began slowly pacing, gears turning in her mind as she played out this chess game many moves ahead on this most unusual board.

"The portal is closed to us," she said, thinking aloud for the benefit of the others. "While the sun's energy coming through it is powerful and has the potential to be utilized in some way, for the moment we are at a disadvantage, and not just for the loss of the pathway to the other galaxy."

Farmatta nodded her agreement. "You are right, of course, Sister. We possess all four Bakana rods, but with the two intended for Charlie and Rika now stuck on this side with us, they are not being utilized as we require. And, of course, there is Master Leif, to consider."

Daisy felt her frustration flare once again. If only they hadn't stopped to investigate that probe they would have probably made it through the portal to the other side.

"*Yeah, or we'd have been burned alive,*" Sarah noted.

Stop reading my mind.

"*Not my fault you think so loud,*" Sarah shot back.

Daisy *was* thinking loud. Her emotions were a churning mess, and for good reason. Her people were in danger and she couldn't do a damn thing to help them. For someone so accustomed to being in control and generally having an aura of overall ass-kickery, it was a horrible sensation.

Farmatta watched her with a tranquil look in her eyes, reading her like an open book.

"Patience, my friend. We are examining other options," she said with that ridiculous calm the Ghalian always seemed to have, no matter how bad things were. "When one door closes, another opens. We will overcome this obstacle."

"Sure," Daisy said. "Only this door is a portal, and it's the only one that exists between our galaxies. Without it we're stuck, and I need to get back and help my family."

"I understand your sense of urgency, and it is not misplaced. But you must also remember, there are powerful casters residing in your realm, and I feel confident Charlie, Ara, and the Geist will do all they can to protect not only your people, but also your homeworld. Now, in the meantime, you must maintain your strength. Come, let us eat as we consider our next moves."

Olo had quietly watched the conversation, not daring interject when the Ghalian were talking. But now that the subject of food had been broached?

"That's a great idea," he said. "I know I could eat a whole Malooki right about now."

"Malooki, however, are not very good eating. A bit chewy, and the hair makes for quite a mess," Zilara said, fully aware his comment was merely a figure of speech.

Daisy looked at the woman, a bit surprised. A Ghalian making a joke? It was as welcome as it was unexpected. "Perhaps I'll stick with something lighter, then," she said. "I wouldn't want to bite off more than I can chew."

"You mean, again."

Oh, bite me, Sarah.

"Better you than a Malooki," she replied with a chuckle.

Amazingly, Daisy felt her mood brighten just a bit. Things were still utter crap, but the Ghalian were on her side. Maybe, just maybe, they'd come out of this on top. But she couldn't stop wondering if the others were safe across the portal.

CHAPTER SIXTY-FOUR

Nakk's people moved far faster than Bawb and the others had anticipated, and within only a few hours all of their captured craft were prepped and ready for flight. Kip's communications relay system was working perfectly, allowing for the synchronized coordination of their movements without utilizing any of the Urvalin gear.

If their understanding of the enemy ships was accurate, in free-flight mode they should be able to travel more or less unnoted. In this place the Urvalin did not operate with any sort of networked navigational system or triumvirate control protocol. It was something they could use to their advantage.

Even so, unusual flight patterns would draw attention, so it was Kip who had been chosen to make the several stealth flights to deliver teams of Nakk's people, utilizing his adaptive camouflage and hugging the terrain near the enemy base.

The leaders of each team were outfitted with small comms units, and when the word was finally given they would begin, staging their attack from all sides, distracting the Urvalin and providing an attention gap in which Kip and the others could make their landings.

By the time all of the pieces were all in place, Charlie had finally roused from his fitful slumber to find an attack plan already underway.

He barely commented on it, which under any other circumstances would have been more than a little distressing. Charlie had an opinion about just about everything and was not shy about sharing it. But with spirits low for obvious reasons, Bawb and the others just let it go.

They were sad as well, but his bond with Ara had been unique. He would be okay, eventually, of that they were sure. But it would take a while.

"You've been busy," he said, scanning the laid-out attack plans on Kip's displays.

"I am glad to see you have decided to join us," Bawb replied. "We could truly use your skills in this conflict."

"What skills? It was Ara that made me special. Now I'm just plain Charlie again."

Hunze shook her head. "Don't you dare say that about yourself. You are more than just your bond with Ara. You are a gladiator. A pirate. A rebel leader. All of those things are *yours*, Charlie. Realize your own worth and own it."

He was about to make a wise crack, but the earnestness of her look stopped him short. She was right and he knew it.

"When did you get so clever?" he grudgingly asked.

A little grin creased her lips. "When you needed to hear it."

Charlie took a deep breath and rolled his shoulders back, standing up a bit straighter. He may have still felt like ass, but he didn't have to let it show.

"Right. So, walk me through this."

Two hours later all of the pieces were in place. Charlie had seemingly gotten his head back in the game and was now geared up in his combat rig, a few extra weapons strapped on just in case. They were going against an unknown number of enemies, and sometimes it was more expedient to simply leave a blade embedded in whomever you'd just slain and draw a new one rather than slow your progress to pull the expended one free.

Where he was well armed, Bawb and Hunze's collection of bladed weapons put even Charlie's to shame. The couple preferred to fight with the clean silence of knives and, of course, their vespus blades. Even lacking their magical potency they were still some of the finest swords ever crafted. And in the hands of Bawb and Hunze they knew no equal.

Dukaan had a weapon for each of his four hands, along with backups, and Nakk, Skohla, and their people designated for the aerial portion of the attack had armed themselves with every last bit of firepower in Kip's armory.

The ground forces would use their spears and arrows to draw the Urvalin's attention, but they possessed only a single pulse pistol set to high. The point was not to cause any real damage with it but rather to get the guards' attention and make them focus all of their response on the ground. And when that happened, the teams would fly in and begin the real assault.

The time for that was now.

"Phase one, begin," Bawb transmitted.

The captured Urvalin ships took to the air, spreading out to make their approaches from multiple directions and altitudes. Anything resembling a formation would draw attention, and that was counter to their goal.

Kip activated his active camouflage and electronic scan-defeating tech and lifted off as well. Whether or not his Earth tech would be sufficient against Urvalin systems was still an unknown, but as Bawb was fond of saying, in battle there were always variables one could not prepare for. All you could do was improvise, adapt, and make the best of the situation.

Kip and one of the captured ships would land atop the structure. Their teams would then enter from that point. Or, at least, that was the hope. The structure they'd identified as the likely entry to the base could very well be the toilets for all they knew. There was only one way to find out.

"Heading down in five," Dukaan said over comms.

"Ground forces, engage," Nakk transmitted from his ship.

This was it. There was no turning back. Either they would take the structure, or they would fail spectacularly, the consequences of which would be severe to say the least.

A roar erupted around the Urvalin base tower, and flaming spears and arrows began raining down upon it. The vast majority just bounced off, causing no harm, but a few did manage to find a seam and lodge there. The fire, however, couldn't damage the structure. The Urvalin would respond regardless, and with force.

"They're coming," Nakk transmitted. "Phase two, initiate."

The captured ships began their approaches from all directions, seemingly reacting to the attack on the ground as a pair of ships also launched from the structure. Nakk's people circled high before beginning to approach the landing areas, allowing the other ships to drop to the surface.

Pulse blasts abruptly flashed into the air, targeting the Urvalin ships. They quickly pulled back, shocked, no doubt, at this unexpected attack. This enemy had functional technology, and that should have been impossible.

"Guys, the top is clear," Charlie said. "I think we need to drop in now."

"Our plan is for a few more minutes," Dukaan replied.

"Yeah, but plans are fluid, as is battle. When the opportunity presents itself, you've gotta take it."

Bawb nodded to the pilot.

"Okay, we're going down," Dukaan said. "Kip, you ready?"

"Yep. Weapons hot and standing by. I'm ready to become visible."

"All right. Nakk, we're going now. Set down at your

coordinates up top. We'll drop in and provide a distraction," Bawb transmitted.

Nakk didn't hesitate or question the slight change in plans; instead, his ship began the approach immediately. "We will be down momentarily," he said. "Good luck."

"You as well," Bawb replied.

The plan was to breach the facility and have two teams split up to find the cells where their people were being held while the others entering from the lower landing zones would search out the transmitter controlling the energy-dampening microsats above. Once they deactivated them, an entire fleet would come back to life.

Or so they hoped.

Nakk's ship gently landed at one of the empty spots atop the Urvalin base without anyone seeming to take note; the battle down below had drawn all of their attention. With eyes elsewhere, the other ships moved into place as well, flying into the landing areas to await their forces' deployment.

"Here we go," Kip said as he deactivated his adaptive camouflage and became visible to the naked eye while simultaneously allowing the Urvalin scans to see him.

Right as he set down on the landing pad with a loud bang.

"Shields up, Kip," Charlie said.

"On full."

Charlie and his friends stood ready at the hatch, awaiting the go signal.

As they had hoped, the sealed door leading into the base opened, and Urvalin guards came streaming out, armed to the teeth.

"Door's open. Hit 'em, Kip," Charlie said.

The ship let off several pulse rounds, forcing the Urvalin to call for reinforcements and take defensive positions. In their tunnel-vision focus, they didn't even question the Urvalin ship parked right beside them. It was one of their own, after all.

"Nakk, now!" Bawb transmitted.

Nakk's ship's door slid open and his forces streamed out. Skohla led the first wave right into the open facility door, preventing anyone still inside from locking them out. At the same time, the others opened fire on the Urvalin response teams from behind, taking them utterly off guard.

"Our turn," Charlie said as the guards spun, now facing attacks on two fronts.

The door slid open, and his crew spilled out onto the landing deck, spreading out quickly while laying down suppressive fire. The aim wasn't to kill the Urvalin, though that would be a nice bonus. Their goal was to drive them back to cover, leaving them exposed from the rear. It was a crossfire, and any sane combatant would realize they had lost and surrender.

Unfortunately, the Urvalin had proven themselves anything but normal in that regard.

The guards fought fiercely even as their comrades fell all around them. It was clear that surrender was not an option, and a few minutes later they all lay dead or dying. After what had happened to Ara, Charlie was fine with that.

"Inside, everyone!" he called out. "Find the prisoners!"

"Teams are in on the other levels," Kip informed them. "Minimal resistance. It seems they sent the bulk of their guards up top. The others went low to mop up the decoy. One of the teams managed to reach the access controls, and the guards are now locked out."

"Then the base is ours," Nakk said with a grin.

Bawb moved toward the open door. "Do not celebrate prematurely, my friend. We must still secure the interior. We must find our people."

CHAPTER SIXTY-FIVE

Bawb and Charlie may not have had the benefit of their shimmer cloaks, or any camouflaging magic for that matter, but they did possess the gift of stealth. Bawb was far more proficient, as was Hunze, but that was only to be expected.

Nakk's people were also adept at silent stalking, courtesy of years of hunting and surviving in the woods of this planet. Not a skill space crews would normally find themselves needing, but then, this was not normal by any stretch of the imagination.

The two groups split up once inside the Urvalin base. The interior was actually far easier to navigate than they'd anticipated, and the teams on the lower level landing platforms had overpowered the resistance and made good progress as well. It was looking like a rout, but that didn't mean there would not still be fighting.

Pulse blasts scorched the wall where a furious barrage had barely missed Charlie's unshielded head.

"Careful," Bawb said. "You are vulnerable."

He was correct in more ways than one. Charlie had been so accustomed to his magic protecting him, those second-nature defenses were hard not to rely on.

"Right, right," Charlie said. "Before that guy nearly took my head off, I saw a flight of stairs up ahead. Looks like they bottlenecked the area as a choke point."

"How can we get past them?" Dukaan asked. "Without magic to provide shielding, we seem to be at a tactical disadvantage."

Bawb and Hunze shared a look, followed by a knowing grin.

"The walls behind them are somewhat close," he said. "That disadvantage may not be as great as you perceive."

"What are you thinking, Bob?" Charlie asked. "Something awesome and unexpected, I hope."

"One could argue that, yes," the assassin replied.

He and Hunze each pulled several small daggers from their hidden sheaths. These were a little different than their normal weapons in that the pommels of them were of added thickness and an unusual shape. Specialty items, it seemed.

"Uh, Bob?" Charlie said, just as the couple stepped from cover and hurled their blades, tucking back to safety immediately.

The knives flew fast and hard, impacting the wall at the far end of the corridor intersecting the staircase. But rather than strike and fall, they redirected that impact energy and bounced, like a bullet's ricochet, hurling off the wall and into the backs of several Urvalin guards.

The men dropped to the ground in pain while their friends turned in shock. It was all of the room to work the pair needed.

Bawb and Hunze raced ahead, throwing a steady stream of daggers, the flying metal keeping their enemies pinned down. Charlie and Dukaan ran right behind them, pulse weapons at the ready.

They reached the corridor and dove, Charlie going left and Dukaan going right, each of them firing off a volley of pulse blasts into the hiding enemy. It wasn't pretty, but it worked, and a moment later the Urvalin lay smoldering on the ground.

"Holy shit, I can't believe that worked," Charlie said. "Where the hell did you learn that trick?"

Bawb grinned, his fangs visible for battle. "I may have taught you all you know of Ghalian fighting styles," he said. "But not all that *I* know."

Charlie couldn't help but laugh. Maybe it was the stress of combat, or the sheer ridiculousness of the moment, but it was a tiny bit of cathartic release he hadn't realized he'd so badly needed.

"It is good to see you laugh," Hunze said as she pried her daggers free and replaced them in their sheaths.

"Indeed, it is," Bawb agreed. "But we have work to do. These guards, do you notice something different about them?"

Charlie looked at the bodies and noted there *was* one difference.

"Key fobs," he said. "They're not just troops. These guys have access."

"Exactly. And by the look of this level, I would wager we are close to prisoner holding."

"Then what are we waiting for?" Charlie asked.

"For both of you to stop talking and start moving," Dukaan said. "Are we ready, here?"

Bawb sheathed his last knife after wiping it clean on a deceased guard's clothing. He pulled free the key fob and tossed it to Dukaan, then did the same with the other key fobs on their victims until each had one.

"*Now* we are ready," he said. "Steel your nerves. We do not know what we will find."

The team moved quickly, checking compartments as they hurried down the corridors. There were a few small rises and dips, the shift in levels covered by small staircases. It seemed the facility had been slapped together from barracks units and altered to suit its current purpose. Storage, maintenance, even small galley areas. But one section had been converted to cells.

"Holy shit! Tamara!" Charlie said when the door swung open.

The metal-armed former commando was sitting on the small bunk in her bare cell, stripped of her flight suit but still clad in her own tank top and pants. Her boots were missing, but while that would be an issue out in the woods, it wouldn't matter much in the clean confines of the base.

"Charlie?" she said. "Oh my God, you guys made it!"

"We did. Are you okay? Did they hurt you?"

She sneered a little. "They tried, but after I busted one fella's nose they just beat on me a bit then left me in my cell. Fuck these scrawny assholes. I didn't tell 'em a goddamn thing."

Charlie couldn't help but chuckle. That was Tamara in a nutshell. A badass to the end. Fortunately, she hadn't met hers. Not yet.

"Who else is here? Have you seen any other survivors?" Hunze asked.

"Shelley is here," she replied. "I saw her when we arrived. There were other pods launched, but I haven't seen any other survivors. I tried to talk him out of it, but the captain went down with the ship. He was trying to reboot Gustavo last I saw him. Did he make it?"

"I'm sorry, Tamara, but Gustavo is gone. Griggalt as well," Dukaan said.

"But Kip clearly made it okay. And Ara, since you're here, Charlie."

Charlie felt a twinge in his gut. "Ara is gone," he said. "It happened after we crashed."

"Oh, shit. I'm so sorry."

"Yeah," he said, a tightness forming in his throat.

They stood silently a moment when Bawb appeared in the doorway. At his side was Shelley, beaten and exhausted, but intact.

"I found but one more survivor. She is dehydrated but otherwise in fair condition."

"Shelley!" Tamara rushed to her and wrapped her up in a tight hug. "How bad is it?"

"I'll be okay," Shelley replied, her voice dry and gravelly.

"Come on," Tamara said, wrapping her ceramisteel arm around her and taking on some of her weight. "We're getting you out of here."

Nakk and his teams were swarming the structure now, searching high and low for the transmitter controlling the power-sapping microsats. Charlie and Bawb decided they would escort the former captives back to Kip before helping with that part of the search.

Only, there was a problem.

"This is all wrong," Nakk transmitted to his new friends. "My people have reported barracks, cells, equipment, and monitoring stations, but no proper command center."

"Wait," Charlie replied. "You're sure they've checked everywhere?"

"Yes. Once we overcame the initial response and freed our people who had been in captivity, the rest of the base turned out to be only sparsely manned. This is not a command base. It is merely a staging center."

Kip had been listening and incorporating real-time updates into his situational processing array. This new tidbit suddenly made several troubling things make sense.

"Guys, I know how their system works now," Kip transmitted. "I thought it was a central command station that controlled them, but now I see it. This is a daisy-chained relay network. They're all interlinked, each of them autonomous but also picking up slack for the others as needed."

Charlie and Bawb knew what that meant, and it was not good.

"So, if this place wasn't controlling them after all, we're screwed, basically," Charlie said.

"I'm afraid so. And worse yet, I've detected a silent alarm."

"Lovely."

"*And* a beacon signal has been activated."

"It just keeps getting better and better," Charlie grumbled. "Okay, Kip, prep for dustoff. We'll be right out."

Silence.

"Kip?"

A shriek of static blasted over the comms.

"The signal is being scrambled," he realized. "We need to warn the others. Quick, outside!"

Charlie and his friends rushed for the exit, hoping that Nakk and his people had been listening in before the signal cut out. Even so, if there was a scrambler in play, that meant one thing. There were other reinforcements out there, and they would be coming soon. The question was *how* soon?

The team paused at the door, not daring to simply rush outside. It *looked* like all was clear, but Charlie had a bad feeling about this.

"Come on, to the ships!" he said, then stepped out and hurried for cover just in case.

It was a good thing he did as pulse fire suddenly rained down from above, peppering the landing platform. Apparently, the Urvalin had several ships in low orbit, now recalled to the base. If not for the fact they didn't want to destroy their own facility, along with their overconfidence at defeating the intruders, the Urvalin could very possibly have killed them all in a single attack.

They had been spared, for now, but the captured Urvalin ship took several direct hits and sat smoldering on the landing site with their attack group looping for another pass.

"Kip, get out of here!" Charlie shouted.

The ship didn't argue, blasting up into the sky in a flash, his weapons firing a blaze of pulse blasts at the Urvalin ships along with a spray of railgun sabots. None hit, but it was at least enough to push the aggressors back for a moment.

Charlie looked up at the sky and realized the futility of the situation. They were outnumbered. Outgunned. Even if Kip could retrieve them, what then? They'd been noticed, and there was no way the Urvalin would let them slip into hiding.

"Charlie, we must retreat to the ground level," Bawb said, rushing to his side.

"Then what? We've got nowhere to run."

Bawb's lack of an answer was all Charlie needed to hear. They both knew they were screwed. Anything they attempted was just rearranging deck chairs on the *Titanic* at this point.

Another volley of Urvalin pulse blasts showered down, and this time it was coming right at them.

"Bob, look out!" Charlie shouted, pushing him aside and casting his strongest defensive spell out of pure instinct.

Miraculously, the spell somehow worked, deflecting all of the attack, leaving the two men unscathed. Bawb looked at Charlie with shock, which was saying something for the assassin.

"Charlie, how did you—?"

"I don't know, dude," he replied. "Something's changed."

And it truly had. He felt power again, and it was getting stronger by the second. But Charlie didn't create his own power. He couldn't. Not without his bond with Ara. His chest suddenly grew warm with an impossible hope.

His wish bore out true when a massive blast of magical fire burst out across the sky, engulfing two of the Urvalin ships and turning them to melted slag.

"Ara!" he shouted, overwhelmed with joy.

"*Sorry I am late,*" she said. "*Now, excuse me a moment, I have something to finish.*"

She spun and dove, her pristine red scales gleaming in the

sunlight as she tore into the remaining enemy ships. One by one they fell to her talons, her teeth, and her flames until none remained.

"*Ara, the satellites are blocking us,*" Charlie told her, reveling in their silent link.

"*Then I will be right back,*" she replied, streaking skyward to the edge of space.

Charlie and Bawb couldn't see what she was doing from that distance, but the small flashes as entire swaths of microsatellites were destroyed was clear enough. Dozens fell, then more, all of them failing as their linked systems abruptly shifted from an advantage to a weakness.

"The energy suck, it's failing!" Kip transmitted as he dropped back down to the landing pad. "The blockage is gone!"

Charlie felt more than just joy at his friend's incredible return. He also felt hope. With the Urvalin satellites down, power would soon start to return to the craft that had survived their rough landings on the surface.

Soon, if all went as he hoped, they would have hundreds of fully functional ships at their disposal. They would have an actual fleet.

Ara soared down in a tight corkscrew, her wings wide and flapping hard as she came to rest on the landing pad. Charlie and Bawb regarded her with amazement. She looked as good as new. Better, even.

"How—?" Charlie began.

"The planet's energy," she said. "The one place I could absorb enough to restore my power. At least for the time being. This place still sucks it away incredibly fast." She glanced up at the sky. "I must get back there and recharge while I still possess the strength to protect myself."

"Protect yourself? From what?"

"The heat, Charlie. The Balamar waters were the key, but my body needed to absorb more power than the tenuous connection with the lava could provide. I was getting stronger, but I knew it would not be enough. Not for a real fight."

"But what did you do?"

"I went to the one place I could absorb enough power," she replied. "I had just enough strength to keep from burning up, though it hurt incredibly at first."

"Hang on, you *swam* in the lava?" he marveled.

"Oh, heavens no."

"I was going to—"

"That wouldn't have been nearly enough," she said with a twinkle in her eye. "I went to the one place this planet was not affected by this magic void. I dove to the planet's core."

Charlie blinked hard. "I'm sorry, did you say you swam in lava to the planet's core?"

"Magma, to be specific. But yes, I did."

Charlie assessed the power once again flowing in his system. It was weakening rapidly, but it did indeed seem to have returned at full strength for at least a little bit.

"And now you need to go down there again?" he asked.

"To replenish my power, yes. My body is healed, but my magic is quite quickly drained."

"And when you come back up?"

"I will once more have all of my strength. For a little while, at least."

"Long enough to escape this planet?"

"Oh, if I'm not engaged in battle, most certainly."

The gears began turning in Charlie's head. Suddenly, things weren't so bad. Suddenly, he had a plan.

"How long, Ara?"

"In my healthy state? Perhaps five hours to recharge. It is still a somewhat slow process in this place. But it will get the job done."

"Great. Then do what you've got to do and meet us back here."

"Of course. And what will you do?"

"Get ready to fly," he replied.

Ara nodded her massive head and lifted off, flying back to the lava pools to swim deep into the planet's core.

"Nakk," Charlie called out to their new ally, "I want you to gather up everyone."

"Everyone?"

"*Everyone*," he replied, his smile growing by the second.

"What are you thinking, Charlie?" Bawb asked.

"I'm thinking that we've got a fleet, Bob. And it's time we use it."

CHAPTER SIXTY-SIX

It had been a tense few hours after Nakk spread the word of their victory to his people. Partly, it was because he had been utilizing their captured Urvalin ships to speed the process, and seeing the enemy drop right down into all of their supposedly protected encampments was disconcerting to say the least.

From then it was a waiting game with all of Nakk's many pockets of survivors rushing to gather all the supplies they had and load them onto the nearest ships. And after so many years stranded, waiting could be just as stressful as action.

Nakk mustered all of his able-bodied pilots to their stations. They had enough people to fly nearly all of their ships, but some would have to be left behind. The final decision of which craft would stay would be made once they all had power. Or so they hoped.

If the energy-dampening field truly was down, then, in theory, the craft should be able to become functional again. How long it would take and at what speed was anyone's guess.

"How's it looking?" Charlie asked as the allotted time approached.

"Power is returning to most vessels, but there are those

whose drive systems appear to have suffered irreparable damage during their crash landings."

"Not entirely unexpected," Bawb mused.

"No, not at all," Nakk said. "We have already begun reallocating their resources and supplies to the functional ships. With all of their foodstuffs, water, and other items from the ground, my people should be ready for liftoff within the hour."

Bawb nodded his approval. "An impressively fast response."

"We have been stranded here against our will for a long time. Believe me when I say, we are *very* motivated."

Charlie knew how they felt. The sooner they could get home, the better. And with new allies at their side, no less. It was looking like they might actually turn this catastrophe into a win, in that regard.

"Let's saddle up and get ready," he said. "Ara will be back soon, and when she is, we'll have a short window to get free of here before the magic drain starts to affect her."

"We will be ready," Nakk said. "I'll be aboard my command ship awaiting your signal."

The alien commander stepped into the waiting commandeered Urvalin ship and departed for his own craft, ready to finally take to the skies after such a long time.

"*Ara, how ya feeling?*" Charlie sent to his Zomoki friend.

"*Quite good,*" she replied, their bond robust even at this distance. "*I will be back to you momentarily.*"

"*Looking forward to it,*" he said.

"*As am I,*" Bawb chimed in.

"*Hey, you're connected again,*" Charlie noted.

"*Yes, as the Wise One's power returned, so did our link.*"

"*Excellent news, man. Round up Hunze and the others. It's time to boogie outta here.*"

The team prepped for liftoff, running through a quick preflight before Ara returned. Fortunately, Kip was in excellent order, and there wasn't much to do.

Faint snores resonated in the ship as Tamara and Shelley were actually napping in their flight seats. They'd eaten well and been treated in the med pod, and with their decades of combined military experience, at moments like this the ability to fall asleep pretty much anywhere was something of a godsend.

"Uh, guys?" Kip said a few minutes later. "I think we may have an issue, here."

Charlie didn't like the sound of that. "Yeah, Kip, what's up this time?"

"I can't be sure, but it's looking like there are ships in orbit. Larger than the ones we've seen so far."

"Urvalin?" Bawb asked, cinching his harness tight.

"I think so. It looks like we're going to have to fight our way out of here."

This was a serious wrinkle in their plans. Ara needed to hang back and keep her magic strong if she was to survive their escape from the magic-blocking planet, and fighting off enemy ships was not conducive to that. But they had one thing on their side that the Urvalin weren't expecting.

"Hey, Nakk," Charlie called over comms. "Kip says it looks like there are some bigger Urvalin craft up there just outside the atmosphere. We're gonna have to fight through them. Do you think your ships are up to it?"

A merry laugh rang out over the comms.

"Oh, we are more than up for it," Nakk replied. "Armaments are functional on seventy percent of our ships, and believe me when I say we are anxious to use them."

"Then you'll get your chance soon," Charlie replied. "I'm going to have Ara hang back when we go. She needs to conserve her magi—*Allpower* for space flight."

"Of course. We will be ready when you are."

It was only twenty minutes before Ara emerged from the molten core of the planet, fully charged with the unusual magic and feeling good.

"I am ready," she said over the new comms unit Dukaan had whipped up for her.

She was still lacking a flight harness, so Charlie would ride aboard Kip for the time being. Once they got home Cal and his fabricators could make a new one, but for now he was content to fly with his friends.

"Nakk, it's time," Charlie transmitted.

"We are ready," Nakk replied. "Follow us out, and shield your friend behind our forces. We will lead the way."

Charlie wasn't about to object to letting the bigger ships deal with the Urvalin. They were not only larger, but they also had quite a bone to pick.

The small craft launched first, making a quick rush to space. The Urvalin had at least ten ships of good size it seemed, and they all converged to crush the much smaller adversary. Nakk's advance ships opened fire with all they had, giving the Urvalin something to think about as the engagement began. They may have been smaller, but they were also more maneuverable for it.

"I approve of our friend's tactics," Bawb said as Nakk then sent up three waves of ships, small and fast to encircle the Urvalin, followed by two flanks of heavy hitters to take them out.

"He's got them pinned down," Charlie said. "As long as they don't warp away for reinforcements we should have them."

"Watch," Bawb said. "All craft are targeting the Urvalin drive systems. We know magic does not function properly here, so once they are unable to warp, it will be a decisive defeat."

It went pretty much as Bawb had anticipated, with Nakk's fleet operating with impressive speed and precision given how long it had been since they'd actually seen proper space combat. In just a few minutes the battle was over, and given the somewhat overkill amount of firepower leveled on the Urvalin, there were most definitely no survivors.

Ara and Kip flew up behind them, finally clear of the planet and its strange magic-blocking properties. Or so they thought. But something else was lurking in the darkness.

"Uh, Ara?" Charlie said, looking at the scans of the system in shock. "Are those what I think they are?"

All eyes were on the displays, both aboard Kip as well as all of Nakk's craft. None had understood just how it was the Urvalin had managed to find a planet where their Allpower was rendered impotent. Now there was an answer, and it was more than just planetary.

"Black holes," Ara said. "Multiple black holes."

"Holy crap!" Kip exclaimed. "This should be an impossibility. I mean, this is totally not a natural occurrence."

Charlie was still in shock as he stared at the sun's light bending toward the dark vortexes. It was no wonder they couldn't connect to the galaxy's flow of magic. The way these black holes were positioned, nothing, not even Allpower, or magic, or whatever you wanted to call it, could reach here.

"The Urvalin did this?" he asked.

"Clearly," Bawb said. "The portal was a perfect trap. An access point to a place you cannot escape. And if somehow the victim did not crash onto the planet, they would be pulled into one of the black holes."

"The amount of power required to achieve this," Ara marveled, "the years upon years of constant expenditure of resources to move not one black hole but several? It is more than could be accomplished in a single lifetime. This is a generations-long endeavor."

Charlie felt a surge of adrenaline crank his senses to eleven.

"Ara, how's your power?"

"Holding, but I fear this changes things. We need to get free of this place, and soon."

Kip was already working on that problem as fast as his AI mind could process.

"There's no way to make it to the portal," he said. "To get to it we'd have to fly into a cross current from the vortexes."

"Kip, we need out of this system," Charlie said. "*Then* we can worry about reaching the portal. Is there a course?"

"I don't see one."

"*I* do," Ara said. "There is a faint stream of particles streaming from the black holes. They are flowing in a different manner than other energy. There must be a pattern to it."

Charlie adjusted his monitor. "Kip, can you see what she's talking about?"

"Hang on. Yeah, I think I picked it up. There, you see?"

The display showed a faint stream spewing from the void.

Charlie couldn't help but marvel at the beauty of it. They were in a bind, but his scientific mind nevertheless reveled in the sheer magnitude of what they were witnessing.

"I'd heard of black hole particle ejection, but I never thought I'd see it in person," he said.

Kip had continued running calculations nonstop and was actually making headway. "Hey, guys. I was thinking. The Urvalin wouldn't just strand a bunch of ships here, so Ara's right. There *has* to be a way out."

"But the black holes," Dukaan said.

"Right, I know. But they were the ones who put them here. And with that in mind, I ran some calculations using the black holes as guideposts of a sort, then cross-referenced their individual subatomic particle streams to see how they interact."

"English, Kip," Charlie said.

"Right. So, long and short, I found a way out. At least I think so. It'll be a serious bit of threading the needle, but if we stay right on the precise course, we should be able to do it."

"And if not?"

"Well, you've always expressed curiosity about what's through a black hole."

Charlie groaned. "Let's not find out today, if at all possible, all right?" He switched the comms on wide, reaching out to all the ships in their fleet. "This is Charlie. We think we have a way out of here, but we'll need to move fast and with precision. There's a gap between the black holes where we should be able to fly without being pulled in. Kip's sending you all the coordinates now. We're heading out immediately. Stay close, and good luck."

With that he shut off his comms.

"Hang on," Dukaan said. "This may get bumpy."

The turbulence was actually minimal as the competing forces caused something of an eddy to form. A tiny route of safe passage just as Kip had hypothesized. The AI ship led the way, a caravan of spacecraft following close behind. Soon a few stars became visible in the distance as they raced for open space. For safety and freedom.

"Almost out," Kip announced.

"I hope there's no one waiting for us once we're clear," Charlie said. "I've already had enough nasty surprises to last a lifetime."

"Sensors aren't picking up anything. No trace of tech or any man-made objects," the AI replied.

"Thank God," Charlie said, letting out a relieved sigh. "We made it."

The newly formed fleet increased their speed as they flew clear of the perilous exit route into the vast expanse of open space, and as they did, the flow of magic washed over them all.

Nakk's people felt the Allpower abruptly reappear, flooding their bodies with whatever limited amounts they naturally possessed. After so many years without so much a drop, good cheer immediately spread throughout the fleet, tangible in the flares of happy Allpower escaping its overjoyed crewmembers.

Bawb and Hunze, linked as they were, each felt identical flashes course through their bodies as well as their potency returned in an instant. He took a deep breath, squeezed her hand, and smiled. They were okay. They were free.

As for Charlie and Ara, they were both already mostly charged from her trip to the center of the planet, but even so, they both felt their tanks topped off and holding strong. Their magic was back as good as ever. They'd escaped the Urvalin trap. And once they got their bearings straight, they'd get their payback. And if Charlie had his way, that payback was going to be a bitch.

EPILOGUE

The makeshift fleet floated silently in the void. Drifting. Powered down to minimal levels as every last craft was surveyed from stem to stern. They had crashed a long time ago and been without power ever since, and any repairs that had been made had been done without the benefit of active systems to ensure the fixes would hold.

A few ships had already suffered failures, but nothing critical to life support or drive systems. Still, the repair teams were working hard, running from ship to ship to help their crews put out proverbial fires.

But something else was off. Something was *very* wrong.

"Charlie?" Ara said. "Do you feel this?"

"I do," he replied, suddenly *very* uneasy. "Ara?" A low panic was already forming in his gut.

Ara sniffed at the magic, getting a sense for the energy flowing throughout the entire galaxy. Linked as they were, Charlie felt her reaction viscerally, his body tensing as hers did.

"Oh no. It can't be," he gasped. "Leila..."

Bawb noticed his shift in posturing, the victorious smile quickly fading from his face. "What is it, Charlie?" he asked.

411

Charlie looked at him with panic in his eyes. "Dude, this magic doesn't feel right. This is different."

"Different?"

"Yeah. And *bad* different. Bob, this isn't my galaxy."

Bawb considered Charlie's revelation a moment.

"Then the portal has taken us back to my—"

"No, you don't understand," Charlie said. "It's not my galaxy. But it's not *your* galaxy either."

"Are you certain?" Hunze asked, reaching out to see if she could feel what Ara had sensed. "Ara? Could there be a mistake?"

"There is no mistake. I am certain," Ara replied. "This is someplace new."

Charlie gazed out at the utterly foreign constellations and felt his stomach sink. Leila was out there somewhere. Pregnant and ready to pop, and he was as lost as the day he'd first met her. Pulse racing, he flopped back in his seat and took a deep breath.

"Where the hell are we?"

Kip scanned his star charts for any reference point at all. He sifted through them all and came up with nothing.

"There are *billions* of galaxies," the AI said. "And we have no idea which one we are in. Worse, I don't think we can get back to the portal to reverse course."

"Wait, what do you mean?" Charlie asked.

"It seemed to be designed to spit out the ships it trapped at speed and send them to the planet below. Without an utterly *enormous* amount of magic, which we cannot access where the portal is floating, it looks like we're stuck here."

Now Charlie was pacing. Not angry pacing. Not upset. He was thinking.

"The Urvalin have the ability to create a portal without requiring a sun or Ootaki hair to power it."

Hunze had been thinking about that as well. "We do not know what sort of power-storage devices they might employ," she said. "We have already gathered the weapons and bandas of their fallen from our prior engagements, and now that we are free of that place, the bandas do appear to hold their Allpower much the way a konus holds magic."

"And who can tell what manner of amalgam of Allpower and technology they may have used to create it," Bawb added. "This is a new galaxy, and one where the two are utilized in tandem, just as your world has started to incorporate magic."

"I know, Bob. It's just, how did they even know to link to *my* galaxy? And how is it our magic works in this one? I mean, what are the odds it would even be compatible?"

"Actually," Ara said over their comms link, "I think I may be able to answer that."

Charlie felt a flicker of hope. "What do you mean?"

"There were legends among my kind. Stories from tens of thousands of years before my time. They were no more than myths, or so I thought. Tales of another galaxy once bonded with our own."

"Yeah, mine."

"No, Charlie. There was another. Legend had it there were *two* other galaxies forever linked with my own. A triumvirate of magical realms, granting those linked to them immense power."

Bawb flashed a curious little look at Hunze. She shrugged, but the look in her eye told him she was thinking the same thing.

"So, you believe this is the third galaxy," he said. "The final link."

"I do believe so, yes," Ara replied. "We are castaways in a place I never actually believed existed. And the Urvalin made it possible."

Charlie stopped pacing. "If they know about this, and the power waiting to be harnessed by linking all three, then they're not just going to invade my galaxy. The Urvalin will come for yours as well."

"That is my concern, yes," she said. "The question is when."

Billions of light years away, Torgus, Fraxxis, and Prin stood on the casting podiums of their respective command ships, each of them far, far away, connecting across the three galaxies.

"The plan is underway," Torgus said. "And despite a few setbacks, we appear to have been successful in our initial ploys."

"You have lowered the portal into the sun, Torgus?" Fraxxis asked.

"Yes. And Prin has confirmed the destruction of multiple resistance ships where she is located in the process, though it appears the one called Daisy escaped. But no worry, we will handle that in good time. And on your end?"

"Charlie and Ara have been reported deceased," Fraxxis said.

"Confirmed?" Torgus asked.

"The messenger came straightaway after our troops stationed there found the wreckage. He said the ship broke apart in the atmosphere, and the only survivors found were a pair of females."

"And the Zomoki?"

"Ara's body was examined where it slammed into the ground. It was burned and most definitely dead."

"Good," Torgus said, feeling the increasing Allpower flow through himself and his partners across the galaxies. "Now we move to the next stage. Now we take control and fulfill our destiny."

PREVIEW: WILD CARD CHARLIE

THE DRAGON MAGE 11

Explosions pummeled Kip, the near misses rocking the poor AI ship like a tiny boat in a big, tumultuous sea. His digital reflexes were up to the task, and he avoided any direct hits, but not for the Urvalin's lack of trying.

What was more concerning was that these attacks were more than just conventional in their nature. Yes, technological weaponry was targeting Kip as he engaged in a frantic dogfight to the death, but also magical attacks of blistering intensity.

But Charlie and his friends knew what they'd signed up for when they picked this fight.

"Ara, a little help, please," Dukaan requested as calmly as he could given the circumstances. "We seem to be a bit outnumbered."

The Chithiid pilot had all four arms moving in a blur of activity as his hands flew across consoles, assisting his AI ship in flight while also targeting the enemy with pulse cannon and railgun rounds. Fortunately, they were not alone in this fight.

They were part of a small attack group of Earth's people along with their new ally Nakk's rebel fleet, this particular wing of which was currently led by Charlie and Ara as the ships engaged the Urvalin battle cruiser and its complement of smaller fighter craft.

Nakk had an additional contingent of heavily armed ships staged nearby as a backup force, not to mention the multiple squadrons concurrently engaged with the Urvalin ships orbiting the planet as well as its two moons. It was a battle on four fronts —three in space and one on the ground—and the advantage was shifting constantly.

The Urvalin, sensing a possible victory, hadn't even noticed Nakk's casters were actively blocking them from jumping away. As for warp, they would target anyone who attempted its drive systems. It was imperfect, but hopefully enough for what they needed.

"Bank hard left," Charlie transmitted over his direct line to Kip and Dukaan.

The pair didn't hesitate, breaking left immediately. The Urvalin ship on their tail followed right behind them, locked on to the ship's energy signature as best it could. It was a different sort of power, though, and that was the only reason Kip had been able to break free repeatedly. But their luck could only last so long.

Fortunately, the Urvalin's was about to run out first.

Ara let loose a stream of magical fire just as Kip flashed past. The Urvalin simply didn't have time to shift course, and moments later the craft was engulfed in flame, reducing it to a lump of drifting slag despite its magical defenses. The Zomoki's magic was incredibly powerful, and the Urvalin had not yet come up with an answer for her attacks.

Kip leveled off and ceased his evasive maneuvers. "Thanks. That was getting close."

"They are proving to be more difficult to handle than we had originally anticipated," Ara replied.

"Yeah, stay sharp," Charlie added. "We've still got a ways to go."

"Copy that," Kip replied, then banked hard and headed back into the fight, weapons blazing.

He was a robust and well-armed ship, and equipped with not only warp tech but also a powerful konus fused to his airframe. Back home that combination made him somewhat special, not to mention a difficult target to say the least.

Here in this new galaxy, however, he was nothing special. Nakk's people as well as the Urvalin used magic and tech together as if it were the most normal thing in the world. And they were damn good at it.

"*We've got to keep their attention up here,*" Charlie silently told Ara. "*The Urvalin have to believe they have the upper hand for as long as we're able.*"

"*Obviously,*" she agreed. "*Fortunately, it would appear they are singularly focused on the three-pronged attack underway in space.*"

"*Yeah, we definitely got their attention, as we hoped.*"

"*Yes. But should they decide to turn their gaze groundward, things might get difficult.*"

It was the weakest part of the plan, and the one they had little control over. The secret ground assault.

In space at least there was the ability to unleash a sudden wave of sheer firepower to try to overwhelm the enemy and keep them focused on the battle. But on the ground? And during a stealth operation? No such overt actions were acceptable. At least, not until it was too late for the enemy to do anything about it.

Bawb and Hunze were on the planet's surface stalking through a wooded area outside a mid-sized city. While the others were in battle above, they were leading a small team of surprisingly talented fighters in an infiltration and capture operation on one of the Urvalin outposts there.

Intelligence gleaned from Nakk's contacts told them that not only was the facility relatively undefended—for an Urvalin base of operations, that is—but it was also reported to be housing a large cache of rather powerful Allpower-storing bandas as well as other Urvalin tech weapons.

With a nascent rebel fleet itching to get into the fight, Charlie and Nakk had both agreed it would be well worth the risk if the intelligence proved true. They'd been picking off smaller targets for a few weeks now, but something substantial was needed if they wanted to truly turn the tables. And this might very well be what they were seeking.

While the Ghalian and his mate took the front position, Skohla provided a rear guard, ready and very able to take out any Urvalin who might stumble upon them before they reached their objective. She'd proven her skills to Bawb already and gained his trust during Hunze's rescue, and the scary Ghalian's approval was good enough for the others.

With their magic working for the most part, Bawb and Hunze were once again a deadly pair to deal with. More so than before, which was saying something. But the magic here also seemed to interact with their other galaxy spells oddly at times, though no one knew how or when such a misfire might occur.

Fortunately, Skohla and her team were adept at casting, and while their spells were somewhat different, they did often achieve a close enough result. And working in threes allowed them to bolster their spells by overlapping their power, just as the Urvalin did. It also made average-strength casters far more difficult to deal with than if they were operating alone.

Bawb stopped in place, the team behind him freezing immediately. He gestured for the others to drop low, lowering to a knee himself. While his shimmer cloak was functional once more, it was not exactly reliable in this galaxy. When this degree of stealth was needed, he simply couldn't risk it.

The bloodshed would have to come *after* they had reached their objective. Anything sooner and the Urvalin would send reinforcements from above, stymieing their efforts.

"Bob, how's it going down there?" Charlie asked.

The Ghalian reached for their silent link, courtesy of Ara, not about to risk a verbal reply. *"We have arrived at the perimeter of the target area. A patrol is nearby, however. We are awaiting their departure."*

"Gotcha. Do what you do and we'll have your back. Everything's going as planned up here."

"Charlie, what is it you always say about tempting that Murphy fellow?"

"Well, yeah. But we've got our power back—"

"And it doesn't always work."

"And we have functional tech as well. We've got these guys, Bob. We just need to drag this out long enough for you to get inside that facility."

"Soon, my friend," Bawb replied, then released their connection.

"Looks like we need to stall these guys a bit longer," Charlie transmitted to the fleet. "Watch each other's backs. Once they've made it in we gang up on—"

A dozen Urvalin ships flashed into the area. They didn't come in with their weapons hot, though. It looked like they were simply arriving at this system to regroup. Unfortunately for Charlie and his friends, that meant that Mr. Murphy had indeed just paid them a visit.

"Shit. We've got incoming!" Charlie warned the others. "Dammit, fall back and regroup. Hit 'em hard! Keep their eyes on us."

Ara spun away from an incoming magical barrage. Charlie, in a makeshift harness instead of Ara's usual one, was thrown to the side.

"Whose brilliant idea was this ambush?" he grumbled.

"Yours, Charlie," Ara replied, unleashing a stream of magical fire at their enemy.

"What was I thinking?"

"That we need resources. Weapons and ships."

"Yeah. And who better to take them from than the Urvalin? I *do* so enjoy taking the Urvalin's stuff," Charlie admitted as he cast what should have been a disabling spell.

The magic flew true, but the result was less than what he'd intended. The Urvalin ship wobbled a bit, and it definitely took a beating from the misfired spell, but it was still flying.

"This is getting out of hand," he grumbled as he let loose with a wide range of spells, opting for the shotgun approach rather than the pinpoint accuracy of a highly specific spell.

"Which is why I suggested we start smaller," Ara said.

Charlie cast again, then let off a few rounds from the pulse weapon he'd mounted to Ara's new harness. The combination of magic and tech caused the Urvalin shielding to buckle, finally doing the trick. The craft fell silent, drifting without power, magical or otherwise.

"Got it!" Charlie exclaimed. "We don't have time to start small. Go big, go home, or die trying, as they say."

"Except we cannot go home," Ara noted. "And in case you had not noticed, the last part is a very real possibility."

ALSO BY SCOTT BARON

Standalone Novels

Living the Good Death

The Clockwork Chimera Series

Daisy's Run

Pushing Daisy

Daisy's Gambit

Chasing Daisy

Daisy's War

The Dragon Mage Series

Bad Luck Charlie

Space Pirate Charlie

Dragon King Charlie

Magic Man Charlie

Star Fighter Charlie

Portal Thief Charlie

Rebel Mage Charlie

Warp Speed Charlie

Checkmate Charlie

Castaway Charlie

The Space Assassins Series

The Interstellar Slayer

The Vespus Blade

The Ghalian Code

Death From the Shadows

Hozark's Revenge

The Warp Riders Series

Deep Space Boogie

Belly of the Beast

Rise of the Forgotten

Pandora's Menagerie

Engines of Chaos

Seeds of Damocles

Odd and Unusual Short Stories:

The Best Laid Plans of Mice: An Anthology

Snow White's Walk of Shame

The Tin Foil Hat Club

Lawyers vs. Demons

The Queen of the Nutters

Lost & Found

ABOUT THE AUTHOR

A native Californian, Scott Baron was born in Hollywood, which he claims may be the reason for his rather off-kilter sense of humor.

Before taking up residence in Venice Beach, Scott first spent a few years abroad in Florence, Italy before returning home to Los Angeles and settling into the film and television industry, where he has worked as an on-set medic for many years.

Aside from mending boo-boos and owies, and penning books and screenplays, Scott is also involved in indie film and theater scene both in the U.S. and abroad.

Made in United States
North Haven, CT
22 December 2024

63284634R00257